Uncertain Destiny

Tears accumulated in her eyes and she wished she'd said something to Jamie, or made love to him. She should have taken a firm grip both on her courage and on the man. In her imagination, she could easily see herself standing naked inside the circle of Jamie's arms, could feel his hands skimming over her while his lips moved against her ear and he whispered everything she wanted to hear.

She threw her cigarette out the window and clutched the steering wheel with both hands. She wasn't going to stop; she wouldn't be defeated by snow and wind. She'd make it through to New York; and, once there, never think about Jamie again.

If only he'd called to say good-bye . . .

Seal Books by Charlotte Vale Allen

Ask your bookseller for the books you have missed

DADDY'S GIRL
DESTINIES
PROMISES

Destinies

Charlotte Vale Allen

Previously Published as
THE MARMALADE MAN

SEAL BOOKS
McClelland and Stewart-Bantam Limited
Toronto

This one is for Barrie,
most beloved Marmalade Man

All of the characters in this book
are fictitious
and any resemblance to actual persons
living or dead
is purely coincidental.

This low-priced Seal Book
has been completely reset in a type face
designed for easy reading, and was printed
from new plates. It contains the complete
text of the original hard-cover edition.
NOT ONE WORD HAS BEEN OMITTED.

DESTINIES
A Seal Book / published by arrangement with
McClelland and Stewart Ltd.

PRINTING HISTORY
Previously published as The Marmalade Man
by McClelland and Stewart, August 1981
Seal edition / July 1982

ISBN 0-7704-1777-9

Destinies

Part 1
Arrivals and Departures 1970

Chapter 1

For months Jamie had been pulling his courage together to make the announcement to Jane. Studying her, he thought sadly of all the years through which they'd traveled together to arrive at this unhappy point. Their marriage, like his education, had been "arranged" by his family, and by hers. It had been expected that they would one day marry, and throughout his years in the Service in Africa, Jane had written faithfully; her letters had been his one tangible link to home and the life he'd lived there. They had created in him a great fondness for her, and that fondness had led him to live up to the expectations of the families. But love—as he dreamed of it in private moments—hadn't ever entered into it. He and Jane had been good friends who'd slept together for a time and who had bred two children, but now no longer had even the friendship in common. He felt like a failure and a coward. One entered into a marriage with the intention of making it work throughout a lifetime. He'd failed because the marriage had failed.

Quietly, after dinner and after the boys had been tucked in bed, he told her, "I think it would be best if I leave. We scarcely see each other these days, and when we are together, we don't seem to have very much to say. I know you've been feeling it too. Of course," he added quickly, "I'll always provide for you and the children. But . . . it's just better if we admit it hasn't worked out."

She sat very still, watching him intently, and he felt foolish, as if he were simply parroting words far too many other men had spoken before. It sounded clichéd: I'm leaving; we didn't make it; I'll make good my obligations. Overheated, miserable, he lit a cigarette and waited for what she'd say.

After a time she lowered her eyes and gazed fixedly at the teacup centered between the fingers of both her hands as if she might suddenly lift the cup and exclaim over the patterns of leaves clinging to the bottom and sides. But her silence held. It made him feel even worse. Was it possible he'd been mistaken, that she'd been content with the marriage?

At last, her eyes still on the teacup, she asked, "Where will you go?"

"I thought I'd take a place downtown, closer ..." He trailed off and drew on his cigarette. To be closer to the CBC, and to the theaters was what he'd intended to say. She knew that.

The crux of the matter was she couldn't take his career seriously. To her it seemed like some sort of game he'd embarked upon. When he eventually returned to his senses and went back to work at a proper job he'd be behaving according to what she'd always expected a husband to do. He simply couldn't make her see that he preferred writing for radio and television, preferred performing onstage, to working in some laboratory, poring over diseased tissues squirming on a slide under a microscope, with the smell of death everywhere. He'd given up his research career in order to have life, and the theater and performing were life. Jane didn't agree. They would never agree, despite his success. He understood that. The confines of her existence had been as rigidly prescribed as his own. The difference between them was that he'd elected to break through the boundaries and seek something that offered him a little pleasure in the course of his working hours. He suspected she would go on until retirement age totting up her columns of figures, lining up debits and credits so that everything would balance perfectly on the final page. He couldn't bear the routine predictability of an existence she found so eminently satisfactory. He couldn't bear the never-ending sameness of the days, of their conversations, of their projected future.

"I see," she said, withdrawing her hands from the teacup. "Well." She took a deep breath, then exhaled slowly. "I can't say I wasn't expecting something like this. I imagine you'll want to tell the boys."

This statement turned him cold. Seconds before, he'd been thinking of his sons as little reproduced packages of Jane. Now he saw them in their reality and knew he'd been indulging in wishful thinking. He was leaving them, thereby destroying the family unity; he would have to try to explain to them why.

"Of course," he said thickly, and took another drag on the cigarette before putting it out.

"When had you planned to go?" she asked, looking around the dining room as if seeing it for the first time.

"I hadn't actually planned. Sunday?" He could stay with any one of a number of friends until he found an apartment. "Whatever's best for you," he said, wanting to be considerate of her feelings. They had, after all, spent eight years together. He couldn't just discount all the shared experiences, the memories, or the reality of the boys. Thinking of Mark and Stephen made his throat ache. He saw himself with them, heard himself telling stories to make them laugh; he could hear their laughter. He didn't want to tell them. Magically, impossibly, he wanted Jane to disappear somehow so that he could go on into the future with his sons. It seemed horribly unfair that his desire for a different kind of life should cost him his children, a very steep price to pay. No, if life were fair, each of them could have taken a boy ... could have ... impossible. He was rarely home as it was. Who'd look after them? Who'd get them off to school, see to their meals, their baths? No, it wasn't possible. The price, mounting by the moment in his awareness, would be his absence from their lives. He would not be there to witness their growth into young men. He was going to cry; he could feel it behind his eyes, and coughed, hoping to dislodge the lump of emotion constricting his throat.

"Well, that's it, then, isn't it?" she said, and stood up to carry her teacup out to the kitchen.

He remained seated at the table, staring at the spot where she'd just been, wondering if she really cared at all that their marriage was ending. He didn't think she did. His announced departure was an inconvenience, that's all, a disruption of the planned passage of their days. She'd adapt; she was extremely flexible. She'd reshape her thoughts and time around his absence and, ultimately, it would be as if he'd never existed, except in the shape of Mark's nose, in the color of Stephen's hair, and in the boys' memories, perhaps, for a time. Until they forgot him. But he wouldn't allow them to forget him.

All at once it seemed as if he were losing everything. He thought of Sherrill and added her to his tally of losses.

Jane was rinsing the cups and teapot. He stood in the dining room doorway watching her as he lit a fresh cigarette. He was smoking too much; his throat felt raw.

"We'll have to move," she said with her back to him. "This place is far too expensive."

"You needn't do that," he said.

"We'll have to move," she repeated a bit more emphatically, shaking the soapy water from her hands before turning to look at him. She was quite a pretty woman, with good skin and clear eyes, but she seemed like a complete stranger to him. "You haven't really thought this through, have you?" she said, not unkindly. "You're going to have to support two households, James, and that's expensive."

It was his turn to lower his eyes. He looked down at his shoes, reminding himself that it was time to polish his and the boys' shoes. He always enjoyed getting out the kit and giving a good shine to the leather. "You're probably right," he said, then looked at her again. She was watching him like a mother, he thought. With consternation she followed all his movements, a disapproving mother.

"Look," he said. "I really am very sorry it's turned out this way."

She nodded, drying her hands on a tea towel.

"I think it would be best if you slept on the sofa tonight," she said, carefully hanging the towel over the handle on the oven door. She switched off the kitchen light, and walked down the hall and up the stairs. He stood in the darkened doorway listening to the sound of her feet climbing the stairs. Her last remark had been unnecessary. He'd been sleeping on the sofa most nights for months, but had been telling himself it was out of deference to her need for sleep and her having to be up early every morning to get the boys fed and off to school before she left for the office. The truth was he'd developed an aversion to touching her. It made him feel too dishonest.

With a sigh, he straightened and turned to look back at the dining room. The wood paneling depressed him with its somber dark gleam. He craved air and lightness, room to move about in. Three more nights in this house and he'd be thoroughly depressed, perhaps to the point where he'd change his mind and stay simply because it required too much energy to go. He switched off the lamp over the dining room table and went quickly down the hall and up the stairs.

"There's no point in prolonging it," he said, going directly to the closet. "I might as well go now and come back on Sunday to have a talk with the boys."

"As you like," she said in the same calm tone with which she had held the entire conversation. Her robe and night-gown over her arm, she shut herself into the bathroom to get ready for bed.

He heaped his clothes into two suitcases, found an old vinyl suit bag and pushed his trousers, sports jackets, and suits into its too small confines. Then he carried the two cases down to the front hall and came back up for his toiletries. "Damn!" he whispered. Jane was in the bathroom. He didn't want to have to see or talk to her again tonight. He scooped up his cuff links and dropped them into his pocket, then loked around for anything he might have missed. Never mind! he told himself. He would collect the rest of it on Sunday.

Downstairs, he rang for a taxi, then was stopped by the realization that he had no idea where he was going. He could call up half a dozen friends—Ron, or Colin, any number of people. The idea of offering explanations at ten o'clock at night, of arriving fully laden with his clothes, defeated him. He'd check into a hotel and do the talking and explaining later.

He looked around the spacious, nicely decorated room, feeling disoriented. It was a favorite hotel for touring companies. The dining room wasn't bad, but it was starting to get a little show-bizzy, with people hanging out in their best gear hoping to be seen. Still, he'd always liked the hotel and felt a bit ill and bewildered now at finding himself alone here with his two suitcases sitting on the bed and his over-crowded suit bag hanging in the closet. He sat down in the armchair, staring at his luggage on the bed. Not yet eleven o'clock. He was hungry. He'd been unable to eat any of the dinner Jane had prepared; he'd been too nerved up, waiting to make his announcement. It was all over now, anticlimactic to say the least, and he was hungry.

"Fuck it!" he said softly, depressed. Pocketing the room

key and his cigarettes, he left and went down to the dining
room.

While he was eating, he thought once more of the boys,
and of Sherrill, and his throat closed again; he lost his
appetite. He signaled to the waitress, who said she'd send
him a barmaid. He pushed away his half-eaten steak and sat
back to wait.

The barmaid approached the table wearing a quizzical
expression. As she came nearer, she broke into a happy grin.
"*Jamie?* It is you! You don't remember me, do you? I'm
Leslie. Remember? We worked together about four years
ago, in Montreal."

He smiled at her, feeling something ease in his chest. "Of
course I remember," he lied, trying to place her. "How are
you?"

"Just great. How are you? Listen, are you going to be
around for a while? I'm off in fifteen minutes. We could
have some coffee, talk. I can't get over seeing you. What're
you doing these days?"

"Just closed another revue last week."

"Terrific! Listen, d'you want a drink? I'd better get it or
I'll just stand here all night yakking."

"Scotch," he said. "A double, neat. And a Heineken.
Please."

She wrote down his order, dropped the pen on her tray
and gave him another beaming smile. "I just can't get *over*
it!" she exclaimed. "I'll be right back."

She wore too much makeup, he thought, but she was
attractive. Watching her walk away in the short costume
the barmaids wore, he decided she had decent legs, although
she was a bit broad in the arse. Her hair looked stiff with
lacquer. Never mind. He was glad to see someone smile,
glad at the opportunity to chat about old times and inconse-
quentials. Anything, just then, was better than sitting upstairs
staring at his overladen suitcases, thinking about the family
he'd just broken up.

It wasn't the first time he'd made love to a woman who
wasn't his wife. In the past few years he'd made love more
often to other women than he had to Jane. Jane had never
cared much for physical displays. But this felt like the first
time. Perhaps it was because he was standing on the brink

of his freedom and knew he could, in the future, have an independent life, enjoying his work. What he wanted and hoped for was to meet someone who'd never bore him by being predictable, someone who'd understand his need to keep his brain alive instead of allowing it to atrophy in some deathly, well-paid, nine-to-five job, someone who'd delight him and bring laughter with her when she entered a room, someone who'd be supportive, caring and gentle, yet passionate, someone who'd love making love, someone he could love unreservedly. A dream woman. Women like that didn't exist, he thought. Obstinately, even stupidly perhaps, he looked for her each day as he moved through the world. Not actively. He was simply keeping his eyes open; he'd recognize her when he saw her. For now, Leslie was a warm, willing body into which he could spill his accumulation of anxieties and small fears. Her breasts were too large, but her legs were good and he liked taking his time touching her. Every so often, she laughed and exclaimed over seeing him again and he tried not to hear. He didn't want to talk or have to listen; he simply wanted to enjoy sensation. The room seemed far less empty and ominous with her in it, with her clothes strewn all over the floor.

"Do you like this?" she asked a little coyly, and he lifted his hips, saying nothing.

"You do like this," she said after a moment and he felt himself becoming irritated with her. At once he disliked himself for his irritability. What was happening to him? he wondered, stroking her stiff hair for a moment before sliding his hand down over the warmer, more welcoming softness of the nape of her neck.

She sat up to look at him and he felt terribly moved by her, so moved that he drew her down into his arms and held her lovingly. We're all such a sorry lot, he thought. Where does it end?

In the morning when he awakened, he felt disgusted with himself. He leaned on his elbow for a minute or two watching Leslie sleep, then got up and went into the bathroom. No toothbrush, no razor. He felt dirty and tired. Under the hot shower he decided to go straight out to buy some toilet articles, then come back with the morning papers and start looking for an apartment. First he had to tackle the problem of how to get rid of Leslie without offending her. He knew if

he had to smile and make small talk to her over breakfast
he'd sink back into the previous night's depression.

She was awake when he emerged from the bathroom, and
sat against the pillows watching him get dressed.

"I'm afraid I've got an early appointment," he lied, tucking in his shirt tails. "And I've got to get out to a drugstore
to pick up some shaving cream, a razor. You understand."

"Sure," she said, not smiling. He didn't think she believed
him. He was unskilled at lying; he hated doing it.

He came over to the bed and bent down to kiss her on the
forehead. Most of her makeup had come off on the bedclothes. She looked younger and far more attractive without
it. For a second or two he wished they knew each other
better, that they had things to talk about. "Look, I'll leave
you the key. Take your time and lock up when you're ready
to go. You can leave the key at the desk for me. I am sorry
about this." He *was* sorry, but he could see she didn't believe
that either.

"Sure," she said again. Then, brightening, she asked, "Will
you be in the bar tonight?"

"I'll try," he promised with a smile, feeling worse by the
moment at compounding the lies. He hoped to be out of the
hotel by the late afternoon. He was being a bastard; he knew
it, but couldn't see any other way to extricate himself from
the situation. He should have exercised more self-control
instead of attempting to soothe his feelings at someone else's
expense. He'd never been the sort of man who used women;
he liked them too well to mistreat them intentionally. Last
night had been a self-indulgent mistake. He didn't think
either of them had benefited from being together. If Leslie
had, he couldn't see how. Her willingness to see him again,
to take whatever attention he might care to pay her, seemed
unspeakably sad. He wouldn't have capitalized on her eagerness in the first place if she hadn't happened along at a
moment when he'd been thinking less than clearly. All he
wanted now was to escape the situation he'd created without doing further damage to either of them. He kissed her
naked shoulder, then straightened and picked up his jacket
from the armchair. Checking to make sure he had his bill-
fold, he made his way to the door.

"Thank you for a lovely evening," he said, and escaped.

It was a bitterly cold morning, with snow underfoot. He

should have worn his topcoat. The wind cut right through to his skin and he hurried up to the drugstore at the corner, anxious to make his purchases and then have breakfast. He'd have it at the counter in the drugstore and look at the ads while he ate. That would give Leslie time enough to clear out of the room. Why was he behaving so badly? This isn't me, he thought, pushing with relief into the warm interior of the drugstore. I don't treat people, women, that way. He loathed the idea of having a reputation as a lady-killer, one of those men who used women like public conveniences.

He wouldn't do that again, he told himself as he collected a can of shaving foam, a razor, some blades, a toothbrush, and a tube of toothpaste and carried them toward the cashier. As an afterthought, he turned back and inspected the bottles of men's cologne, deciding to treat himself to some Chanel after-shave. He gave the cashier his MasterCharge card, then waited impatiently, made hungry by the smell of frying bacon, while the woman checked his card against a lengthy list of numbers on an orange sheet. Satisfied, she rang the charge, had him sign the slip, then put his purchases into a large brown paper bag.

He ducked outside to buy a *Globe and Mail* and a *Star,* then returned inside to seat himself at the counter, placing the bag at his feet. He was famished, and ordered two eggs, a double order of bacon, a side order of grilled tomatoes, whole wheat toast, and coffee. While he waited for the food, he opened the *Globe* and folded it open to the Apartments to Rent section. He marked several possibilities and sipped at his coffee. He was starting to feel a little better. The waitress behind the counter smiled at him as she set down his food. He returned her smile, then placed the paper beside his plate in order to continue scanning it while he attacked his breakfast.

Halfway through, he thought about Mark and Stephen and once more lost his appetite. He could too clearly see their small, earnest faces and felt again a coward and a traitor. The guilt was compounded by his treatment of Leslie. He'd finish eating and get back to the hotel. If she was still there, he'd make up some story about his appointment having been canceled, buy her a bang-up breakfast, and see her on her way properly. Picking up his knife and fork, he went back to work on the food and quickly finished. The waitress, bestowing another smile upon him, refilled his coffee cup and deftly removed the empty plate.

"Rotten day, eh?" she observed, looking over toward the window.

"Hmmm," he murmured, folding open the *Star*.

"You must be freezing," she said, "going out without a coat. But you're English, eh? You people never feel the cold, do you?"

"Oh, we do," he answered, wishing she'd leave him to get on with the ads. "I'm staying just down the road. Not out long enough to get cold."

"Yeah, well . . ." She carried the coffeepot on down the counter to refill other cups.

"Jesus!" he whispered under his breath. He reached for his cigarettes only to find he'd left them back at the hotel. Putting down the paper, he walked over to the far side of the drugstore to buy a pack of Gitanes. When he got back, his *Globe and Mail* was gone. Turning, he saw the man who'd been seated two stools down from him going out the door with the newspaper tucked under his arm, still folded open to the classified section. Defeated, Jamie retrieved the *Star* and his paper bag, dropped some money on the counter, and pushed out of the drugstore to buy another *Globe*.

Half-frozen, he got back to his hotel room to find Leslie gone. On the desk was a note with her telephone number. "Call me," the note read. She'd signed it "Leslie" and had dotted the *i* with a little circle. He left the note on the desk and opened the *Globe* to go over the ads again.

Chapter 2

Sherrill was supposed to do the curtain raiser of the second act nude from the waist up. She simply couldn't do it. With Della's permission—she'd been in two other shows Della had produced and felt close enough to the woman to confide her anxiety—she'd sewn a short lace top that would, from the rear, lend the illusion of nudity but allow her to move about in the tiny backstage area comfortably covered.

There were only the three of them backstage during the show: Ron, Jamie, and herself. She didn't include the stage manager in her tally since he rarely looked away from the lighting board or the paperback science fiction novels he read between acts. Neither Ron nor Jamie would have said or done anything to embarrass her; they were both long-term professionals and undoubtedly accustomed to seeing their female co-players running about backstage in various stages of undress. The problem was entirely within herself. She was not sufficiently beautiful or courageous to risk either their commenting or their ignoring her altogether. Tonight was the last time she'd have to consider the matter; the show was closing.

Jamie was already onstage in the dark, and she moved past the black velvet curtain that closed off the minimal wing areas to position herself in his arms. As had happened every night of the run, she experienced an odd interior flutter as she fitted her arms around his neck and breathed in the fresh, sweet scent of his after-shave. His hands stroked down the length of her exposed spine and she breathed deeply, raggedly, wondering if he knew the effect he had upon her. His hands moved over her back—appreciatively, she thought, sensing all sorts of messages yet refusing to investigate them—touched at her waist for a moment, then his arms came around her and he whispered in her ear. His voice was rich, hypnotic, soft.

"Gorgeous skin you've got." His lips moved against her ear.

She couldn't speak. If she attempted to reply, a gusher of words might erupt from her mouth: declarations of caring that had no foundation in reality. Reflexively, her arms tightened around his neck. For a few seconds she closed her eyes to savor the breadth and solidity of his body, fully clad, against hers. She had the sensation of sinking right through his chest and into the interior of his body. She felt serene, even euphoric, for these few seconds while, like vapor, she filled his interior and turned—utterly shielded and protected by his substantial frame—to survey the world through the different vision of his eyes. Nothing in her experience had ever been so appropriately fulfilling as these nightly moments when she was able to pretend that she and this man might go directly from this embrace into a tacitly agreed-upon future together. She could effortlessly project the two of them into scene after scene of harmonious involvement. Absurd, she thought, these full-blown fantasies she created out of nothing. She doubted Jamie was aware of her at all, except as a body that seemed to please him for these few moments.

Following the thick muffled movement of the curtains parting, the lights came up to a third; a pause, then Ron delivered his offstage lines. Jamie delivered his, gave her bottom the prolonged caress called for in the script, released her, and she slipped silently offstage.

In her corner of the crowded storage room they all shared as a communal dressing room, she untied the lace coverup, stepped into her slip, then her dress. The audience was laughing. They were receptive tonight. The closing would leave a good taste in everyone's mouth. Dressed, she went to stand in the wings, watching through a slit in the blackout curtain. Her heart beat too fast and she was perspiring; she was keenly aware of her nakedness under the clothes. She wished she were the sort of woman who found it easy to be in the company of men, the sort who could approach Jamie and say, "Look, we both feel it. Why don't we do something about it?"

She didn't appear again onstage until the next skit, and she was grateful. She couldn't have delivered lines after those heated intimate moments with Jamie that made her horribly nervous. Infused with a brief, hopeless yearning, part of her brain had long since concluded that she was more than a little in love with the man; the rest of her consciousness avoided the idea.

She had a minute or two more before the next number, a vocal she did alone at the piano. Invariably she brought to it a tremendous amount of energy that had been generated by Jamie's soft mellow voice murmuring in her ear as his hands glided over her. The pleasure she still felt was so acute that her legs trembled. She was relieved that the show was closing, that she'd be leaving the city in a few days' time. She'd be able to remove herself completely; there'd be no temptation, no reason for her to think about calling him up again and inviting him over for tea, or a meal. Jamie was married and had, she knew, several children.

He knew it made her nervous, but he couldn't resist teasing her. Was it teasing, though? he wondered. True, she did have lovely skin, soft and velvety, but it wasn't merely a matter of the physical appeal she had for him. The curtain raiser afforded him an opportunity, in the dark, to measure her narrow dimensions with his hands while her head lay against his shoulder—an illusion of vulnerability and of belonging—and her short hair tickled his cheek. He felt contentment for those few seconds and he was startled every time by his desire to have those seconds expanded.

She was an odd girl. Not beautiful. There was a quality about her eyes, large, gray-blue, haunted eyes, that touched him and aroused his protective instincts. She seemed impossibly young. Perhaps that was why he thought of her as a girl when she was, in fact, twenty-five. She dressed like a schoolgirl, in pinafore dresses and knee socks, and he wondered why when she had the figure to carry off far more sophisticated clothes. In all, she looked about eighteen, except for her eyes. She had fine bones, an appealingly heart-shaped face, and a splendid wide smile. Her eyes, though, intrigued him. She was too young to have such old, old eyes.

He liked her; he would have enjoyed knowing her better. But she was too—fragile, too highly charged to approach, although that evening a while back when she'd given him a ride home from the theater, he'd sensed something, a possibility perhaps. He'd asked if she wouldn't mind parking at the corner, and she'd understood that he hadn't wanted to create any problems with Jane by having her see him climbing out of Sherrill's car. They'd sat talking for a few minutes and the air inside the little Volkswagen had been electric with tension. He'd known intuitively that if he'd made any sort of move toward her they'd have become quickly involved. He'd wondered a number of times how it might be to learn about her, to share her thoughts, to hear of her experiences, to make love to her. They'd just talked, and after a few minutes, he'd put his hand on the door, ready to get out. Then, on impulse, and out of genuine affection for her, he'd leaned over to kiss her cheek. Her eyes had gone wide and

she'd appeared to hold her breath, as if frightened. He'd
purposely told a joke to make her laugh and put her at ease
before he got out of the car, to stand on the sidewalk watching her drive away. Then he'd turned toward home, trying
to decipher his feelings for this girl.

Jane had, he remembered, gone to bed. She rarely waited
up for him. Naturally the children had been asleep for
hours. He'd gone up to look in on the boys and straighten
their bedclothes, then, with a beer from the refrigerator and
a glass of Scotch, he'd gone to sit in the living room to watch
television with the sound turned down. He'd drunk the
beer, then lit a cigarette and sat slowly sipping the Scotch
while he gazed at the screen. His mind tried to imagine
Sherrill, where she'd go, how she'd end up, and what sort of
woman she'd be.

She had considerable talent: she sang well in husky, surprisingly deep tones far lower than her speaking voice; she
was a skilled pianist, and had written and performed several excellent numbers for the shows they'd done together.
She brought imagination to her acting and got a lot of laughter from audiences, but she wasn't funny. She was too
serious, too intelligent to play the clown offstage. Perhaps it
was the underlying sobriety that made her so delightful
onstage. Like all good comediennes, she displayed a touch of
pathos that tempered her apparent youth and made her
lovable.

One might have expected her to fizz offstage, like so
many of the other pretty confections he'd performed with
in the past. Sherrill offstage, however, was almost totally
unrelated to Sherrill onstage. Without makeup, clad in her
girlish clothes, she spoke softly and earnestly; she listened
with the diligence of a good student and absorbed information with small, assenting nods of her head. Onstage, she
dazzled at some moments, was forlorn, almost waiflike, the
next.

He questioned why he spent so much time thinking about
her. They were simply friends, if one cared to put a title to
their relationship. She had invited him for a cup of tea one
afternoon several months earlier, and he'd gone out of curiosity primarily. He'd admired the living room while she was
in the kitchen getting the tea. The entire time he'd been
there she'd seemed so nervous he'd felt sorry for her, won-

dering why she'd extended the invitation when it was so obvious that his presence there rattled her. She couldn't seem to relax, could scarcely seem to talk coherently. Every so often her eyes had come to rest on him almost fearfully. He had wished he could reassure her that he was there only for tea and not to throw her down on the living room floor and ravage her. He'd told several long, funny stories that had made her laugh, and then he'd left, exhausted as if he'd just done two shows back to back with no interval. He'd have loved to make love to her. He smiled to himself over his contradictory impulses.

While she was onstage, he collected his props for the blackout and went to stand stage right and watch her. He did like the way she sang. So did the audience. He didn't think they knew quite how to react to her. The emotional content was so powerful that it always took them a moment or two, once the number had ended, to respond. Even then, they were still so under the influence of the sight and sound of her—all softened and aglow in a surprise-pink spot—that they didn't applaud quite as heartily as they might have, which led Sherrill to complain to him that they didn't like her.

"There's always that pause," she'd told him. "I sit waiting for them to clap, afraid they're going to come running up on the stage and slam the piano lid on my fingers." She'd laughed self-deprecatingly.

"They adore you, love," he'd assured her, tempted oddly to say that he did, too. She hadn't believed him; she didn't understand the impact she had on people. She could, if she cared to risk the disappointments and uncertainty, not to mention the humiliation, of the theater, have an outstanding career. Not the best singer, or the most beautiful girl, she did have an overwhelming presence, an almost unbearable poignancy with those great round eyes, and lovely body: long-legged, slim-waisted, small-breasted. He wished he knew how to get her to relax. The image of the two of them, sitting, chatting companionably, strongly appealed to him. Perhaps once he was on his own he'd invite her round to a meal, or out to see a movie . . . something.

After the show, the silence backstage was dispiriting. Out front, the waiters lethargically cleared the last of the tables.

Sherrill collected her makeup and looked around for her shoes. Every night, without fail, somebody managed to kick her shoes out of the way so that they got hidden under a box or some props. Dressed in her favorite outfit of long-sleeved white shirt and gray jumper, but with tights on instead of the knee socks she preferred, she padded around backstage searching for her shoes.

Ron and Jamie were headed for Yorkville. Jamie stopped to ask, "Want to come? There's a party."

She looked up and smiled. "No, thanks. I can't find my goddamned shoes."

"I'll meet you there," Jamie told Ron, and came over to help her look. He was smiling; he liked the way she swore. She was one of the rare women he'd met who could make swearing seem a natural and spontaneous part of everyday speech. Most women came across as highly uncomfortable and overly aware of themselves when they risked interjecting a profanity into their conversation. Sherrill swore with feeling and great appropriateness. It was one more thing he enjoyed about her. He found her shoes in an unlikely place, under the lighting board, and sat down on the stage manager's stool to watch while she put them on.

"Where do you go from here?" he asked, admiring her well-shaped, elegant legs. He'd have liked to see her putting on a pair of expensive high-heeled sandals.

She felt awkward under his gaze. His eyes seemed to penetrate her flesh. She wished she had the courage to hold her hand out to him, to lead him into the storage room, where, with the door carefully locked, they'd make love among the packing cases and filing cabinets. "I finally got my green card," she said with forced brightness, smiling again at him. She prayed her feelings didn't show; she wanted to seem casually in control of herself.

"Good girl!"

"Yup! I'm off to New York." For a moment she looked uncertain. Her eyes seemed darker; she appeared suddenly smaller. Then her smile returned and she said, "I've got an agent lined up, and some auditions. I'll be staying with my friend Michelle until I can find an apartment. Have you been to New York?" She was talking too much, she was certain. She always went on and on when she was unsure of herself.

"Once or twice," he said quietly, absorbing the fact that she would be leaving town.

"Did you like it? I loved it. I can't wait to get there."

He nodded, reached into his pocket for his cigarettes, and offered her one. She shook her head. "No, thanks." Standing in front of the black velvet curtain, she looked, at that moment, perhaps twelve years old with her short, shaggy hair and childish clothes. He realized that the only times she seemed fully grown and womanly were when he held her for the second-act curtain raiser and she stood, like something barely tamed, within the circle of his arms. She was an extraordinary mix of virginal child and sexual woman.

"What about you?" she asked, looking out at the deserted dining area. She wished she were brave enough to risk attempting to bring fantasies to life. Why did she have to find his face so attractive, his voice with its precise British diction so captivating? She wanted to stay there, talking with him, forever; she also longed to get away from him so she could put her feelings back in order. The sight of his aristocratic features, his pointed chin and strong nose, his fine skin, made her yearn to touch him.

He considered telling her that he planned to get out, that he felt he was suffocating, that he was leaving Jane, to see about living some more satisfactory kind of life. He considered discussing how he felt about the prospect of leaving his children; he loved the boys and couldn't bear to imagine how they'd react to his going. He wondered what her reaction would be if he told her how lovely and lovable he found her, or what her answer would be if he asked why she'd decided to move to New York just when she was starting to make a real name for herself here. Instead, he shrugged lightly and said, "More of the same, I expect."

She loved the sound of his voice. It was even fuller, richer, now with the place empty and everyone gone; it seemed to swell out over the stage, down across the empty tables and chairs; she could feel it reaching inside her and it worried her. She didn't want to react to him, didn't want to feel anything but friendship for him. She wondered why and how he'd decided to become an actor. Why hadn't she ever asked him about himself? Had he been a performer in England before he'd come to Canada? She seemed to recall his mentioning some other career, but she couldn't remem-

ber what it had been. "Can I give you a lift?" she asked,
feeling herself being drawn too stongly toward him.

"If you wouldn't mind," he said, and stood down off the
stool. "I'd appreciate it."

"I'll get my coat." She went back into the storage room
and retrieved her coat. Her hands were damp; she was
perspiring again.

He insisted on helping her on with her coat and she tried
not to mind his proximity. She felt more able to breathe
when his hands had gone away.

"Don't you have a coat?" she asked. "You never seem to
wear one. Don't you feel the cold?" Oh, God! Shut up! she
thought. Just shut up!

"It isn't particularly cold," he said, holding the door open
for her.

"I'm parked in the lot across the street," she said, standing on the curb looking up and down Bay Street, dimly lit
and deserted. It was after midnight. She turned to look
briefly at Jamie, who was suddenly quiet. She had no idea
how to read him, what to make of him, and wished she did.
His sometime, sudden silences intimidated her, made her
wonder if she bored him and he was simply politely tolerat-
ing her.

He threw away his cigarette and waited to open the car
door for her. His good manners put her on edge: somehow
his rather old-school ways deprived her of control in the
situation. She needed to feel she was in charge of her own
actions. She hadn't ever, in the two years of working together, felt entirely at ease with Jamie. It had to do with his, to
her, pleasing looks, and his dignified demeanor, his impec-
cable manners, and her ludicrous fantasies involving him.

Jamie wasn't like any other man she'd known. She'd never
seen him lose his temper, or heard him speak badly of
anyone or display any negative emotion. She'd seen him
smile frequently, and laugh; she'd heard him tell his marvelous long funny stories, but she didn't think she'd ever
actually *seen* him. Now they were parting to go in different
directions and she had no real idea who he was or if he
liked her at all. He most likely thought she was a little silly
and not very good-looking. Most men were put off by her.
She was ambitious and highly energetic, but she couldn't
help that.

"I'll just hop out at Avenue Road and Yorkville," he said, settling himself on the passenger seat of the Bug. "You do go by there, don't you?"

"I'll be glad to take you wherever you're going. It's no trouble." Did he find her overly accommodating? she wondered. She sounded to herself like one of those doormat women who'd do absolutely anything to make themselves attractive to men.

He gave her a small smile and turned to look out the window, still apparently preoccupied. She wouldn't think about it. She'd drop him off, go home, remove the thick-feeling stage makeup, watch a late movie, have a sandwich and a cup of tea, then go to sleep. Everything was packed. The movers were coming to take her things to the warehouse for storage first thing Monday morning. Monday afternoon, she'd get into the Bug with her big brown envelope of documents and take off for New York. New York was the ultimate challenge, the big, always exciting place where she'd make a name for herself. New York was five hundred or so miles away from here, away from Jamie; far enough away so that she wouldn't have the time or inclination to think about him. There was no point whatsoever in daydreaming about a man who evidently was quite content with his life as it was.

He gazed out the window, feeling a completely unexpected sense of loss. She was leaving. He'd heard her talk about her plans, but nothing had really registered. Suddenly, with a sinking sensation he understood that they mightn't ever see each other again, and was shaken by the piercing depth of his reaction.

"Do you know where you'll be?" he asked as she was driving across Bloor Street.

"I've got Michelle's address, if that's what you mean."

"Write it down for me," he said, shifting in his seat to look at her. "I'll send you filthy postcards." He smiled. She felt like crying, but she managed a laugh as she pulled over at the corner of Yorkville. She put on the turn signal before groping in her handbag for something to write on. She gave him her address book and a pen, saying, "Write down your address for me. I'll write to you."

"Promise?"

"I promise."

He printed his name and address, then returned the book
and pen to her, watching as she wrote Michelle's address on
the back of an envelope. She had good hands, large and
capable-looking. He accepted the envelope, looked at it for a
moment, then folded it in half and tucked it into his jacket
pocket.

He debated kissing her good-bye, but saw something shad-
owy in her eyes and decided against it. Giving her hand a
squeeze, he said, "Thanks, love. Take care of yourself, and
be sure to let me know how you're getting on," and got out
of the car to walk away down Yorkville.

Feeling all at once very alone, she returned everything to
her handbag and watched him—an urbane man in a dark
gray suit, white shirt, and tie—stroll away down the street,
probably headed toward laughter and drinks and people
infinitely more fun to be with than she. Wasn't he cold? It
was only about forty degrees tonight. He didn't seem to be
cold. He crossed to the far side of the street and walked on.
She put the Bug in gear, checked the rearview mirror, and
pulled away from the curb. His parting words echoed inside
her skull. What if she parked the car and ran back to meet
him? No, she thought. No.

Halfway down the block, he stopped and turned, to see
the light blue Bug disappearing up Avenue Road. Perhaps
he should have said something. What? What could he have
possibly said? For a few seconds, unaware of the damp cold,
he stood staring into space, fixed on an interior scenario:
hand in hand, laughing, he and Sherrill—that delicate yet
admirably determined young woman—ran off together. The
notes of their laughter seemed to transcend his imaginings
and, hearing music, he continued on down the street, past
the window from which the music came.

Chapter 3

As Dene rode the bus out to La Guardia, she felt strongly that returning home was a good idea. At some point she would have to see her mother, and Jake's parents, but it wasn't something that had to be done the moment she arrived. Once she was settled and reacclimated to the city she'd contact the families. It was entirely possible she'd be able to deal with that now. Time and distance had dulled her feelings.

She felt a definite excitement, as if this preliminary trip back might offer more than just an alternative place to live. She was actually beginning to feel alive again and, considering this, she felt guilty. Surely, she reasoned, she couldn't be expected to grieve forever. It wasn't as if she'd forgotten any of it; she was simply emerging from the frozen depths of shock and loss. Four years ago she wouldn't have believed she'd ever recover. Now, she told herself, it was all right. No one could reasonably expect her to remain in a state of perpetual grief.

What was left? Friends? She grew enervated merely thinking about contacting people from the past. Perhaps it would be best to return with an entirely new personality: she'd create it around the sketchy identity she'd assumed during these past four years. That was safest. Were she to attempt to reconstruct any aspect of her previous life, she'd be compelled to discuss Jake and Mimi at length and often. She simply couldn't do it. It was one thing to find herself recovered, but quite another to tread in the dangerous territory of prior friendships, where an exchange of questions and answers was bound to take place. So she would not go seeking apartments in Rosedale, or get in touch with old friends, or make any attempts at reconstruction. She would begin anew, or continue on as the someone else she now was. But who was she?

*My name is Dene Whitmore. I am thirty-four years old. I design
toys. Once upon a time I had illusions about art; I wanted to
be a painter. Now I have no illusions. I live alone, I am alone.
I . . . I want to go home.*

A few minutes before the announcement that the plane
was boarding she swallowed a Dramamine tablet, then stood
in line in the lounge, waiting to present her boarding pass.
She hated flying. It was, she thought, a sign of newly reborn
courage that in her eagerness to see the city again she'd
chosen to fly rather than take the train or a bus. Years ago,
she'd have rented a car. Without a second thought, she'd
have called Hertz or Avis, driven the rental car the five
hundred—odd miles, and when the bill came, she'd have
paid it as a matter of course. It was astonishing to think of
how cavalier she'd once been about money. Jake had always
encouraged her to spend. She'd never had any real sense of
it; money had simply been a plentiful commodity and she'd
used it as such.

Don't blame it on money! she warned herself. But the
money had determined the life-style, and the life-style had
determined its own end. What else could be responsible?
She gazed out the plane window, admitting finally that no
one and nothing could be blamed. Placing blame was for
small children who hadn't yet come to terms with life's
realities, not for a thirty-four-year-old woman who knew
she could attribute responsibility only to time and circumstances. *If the weather was bad and the roads were slickly
treacherous . . . If the wind velocity was strong and snow fell
more quickly than the wiper blades could clear it . . . If other
people in other cars were suffering under the same conditions
. . . If, if, if . . .*

She kept her seat belt fastened even after the signs clicked
off. Her only concession to the SMOKING/NO SMOKING and
FASTEN SEATBELT signs was to light a cigarette and pull out
the minute ashtray in the arm of her seat before turning
again to the window. There was nothing to see but her own
reflection, and she studied this black-on-black portrait for
several minutes, wondering why nothing showed on her
face. Except for the absence of the meticulously applied
makeup she'd once worn, she looked much as she always
had. Older, but the same. Not years and years older, as she
felt, but just older. It was amazing. It would have been far

more appropriate, she thought, if the image had whitened hair and deep creases framing her eyes and mouth: exterior signs of interior anguish.

She thought back to the day before. She'd been standing in front of a discount drugstore on Third Avenue, looking into the window, when it occurred to her that there were no bargains here, and that she was tired of New York. She'd turned to study the midday crowd surging down the avenue and felt exhausted at the thought of reentering the stream of traffic.

It should have seemed strange, she'd thought, to see a tall, gaunt young man with a wild, Bride-of-Frankenstein afro swinging along the sidewalk with an enormous radio-cassette player in his hand and an ornately painted set of headphones over his ears. But it hadn't; she'd become accustomed to the bizarre after four years in Manhattan, just as she'd come to accept the current craze for deathly white makeup, charcoal eyeshadow, and plum-colored lipstick that rendered pretty girls and no longer pretty older women into leagues of what looked like the walking dead.

Suddenly, the full impact of the crowds and of the city itself overwhelmed her. Where had everyone been going, and why were they in such a rush? What would possibly happen if all these people were to slow down to a reasonable pace? If they slowed down, would they see the rubbish littering the streets, or the adolescent girls standing in the doorways along Forty-fourth Street near Broadway? Would they see, as she had, the overpowering height of the buildings, and their own accordingly reduced stature?

I want to go home, she'd decided. *I want to get out of here.*

The shifting crowd had swelled past her. One or two people had glared angrily at her for disturbing their direct passage down the avenue. She'd been jostled, pushed. On the far side of the street, at the corner, a shopping-bag lady had calmly gone through the contents of a trash can. She'd pulled a newspaper from the can, shaken it, then pushed it into one of the several very full bags on the ground around her feet. Immensely fat, she'd had closely cropped gray hair and a very pale, dirt-streaked face. With oddly delicate gestures, she'd continued sifting through the refuse in the trash can. She'd been clad in a too small black cardigan over a torn red blouse, and a long brownish-red skirt that had

come almost to her ankles. Her feet were covered by filthy
sneakers and her ankles were puffed and grimy. Dene had
looked away. She'd had an appointment with John Stevens
of Regular Toys, to sign a contract and collect her advance.

Headed across town to Madison and Forty-seventh Street,
she'd been aware of sounds and smells and the bodies all
around her as she'd never been before. She'd been a robot,
she'd thought, working mechanically and without real inspi-
ration, because she'd needed the money to live. Even that
wasn't the truth, though. She'd never touched the insurance
money; it was still in her Toronto account at the Bank of
Montreal, gathering interest. To ignore the money had been
to deny what had actually happened. Tainted money, death
money, she'd been unable to bring herself to believe in its
existence beyond the necessity of placing it in the bank for
safekeeping.

There'd been a contract to sign and a check to accept.
After that, she'd decided she'd fly up to Toronto and find a
place to live. Then she'd come back and start packing, do
something about breaking the lease on the Seventy-fourth
Street apartment, her so-called garden apartment: one room,
twelve by sixteen, with a pullman kitchen, two closets, and
a tiny bathroom. The garden was larger than the apartment,
weed-strewn but still bearing evidence of the previous tenant's talent and imagination. At the foot of the garden, its
base tangled with weeds, stood a stone bird bath. What had
once been carefully laid-out flower beds still showed dis-
cernable borders. She'd planned to restore the garden but
had never done it.

Sometimes, on summer evenings, she'd taken one of the
living room chairs outside to sit, smoking a cigarette and
pretending she wasn't surrounded on all sides by towering
high-rise apartment buildings: a dark shape perched on a
wooden chair, staring into space—a dot on the landscape.
She looked up at the lighted windows all around, hearing
music drift down at her from somewhere, and an occasional
bark of laughter, or a shout. City noises: the 3 A.M. crash of
glass as a bottle was thrown from one of the windows and
smashed against the fence or the concrete patio of one of the
garden apartments; the 5 A.M. clatter of garbage cans being
emptied and returned to the sidewalk; sirens, and car horns,

and footfalls from the apartment above; the smell of cabbage, or fish, or incense, in the hallways and lobby.

The super was an elegant lush who'd once been, it was rumored, a professional man of some sort, but who now spent most of his time downstairs in the laundry room, watching the laundry float past the windows of the dryers while he nursed a bottle of Chivas Regal and chain-smoked. He was rarely sober, but he was inoffensive and exquisitely mannered. All the tenants liked him. Charlie was an expensive charity case indulged by the two hundred or so people who populated the ten-story building. His apartment was next door to hers, and often in the summer she had stepped outside into her garden to hear Charlie singing to himself as he troweled another layer of mortar along the wall separating their gardens in order to implant yet another row of wine or liquor bottles. In the sunlight, the bottles looked quite beautiful up there. In their staggered rows, there was a kind of lunatic symmetry to their arrangement that pleased her, as did Charlie's wardrobe of threadbare button-down shirts and baggy cords and what looked like old-school ties.

Dene thought he looked like the former headmaster of some good boys' school, or the vice-president, perhaps, of a small New England bank. He had the English-influenced kind of New York accent one heard used only by the older residents of the city, the ones who'd been New York born and bred and attended first-class schools. It spoke of money, and bootleg hootch in the twenties; of Packards and live-in help and indulgent parents; of a way of life that had come to an end with the Second World War. Charlie was a dinosaur. Everyone seemed to know it and treated him accordingly, with good-natured respect and tolerance. And anyway, he sang wonderfully well. Often Dene left her back door open in the hope of hearing Charlie sing part or all of the libretto of *H.M.S. Pinafore* or *The Mikado*. He was partial to opera, and if he wasn't actually singing in a surprisingly pure tenor, his record player was sending out, in rather tinny tones, the last half of *Madame Butterfly* or some other Puccini opera.

Images slipped into her brain like slides and she experienced a rush of excitement for Toronto, for the sight of familiar streets and moments: the junky little stores on Queen Street; the Rosedale subway station; the lakeshore;

the St. Lawrence Market on a Saturday morning, with its smells and colors; the crowds of shoppers and tourists; the Royal Alexandra with its small foyer and its aura of other, grander times; her mother's house.

She opened her eyes to put out her cigarette and for the first time took stock of the woman beside her, who looked like somebody's grandmother. She had light silvery hair, a tweed skirt, and a cardigan over a milky-white blouse, small gold hoops in her ears, a dusting of face powder and circles of rouge on her cheeks, gold-frame reading glasses. She was scanning a copy of *Newsweek* and making marks here and there on the pages with a red felt-tipped pen. Dene tried to see what she was writing, but couldn't read the woman's script. She was reminded of her college days, of frantic note-taking during a lecture, and of being unable, afterward, to decipher her hasty scrawl.

Years ago she'd have asked the woman what she was doing, and why. Then she hadn't been in the least adverse to talking to strangers. In fact, she'd made several good friends that way. Now she couldn't help feeling that a question might be construed as an intrusion, and since she didn't encourage other people's interest in her, she couldn't very well violate this woman's privacy. So she was surprised when the woman looked up suddenly and smiled— reducing Dene's estimate of her age by a good ten years in the process—and said, "I'm a researcher. I go through periodicals and newspapers and make notes of anything pertaining to the research."

Stupidly, Dene said, "Oh."

"I couldn't help sensing you were wondering," the woman went on. "It usually happens."

"People ask what you're doing?"

"Regularly." She recapped her pen and used it as a marker as she closed the magazine. "I'm used to it. When I first started the work, it embarrassed me. But not anymore."

"What sort of research?" Dene asked, not really interested.

"Free-lance. Right now, I'm working for a man who's doing a book on politicians' wives."

"Their wives? Why?"

"Haven't the foggiest notion," she said with a laugh. "I just do the job and submit my bill."

"Politicians' wives," Dene repeated, considering that. "I

suppose people might be interested in knowing what sort of women marry men with political ambitions."

"The ambition usually comes considerably after the marriage. Anyway, it's not quite as deadly as my last job. That was an analysis of housing starts and boring as hell." She reached for an expensive-looking black leather handbag and took out a pack of Rothman's and a gold lighter. With the cigarette lit, she removed her reading glasses, then lowered her seat back.

"Are you from Toronto?" Dene asked.

The woman turned her head and Dene studied her, finding her quite beautiful. She must have been, Dene thought, a stunning young girl.

"I live there now," the woman answered, appearing enviably relaxed. "I was born in Connecticut. My husband was from Toronto. After the divorce, I decide to stay on. Oddly enough, he now lives in Connecticut. The company transferred him to New York a few years back and he and his second wife live in Old Greenwich."

"Is that where you were from?"

"Hartford. But we met in Boston."

"It sounds complicated," Dene said.

"Oh, it wasn't. We were both at school there. It was all really very simple and uncomplicated. Where are you from?"

"Well," Dene began, wishing she hadn't started this, "I was born in Toronto, but I've been living in New York for the last four years. I've just decided to come back."

"I liked New York," the woman said. "We lived there for six months years back when Frank was taking a refresher course." She smiled suddenly and extended her hand. "Anne Reynolds."

"Dene Whitmore." The woman had a good solid handshake.

"What've you been doing in New York?" Anne asked.

"I don't honestly know," Dene said truthfully. "I think I've been in a coma."

Anne laughed appreciatively.

"Actually, I design toys."

"Isn't that fascinating? What kind of toys?"

"Families. They come complete in their own little log cabin, or tepee, or igloo. But I've just about run dry. There are only so many you can do. I'm not sure what I'll do next."

Anyway, it's down near the bottom of my list of priorities. I'm up for the weekend to find someplace to live."

"Toys," Anne said thoughtfully, puffing on her cigarette. "It sounds like a pleasant way to earn a living."

"It's all right." Dene felt tired all at once. She'd talked more to this woman than she had to anyone in years and she'd grown out of the habit. She lit a fresh cigarette and stared out the window again. Maybe coming back wasn't such a good idea after all, she thought, and then wondered why she thought that.

"Are you on your own?" Anne asked, after a time.

Dene turned back from the window and nodded.

"Divorced?"

"I'm a widow."

"That's sad," Anne said soberly. "Were you married long?"

"Six years." She prayed this woman wouldn't pursue the matter.

"Look, I know this will sound strange, but I have a house with an apartment downstairs. I was going to start advertising this weekend. I don't suppose you'd be interested?"

"A house?"

"My tenants are moving out at the end of the month. If you're interested, I'd be glad to show you the place. It's a very nice apartment. Nothing grand, but the rent's reasonable and the neighborhood's pleasant. We're not far from the subway and within walking distance of the stores."

"Where?" Dene asked, wondering how this could be happening.

"Roughly, Eglinton and Yonge. Duplex and Castlefield, to be exact."

"I know where that is," Dene said, feeling stupid again.

Anne opened her handbag and took out a card. "If you decide you'd like to see it, just give me a call. It's a one-bedroom and the rent is two hundred."

"Thank you." Dene took the card and tucked it into her bag. You didn't meet someone on a plane and rent an apartment from them. That wasn't the way things worked. Was it?

Anne put out her cigarette, closed her eyes, and slept throughout the rest of the flight. Dene looked over from time to time, then put their conversation behind her and gazed blankly at the dark window. She had a mental image of a luxurious high-rise apartment with walls of tinted glass and a panoramic view of the city, lights dotting the night-scape. Ridiculous! She didn't even like high-rise buildings. What would she use as furniture to fill the vast rooms of her imagining? No. Something small and cozy, with a fireplace, possibly, and a window in front of which she could place her drawing board. Good light and a reasonable amount of space was all she wanted.

She decided to go through the customs and immigration line marked VISITORS, and explained to the official that she was simply visiting and had nothing to declare. He gave her a white card with NOTHING TO DECLARE encircled and she headed toward the baggage claim area. She saw the woman who'd sat beside her on the plane, but couldn't remember her name. She considered searching for the card but decided not to. Her bag was one of the first offloaded. She grabbed it from the carousel and started toward the exit.

Anne Reynolds called out something Dene didn't catch. She turned to smile blankly at the woman before presenting her card at the exit barrier, then made her way past the crowd of people waiting to greet arrivals. She stopped and scanned the row of car rental booths, then went over to the Budget Car Rental desk and requested the smallest, least-expensive car available.

"For how long?" the girl behind the counter asked.

"Just the weekend."

"How about a Pinto?"

"Fine." Dene showed her driver's license and her Master-Charge card. She was told where to locate the car and found the Pinto with no trouble. She pulled in at the first hotel she saw, left the car parked by the entrance, and went inside to find that they did have a single room. She regis-tered, was given a room key and told where to park and also what time the restaurants would be closing.

On her way back to the car, she paused to buy a *Globe and Mail* and a *Star*.

The room was exactly what she'd expected: sterile and uninviting, with a double bed, a color television set, a paper strip across the toilet seat, and water glasses in little paper bags. She put the suitcase down on the low bench beside the desk before sitting on the edge of the bed to open the *Star* to the classified ads section. It was still early enough—only nine o'clock—to telephone and set up some appointments.

She couldn't believe the number of ads. There were dozens of them. She lit a cigarette as she went up and down the columns, circling ones that looked reasonable. She'd forgotten a lot of the streets. Where was Cummer? She couldn't remember ever having heard of it. She knew that she wouldn't care to live as far east as Victoria Park or as far north as Finch. Something between St. Clair and Eglinton, say, between Bathurst and Yonge. In all, she circled fourteen ads, nine in the *Star* and five in the *Globe*. Six of the numbers she tried rang unanswered. Two of the apartments were already rented. She made appointments to see six of the listings the next day, allowing an hour for each viewing. This wasn't going to be difficult at all, she thought, after the last of the calls. She'd easily find a place in one weekend.

Feeling reassured, she gathered up her cigarettes and the room key and went down to the lobby. The dining room and coffee shop were still open. She stood midway between the two, debating, and finally decided on the dining room. She'd treat herself to a good meal, and some wine, to celebrate her return.

Once seated in a far corner of the room, her order taken, she thought again about the woman on the plane. She looked through her handbag and found the card. Anne Reynolds. An address on Duplex and a telephone number. Down in the corner of the card was printed RESEARCH. Imagine offering a complete stranger an apartment in your own home? But why not? she thought more temperately. Why shouldn't she have offered Dene a chance at it? After all, she had an apartment to rent and Dene was looking for one. Still, it didn't feel quite right. Renting an apartment in someone's home would undoubtedly lead to an exchange of confidences, a familiarity that didn't interest her. Anne had already managed to elicit the information that Dene was not divorced but widowed. Next she'd want to know how and why, and Dene couldn't stand the thought of that. No. It was best to maintain her anonymity. She'd find an apartment through one of the appointments she'd set up; she was bound to. She wanted a standard lease from a standard corporate landlord, not rooms in some researcher's home.

The meal was disappointing. The wine was watery and

acidic, the salad consisted of plain lettuce and pallid tomatoes and was overdressed, the steak was tough and underdone. The baked potato wasn't bad, but the coffee was thick
and bitter—obviously the bottom of the pot. She passed up
dessert, signed for the meal, left the dining room and returned
upstairs to open the curtains and stare out the window,
watching planes take off. Finally, chilled, she drew the
curtains and turned to survey the room. With a sigh, she
unpacked and carried her nightgown and toiletries bag into
the bathroom. A hot shower would ease her muscles and
enable her to sleep.

Her reflection in the large bathroom mirror startled her.
She hadn't confronted a mirror of this size in a very long
time and wasn't sure how to react to what she saw. She'd
become a stick doll, she thought, horrified by the ridge of
bone running down her chest and the pointy angularity of
her shoulders and hips. She wanted to cry. What had become
of the woman whose image she'd once known so well, an
image with good breasts and rounded hips? This woman in
the mirror was all angles and concavities, lacking substance.
What had been her breasts were shrunken pouches of flesh
that would have looked more fitting on a twelve-year-old.
Quickly, she turned away, pulled on her shower cap, adjusted
the water temperature, and stepped under the blast of hot
water.

There were several dreams she had regularly, frighteningly. This time she had the dream of Jake and Mimi, and
awakened sobbing. She sat against the headboard and smoked
a cigarette in the dark, waiting for the dream to recede. She
listened to the night silence, feeling bereft and dislocated.
She thought about her mother's house with its gleaming
hardwood floors, its vases of fresh-cut flowers, its attic full
of trunks and boxes. She could hear footsteps clicking smartly
along the hallways and could see, finally, her mother's sad,
pretty features. For the first time in four years she wanted
to see her mother. She could almost feel herself sinking into
a welcoming embrace, could almost smell the familiar scent
of Joy and hear the soft English articulation of her mother's
comforting words.

The dream displaced, she extinguished the cigarette and
lay down to sleep.

Chapter 4

Sherrill had visited her mother a few days earlier to say good-bye. All that remained was the telephone call she'd promised to make to her mother before she actually locked up the apartment and went out to get into the car.

She put off making the call as long as possible, thinking Jamie might call to say good-bye. Why would he? she asked herself. As far as he was concerned, she was a working acquaintance. He'd said his good-bye on Saturday night. It would be wonderful, though, if he'd called. She told herself to forget it and dialed the office number. Her mother's secretary wanted to chat, as if this were one of the routine calls Sherrill made regularly. At last Sherrill interrupted to say, "I think my mother's expecting my call, Mary. I'm just about to leave."

Mary said, "That's right! I must be crazy. Hang on, hon."

The sound of her mother's voice gave Sherrill a sudden, inexplicable lump in her throat. She hadn't expected to have any reaction at all, but as their brief conversation wound to a close, she felt cut loose, already separated from the one person who'd always been wholeheartedly support-ive. She managed to say good-bye and fumbled the receiver back into the cradle.

She was actually leaving, going off to New York. She'd gone down a few months earlier to see if she could get an agent, and if she'd have any chance of getting work. Michelle, an old London Academy friend who made a lot of money doing voiceovers for commercials and dubbing foreign films, had taken Sherrill along to meet her agent, whose interest had been immediate. He'd liked Sherrill's voice tape and photographs, and had been impressed by her credits as a revue writer and composer. He'd agreed then and there to take her on, and Michelle had treated a bemused Sherrill to a celebration drink at the Plaza.

Everything had happened very quickly, far more so than she'd expected. She hadn't thought she'd come away from her week-long visit with anything more than some first impressions; instead, she'd returned to Toronto as a performer with an honest-to-God New York agent. John, the agent, and Michelle had written their To Whom it May Concern letters of reference on Sherrill's behalf. After the applications for a visa had been filed, she'd gone downtown to the American Consulate on University Avenue and been granted one. Every step of the way she'd been waiting for the snag that would put an end to the dizzying momentum of events. It hadn't happened.

Now she sat on the floor of her denuded apartment, her hand still on the telephone, feeling she'd just severed the last connection tying her to the first twenty-five years of her life. She was stricken with a feeling akin to terror. A whim, a week's vacation, a visit to an old friend had resulted in a complete redirection of her life, and she wasn't at all convinced that any of it was what she wanted. The New York State road map lay open on the floor, her pack of cigarettes centered over Lake Ontario.

"Jesus!" she whispered, and reached for a cigarette.

Her insides were clenching, unclenching. She lit the cigarette, took a hard drag, and told herself to pick up the pack of cigarettes and the road map and get going. She couldn't move. Sure, she'd liked New York while she'd been there; she and Michelle had had a great time seeing the shows, window-shopping in the Village, eating in exotic restaurants. She'd loved it—for a visit. But to live there, how would that be?

Seven years ago, when she was preparing to go off to London, she'd felt only a strange rightness to the move. She'd wanted to go to a good theater school, and LAMDA had accepted her. She'd packed up and flown off to London filled with excitement and anticipation. After her two years at school, she'd returned to Canada, again in high spirits. She'd been returning home to capitalize on all she'd learned at the academy. There'd been logic to those moves. She failed to see any in this one.

She'd established a good reputation here; she was working regularly, even getting billing now and then. Why give that up to go to a city five times the size to compete with

ten times as many actors! Because Canada had no star
system and didn't nurture its artists; Canada didn't support the arts. All the old stock lines, but they were true.
She'd never achieve any real success if she stayed here.
She'd go on, getting work, but never really rising, because
the business here didn't have any top. There was only,
ultimately, the plateau of continual employment. She felt
frustrated here, from time to time, by the lack of real challenge. She had constant daydreams about a man who was a
total enigma to her. She tossed the cigarette into the grate,
picked up the map, got slowly to her feet, and took a last
look around.

She'd never again have an apartment quite like this one,
with its many mullioned windows in the living room, its
good oak floors and wide fireplace; the cosy bedroom, the
tiny, cramped kitchen. She'd spent five years in these rooms,
had grown accustomed to the hiss of heat steaming into the
radiators in winter, and the spring sign of forsythia creeping yellow over the windowsills.

The place looked devastated now. And St. Clair had
changed in five years. Many of the old houses had been
either torn down or taken over for medical suites. A huge
new Loblaws supermarket had been built near Bathurst,
and just down from St. Clair, twin apartment towers—called
a luxury complex—had recently been completed. The area
didn't feel so much like a neighborhood now; it seemed to
have been depersonalized, sanitized, made sterile, perhaps
for the hundreds of people who'd move in to populate those
twin white towers dominating the horizon.

Of course the streetcars still ran, and the noise of the
traffic outside had lulled her to sleep at night. The park
across the way hadn't changed, but a lot had. She felt as if
she were one of the old things that should have been left
alone. Her own drive, and a reluctance—or was it an
inability—to say no, were forcing her out of the comfortably
safe and well-known life she'd created, into a vast, potentially empty landscape that might swallow her. Well, she
damned well wouldn't go down without a fight. She'd see
this move through even if it turned out to be an unmitigated
disaster.

He wasn't going to phone.

She left the apartment keys in the landlady's mailbox, as

arranged, then walked across the road to the Bug. Her insides were still quivery, unsettled. A reasonable, inner voice told her she didn't have to go; she could unpack the car, call the movers, and tell them to bring her things back.

"No!" she cried aloud, her eyes on the wet pavement beneath her feet. No! She climbed into the car, threw the shift into reverse, and backed out of the lot. If she didn't go now, she'd spend years poring over the if-only's; she might never be able to be satisfied with anything.

Headed for the Queen Elizabeth Way, she looked at the city. She was wise to leave in November when the city was in the first throes of what was predicted would be an especially hard winter. She could have waited until spring, but she'd have been unable to leave when the trees were in bud and the grass was starting to turn from brown to green. When the flowers began to come into bloom the city would assume its other personality, the lush summery one that made her chest feel too small to contain all the pleasure the city gave her. Right this moment, with the streets gray and shiny with the imprint of rain, and the wind sharp enough to make it hurt to breathe too deeply, it wasn't all that difficult to leave.

She reminded herself of the impact Manhattan had had on her in the early summer when she'd been there. The people on the streets had been fascinating, far better dressed than Torontonians, sharper, more elegant, even more alive. Everyone moved so quickly; everything seemed to happen at an accelerated rate. By comparison, Toronto was suburban, behind the times. She'd be able to see all the foreign films, plays, and musicals she cared to. There was every kind of food in the world waiting to be sampled. There were opportunities of a magnitude and variety that could never exist in Canada. She'd make the most of all of them.

She thought about Jamie Ferrara, again seeing him walk away down the dark, empty street in the cold. For a few seconds, she had a distinct sense of the man, an impression of his identity. It was a nebulous, purely instinctive insight into who he was, and why; an understanding all at once of his integrity, his pride, and—startlingly—his aloneness.

She understood the aloneness. She'd felt it herself most of her life: a separateness, a knowledge of being different, of being "other." She'd never attempted to articulate this mat-

ter of otherness to anyone for fear of sounding foolish and of
revealing herself to be odd. It wasn't odd, though. It was
simply a matter of her awareness of the distance between
herself and other people. The distance seemed to have existed
always, and she hadn't so far learned how to bridge the
sometimes considerable gap in order to participate more
fully and actively in the lives and interests of others. Perhaps she and Jamie were both victims of their inability to
step beyond themselves and make contact. Maybe she should
have tried to talk to him about it. But how, when? Their
conversations had revolved around observations about the
weather, or had had to do with the shows they'd done.
There'd never been an opening—for either one of them.

She was too analytical, she told herself. It was a view her
mother held of her, as well.

"You're in the wrong business," her mother had once told
her. "You want people to admire you for your logic and
intelligence, but you show them your legs and sing for them
and hope they'll notice that you do it *intelligently*. You don't
need a great brain to be a whiz in show business, Sherry.
Look at all the people who've bluffed it out with good looks
and a nice speaking voice. A clever director can make anybody look good. I'm not denying you're talented. You are.
But there are half a dozen other businesses you could be in
that would give you what you want. I just can't help wondering if this one's going to give you what you're after."

Josie Westcott was no fool, and Sherrill knew it. But
whenever she'd contemplated her alternatives, none of them
offered her the possibility of the kind of success she hoped
to attain. She wanted freedom and independence and the
money to maintain both. She couldn't get that working in an
office or writing specialty material for other people. Periodically, her mother's comments nagged at her with their
inescapable truth. She'd never discounted her mother's comments because, almost always, her mother was right.

Their relationship was admittedly unusual, owing in no
small part to Sherrill's father having decided to abandon
both mother and child when Sherrill was three and her
mother twenty-three.

"I knew I should never have married him," her mother
had said over the years when Sherrill asked about him. "He
was too damned attractive."

When asked what she meant by that, Josie had explained, "He enjoyed being good-looking, having women fawn over him. He wasn't a bad man, just weak. I can practically guarantee you he's lived with dozens of women since he left—spreading himself around." She'd always smiled when speaking of him, as if privately glad to have partaken of his charm.

After he'd left, Josie had filed for divorce and, with the help of her parents, had gone back to school. For the next four years, she and Sherrill had been what Josie wryly called "schoolgirls" together. In the evenings mother and daughter had sat together at the kitchen table doing their homework. When she thought of her childhood, Sherrill always recalled those evenings in the kitchen, and how the light had cast a sheen over her mother's bent head.

By the time she was thirty, Josie had opened her own office as a CPA. She had since managed to build to the point where she now had fifteen employees and a substantial clientele. She had dated regularly over the years, but chose to remain single. She still dated, but not so often as before.

"I'm getting too old for it," she'd told Sherrill recently, and had narrowed her men down to two: Larry Harwood, a lawyer she'd been seeing for close to ten years, and Dave Atkins, a contractor she'd known since high school. Sherrill had as a child and, later, as a teenager accompanied her mother and one or the other of these men on countless outings. Larry was tall and slim, with a penchant for expensive, hand-tailored Italian suits. He liked dimly lit French restaurants, open-air concerts, and Josie Westcott. When in his company, she and her mother were quieter, even solemn, perhaps because the quality of their time together was exceptionally high. By contrast, Dave was a ruddy-complected, solidly built outdoors man whose interests ran to baseball games, picnics, camping trips, and Agatha Christie novels. Sherrill like both men equally well; evidently so did her mother.

At forty-five, Josie looked, Sherrill thought, better than she had at thirty. She belonged to a health club and played tennis at least twice a week, swam almost every morning for an hour, and had become a vegetarian the previous year.

She cooked superbly and Sherrill herself was toying with
the idea of dispensing with meat.

Her mother had met Jamie, and had liked him.

"He's a gentleman, Sherry. A rare breed nowadays. He
likes you, you know."

Her mother's words had, for some reason, alarmed her.
"He's married," Sherrill had said defensively.

"I simply said he *likes* you," Josie had replied with lifted
eyebrows.

"He likes everyone," Sherrill had said. It was the truth.
Everyone also liked Jamie. He *was* a gentleman. He was
handsome, charming, witty, talented, and married. She imagined his wife to be beautiful, in an understated English
way, and probably blond. She was undoubtedly everything
Sherrill was not. She couldn't bear even to imagine Jamie's
wife, or his children. It couldn't possibly do her any good to
think about him, or his private life. The odd thing was that
he seemed to her to be someone who didn't *have* a private
life. She'd never heard him speak of his family. Was he
happy? she wondered. Somehow she didn't think so. Forget
it! she told herself. What she had was nothing more than a
schoolgirl's crush on an attractive man. By the time she got
to New York she'd have forgotten all about him.

Once past the Hamilton, the traffic thinned out and she
relaxed a bit, raising the volume on the radio and rolling
down the window a crack to let the car air out. The rhythm
and motion were taking her over; she had begun to feel like
an extension of the machinery. It was not an unpleasant
sensation; in fact, she enjoyed driving.

The wind was high, buffeting the little car as she headed
toward Niagara Falls. Just past Vineland, she looked over to
the left side of the road to see the lake. It was within a
hundred feet of the highway at this point, and she always
felt a thrill of excitement at coming down the long stretch
and up the slight rise to see the greenish-white lake waters
so close to the highway. Quite often there would be people
walking at the side of the road carrying fishing rods and
buckets, on their way to the shore to spend a few hours
casting their lines into the polluted water. Today there
were no cars parked on the service roads, no fishermen

ambling down the road. The lake waters were choppy and the air was stingingly cold.

The closer she got to Niagara, the more nervous she became about making her official entry into the United States. She had all her documents: the affidavits, the chest X ray, the signed and sworn applications, everything required to allow her to live and work in this other country. All her life she and her friends had spoken disparagingly of Americans, and their negative influence on business and industry in Canada, of their general ignorance when it came to the country and its people, of their lack of interest in anything but money and power.

Now she felt like a traitor, having paid a firm of consultants three hundred and fifty dollars to assist in securing her right of way into this country she'd privately and publicly maligned. She had, once, in London approached a newspaper vendor to buy an *Evening Standard.* The man had held back the folded newspaper, asking, "You an American, then?" Taken aback by the question, she'd said, "No, I'm Canadian." "That's all right, then," he'd said. "We're fed up with Americans 'ere." She'd paid for and received the newspaper, then continued on her way, wondering what the brief exchange had signified—if anything. She'd felt guilty. What difference would it have made if she'd been American? No one ought to be judged by his nationality. It was the individual who counted. She'd thought often of that newspaper vendor and wished she'd said she was American just to know what he would have done. Perhaps all nationalism, on a certain level, was silly. Her reasoning, however, did nothing to assuage her mounting ambivalence about this move, and it was growing larger minute by minute as she neared her point of entry.

Her border crossing took less than ten minutes. Her documents were checked, her chest X ray ignored. She was told her green card would be mailed to her at Michelle's address, and that was that. Feeling very let down—had she, perhaps, been hoping to be refused entry?—she got back into the Bug and drove over the Rainbow Bridge, on her way to the New York State Thruway.

She'd been expecting something of significance to take place at the border—a ceremony, possibly, or some elaborate ritual of welcome. It had been a pedestrian, even squalid,

ten minutes while she'd stood on one side of the counter
and the immigration officer had stood on the other, perfunctorily checking her documents before keeping some and
shoving the others back into the brown envelope, stamping.
this and that, then waving her on.

What had she expected? Brass bands and banners? But
how mean an entrance, how small and unnoticeable her
slide into the stream of American traffic!

By the time she reached the entrance to the thruway it
was snowing. The wind pushed at the small car so that it
was hard to stay in her lane. Her common sense told her to
find a motel and stop for the night, or at least until the
snow blew past. She kept going. She wanted to put more
distance between herself and her recent past; she wanted to
get to Manhattan and Michelle's apartment and begin the
next part of her life. She told herself she was crazy. The
snow was quickly getting thicker and the fragile windshield
wipers seemed barely able to shift the weight of the accu-
mulating snow. Visibility was rapidly diminishing, and the
monotony of the unraveling snowscape ahead was starting
to make her sleepy. The whole venture had taken on the
overtones of a disaster: *Actress makes entrance into the United
States, set for glory, only to die on snowbound thruway.* She
raised the volume further on the radio, hoping for some
local weather reports as she played with the dial, found a
strong station, and lit a cigarette. The ashtray was already
half filled. The heat gushed back from the defrost vents and
swirled around her head. She wound down the window and
tried to ignore the snow rushing in as she leaned forward
over the wheel and narrowed her eyes as if that might
enhance her vision.

Tears accumulated in her eyes and she wished she'd said
something to Jamie, or made love to him. She should have
taken a firm grip both on her courage and on the man. In
her imagination, she could easily see herself standing naked
inside the circle of Jamie's arms, could feel his hands skimming over her while his lips moved against her ear and he
whispered everything she wanted to hear.

She threw her cigarette out the window and clutched the
steering wheel with both hands. She wasn't going to stop;
she wouldn't be defeated by snow and wind. She'd make it

through to New York, and, once there, never think about Jamie again.

"You made the damned decision," she said aloud. "Now you stick with it!"

What, though, had she actually decided?

Never mind, she told herself. Just get there and do it one step at a time!

If only he'd called to say good-bye . . .

Chapter 5

Nothing Dene saw was right. Both of the duplex apartments were dark and musty-smelling; three apartments were all too far from public transportation routes; the last one she simply disliked. She bought the Saturday papers and again went through the ads. There were half a dozen new listings, three of which she went to see. Two were in Rosedale. She liked the second of them, but was so inundated by memories just being in the area that she knew she couldn't possibly live there. She returned to the hotel late Saturday afternoon exhausted and depressed.

She ordered dinner from room service and ate a shrimp salad while watching an old movie on television. She'd forgotten how mindlessly pleasurable and absorbing television could be. Intermittently, she saw pictures of herself at work in the New York apartment, with the back door open and Charlie's drunken tenor wafting in from outside where he was cementing more bottles to the top of his wall. It was a safe image—a still life of her existence. Loneliness, isolation, and loss of identity accompanied the picture, and she was forced to admit to herself that she no longer cared to live completely alone. Out of all the ads she couldn't find one place that suited her, and that was a little distressing.

After setting the room service tray outside the door, she hooked the DO NOT DISTURB sign over the outer doorknob, doublelocked the door, and sat back down on the foot of the bed to watch the eleven o'clock news. It was strange to hear about local politicians and items of especially Canadian interest. But this was another country, after all, not a northern suburb of some American city, a separate country with decidedly different views and ways of doing things. This realization warmed her. Even if some of the street names and the goings-on here were unfamiliar after so long away, nevertheless they were *her* politicians, and the streets were *her* birthright. She had a sense of belonging, of home, she hadn't had in New York. She could extend her stay, buy the newspapers each day, and go on looking until she found an apartment that suited her

Call the woman! her interior voice told her impatiently. She'd been nice enough, even witty. What on earth have you got to lose?

She reached for her handbag, and found Anne Reynolds' card. She studied it for several minutes, debating, then got up to wedge the card into the telephone dial where she'd be sure to see it when she woke up in the morning.

She was up far too early and dawdled over breakfast—the best meal she'd so far had in the hotel—as long as possible before returning to her room. It was still too early to call. She stood for a long time in front of the window, watching planes take off. Finally, at nine o'clock, she went down to the lobby, where the gift shop was now open, and bought all the Sunday papers. Back in her room, she gazed at the sizable stack of papers, unable to summon the energy or the interest to look through them. She returned to the window to watch the planes.

At a quarter to ten, she went to the telephone.

The instant she heard the woman's voice she became doubtful again, and there was a lengthening silence as Anne Reynolds said, "Hello," several times. At last, Dene managed to get out a thick "Hello." "This is Dene Whitmore," she began, positive the woman wouldn't remember. "We met on the plane Friday night."

"Of course. Have you decided you'd like to see the apartment?"

"Well . . . yes, I would."

"Good! My tenants are away for the weekend. So, if you like, you could come now."

"Yes, all right."

"You know how to get here?"

"Yes, I do."

"Good! See you soon," Anne said, and hung up.

Slowly Dene put down the receiver, and stood staring at the telephone. This was a mistake. She was crazy even to consider renting a place from this woman. She was so ... decisive. Maybe she was the type of woman who'd want to make decisions for Dene.

"Nuts!" she said aloud and went into the bathroom to brush her hair and, on second thought, apply a bit of make-up. Since the previous night's encounter with the mirror she'd become overly conscious of her pale, unpretty appearance. She unearthed a stick of Erace and an old compact of powdered blusher and went to work on the dark areas under her eyes, and her cheeks. The end result, she thought, was garish. She washed her face, turned off the bathroom light, pulled on her old London Fog raincoat, and went down to the car.

As had happened the day before, she experienced a quiet euphoria as she drove along the 401, heading for the Yonge Street exit. She opened the window to feel winter in the air. It had a certain edge and weight that told her it would probably rain later in the afternoon. It surprised her that she was still able to read the air. Jake used to laugh when she'd predicted rain or snow. "But I can tell!" she'd insisted. "I can feel it in the air." He'd called her "Swami" and laughed. In time, he'd started asking what sort of day she'd thought it would be and if he needed to take an umbrella or a hat, because she was rarely wrong. Jake. No.

The house was a large, detached red-brick right on the corner of the street. She drove slowly past, craning to get as complete a viewing as possible, and saw additions at the rear that were probably sun-rooms on the ground and second floors. There was a double garage and a good-sized paved area where a grimy white Mercedes was parked at an angle. She pulled in beside the Mercedes, got out and stood for a few moments looking at the house. White-painted shutters enclosed all the rear windows. The house looked and felt right and she knew that not only was she going to like the apartment, she was going to want to live there.

The woman who came to the door did not look like someone's grandmother. In a silky, pale green caftan, with her hair coiled loosely into a topknot, Anne Reynolds looked vital and healthy and considerably younger than Dene had assumed she was.

"You're in time for coffee," Anne said, holding open the door.

Dene stepped inside and followed Anne upstairs to the living room, where a longish-haired, heavily bearded young man sat sprawled in a very modern armchair.

"Come in and sit down," Anne said. "This is my nephew, Charlie."

Charlie hauled himself up out of the chair, with a grin offered his hand to Dene, and said, "Hi."

Dene shook his hand, then freed herself and looked around uncertainly.

"Make yourself comfortable," Anne called, on her way to the kitchen. "Cream and sugar?"

"Black, please." Dene sat on the edge of one of the armchairs as Charlie said, "I hear you're moving back from New York."

"That's right."

"Been away long?" he asked, lounging with one leg resting atop the other at right angles.

"Four years."

"The city's changed, eh?" he observed, smiling.

"I haven't really seen enough to tell."

"Oh, you will," he said confidently. "It's a pretty good place to live, these days. Anne says you design toys."

"Yes, I do."

"Am I making you nervous?" he asked incisively.

"No," she lied, meeting his eyes. He looked young; at least what she could see of his face—round blue eyes and a well-shaped mouth—looked youthful. The rest of his face was hidden behind a curling red-blond beard; it and his hair looked impossibly clean, as did his faded denims and plaid work shirt. She guessed his age to be about twenty-four or -five.

"It's okay," he said, still smiling. "I talk a lot, ask a lot of questions. If it gets to you, just tell me to shut up."

Anne reappeared carrying a tray with three mugs of coffee and a plate of doughnuts.

"He does talk a lot," she corroborated. "After a while, it just becomes background music."

Charlie made a scoffing noise as he helped himself to a mug and two doughnuts, which he began to devour in huge bites.

"The other Charlie I know does make background music," Dene said.

"Oh?" Anne offered her a doughnut, which Dene refused, then went to sit in the middle of the long, deep, lushly upholstered chocolate-brown sofa that took up the center of the room.

"My super," Dene explained, wishing she'd said nothing. "He sings arias while he puts his bottles on the wall."

"What does he do?" Charlie asked, licking powdered sugar from his fingers. "Shoot them off?"

"He cements them on top of the wall. They look ... beautiful," she trailed off.

"It sounds like New York, all right," Anne said, sitting with her legs tucked under, holding her mug with both hands. She watched Dene take a sip of coffee, then set the cup down carefully on the table beside her while she opened her bag for her cigarettes. She exuded sadness, Anne thought. "Charlie," she explained, "is my brother Ted's son. He's undoubtedly the world's oldest draft dodger. He likes to hang out here Sunday mornings," she said, giving him an affectionate smile. "He also likes to clutter up my garage with his memorabilia—which is why my car is parked outside."

Charlie snorted with laughter. "I like to think of them as artifacts," he told Dene. "And I'm not a draft dodger. I'm an aging conscientious objector. Anyway, I've got citizenship now."

"What are your artifacts?" Dene asked, somewhat thawed by the easy camaraderie of this woman and her tall, powerful-looking nephew.

"Comic books," he said. "I sell them, among other things."

"What other things?"

"Big Little Books. Remember those? Stuff from the thirties and forties. All kinds of things."

"He's got a junk store," Anne clarified.

"Hey! Some of my stuff's pretty good," Charlie said, mock defensively. "Just because you go in heavily for Italian mod-

own dooon't moan a whole lot of poopio don't go how my otubb.
I've got some honest-to-God art deco jewelry that's sensational. And some nice brass pieces, too."

"Where's your store?" Dene asked.

"Queen and McCaul. Come on by sometime. I'll bet you
get a charge out of my place." He pushed back his sleeve to
look at his watch. "I've got to go," he said, and gulped down
his coffee. "Don't get up," he told his aunt as he set his mug
on the mantel. "Take the apartment," he said to Dene. "It's
dynamite and a good deal." He bent over Anne to kiss her
on the forehead, waggled his fingers at Dene, and walked
out, pausing to retrieve the corduroy jacket he'd left hanging over the newel post at the top of the stairs.

After the front door had closed, Anne sat looking at Dene,
thoughtfully sipping her coffee. Finally she said, "He's a
sweetheart."

"Is he really a conscientious objector?"

"Never! He's far too old. But he looks like a kid, doesn't
he?"

"Isn't he?" Dene asked.

"I'll bet you five dollars he's older than you are."

"You'll lose," Dene warned.

"Five says I'll win."

Dene smiled slowly, studying the older woman's expression. "All right. I'll be thirty-five next month."

Anne laughed happily. "You owe me five. He'll be thirty-
seven in February."

"You're joking!" Dene exclaimed disbelievingly.

"My brother Ted's twelve years older than me. Charlie's
his youngest. Hal's thirty-seven, and Claire's thirty-eight.
Ted and Joan had the kids like they were entrants in some
kind of contest. Bang bang bang. I don't honestly know how
the poor woman survived the first five years of their marriage. At one point she had three kids all crawling around
on the kitchen floor. But if you knew Ted, you'd know it
was typical of the way he does things. Anyway, Charlie's a
love."

"Do you have children?" Dene asked, violating the promise she'd made to herself not to get on personal terms with
this woman.

Anne laughed again. "Not after seeing my sister-in-law go
through what she did with her three. I wasn't much more

than a kid, but I swore I wouldn't go through that. And I didn't. How about you?"

"Do you think I could see the apartment now?" Dene looked down, paying close attention to putting out her cigarette in a small porcelain ashtray she'd found on the table beside her.

"Sure," Anne said after a moment, and uncoiled herself from the sofa. "Let me get the keys."

She went back out to the kitchen and Dene got up, clutching her handbag, feeling vaguely threatened. Anne came back carrying a ring of keys. It hadn't escaped her that Dene had gone very tense during their talk of children and had actually paled when asked if she had any. She also hadn't answered the question, Anne realized, and she wondered what kind of tales Dene might have to tell. There was definitely a story here, she thought; but tact and consideration kept her from asking further questions.

"You're quite tall, aren't you?" she noted aloud as she and Dene were going down the stairs.

"So are you," Dene replied, waiting while Anne unlocked the door.

"Not as tall as you. This is the living room, obviously," Anne said, standing aside to allow Dene a viewing of the room. It was about twelve by fifteen, with a bay window and what looked to be a functioning fireplace, flanked by built-in bookshelves.

"It's very nice," Dene said inadequately, trailing after Anne to an open expanse.

"This is the dining area. The kitchen's fairly big, so it could be a workroom, I suppose. This is the bedroom," she went on, opening the door to reveal an unmade king-sized bed. "Ooops." She gave Dene a smile of complicity. "You get the general idea, though. There's loads of closet space. And the back door there"—she indicated the rear of the kitchen—"takes you outside. I had the lawn paved over. I got fed up with taking care of it."

"It really is very nice," Dene said, wandering away to have a second look around. The living room was cluttered with far too much furniture, but with just a few, well-chosen pieces, it would be a lovely room.

"Oh, I forgot to tell you the sun-room's off the bedroom," Anne said from the doorway.

Take it! Dene's inner voice ordered. It's absolutely perfect. You'll never find anything better for the money. Take it!

"Well," Anne said, watching her. "What d'you think?"

"Is the heat included?" Dene asked, stalling.

"Everything's included but the telephone, and cable TV, if you want it."

"You're not asking enough," Dene said bluntly.

"I don't need the money," Anne said, her voice husky and soft. "I need people in the house. I like to know that if I scream someone's going to hear me."

Slowly, Dene turned to look at her. She really was a very beautiful woman, with fine features, large eyes and a delicately sculpted mouth.

"You know what I mean," Anne said in that same hushed voice. "You must, having lived in New York for four years."

"I know," Dene said quietly. Why, she wondered, was she surprised? Any woman living alone felt afraid at times. It wasn't the fact of this woman's fear that was so startling, but her frank admission of it.

"It's available December first," Anne said. "You can have a lease, or go month by month. It's all the same to me. Would you like me to leave you to take another look around?"

"I don't think so, thank you."

"Yes?" Anne asked.

"Yes."

"Good. Let's go back and finish our coffee while we work out the details."

Anne had frail-looking wrists and ankles, Dene noticed. Her hair looked as if it would be soft to the touch. With it pinned up, the angles of her face were attractively revealed, and it was the absence of face powder and rouge that made her appear so much younger today. Suddenly, Dene wondered how she appeared to Anne. She resisted the temptation to run her hand over her hair, guessing that she probably looked disheveled and unrelentingly plain.

Before Dene had a chance to sit down, Anne asked, "Would you like to see the rest of the house?"

"I'd love to," Dene said with enthusiasm, surprising herself.

Anne showed her the large, sunny kitchen, and the spare bedroom with its adjoining sun-room, then moved toward the stairs that had, in former times, led to the attic. What had been the attic was now two large rooms, one an office and the other Anne's bedroom. On the outside wall of her bedroom was a pair of large sliding glass doors that gave onto an enclosed redwood patio where there was a round table with two chairs and a variety of plants in tubs. The bedroom itself had a thick apricot-colored carpet; the walls were painted white and had been left bare. Placed squarely in the center of the far wall was an ultramodern all-in-one oak unit consisting of a low-slung bed, headboard, and two side tables, each holding round white lamps with pleated apricot shades. There were flowered covers on the pillows and a matching cover on the comforter. Aside from a long, low chest of drawers, also in oak, there was no other furniture in the room. The oak was golden, with a matte finish, and looked very expensive. In the right-hand corner of the room a door stood ajar, revealing a bathroom completely tiled in large white squares.

"It's beautiful," Dene said. "You've got wonderful taste."

"Thank you. Charlie just finished the deck last weekend. It's taken months to have all the work done up here. I've been wanting to do this over for years but didn't have the money. Old Aunt Grace finally died last year, at the age of a hundred and four, and Ted and I inherited her money."

"Is Charlie a carpenter?" Dene asked, on the way back downstairs.

"Charlie? He's everything. There's very little Charlie can't do," Anne said, curling up again on the sofa. "Except, perhaps, sustain a relationship. He has a little trouble with that. He's been married twice. The first time when he was nineteen. That lasted three years. The second time when he was twenty-seven. That one lasted three years, too. I think he's finally given up. It's a pity. He really is a sweetheart. You work at home, I take it?"

"Yes. Does that matter?"

"Not in the least. So do I."

"That's right. I'd forgotten you do research."

"Politicians' wives," Anne reminded her with a smile. "Why do you look so—dumbfounded? You've looked that way since you walked through the door."

"Do I? I'm sorry." Dene could feel the blood rushing up into her face and looked down at her hands. Was she so transparent, so easily read?

"There's no need to be sorry," Anne said kindly. "I was just curious to know what in particular surprises you here."

"Well," Dene hedged. "The house . . . I mean, it's lovely . . . I . . ."

"Would you like a lease?" Anne asked to help her over the rough patch. "Or would you prefer to go month by month?"

"Whatever's best for you," Dene said, eager now to get away and be on her own. She wanted to think about this woman, and her nephew, and the apartment, and that extraordinary bedroom. Anne's presence, for so slight a woman, was powerful. Dene could feel it wrapping itself around her like a blanket.

"Make a decision," Anne said gently. "It's something women alone have to get used to doing. It's a good, healthy process."

"A lease, then," Dene said.

"One year or two?"

"Two."

"Good."

"What about a deposit?" Dene asked.

"Oh, give me whatever you like. We'll get it squared away when you move in."

She was so casual about this, Dene thought. Surely it was bad business to be that casual. She got out her checkbook and dug about for her pen. "It's a New York check. Will that be all right?"

"Fine. I'll let you know what it works out to with the exchange and we'll tie up the loose ends at the first of the month. Do you have much furniture to ship?"

"None," Dene answered, making the check out for four hundred dollars to cover the first and last month's rent. At least she'd be businesslike about this, if Anne couldn't or wouldn't. "A few suitcases. I'll buy what I need when I get here."

"Have you been living in a furnished place?" Anne asked.

"No. But what I've got is secondhand junk and I don't see any point in paying a fortune to have it shipped here."

"What lovely hair you have," Anne observed. "It's a remarkable color."

Again, Dene was thrown and said, "Thank you," as she tore the check out of the book, then wondered what to do with it. Anne was way over on the other side of the room and Dene felt suddenly awkward.

"Just leave it on the table," Anne said, studying Dene. "There's a laundry room in the basement. Don't be surprised if you find Charlie down there from time to time. He likes to bring his laundry here. I used to do it for him until it occurred to me one day that he was a grown man and more than capable of doing his own laundry. When I was first married, I thought I'd be a perfect wife and hand launder Frank's shirts. After the third shirt, I gave up in disgust and took them to the laundry. I wasn't perfect-wife material." She laughed softly, aware that Dene was anxious to leave. She wished she knew what to say to relax her. "Would you like to stay for lunch?" she invited, positive Dene would refuse.

"Oh, thank you, but I couldn't." Dene closed her handbag with a snap and stood up. "I've really got to go."

Languidly, gracefully, Anne unfolded herself from the sofa. "You really don't have to go," she said disconcertingly, "but I understand. Next time, I'll feed you. There's nothing to be afraid of here—a couple of mildly eccentric people wandering around, but nothing sinister. I had a lover, but he's been gone for months now."

Dene didn't know what to say, so remained silent. Anne's openness intrigued and confused her. She was curious to know more about this woman's life—references to a "lover" and to Charlie puzzled her—but felt she simply had to get away from here in order to think things over.

At the foot of the stairs, Anne placed her hand on Dene's arm, and withdrew it at once when Dene jumped and turned abruptly to look at her, wide-eyed.

"It's all right," Anne said. "I'm someone given to touching. That's all."

"I've got to go now," Dene said wildly. "I'll . . . I'll be in touch with you from New York."

"Do you have family here?" Anne asked as she opened the front door, suppressing a strong maternal desire to hold this fragile young woman in her arms and relieve her suffering.

"My mother. And my husband's parents." Her throat was choking closed. She uttered a strangled "Good-bye" and had to restrain herself from running down the front steps. She

made an effort to smile, then turned and walked woodenly
down the path. She could feel Anne's eyes on her and kept
her spine very straight as she went along the sidewalk and
turned the corner. Once inside the Pinto, she exhaled, then
folded her arms across the steering wheel and rested her
head on them. She felt as if she'd just sprinted ten miles. At
least, she thought, straightening with a deep sigh to fit the
key into the ignition, she'd found a place to live.

From the upstairs kitchen window, Anne watched Dene
climb into the car and collapse over the steering wheel. The
hour they had spent together had been a mild torture for
Dene, Anne knew, and wondered why. A pretty young woman
who seemed held together with fine wires. What happened
to you? Anne asked silently. Why are you so shattered?

Dene drove away at last, and Anne turned from the window. What a pity she couldn't have come sufficiently past
her fear to stay for lunch, Anne thought. It was too much
trouble to cook for one, so she decided to skip lunch.

Chapter 6

Dene drove back to the hotel, angry with herself for having behaved so absurdly, for reading too much into words
and gestures. That woman and her nephew were in no way
threatening, and she knew that. No, the threat and suspicion existed stubbornly within her, and she was going to
have to rid herself of them. She'd been foolish, even rude, in
turning down Anne's lunch invitation. Now she was left
with seven hours on her hands before her flight was scheduled to depart.

She telephoned the airline to find out if there was a seat
available on an earlier flight. There was. Hurriedly, she
repacked her bag and checked out. She drove the Pinto back
to the car rental area at the airport, then walked over to the
terminal and checked in.

While she waited in the boarding lounge, she went over

the logistics of the move. It was now the fifteenth of November. In the next two weeks she'd have to break the lease on her garden apartment, or sublet it, arrange to dispose of the little furniture she had, close out her bank account, file a change-of-address card with the post office, and advise Regular Toys of the move. Aside from the problem of the apartment, everything else could be accomplished in one day. What would she do for the other fifteen or sixteen days remaining before she could claim the apartment in Anne Reynolds' house? Sightsee? Go to movies or the theater? Try some of the restaurants for which New York was famous? She had no desire to do any of it. She was rushing to New York in order to come rushing back here. Perhaps she really was losing her mind.

Who was Anne Reynolds, with her quick-change artistry that had her looking like a grandmother one day, and like someone half that age the next? She certainly wasn't the fifty-five or sixty Dene had originally thought. Dene saw the two of them again sitting on the plane, and Anne's head turning slowly; she saw the woman smile, showing small, even teeth, and heard her say, "I couldn't help sensing you were wondering." She wasn't perfect-wife material. What an amazing thing to say! How did a person know what she was or wasn't suited for? Dene wondered. She herself had very little idea; she'd simply fallen into whatever was available—always. After her cash supply had run out in New York, she'd tossed off some drawings of the First Family, then started calling toy companies to ask for appointments. She'd never stopped to consider whether designing toys was something she wanted to do, or liked. She'd just done it, and had kept on doing it because it brought in the money she needed to live. Yet that wasn't the truth, because the death money was sitting in the Bank of Montreal savings account, gathering dust and interest. Jake had been very particular about things like insurance, so there was quite a lot of money in that account. Touching any part of it, though, was acknowledgment of a reality she'd managed to keep at bay for more than four years. She'd never even bothered to look at the bank statements. They were sitting unopened in a brown paper bag at the rear of the shelf of the second closet, beside the small box containing the few things she'd frantically collected from the Rosedale house before taking flight. One of these days she was going to have to confront the evidence of her former life. But not yet.

The Dramamine tablet was making her drowsy. She checked the time. A few more minutes and they'd be boarding. She looked around at the other passengers and was all at once completely and terrifyingly disoriented, even more so than she'd been a few days earlier, standing by the drugstore window. She had to concentrate hard on where she was going and where she'd been, what she was trying to accomplish. With a jolt, she realized she hadn't contacted her mother. Now it was too late. She couldn't possibly telephone to say hello, and good-bye again.

What she needed was a list. She got out a small note pad and her pen and, at the top of the list, wrote: "telephone installed."

She would telephone from New York to arrange the installation. For some reason, this struck her as funny and she laughed aloud. Then, distressed by her behavior, she looked around to see if she'd attracted any attention. Fortunately, she hadn't. The boarding announcement began just then. She returned the notepad and pen to her handbag and stood up to join the queue.

Charlie had seemed shattered by her announcement that she was leaving. He'd been sober for a change, and looked pale and unhealthy. She thought it strange that he always appeared to be far healthier when he was drinking.

"I'm used to having you next door," he said, sadly encountering her in the hallway a week later. "You get used to people, you know. The next tenant's a complete unknown, complete. I hate changes. Your entire lifetime's nothing but changes, one after another. Why are you leaving?" he asked plaintively.

"I'm going back home to Canada. I don't really like it here."

"Nobody really likes it here. But it's cold up there. Why do you want to go where it's cold?"

"It's no colder than it is here, Charlie." She smiled, moved by him. He did seem, as he'd said, unequal to life's changes. "I don't mind the cold. I feel stronger in the winter. Heat drags me down. I can never get much of value done in the summer."

"Well, at least let me buy you dinner before you go."

"You don't have to do that, Charlie," she protested, taken off guard.

"I'll buy you dinner," he declared. "What's a good night?"

"Well, if you're sure you want to, tonight's fine with me." She thought he might stay sober if he made a commitment to her.

"Okay," he said. "Seven o'clock."

He studied her for a moment, looking dismayed, then went off to hold open the lobby door for the elderly blue-haired woman who lived in one of the penthouses. Dene watched him make a gentlemanly display of carrying the woman's shopping bag. At last, with the elevator doors closed on Charlie and the old woman, Dene turned to let herself into the denuded garden apartment.

She'd managed to sell everything but the bed, and Charlie had staked a claim on that. "Whatever you can't sell, I'll take," he'd said. Getting rid of her few things had been almost too easy. She'd taped a note inside the elevator, and within two days, various tenants had come down to buy up her belongings. Not one of them had questioned her, or expressed any interest in why she was going, or where. They'd examined what was for sale, made their selections, paid in cash or written out checks, taken their purchases or arranged to come back for them later, and gone away. She might have been a shopkeeper for all the notice they took of her, which was fine, because she had no wish to explain herself or to answer questions. Charlie's invitation and his expression of upset did come as a genuine surprise, and she stood staring into the apartment, thinking about it.

The room looked far larger now that it contained only the bed. Stark and dim, it was like a prison cell. Beyond the rain-spattered window she could see the shiny gray stone of the apartment building opposite. She walked over to the back door, opened it, and stood on the threshold slowly looking at the surrounding buildings. Hundreds of people lived in hundreds of cells on all sides of her. How could they bear it? The only reason she'd been able to tolerate this place was because of the garden and the illusion it offered of space and greenery. Only weeds and plane trees flour-

What here Wasn't it, she wondered, a plant free that had grown in Brooklyn? Surely that was what it had been—one of those indomitable weeds that would grow and grow and become a tree if not uprooted at once. Was that the correct name? Did it matter if it was? She turned to study the room from this vantage point, deciding she'd dress for the occasion, in the blousy dark blue jersey with long sleeves.

Charlie was still sober when he came tapping at her door, and his ashen features reshaped themselves into a smile as he said, "You look wonderful!"

She thanked him, locked her door, then followed him out through the lobby and onto the street, where he ambled along at her side in silence for several minutes. When they got to Third Avenue, he looked over at her and asked, "Is Allen's all right?"

"Fine," she answered, familiar with the restaurant. They specialized in hamburgers, along with reasonably good salads, and excellent home fries. It was a neighborhood hangout. On Friday and Saturday nights, when the weather wasn't bad, there was usually a sizable crowd milling about on the sidewalk in front. Tonight the place was relatively quiet. They found a booth by the side windows and the waiter came over to put two menus down in front of them.

"Drinks?" the waiter asked.

Dene looked questioningly at Charlie.

"Tonic with a twist," Charlie said.

"I'll have the same," Dene chorused. If she had a drink it might get Charlie started, and much as she liked him she didn't feel up to coping with a drunk. Still, she couldn't resist asking, "Are you on the wagon, Charlie?"

He smiled again, showing his large teeth. "Every few months, I get religion," he said self-deprecatingly. "Somebody or other talks me into an AA meeting and I go. I listen to them talk about how the old demon booze wrecked their marriages and their careers, and how AA's put them on the right track again, and I think maybe I'll give it the old college try. So, for a week or two, I drink tonic. Then I start to wonder what the point of the whole exercise is, and give it all up. Being sober isn't all it's cracked up to be," he concluded, still smiling.

"What did you do?" she asked. "Before, I mean."

He folded his hands together on top of the menu and

stared at her as if debating the wisdom of confiding his past to her. At length he said, "I was just one of the boys in the Brooks Brothers suits."

"Doing what?" She offered him a cigarette. He declined with a little wave of his hand.

"Doing what," he repeated. "Do you really want to know?"

"Yes."

"I was a buyer for Abercrombie & Fitch."

"What did you buy?"

"This and that." He slid down a bit in his seat and smiled again. "There I was with my paper from Yale and my closet full of gray flannel and pinstripes, buying fishing rods and tackle bags. It occurred to me one day over lunch that it was the biggest waste of time ever. So I stayed on at lunch, had several more wonderful drinks, and decided that if I was going to waste my time I might as well waste it productively. Productive waste consisted of sitting among convivial company and sporting a pleasant glow. I like drinking. I *love* drinking. I don't have a good story to tell them, you see. I mean, it's all right to stand up there in front of a group of us alkies and tell how you lost the wife and little kiddies, the house and the career, the whole damned shooting match. I never had anything to lose and still don't. It seems to me that if you're going to go to the trouble of getting a degree from a good school and all the rest of it, there ought to be something better waiting at the other end than a poorly paid, glorified salesman's job at Abercrombie's."

"I agree," she said.

"But I like to keep my hand in," he went on. "So I let myself be talked into going to meetings every now and then. They have such fervor, reformed drunks. Anyway, I go, and I let whoever talked me into it think he did a good job. I stay off the sauce for a few weeks. Then, when it all starts turning a bit too black and white, like those Swedish films, I get out the Chivas and tone down the edges. Now," he said, straightening a bit, "let's order some of their abominable hamburgers. Home fries?"

"Definitely." She smiled, wishing she'd taken the time long before this to get to know Charlie. He was something of a philosopher, and his philosophy wasn't entirely unreasonable.

After their drinks and the food had been served, Charlie asked, "Who were you?"

"The female equivalent of you," she answered truthfully. "I thought I'd be a painter. Actually, I didn't think very much about anything else. After I finished college, I took two years of a four year art course. I quit because I thought I'd learned enough. I also didn't want the courses to interfere with my originality. My husband once made what I thought was a very profound observation. He asked me to name six successful authors who were the products of an academic environment. I could only name two, Fitzgerald and Donleavy. He actually could name six. But the point he made was that the best creative writers were the ones who'd learned from life, like Hemingway, and not from English lit classes. I felt that way about the art college, so I quit. I never did do more than fill half a dozen sketch pads, and some ethereal watercolors. Then . . . I quit."

"What happened to the husband?" Charlie asked around a mouthful of food.

"He died," she said, low.

"Did you care?" he asked.

"Yes."

"Too bad." His eyes held hers for another second or two, then he continued eating. She'd lost her appetite. She pushed the food around on her plate, ate some more of the home fries, then put down her knife and fork and waited for Charlie to finish. While she waited, she contemplated him. He was quite a handsome man. Tall, with a full head of thick dark brown hair, he had good, strong features and an appealing smile. There were probably, she thought, thousands of people like her and Charlie, all hiding out for one reason or another.

Charlie finished and summoned the waiter over to order coffee for both of them. Then he looked at her for a long time before saying anything. At last he said, "It's over now, huh, and safe to go home?"

"Something like that."

"I lied," he said flatly. "You're a nice woman. A little too naïve for your own good, but nice. I've never been above the second floor of Abercrombie's in my life. I was a broker on Wall Street, senior partner in a good house. I had a wife and two kids in Larchmont and I rode the commuter trains back and forth every day. I started drinking way back in prep school, with all my friends, and drank my way through Yale and grad school. I kept drinking right on through the partnership, and the marriage, and the kids. I'm like every other pathetic bastard who gets up at those meetings and talks about all he threw away. I'm *exactly* like them. Do you have any idea how demoralizing it is to know you're a walking cliché? I am, you know. I hate being so damned typical. Anyway, old friends of the family took pity and gave me my job. They'll never fire me as long as I manage to keep an eye on the boiler, keep the lobby reasonably clean, and make sure nobody starts ripping off the tenants. It's amazing how people always prefer to believe the made-up story. That's because the make-believe is a lot more interesting. There's nothing that interesting about a fifty-five-year-old drunk with a past history of wasted opportunities. If I had anything left to go home to, you'd better believe I'd go. But it's gone, all of it. I think," he said momentously, "I'll have a drink. To celebrate," he added, "this brief moment of truth. I usually stick with the lie."

"You sound so bitter, Charlie," she said quietly.

"Nah. I'm just sober. It always brings out the worst in me. Listen, Dene"—he placed his hand over hers for a moment— "get the hell out of this city and don't look back. You'll be okay. The time is right for you, I can tell. Why don't you run along now and finish your packing or whatever. I know you don't want to sit here and listen to any more of this."

"I don't mind . . ."

"It's okay," he said, giving her hand a brief squeeze. "You really are a nice woman. You'd be a damned good-looking one, too, if you ate now and then, and took some interest. Whatever happened, I'm willing to bet it wasn't your fault. But you're blaming yourself. Don't do that," he said, "or you'll never be able to put it back together. You go on now. And thanks for coming out. I enjoyed it. It's not too often I get a chance to talk these days."

"Are you sure?" she asked, reluctant to leave him alone.

"You look good in that dress." He smiled, then turned to signal the waiter.

"Well, if you're sure." She hesitated, not certain whether she should allow herself to be sent off this way.

"The usual," Charlie told the waiter. Then he reached

over and put his hand on Dene's hair. "Don't ever cut it. I knew it would feel like silk. Scram now. Go get living again."

She made her way slowly to the door. When she turned to look back, the waiter was setting a drink down in front of Charlie, and Charlie was smiling happily.

She felt much better about everything. Charlie had managed to give her departure additional dimension and meaning. As she walked back along Third Avenue she felt years younger, and lighter, as if something terribly heavy had just been lifted from her shoulders.

Chapter 7

He'd bred two perfect little English gentlemen, Jamie thought. Mark and Stephen sat quietly and listened to everything Jamie had to say, absorbing his words with little outward reaction. Did they understand what he was telling them? he wondered. Or had they, too, fallen into the apathy that he and Jane had displayed toward one another for so long? Their failure to react defeated him, gave him the sense that nothing really mattered. For the past four days all he'd been able to think of was this afternoon and how he'd tell the boys he didn't intend to live with them in the future. He'd shuffled words and gestures as he'd paced the floor of his empty new apartment on Walmer Road; pacing back and forth, he'd meticulously discarded this word, inserted that, until he'd had what seemed a reasonable presentation with all possible areas covered. He'd arrived at the house this afternoon prepared for a highly emotional scene. Instead he was confronted by their two unyielding little faces and the dark, glossy mirrors of their eyes. He wanted to shake them to get some sort of true response from them. They had to care about this. If they didn't, then why did he care as much as he did?

He talked to them; he promised them weekend visits and

summer holidays together; he spun out a lengthening monologue as he spoke of the future and trips the three of them might take together. Throughout, the two boys sat rigid, their eyes fixed on him, revealing none of what they were feeling. Finally, with something like despair squeezing at his lungs, Jamie went silent and stared back at them. He lit a cigarette, waiting and hoping they'd say something. Nothing. He took a few puffs on the cigarette, deciding Jane had coached them into this perfect silence. She had to have. These two effigies weren't the sons he'd played with, had made laugh, had taken on outings all of their lives. They were simply lifelike replicas of his boys. Grief gushed up into his throat at the idea that he'd already lost them. In less than a week away he'd lost what he'd thought he'd have for a lifetime: his fatherhood. He couldn't believe it.

With rage and sorrow doing battle inside him, he crushed out the Gitane and got to his feet. This was hopeless, impossible. He wanted to throttle Jane for whatever it was she'd said to the boys. Did she care so little for him that she could, in just four days, thoroughly undermine all the feelings they'd had for their father? He didn't know what to do. He felt, more strongly by the second, that what he was attending here was some sort of funeral for the man, the father, he'd been. There'd been a death here and he'd been the victim. The terrifying aspect of it was that he was still around to be a witness to the spectacle. He felt he had to get away, get out of there, and try to deal with the surging emotions the past half hour or so had created in him.

"I'll ring you during the week," he said a little weakly, watching both boys closely, still hoping for some sign. "Just to say hello, see how you're getting on."

The boys, little robots, nodded.

He left the room and walked down the hall to the kitchen, where Jane was seated at the table with a cup of tea and a paperback novel open on the table before her. She was reading and didn't look up for a moment. Then she turned the book over so that it lay face down on the table, and lifted her head to look at him.

"What have you said to them?" he asked almost inaudibly.

"Just that you weren't going to be living with us from now on."

"*How* did you say it to them?" he asked.

"I simply told them."

He wanted to shout accusations at her, to confront her with her crime against him, but he could hear in advance the sound of his own ranting voice and knew that anything he said would sound ludicrous. "I see," he said. His hands felt peculiar, numb. He felt chilled. "I said I'd ring during the week to talk to them."

"As you like." Her eyes dropped and she looked at the cover of the paperback. She seemed more anxious to get back to her novel than she did to talk to him. "Would you like a cup of tea before you go?" she asked.

"No. Thank you." He stared at her a moment longer, then turned and went back down the hall to the front door. Pausing, he glanced into the living room. The boys were still sitting together on the sofa, but Mark had his hand cupped around Stephen's ear and was whispering something to him. When they sensed his presence, both boys turned and gazed at him.

"Are you going now?" Stephen asked, rather formally.

"I thought I would."

"Will you really take us on a super trip next summer?" Mark asked, glints of excitement in his eyes.

With hope inching its way back inside him, Jamie carefully answered, "If you want to go."

"Where?" Stephen, the older, more cautious one, wanted to know.

"I don't know. We'll have to talk about it, make plans. We've got lots of time to discuss it."

"What time are you going to phone? Which day?" Mark asked.

"I'll ring Wednesday, at seven-thirty, before bedtime."

"What if we're not here?" Mark pursued it.

Stephen turned to look at his younger brother with an expression of disdain. "You're going to be here," he stated, then turned to look back at his father. "What'll we do next weekend?" he asked.

"The zoo?" Jamie offered. It was their favorite place to go.

Mark let out a whoop and grinned, revealing the gap where his two front teeth were missing on top. Jamie allowed himself a small, responding smile. Still Stephen showed no reaction. "Will that be all right with you, Stephen?" Jamie asked him.

"I guess so," he answered a little sullenly.

"Well, I'll be off now, then."

"What time next Sunday?" Stephen asked warily.

"Midday, I thought. We'll have lunch out."

"Oh boy!" Mark crowed. "Where?"

"I don't know yet. I'll let you know Wednesday when I ring."

"Okay! Oh boy!" Mark was bouncing up and down on the sofa, but Stephen remained rigid, his eyes boring into Jamie's.

Jamie wanted to hold them, to put his arms around them and feel their small, sturdy bodies pressing against his chest, to touch his lips to their soft cheeks, to the somehow too thin skin stretched across their temples. He waited for some sign. Mark looked willing, even expectant. But Stephen's wariness stood between Jamie's desire to embrace them and his ability to move toward them. He wanted to light another cigarette; he wanted a large drink; he wanted simply to evaporate and find himself out of there; he wanted his sons to indicate, even in the slightest fashion, that they loved him and that it mattered to them that their life together as they'd always known it had come to an end. They continued to sit side by side on the sofa, watching him. At least Mark had displayed a bit of enthusiasm for the promised telephone call and next Sunday's outing. Stephen had yet to show more than suspicion.

Jamie took a step back from the living room door, and then another, his eyes clinging to the boys. He felt he was at the end of a long, long rope and these two little boys held the other end in their hands. He dangled; he hung suspended, each second ticking noisily away in his consciousness as he awaited some sign. He took another step and turned toward the door. Now he could no longer see them. He could only feel their presence. How could they just let him go away from them this way? he wondered, his brief-lived hope as distant now as something that might have happened in his own childhood. He extended his hand—it felt heavy and looked monstrously ugly to him—to the doorknob. His fingers closed around the knob and he turned it. He could die now and it wouldn't matter. He'd failed not only at the marriage, but as a father. Failure seemed all at once to adhere to him like a foul odor and he was desperate for fresh air and the sight of something other than the wood-paneled interior of this rented house and of his wife, uncaring, at the kitchen table, more absorbed in some dollar Gothic romance than she'd ever been in him. His sons were letting him go without even a good-bye. He got the door open and stared out at the street. His chest was heaving; there was a pounding in his ears. Hearing a slight noise behind him, he turned to see Mark and Stephen standing in the living room doorway watching him.

Why, Jamie suddenly wondered, was he placing the burden of his expectations on these two children? He was the grownup. He was the one who'd made this decision to separate himself from them. He turned, his arms flying out, and gathered them to him like a harvest; holding the boys hard in his arms, he laid his cheek against the top of Mark's head, then Stephen's. He felt something inside himself break with a small, exquisite pain. Opening his arms, he released them as abruptly as he'd drawn them to him, and turned to go off down the front steps and quickly up the street. Behind him, he heard the front door close. He walked as fast as he could, reaching into his breast pocket for a handkerchief, or a tissue. He hadn't either, and it annoyed him. He wiped his eyes on the sleeve of his jacket and stopped to light a cigarette before hurrying on, almost at a run.

It was wretchedly cold, the sky black with an accumulation of something that would come down as either freezing rain or thick snow. Again he'd come out without an overcoat. The cold didn't bother him particularly. He was simply aware of it—another external—as he was of the three other bundled-up people at the streetcar stop, as he was of the cars passing on Bloor Street, as he was of the wind that sliced against his face and made his damp eyes smart. The cigarette made him cough and he dropped it, then stepped on it to extinguish it. He put his hand into his trouser pocket for some change for the streetcar, remembering, as he did, that he'd forgotten to ask Jane if there'd been any mail for him. Fortunately, all his checks went to the agency. His personal mail went to the house. He'd have to start giving people the agency's address. Knowing the postal service, it would be impossible to put in a change-of-address card solely in his name. The result of that would be his receiving the mail for the entire family. No, he'd have to start telling people to get in touch with him through the agency. Matt wouldn't mind. At least half Matt's clients had their mail sent to the office. Privately, Jamie had always thought Matt enjoyed the little services he provided for his clients. There was an outsized shoe box in the reception area with mail, in alphabetical order, for the clients who dropped in from time to time to collect it and have a chat with Matt. Jamie would simply become another of them.

The streetcar came swaying along the tracks and he climbed on, dropped his money into the fare box, and went to sit at the rear of the car, turning at once to look out the window. The day was so dark that he was reflected in the window and he stared for a moment at his image, hating the sight of himself: a funny-looking fool who hadn't the wits to deal with two small boys and their mother.

At Spadina Road he got out and stopped in Becker's for a newspaper, a pack of cigarettes, and a tin of Melitta coffee. Then, walking slowly, he went back along Bloor to Walmer Road. In the apartment—unfurnished except for a folding cot he'd borrowed from Ron along with a bridge table and a chair—he put a potful of water on to boil for coffee and stared at the ruled pad where he'd started work on the radio script. He'd done only a few pages, wasn't even a quarter of the way through it. He had to get it on to the CBC by Thursday, but he didn't feel like working. Sliding open the door, he stepped out onto the balcony and looked up at the sky—darker still now—then down at the street below. He felt completely isolated up here on the eighth floor in this set of boxes he'd rented. Turning, he leaned against the balcony wall and stared in at the apartment. The floors were good—parquet. The living room was a decent size. The bedroom was little more than an outsized closet, and the kitchen was merely serviceable and hidden behind a bamboo curtain on a track. Jane had been right: this was going to be expensive. He felt the beginnings of panic when he considered what it would cost him to accumulate the bare necessities he needed to live with, along with the monthly sum he'd have to give Jane. He'd never before worried about money; it had come along. He'd worked steadily, and with Jane's salary, they'd always managed. Now, if he missed more than two or three weeks' work, he'd be in trouble.

"Jesus!" he said aloud, and shivered. It was starting to snow. He looked down again at the street. Snow from the previous week's fall lay humped in the gutters like discarded rags. Patches of it, soot-smeared, sat centered on nearby lawns. He didn't even have a pair of overshoes; he'd have to get those, too. What the hell was he doing? he wondered, gazing unblinking at the street. He was trading in one kind of futility for another. Wasn't there something more? He didn't even have a damned radio. Something more he'd have to buy. And he'd forgotten his records. They were still at the house, which meant another trip out there, another senseless meeting with Jane, another session with those two frozen little people he'd once recognized as his children. It was too late to change any of it. This was what he'd wanted: his freedom. Now he had it, and it was far more expensive and complicated than he'd ever dreamed.

He'd thought longingly, for years, of one day reclaiming his freedom. In his thoughts there had been no complications, and no real cost. He'd seen himself traveling unencumbered through the days, working, enjoying his off time, seeing women if he cared to, living life by his own rhythms, according to his own whims and impulses. Now he could see that his fantasizings had been as self-indulgent and unrealistic as any child's. He'd claimed his freedom only to discover that it had certain well-defined limitations he might never get beyond. Because even when, one day, he and Jane were no longer legally tied, he would always and forever have the responsibility of the boys. He didn't mind that, but the financial part of it frightened him. He was going to have to take every job offered him, no matter what it was. He simply couldn't afford to be selective. At the very roughest estimate he was going to have to come up with at least three hundred dollars a month to contribute toward the support of the boys. If a divorce did come into it, there'd undoubtedly be alimony, to boot. He felt, standing out there on the balcony in the snow, as if someone had strapped lead weights around his neck, arms, and legs, and that he would, if he wasn't careful, sink to the ground under the weight of them.

He tried to light a cigarette, but the wind kept blowing out his matches. Then he remembered the water he'd put on to boil and stepped back inside the apartment, pulling the door closed after him. The air inside seemed hot and heavy after the balcony. He loosened his tie and took off his jacket, draping it over the back of the folding bridge chair Ron had loaned him.

He fitted a filter into the Melitta cone, then went to open the tin of coffee, only to find that it was, of course, sealed. He didn't have a can opener. Near tears again, he snatched up his jacket, pulled it on, pocketed his keys, and stormed out of the apartment to go back down to Becker's to buy a can opener.

As he marched along the slushy pavement, the snow falling more and more thickly, he promised himself he'd make a list. He needed a sofa, a bed, a table, a couple of chairs, some kitchen gear. He'd make do with the minimum until he got a bit ahead with some money. Along the way he'd add bits and pieces. It would be idiotic to be so easily defeated now when he'd finally attained his dream of freedom. He just needed some time. And some money. Jesus! He really was going to have to take any damned thing that came along. He'd have to start popping in on producers, socializing regularly to keep his face forefront in their minds. And the bloody telephone wasn't going to be installed until midweek. Life would be easier once he had the telephone in.

A matter of weeks and it would be Christmas. He'd have to get gifts for the boys, perhaps take them out somewhere. To a matinee, possibly. He'd see about some tickets. Once he had some furniture, he could have the boys stay overnight now and then. A sofa bed, he decided, would make sense. That way, he'd have a place for Mark and Stephen to sleep.

He had, he suddenly realized, left the pot of water boiling on the stove. He quickened his pace and hurried into Becker's, found a can opener, paid for it, and started to the apartment. Make lists, he scoffed. He'd never in his life been someone who made lists. If he couldn't remember what he needed, then he'd just have to do without. At least he'd been invited out to a party next Saturday, so he wouldn't have to spend the weekend eating alone in some bloody restaurant. First thing he had to do was get some kitchen gear so he could start cooking. He was fed up with restaurant food, sick to death of it. And he liked cooking.

As he walked through the snow, he thought about a roasted

leg of lamb, with roast potatoes and fresh peas and mint
sauce. He'd do one up, invite a few people around. Just as
soon as he got some furniture and something to hang on
those stark white walls. At least the party next Saturday
was something to look forward to.

Chapter 8

Sherrill was a little disappointed in Michelle. She wasn't
at all as Sherrill remembered. She left things lying about
without actually being sloppy; she tried on Sherrill's clothes
and used her makeup without bothering to ask if she might;
she spent hours almost every night on the telephone talking
to her married boyfriend, and hours afterward miserably
bemoaning her bad luck in falling in love with a man who
had a wife. Sherrill's patience was rapidly running out. If
she didn't find an apartment soon and get off on her own
she might make some comment, or offer some criticism,
she'd later regret. It felt as if she'd been living, at too close
quarters, with Michelle for months.

She'd already found one apartment and had excitedly
called Michelle to come to see it before the lease was signed.
Michelle had arrived and without a word took Sherrill by
the arm, said to the super, "Never mind. She's decided not
to take it," and marched her out onto the sidewalk where,
red-faced, she'd half-shouted, "Are you *crazy*? Do you know
what this place *is*, for God's sake?"

Turning to look back at the building, Sherrill had said,
"But it's quite a nice apartment and it's only a hundred and
eighty."

"It's only a hundred and eighty because this is Hell's
Kitchen, and if you survived your first month here the
police department would probably give you some kind of
award. I thought you knew something about the city."

"How could I? I've only been here once before, and now."

"Okay, okay." Michelle backed down. "I'll help you find a

place. If I don't, you'll probably wind up getting yourself raped and murdered. Come on," she said, starting off down the street. "I'm sorry I screamed at you. But, Christ! Even if you didn't get raped and murdered coming home one night, they'd be breaking into that apartment twice a day and three times on Sundays."

Sherrill was anxious to go out looking again today, but Michelle was still asleep, exhausted from the dinner party she'd given the night before. Sherrill had thought perhaps the married lover might show up, but all the guests had been medical men and actresses. Sherrill had spent most of the evening sitting on the sofa talking to an ear, nose, and throat specialist who'd insisted she give up smoking because he could, just by placing his ear against her chest, detect a decidedly unhealthy wheeze. "What're those you're smoking, anyway?" he'd asked, picking up her pack of Rothmans.

"Canadian cigarettes."

"Oh! Been up there?"

"I've just come from there."

"I hear it's a beautiful country. One of these days I've got to get up there and do some fishing."

"We've got quite a few big cities," she'd said, in her pleasantest voice.

"Yeah. Toronto and, what is it, Quebec? Montreal?"

"Do you know how many provinces there are in Canada?" she'd asked, mildly irked by this arrogant man.

He'd looked off into space, trying to come up with an answer. "Wait a minute," he'd said, sensing she was about to tell him. "Twelve!"

"Ten."

He'd stared at her for a moment, then turned to talk to the actress on his right. She'd bored him, but that wasn't important. She'd felt terribly uncomfortable and out of place. Doctors, dentists, and actresses all crammed together: Michelle's idea of a party. Everyone had talked about symptoms of one sort or another, except for the two internists who'd discussed in depth a surgical procedure that sounded grotesque. The last of the guests had left at three-fifteen. Michelle had pulled open the sofa bed and flopped down to sleep in her underwear without bothering to remove her makeup. Her underwear, Sherrill couldn't help noticing, was on the gray side and decidedly tatty.

She simply had to get a place of her own so she could
begin to enjoy her life here. She'd brought the *Times* in
from outside the apartment door and had already circled
three ads, but it didn't look as if Michelle would be up for
hours. At last Sherrill carried the telephone into the bathroom, quietly closed the door, and started to make calls,
setting up appointments.

She left a note for Michelle on the counter in the tiny
pullman kitchen, made sure she had the keys Michelle had
given her, and let herself out. It was a sunny day, quite
mild, and she headed toward Second Avenue, glad to be out
on the streets of the city. There was a definite excitement
to her presence here, but it was an excitement that didn't
have as much to do with the city as it did with her desire to
conquer it. She could succeed here, make an important
career for herself. Opportunity whispered at her like a
small voice under the breeze. She could be a success and
have a townhouse in the East Sixties, with dinner parties
attended by her friends; she could have men seeking her
out, pursuing her with offers of trips to the West Indies and
gifts from Tiffany's.

That was garbage, stuff from old movies. What she might
have was a chance to work and gain some recognition. Some
man she'd meet might decide to love her. She knew him;
he'd lived in her dreams all her adult life. He was sensitive,
understanding, and, above all, kind. He liked to dance, he
was generous, and he loved her to the exclusion of everyone
else. Whoever he was, he was out there right now hoping to
meet her. They'd know one another at once, without any
need for words. He probably lived on one of these streets.

As she crossed Third Avenue and headed for the bus
stop, she admitted that there were things about the city she
didn't like, things that threatened to outweigh her ambition,
her dreams. It was so dirty and so dangerous. It confused
her to discover herself in an elegant neighborhood of expensive, well-tended houses and then to turn a corner and, in
the next block, find falling-down slums and decaying brownstones where surly-looking people sat hunched on the stoops,
eyeing her as she went past. Wealth and poverty lived back to
back here, carefully tended gardens abutting the rectangular
repositories for broken bottles and garbage tossed from upper-
story windows. When the sun shone, as it did today, the city

seemed harmless, a place where nothing bad could ever happen to her. On wet, windy days, or at night, she felt afraid as she never had before. There was an irrational element here, something unreasoning and violent. Her common sense cautioned that it would be foolhardy to venture out of doors for a late-night stroll, or to come home alone from an evening out unless it were in a taxi or by private car.

The first apartment was on the top floor of a converted house in the East Forties. Three small rooms—kitchen, living room, and bedroom—jumbled together in somehow random fashion, at two hundred and twenty-five dollars a month. It had a fireplace, which the man who showed her the apartment pointed out several times, as if it was an extraordinary feature of the place. She thanked him, then ran quickly down the five flights of steps to the street. She hated it.

The second apartment was on East Eighteenth Street. One large room, about fifteen by twenty, with a bathroom, a kitchen built into a closet and hidden by a curtain, and a sleeping loft built over the front door. The ceiling was at least fifteen feet high, and there were three floor-to-ceiling windows overlooking the street. Her instinct told her to take it even though the rent was somewhat more than she'd budgeted. It was a small building, privately owned, and the landlady herself showed Sherrill the apartment. She leaned against the front door while Sherrill moved about the room, pausing to look out the windows.

"What d'you do?" the landlady asked, her hands jammed deep into the pockets of her voluminous print dress.

Sherrill debated telling the truth. The woman looked a bit arty, with dyed red hair coiled into a knot, and big hoop earrings dangling from her ears. She had a hard but pleasant face. It was difficult to read her.

"I've just arrived from Canada," Sherrill hedged.

"The place is a gem," the woman said tonelessly, as if she'd failed to hear Sherrill. "It's a bargain at two-fifty. You won't find anything to touch it for the price. If you want it, take it, 'cause the phone's ringing off the hook and it'll be gone in another hour. What've you come from Canada to do?"

"I compose," Sherrill lied.

"Yeah?" The woman smiled for the first time, showing large teeth and dimples. "I heard any of your stuff?"

"Probably not." Sherrill smiled back. "I write specialty material, show pieces for revues, that sort of thing."

"I used to be on the stage," the woman said, her expression warming.

"What did you do?"

"I was a dancer, a hoofer, a hundred years ago." She straightened; her smile thinned out. "Well? What d'you think? You want? You got a piano?"

"A piano? No."

"Be a pain in the ass tryin' to get a piano up here, but you could have one. It doesn't make any difference to me. I like a little life around the place. You know?"

"What about a lease?"

"Two years."

"Okay," Sherrill said. "I'll take it. When could I move in?"

"Soon's your check clears the bank."

"I don't have a bank account here yet." She experienced a sudden alarm. She couldn't find the perfect place and then lose it because she didn't have a bank account. That wouldn't be fair. "I've got traveler's checks. That's as good as cash."

"Better," the woman agreed. "What d'you say your name is?"

"Sherrill Westcott."

The woman thrust out her hand and enclosed Sherrill's in a solid handshake. "I'm Rae," she said, smiling again. "Come on downstairs and we'll get you signed on the dotted line. How the hell old are you, anyway? You look about fifteen."

Sherrill laughed. "I'm twenty-five."

"No shit!" Rae exclaimed. "Wouldn't've put you past twenty. Swear to God, you look fifteen."

Out on the street again, Sherrill stopped for a moment to admire the windows of her new home. Then she continued on along Eighteenth Street to Third Avenue, searching for a bank. She found one on the corner of Twenty-third and Third and went in to open checking and savings accounts. That done, she flagged down a taxi and returned to Michelle's apartment to tell her the good news.

Michelle was still asleep. Sherrill's note was on the counter where she'd left it. After tearing up the note, Sherrill put on some coffee, then took the telephone into the bathroom to call the moving company in Toronto. She was told it would be three to six weeks before delivery. Upset at this unexpected delay, Sherrill hung up and made a note of the call on the list she was keeping in order to reimburse Michelle later.

She poured two cups of coffee and carried them into the living room, where she sat on the edge of the sofa bed studying Michelle for a few seconds. Michelle had lovely features and a wonderful velvety complexion. How ironic, Sherrill thought, that someone as photogenic as Michelle should make her living with her voice, and never be seen. It was Sherrill who made her living being seen, appearing onstage, and she was nowhere as good-looking as Michelle. At least, she didn't think so. Michelle was tall and slim, striking. People stared at her when she was out on the street. She wore expensive, vividly colored clothes that flattered her pale features and blond hair. Sherrill had gone through a brief stage, upon returning from England, of dressing exotically. She'd been unable to sustain her enthusiasm either for the clothes or for whatever effect she'd created; she'd chosen to be comfortably unobtrusive in what she wore, despite the fact that her choice of clothes tended to make her look years younger than she was.

After a moment, eager to share her excitement, she put her hand gently on Michelle's shoulder and said softly, "I made coffee, Misha. It's almost two-thirty. Michelle?"

Michelle opened her eyes and smiled. She always awakened cheerfully. She said, "Hi. You're dressed already. How come?"

Sherrill handed her the coffee. "I've been out and found a terrific apartment. I can move in anytime after today."

Michelle sat up, holding the coffee cup with both hands. "You're kidding! Where?"

"Eighteenth Street near Third Avenue."

"Gramercy Park. Not bad." Michelle sipped at the coffee. "What's it like? Tell me all about it."

Sherrill told her, then said, "I called the movers. It's going to take anywhere from three to six weeks for my furniture to get here."

"Rent some stuff," Michelle said easily.

"Really?"

"Get the Yellow Pages and we'll make some calls. What's the matter?"

Sherrill looked over at the heavily curtained windows and breathed deeply, aware of the sleepy scent of Michelle and the rich flavor of the fresh-ground coffee. "I don't know," she said. "I was so anxious to get here. Now that I'm here, I keep wondering if I'm not crazy, if I shouldn't turn around and go home right now. It's not the way I thought it would be. I mean, I can't even use the car because there's never anywhere to park. What good is it going to be stuck in a garage at Ninetieth Street and First Avenue?"

"Don't get rid of it!" Michelle warned. "The car's important. You'll need it to get out of town. Everybody has to get out of here, take a break every so often. Keep it! I'll make a deal with you: let me use it now and then and I'll pay half the parking."

"Really?"

"Sure. Absolutely."

"Well, all right. You're sure?"

"Positive. What else?" Michelle asked incisively.

"What do you mean what else?"

"You look down."

"Oh, I'm not." She made herself smile. "I'm just going to have to get used to it here. I set myself up for things," she explained. "I get carried away with the *idea* of something, then I'm defeated by the logistics. But I've got an apartment now. Things'll work out." She refused to acknowledge the depression that had begun to creep into her chest. She couldn't understand how it was possible that she'd loved New York as much as she had just a few months earlier and could find so much to fear now. She felt totally alien, as if no matter how long she stayed she'd never learn to be like the people who lived here; she felt frightened, too, as if she were standing atop a pyramid of precariously placed, very rickety boxes and one misstep would send her crashing down through the flimsy boxes. The future she'd envisioned—childishly, she now thought—wasn't going to be at all as she'd imagined it; nothing was.

She was lonely for her Toronto apartment, her mother, and the parking lot where she'd kept the Bug and had had unlimited access to it. She missed Della and Ron and Jamie.

She wouldn't think about Jamie. She missed the cleanliness of Toronto and the safe feeling she'd always taken for granted coming home late nights from the theater. She missed the many, many trees, the gardens everywhere, and the knowledge that there were people she could call up and go visit when she didn't feel like being alone. Everything inside her was shouting GO HOME! It was too late. She'd given Rae seven hundred and fifty dollars as first month's rent and two months' security. If she changed her mind and called Rae to say she'd decided not to take the apartment after all, Rae would say sorry, and keep Sherrill's deposit for the inconvenience. The money she'd saved wasn't going to last very long at this rate. She'd have to get work, and soon; she'd have to attend every audition going. She didn't want to.

All her ideas of success had been, she now saw, purely illusory. She'd made a rash decision and was going to have to live with it. She felt utterly unequal to this move she'd made. Because of the commitments she'd already made, she'd have to put a good face on it; she'd make the rounds diligently and give out her eight-by-tens and résumés; she'd have to make a go of it. For the first time in her life she felt deeply afraid and didn't know any other way to cope with her fear except by going doggedly forward. She did have an apartment, and a garage for the car—for which Michelle would pay half; she had an agent and two auditions already scheduled for the coming week: one with an ad agency for a voiceover, the other with a producer who was looking for a replacement member of a small revue company that performed in a club in the East Fifties. She'd get both jobs, she promised herself, and maybe rent a piano. That wasn't such a bad idea. At home she'd worked on the piano at the dinner theater after hours. Della had arranged it. If you could, as Michelle had said, rent anything here, then she might as well go ahead, rent a small piano, and really cover all the bases. She might pick up some work writing special material.

Michelle sat cross-legged on the bed drinking her coffee, watching Sherrill. After a time she said, "It's incredible! You've got the most amazing face. Really. You've gone through about ten changes while I've been watching you."

Sherrill turned to look at her. Then she smiled. Her insides seemed unconnected and were racing around inside her like small, crazed animals. "I've decided to beat the system," she said. "I'll be damned if it's going to beat me."

"The thing of it is," Michelle said soberly, "not to let them know any of it matters to you. When they see that you care, when it shows that it means something to you, they'll do it to you every time. It's scary, isn't it? At the beginning, I was a wreck. Now I don't even think about it anymore. You kind of make your little nest and go from there. You'll be all right. John doesn't take just anybody on, you know. I knew right away he thought your tape was terrific. And he liked you."

Sherrill looked at her a moment longer; then her eyes shifted to the window—a lighter square in the dark blue of the curtains.

Sherrill was going to make it big, Michelle thought. There was something about her, a quality Michelle couldn't define. You could see it, could almost reach out and touch it. *A defiance, maybe, a scared defiance.* If it had been anyone else, Michelle would have been jealous. But how could she be jealous of what felt so—inevitable? If it had been anyone else, Michelle would have put an arm around her. You couldn't make gestures like that with Sherrill. You never knew how she'd react. She had an innate, almost rigid reserve that was hard to penetrate. She might accept an arm around her shoulder, or she might subtly slip away to go stand at a distance, refusing to accept the offer of comfort. She was complicated and unpredictable, as Michelle had learned years before when they'd been together at LAMDA. Nothing Sherrill ever did was what others expected. She seemed like such a kid sometimes that, by comparison, Michelle felt twenty years older. It was a mistake, though, to be taken in by her youthful appearance, because any number of times Michelle had seen her pick herself up from defeat and walk straight into success. Nothing could keep her down. The only person who could defeat Sherrill was Sherrill.

"You'll be all right," Michelle repeated, and risked placing her hand on Sherrill's arm. To her gratification and relief, Sherrill patted her hand and smiled.

"Damned right," Sherrill said, then returned to gazing at the window. She wished Michelle would get dressed so they could pull the curtains and let in some light. She had no right to be as impatient with Michelle as she was, and reminded herself of that. They were entirely different people with entirely different ways of doing things, of living. I've got to learn to be more tolerant, she told herself, not for the first time.

She was also going to have to learn to control the mood shifts that had her high one moment, low the next. She drank her coffee, mentally planning where her furniture would go in the new apartment. She would, she promised herself, be far more relaxed and comfortable once she was settled, once she got past the temptation of thinking about Jamie.

Chapter 9

Unexpectedly, Dene choked up when it came time to leave. She stood at the door looking down the length of the room—stripped now and forlorn—and felt a pang of nostalgia for the loss of this hiding place. It had been safe here, all things considered, and had been neither pleasant nor unpleasant, but rather a time entirely devoid of feelings. In leaving, she was surrendering her anonymous safety. Returning to Toronto not only meant going back to the place where she'd once been happy, it also meant she'd be obliged to confront fragments of the past that might be painful.

Charlie came up behind her. "I've got a cab," he said, then fell silent as he, too, studied the denuded room. At last he cleared his throat and said, "New tenant's moving in this afternoon. The stinking landlord's too cheap to paint the place for him." He shook his head, picked up two of her four suitcases, and carried them out to the cab.

She closed the door reluctantly and followed. She had a newborn feeling, as if she were being thrust for the first time, at almost thirty-five, into the world. Charlie was standing with his hand on the hood of the car, talking to the cabbie. He noticed her and hurried to relieve her of the last two bags, got them into the back of the car, then looked abashed at not knowing how to say good-bye. She rescued the moment by forcing herself to smile. She kissed his cheek, pressed an envelope into his hand, slid into the rear of the taxi, and they were off, the cab accelerating down the street. She turned to see Charlie waving good-bye with the hand holding the white envelope. She faced forward after a moment and relaxed against the seat. The fifty dollars in the envelope would buy Charlie quite a lot of Chivas. If that was what made him happy, it was what she wanted him to have. She hoped, though, he'd use the money to buy himself some warmer winter clothes than the ones he habitually wore. She doubted he would. Again she wished she'd taken the chance to get to know him better. She suspected that for years to come, at random moments, she'd find herself thinking of Charlie out in the garden with a bag of ready-mix concrete and half a dozen new bottles, singing as he further glorified the wall.

Anne had had the apartment painted. Every surface gleamed. Dene stood just inside the kitchen, holding the set of keys Anne had, by arrangement, left in the milk box by the back door. The window glass shone, the kitchen floor was slick from recent waxing. She went back out to bring in the last of the suitcases, parked them to one side of the kitchen door, then went slowly through the rooms. It was as if she had never seen the place before. As she'd imagined, the absence of the previous tenants' bulky furniture made the rooms appear large and gracious. Sun poured in the windows, turning the floors golden. On the mantel in the living room was a small Boston fern and, propped against it, a note from Anne. In a large, relaxed script, it read: "I'll be back by six. Plan on having dinner with me, Anne. P.S.: Welcome home!"

Dene returned the note to the mantel and walked through the rooms, pausing to admire the bedroom and adjoining sun-room, which was about eight by ten, with windows on three sides. It would be the perfect place to work, she thought, and could readily see her drawing board placed at an angle in the corner, with hanging plants in front of the windows. She breathed deeply, elated by the clean spaciousness of her new home.

The telephone, as instructed, had been installed on the kitchen wall, a set of directories sat on the counter near it. She reached for the Yellow Pages and flipped through the rentals section. She called the first number listed and arranged to rent a folding cot, a table and two chairs, and, on a whim, a television set. That done, she left and walked down to the subway station at Yonge and Eglinton. Her first stop would be the Bank of Montreal. She had decided on the flight up from New York that she'd use the death money. She wanted some good-looking furniture and a decent drawing board. She was tired of her transient life-style. Possessions would alter that and give some sense of permanence to her existence.

She was staggered by the amount of interest that had accumulated, and pleased, too, because she'd be able to use the interest and not touch any of the money that had generated it. She opened a checking account, transferred the interest into it, changed her American dollars for Canadian, was given a temporary checkbook, and was out of the bank in under an hour. She stood on the sidewalk, her momentum lost. What should she do next? The rental furniture wasn't going to be delivered until late in the afternoon. Food. She'd go to the supermarket. She'd noticed that there was a Dominion store on Eglinton.

The spacious cleanliness of the market was overwhelming after the New York stores. She wheeled the basket up and down the aisles, enjoying herself, and ended up with ninety-odd dollars' worth of groceries and sundry other items. She then found herself with the problem of how to get these things home. In the end, the store manager graciously helped her carry the many bags out to the street and waved down a taxi. She felt positively idiotic. Why hadn't she considered how she was going to get everything home when she'd been giddily wheeling the basket up and down the aisles? What she needed, she thought, as the cabdriver helped her unload her purchases at the kitchen door, was a car. It would certainly make life a lot easier.

After the groceries had been put away, she sat down on the living-room floor with her back against the wall and looked contentedly at the room while she smoked a cigarette, holding the cheap glass ashtray she'd picked up at the supermarket on the worn-through knee of her faded jeans.

She was hungry, and a little sleepy, but too keyed-up to nap. It was too late for lunch, but not too late to take a walk around the neighborhood.

There were, she discovered, many charming little shops on Yonge Street. She strolled along, savoring the atypically mild December air, looking in shop windows. On impulse, she stopped to buy half a pound of Earl Gray tea and two white mugs painted with rainbows, then walked on. There seemed to be many elderly people out and about, certainly more than she ever recalled seeing on the streets of Manhattan. But then, in view of how regularly the elderly were mugged there, it made sense that you'd rarely see them outdoors. She breathed deeply, more gratified by the minute at her return.

The still-dirty white Mercedes was parked outside when she got back to the house. She let herself in and, hearing Anne moving about above, realized she was looking forward to seeing her again. She put away the tea, rinsed out the mugs, then went to inspect herself in the bathroom mirror. She looked tired, she thought, inspecting the dark circles under her eyes.

The ringing of the doorbell startled her, and she went through to the front door wondering who it could be. She'd completely forgotten about the rental company, but there in the hallway were two men with her furniture. With quick efficiency, they brought in the few pieces, had her sign for the delivery, gave her a yellow carbon copy of the order, and were gone. From the largest of her four suitcases she got out the pair of sheets, the tiny boudoir pillow, and the two blankets she'd crammed in along with four towels, two washcloths, and two dish towels: her supply of linens, threadbare and old. The cot made up in the bedroom, the various towels hung away, she again surveyed the rooms. The small bridge table and the two chairs looked ridiculously dwarfed in the dining area. She moved them into the kitchen, studied the effect. Satisfied, she washed her hands, brushed her hair, and went to ring Anne's bell. Her palms were damp; she was nervous.

Anne greeted her like a long-lost friend. Dene wondered why. She'd done nothing to inspire any feelings of fondness in this woman; at least, she didn't think she had. Perhaps Anne was an enthusiast, someone who made overt displays of liking for people in general. Dene could see that Anne would have liked to embrace her, and was glad she didn't.

"Well, you made it!" Anne smiled widely, her hands hovering in the air for a moment before dropping into the pockets of the heavy white cable-knit cardigan she wore over a white blouse and a gray wool skirt. "Come on up! We've got time for a drink before dinner. How was your flight?"

"Fine. You had the apartment painted."

"I always have the place done over for new tenants. Don't you like it?"

"Oh, I do. I hadn't expected it, that's all."

Anne directed her into the living room, asking, "A glass of wine?"

"Yes, thank you." Dene sat in the same chair as the last time and silently admired the room. Without Charlie lounging in the other chair, the room seemed larger. And emptier.

"You're used to the New York way of doing things," Anne said, returning with two glasses of white wine. She gave one to Dene, clicked glasses with her, and said, "Cheers." She then curled up in the center of the lush brown sofa with her legs tucked under. Her hair was down, as it had been when they'd met, and didn't suit her nearly so well as it did up.

"I suppose I am," Dene admitted, trying not to stare.

"You're looking surprised again," Anne observed. "What is it this time?"

"Am I?" she asked distractedly.

She seemed, Anne thought, far younger than she'd said she was, young and sadly defenseless. "It's all right," Anne said indulgently. "I'd probably look that way too if I'd just come home after years away. I was going to invite Charlie to join us tonight—I feed him fairly often, otherwise he'd undoubtedly starve to death—but I thought you'd probably prefer to have a quiet, early evening on your first day back."

Dene nodded, then took a sip of the wine. "I went out for a walk this afternoon. I like the neighborhood. It's changed a lot from what I remember."

"For the good," Anne agreed.

"Are you still researching politicians' wives?"

Anne laughed. "That one's finished. I'm taking a break now until after the first of the year. One of the nice things

about tree-lancing is being able to choose when I work. I do
the job only to keep my brain alive. I've got to do *something*."

She said this in much the same way she'd spoken of
wanting someone to be there to hear if she screamed, and
Dene studied her, noticing more details every time her eyes
came to rest on the woman. Anne was slim, with narrow
hips and shoulders, a long neck, and graceful hands. She
was wearing face powder and rouge again, and they sat over
her delicate features like a mask. Dene suddenly wanted to
tell her that the makeup added years to her age, but that
would be cruel.

"You have family in town, isn't that right?" Anne asked,
apparently unbothered by Dene's inspection of her.

"My mother, and my . . . in-laws."

"Do they know you're back?"

"Not yet. I meant to call my mother but . . ." She shrugged
and looked over at the fireplace. "I haven't spoken to her, or
written since I left. I'm not sure . . . I mean . . . For all I
know, she thinks I'm dead." She turned her head back
slowly, her eyes meeting Anne's.

"I see," Anne said soberly. "You're not close, then?"

"We were. Suffocatingly close."

"I *see*." Anne nodded thoughtfully, then took another sip
of wine. She set the glass down on the coffee table and
uncoiled herself from the sofa. "I'll just check the vegetables," she said, and went shoeless back to the kitchen.

Why was it, Dene wondered, she suddenly felt like confiding in this woman? Why was she so strongly tempted to
talk to her? There was a quality about Anne, an earnest
aspect to the way she listened, and to the incisive questions
she asked, that urged Dene to confide in her. Instinctively,
she wanted to trust her, and that was very odd.

"About five minutes," Anne said, returning. "I hope you're
hungry. I've made enough food for half the neighborhood."

"I'm starved." Dene smiled slightly. "Now that I think
about it, I haven't eaten since yesterday."

"You can't afford to skip meals. You'll wind up in the
hospital with a fine case of malnutrition."

"I don't have much of an appetite."

"What are you doing for furniture?" Anne asked.

"I've rented some things. I thought I'd start looking for
new furniture tomorrow."

"Do you have any idea where you're going to start?"

"I . . . no."

"I love shopping," Anne said eagerly. "I'll go with you, if you like, take you to some of my favorite places."

"You're probably busy," Dene began.

"I'm not doing a thing until after the first of the year," Anne reminded her. "Just some Christmas shopping, and not much of that. I'd love to go with you."

"Well, all right."

"Good! I'll come down for you in the morning at about ten. Okay?"

"Okay."

"Come keep me company while I dish up," Anne invited. "I'm one of the ones who actually likes having people in her kitchen."

"So am I," Dene replied automatically, remembering the kitchen in Rosedale and how people had invariably gravitated to it. She could, too clearly, see and hear the laughing conversations that had taken place in that wide, warm room. *I want it back!* she thought, anguished. *I can't live without you.*

"Are you all right?"

Dene felt Anne's hand on her arm and looked down at it.

"All the color drained out of your face," Anne said, her hand remaining on Dene's arm. "You look as if you're going to faint."

"No, I'm all right." She looked up to notice that Anne had very round blue eyes. She wanted to rest her head on Anne's shoulder and say, "I'm not all right. I don't know if I'm ever going to be all right again." Instead, she moved away from Anne's hand, asking, "Do you need help with anything?"

Anne didn't respond for a moment, her eyes still fixed on Dene's. "Just sit down there," she said, "and talk to me. Everything's ready. I've only got to bring it to the table." While she spooned rice from the pot into the serving dish, she told herself it was none of her business, and that she shouldn't involve herself. But from the beginning, on the plane, she'd felt an immediate caring for this young woman. It didn't make a bit of sense. Feelings, though, were rarely rational. One liked or disliked people often for highly arbitrary reasons. There was something so palpably sad and so touchingly vulnerable about Dene that it was impossible for

Anne not to respond to her. Just don't pressure her, she cautioned herself. She turned with a smile and carried the rice and the bowl of steamed vegetables to the table, then went back for the veal. "Nothing exciting, I'm afraid," she said, pouring more wine into their glasses.

"It smells wonderful."

"When in doubt," Anne said, "cook veal. Help yourself. If you haven't eaten since yesterday, you probably *are* on the verge of fainting."

Dene made no move toward the food. Softly, she said, "It's very kind of you to do all this for me."

"Not at all. Don't you think you deserve to be treated well?"

"No."

"No? For heaven's sake, why not?"

"I . . . uh . . . don't know why. I just don't."

"Well, that's nonsense. We all need people to be kind to us."

"What we need," Dene said slowly, "isn't always what we get."

"No, that's true." Seeing that Dene wasn't going to start, Anne reached across the table for her plate and served her. "Eat," she said quietly. "I don't like the idea of people fainting on me." She smiled coaxingly and Dene seemed to emerge from her brief trance and returned the smile.

"I'm acting like a fool," she said, picking up her knife and fork.

"No you're not," Anne said, serving herself. "There's no need to be self-conscious, or to apologize. I understand."

"Are you this way with everyone?"

Anne laughed delightedly. "No," she answered. Suddenly serious, she said, "Not everyone. But I can't help feeling someone should be kind to you. You seem so in need of it. And it makes me feel better about myself."

"I know," Dene said, thinking about it, remembering Charlie. "I'm a little embarrassed."

"Don't be. Eat!" Anne smiled that coaxing smile again and Dene started to eat. Anne watched her for a moment, then began on her own food.

Chapter 10

Dene dreamed the slow-motion dream, the one in which she and Jake tried to move toward each other through a thick, gluelike substance that rendered their movements heavy and slow. It was the dream where, no matter how hard they tried, they couldn't meet. They strained and cried out in frustration but remained apart. She made herself wake up, and sat on the lumpy cot in the dark with her head in her hands, her heart beating too quickly, waiting for the dream to leave her. After a time, she got up and walked out to the living room to stand at the window staring at the deserted 3 A.M. street, her fists resting on the windowsill, feeling the emptiness at her back.

Why was she alive? Why did she have this blind, tenacious grip on life? There was nothing left, so why go on? But she couldn't, simply because she wished it, will herself to die. She wasn't prepared to take an active part in putting an end to her life. Therefore, she lived. So simple. She sighed, her fists unclenched, some of the stiffness left her spine. Shivering, she returned to the cot and curled up on her side, feeling small and alone.

Sleep wouldn't come back. She turned toward the wall and closed her eyes tightly, but when she did, an image of Jake, starkly clear and minutely detailed, took shape on an interior screen. Too tired to fight, she succumbed and studied the image: it smiled and smiled at her, and she felt herself crumble inside, the parts of her tumbling down into bottomless emptiness. Tears ran irritatingly down the side of her nose. She wiped her face with the sheet and burrowed deeper into the blankets.

At last she slept, but restlessly. She got up at eight, feeling achy and exhausted as she made a cup of instant coffee and carried it with her to the telephone. It took several minutes before she could lift the receiver and dial the well-remembered number on the wall phone. The ringing began at the other end and she counted. One ring, two, three. Midway through the fourth ring, the voice she'd known all her life said, "Hello?"

For a second, Dene couldn't speak. Then she said, "Mother?" in a thin, wispy voice she scarcely recognized as her own.

"*Dene?*" Her mother's voice was high and tremulous, filled with shock. "Is it you, Dene?"

"It's me."

"Where *are* you? Are you all right? Where are you calling from, Dene?"

"I'm here, in the city."

"You're here? Where? Have you been here all along, or have you been away and just come back?"

"I've just come back. From New York."

"Ah! I knew you hadn't stayed. Will you be going back there? Am I going to see you? How *are* you, darling?"

"I'm . . . How are you?"

"I'm fine. But you . . . Are you going to be staying?"

Dene could picture her easily. She'd be sitting on the little Queen Anne chair in the foyer with her slim legs carefully crossed, both hands curved around the receiver. She'd always held the telephone as if it were a cherished object.

"I'm staying," Dene said finally. "I've rented an apartment. I'm going out this morning to shop for some furniture."

"Have you been in touch with the Whitmores?"

"Not yet. I . . . not yet."

"I don't understand," her mother said, a bit impatiently. "You're going out to buy furniture?"

"That's right."

"But everything . . . all your things are in storage. I've been paying the charges all this time."

"I don't *want* them!" she cried. "I don't *want any* of those things!"

"All right, darling," her mother said appeasingly. "I quite understand."

"Do you?"

"Of course I do. Come this evening. I had plans, but I'll cancel them at once. I do so want to see you. Where is your apartment? Have you a telephone?"

Dene gave her the address and telephone number. "I'll come at six. All right?"

"Naturally it's all right! You can't imagine ... No, I won't say that. I'm so pleased!" she said softly. "I'll ring off now and see you at six."

The call ended, Dene picked up the mug of coffee and held it with both hands. She was trembling. She drank some of the coffee, then sat down at the rickety rented table, studying the way the sun came through the kitchen window. She got up, found a sketch pad and some pencils in one of the suitcases, and returned to the table to sip the coffee while her hand made a quick rendering of the kitchen window in the sun. She felt even smaller and more alone than she had in the middle of the night, like a little girl who'd done something naughty and was about to be punished.

Anne came to the door on the dot of ten. Clad in well-fitting black trousers and a black cashmere turtleneck sweater, she looked elegant and rather mysterious. Her hair was once more twisted up into a topknot and her only makeup was a reddish brown lipstick that suited her well. She carried a mink jacket over her arm and the black leather handbag, and stood in the middle of the living room waiting while Dene went for her coat and bag.

"That outfit really suits you," Dene said as she pulled on her duffle coat. "I'm not sure I'm fit to be seen with you." She had, Dene thought, a superb figure for a woman her age—whatever age she was—with full breasts and a very small waist.

Anne laughed and fitted her arms into the sleeves of the mink. "You look just fine. If I could get away with jeans and T-shirts, I would. I happen to be a little too far over the hill for them."

"You're not that old," Dene protested as they went out to the car.

"You're sweet," Anne said, opening the passenger door.

Dene leaned across the seat to unlock the door on the driver's side. Anne said, "Thank you, that was thoughtful," as she slid in and fastened her seat belt. "Would you mind doing up your belt?"

Dene pulled the belt around her. Anne fitted the key into the ignition. The car started with a low growl, and she slid

the shift into reverse. "I'm forty seven," she said, her eyes
on the rearview mirror. "And I look every day of it."

"No you don't."

"You're sweet," she said again.

"I'm truthful," Dene persisted.

"You're *sweet!*"

Dene laughed, then listened to the rare echo of her own
laughter inside the luxurious car and wondered at the sound
of it as she tried to remember when she'd last laughed, or
felt like it. "I spoke to my mother this morning."

"And? How was it?"

"I'm not sure what I expected, but it was fine. I'm going
for dinner tonight."

"What's she like, your mother?" Anne asked, curious.

"Petite, very good-looking, a smart dresser. She's English.
I was born in England, actually. I had dual citizenship, but I
surrendered my British passport when I was eighteen. My
mother's always kept hers. After thirty years, she still thinks
my father's going to come to his senses, give up his second
wife, and come back to her. At least, she used to think that.
I don't know if she still does."

"How sad," Anne said.

"I never used to think so. After I talked to her this
morning, it occurred to me that it really is sad. They were
married when she was eighteen and he was twenty-four.
She was only twenty-three when he left her. It seems very
young to me now."

"Are you in touch with your father?"

"No. I visited once. I nagged and nagged until my mother
gave in and wrote him to ask if I could come visit. Then,
once all the plans were made, I didn't want to go. I hadn't
seen him in five years. I was afraid I wouldn't recognize
him, or that he wouldn't show up at the airport to meet me.
My mother told me not to be foolish, and off we went to the
airport.

"I'd been flying for years. My mother's a great traveler.
I'd been with her to Jamaica, and Nassau, and Palm Beach,
to Paris, and, of course, London. But this was my first trip
to London alone and I was terribly nervous, especially since
I didn't think I really wanted to see him after all.

"He was at the airport. I recognized him at once. He was
tall, with red hair like mine, and the same dead-white

complexion. He was wearing a dark gray Savile Row three-piece suit, a black topcoat with a velvet collar, and a black homburg. Incredibly elegant. We smiled and shook hands and he took me out to his Daimier. We sat in the back, my father tapped at the partition with one manicured finger, and the driver touched his cap. It was like a movie.

"His second wife was very nice, nowhere near as good-looking as Mummy," she said, lapsing into childhood expressions. "Anyway, they took me to the theater, and the ballet at Covent Garden, to Madame Tussaud's and the Planetarium. We went to what they called 'charming little restaurants' for lunch and dinner. And every night we said good night very formally, and then I was by myself in their guest room. They had a pied à terre in Berkeley Square. Unbelievable!" She shook her head, then went on. "The most personal remark he made the entire time I was there was to say I'd gone 'quite American.' I corrected him and he just smiled and said, 'As the case may be.' Then he asked after my mother, but he called her 'Moira,' not 'your mother.' I said she was fine and he said, 'I expect Moira will remarry.' "

Anne laughed appreciatively at Dene's put-on upper-class English accent.

"I told him I didn't think she would, because she'd told me she didn't want to. He looked, not angry . . . displeased, for a moment or two. Then he smiled very quickly, as if revealing emotions simply 'wasn't done.'

"It was a pleasant enough week. But I came home feeling as if I'd spent the time with a stranger. When I told my mother that, she said, 'Precisely as I expected,' and that was the end of it. I haven't seen him from that day to this. My mother used to talk about him all the time, with such regret, and longing, as if there might have been something she could have said or done to alter the course of events. I'm sure that in the back of her mind she's always believed that one day my father's 'frivolous affair'—her words—with this other woman would end, and he'd come to his senses and fly over to get her. I once ventured to ask her if it wasn't possible that he'd simply fallen out of love with her, and then watched her come unglued. Literally." She turned to look over at Anne. "It was awful. She blamed everything on my father's second wife. Well," she sighed, "over the years, she stopped talking about it quite so much, and by tho timo I loft, she rarely used to mention him. For years and years I hoped she'd find somebody else to love. But she never did."

"That's quite a story," Anne said. "What did your father do?"

"He was just a businessman. Well, not *just*. He inherited the family business and turned it into a small empire. Paper products."

"Where does your mother live?"

"On Russell Hill Road, just south of St. Clair. It's an enormous house, far too big." Why was she talking such a lot? she wondered, glancing out the window. Because they were going through Rosedale and she didn't want to have to think about how it had been, living here. "When I was little," she went on, her eyes on the fine old houses either side of Mount Pleasant, "I believed we had ghosts in the attic because when the wind blew I could hear all kinds of strange noises up there. Then, when I was older and going to college, I decided the attic had great romantic potential and I nagged Mother for months to have it done over so I could have my own apartment. She wouldn't. She was right, really. It would have made the house that much bigger and Mrs. Wicks, the housekeeper, could barely look after the place as it was. My mother," she explained, "keeps three in staff. She's a dinosaur, like Charlie, the super. It would be impossible for her to function without a cook, a housekeeper, and a driver. Every morning, after coffee in bed, she bathes and gets dressed, then goes down to the kitchen to plan the day's menus with Mrs. Forbes, the cook. She entertains quite a bit. I don't know," she said, winding down now that they were safely out of Rosedale. "I've gone through so many stages with her, from being impatient to belittling her, I'm not sure I know who she is. It's going to be strange, seeing her again. I have a feeling we're not going to know each other."

"What happened?" Anne asked softly, looking over.

"I can't talk about it," Dene replied, stiffening.

"Surely your mother's going to want to talk about it, whatever it was."

"I know," Dene said somberly. "It's what I'm most afraid of. Please don't think me rude. You've been ... It's just that I can't."

"It's all right."

Dene exhaled slowly and turned to look out the window.

She found quite a number of things she liked: a pair of beige corduroy love seats with rounded, comfortable lines, a low butcher-block coffee table, a three-piece kitchen set, a square white dining table with four chairs, several area rugs, and, finally, a brass headboard.

At one point, Anne asked, "Are you sure you can afford all this?"

"I have death money," Dene said coldly.

Chilled, Anne stared at her for a moment, then decided not to pursue the matter.

"I've been thinking about buying a car," Dene said, in a more normal tone of voice. "I didn't really need one in New York. I mean, there wasn't anywhere to go. But now that I'm back ... and the city's so spread out ..."

"You don't really need a car here either," Anne said. "The TTC's very good. Unless you're intending to do a lot of visiting way out in the suburbs."

"I still have my Ontario license," Dene said. "I kept renewing it. I don't know why. So many things ..."

"How about some lunch?" Anne suggested to break the sudden tension. "I know a marvelous Greek restaurant. Do you like Greek food? It's almost two. You've got to be hungry. I know I am."

"I'm sorry," Dene said earnestly, searching the depths of Anne's eyes. "I've been completely alone for the past four years. I've forgotten ... how to be with people. I keep saying and doing things I don't really mean."

"It's all right. Greek food?"

"I adore it. Why are you being so indulgent with me?"

"I like you," Anne said simply. "Let's go eat."

Dene wanted to say, "I like you, too. Very much." But she couldn't speak at all. It was as if she'd worn herself out with all the talking she'd done earlier in the car.

Before Anne left to go back upstairs, Dene hesitantly asked, "Would you like to have dinner with me, tomorrow?"

"Charlie's coming tomorrow. We could make it Monday night, if that's all right with you."

"Fine," she said disappointed. "Monday."

Anne went off and Dene stood surrounded by her pur-

chases, wishing Anne had invited her to dinner with Charlie. It might be nice, she thought, to see him again. He'd
seemed so relaxed and easygoing.

Dene was taken completely off guard by the fact that
Moira herself came to the door and not Mrs. Wicks, as Dene
had expected. She looked even lovelier than Dene remembered, her hair more silver now than blond, and her features becomingly flushed as she drew Dene inside and into
an overpowering embrace. Then, tearfully, she held Dene
away and studied her for several moments. "You're so thin,"
she said at last. "I wouldn't have known you."

"You would have known me." Dene smiled, feeling
strangely shy.

"Take off your coat and come inside. I want a good look at
you."

Dene shrugged off the duffle coat and, from years of
habit, draped it over the foot of the banister, then, with her
mother clinging to her hand, went with her into the living
room, where they sat side by side on the sofa.

"You've done the place over," Dene said, looking around.

"A great deal has changed since you went away, Dene."

"Has it? You look wonderful, absolutely wonderful."

"Oh, thank you. I'm not sure I know quite where to begin.
Oh, Dene," she exclaimed, "you really do look frightful.
You're so pale, and you can't weigh more than a hundred
pounds. Are you all right, darling?"

Dene laughed for the second time that day. "I weigh
considerably more than a hundred pounds."

"I'll wager you don't. Someone your height should be
carrying far more weight."

"What's become of Mrs. Wicks?" Dene remembered to
ask, unable to take her eyes off her mother. Moira seemed to
be aglow.

"I retired her two years ago. We have a Mrs. Sanderson
now."

"I don't remember you favoring the imperial 'we,' " Dene
teased, beginning to take pleasure in her mother's company.
She was familiar, after all.

"I don't. The thing of it is ... This is frightfully
awkward!"

"What is?"

Again her mother flushed, so that she looked young, even

girlish. How extraordinary, Dene thought, that this woman could be her mother! She was familiar in the way that certain landmarks and old memories were, but very much of a stranger, too. "What is it?" Dene prompted. "I know! You're seeing someone."

"Actually," Moira said, her hand tightening around Dene's, "I've remarried."

Part 2
Attachments
1970

Chapter 11

The party, Jamie thought, was a bore. He had mixed feelings about parties in general. When he drank enough, he could have a wonderful time. But if his quieter side—his more real side, he believed—held sway, then he drank moderately, smiled every so often, had very little to say, and just waited out the event until it ended; the hours stretched interminably and he felt lonely and isolated.

Tonight's bash was typical of dozens of others he'd attended: too many people crowded into several small rooms, the air thick with smoke and laughter, a constant ebb and flow of new arrivals, departing couples. The food wasn't bad, though. He helped himself to a large plateful from the buffet and wedged himself into a corner. He felt as if he were watching a play with uninspired dialogue and a cast who felt obliged to overact. He ate mindlessly; his eyes moved over the faces—some overly animated, others empty— coming to rest on a woman in the far corner of the room by the door. She stood listening to a tall, earnest-looking man who seemed to be talking importantly, bending slightly toward her, as if for emphasis, as he spoke. Jamie couldn't hear what he was saying, the music was far too loud, but he watched, intrigued by the way the woman made an obvious effort to pay attention. Every so often her eyes left the face of the man and searched space as if for an exit she might discreetly slip through.

She looked soft, Jamie thought. A tall, slim woman in a black dress, with a string of pearls falling midway down her bosom. Her hair was a fine silvery color and it, too, looked soft, but he thought it would have been more attractive fixed in some other fashion. Hanging down over her shoulders as it did, it failed to enhance her features. Her makeup wasn't at all flattering to her exquisite features. He shifted closer to have a better look at her.

She was drinking either water or neat vodka, possibly gin. From time to time she took a sip from the glass in her right hand and regarded her companion over the rim. Jamie settled opposite the doorway and continued to study her. On the middle finger of her right hand she wore a handsome gold dress ring with a large square-cut stone that looked to be a citrine. She had on gold hoop earrings that were revealed when she turned her head or pushed the hair back from her face. She was lovely, Jamie decided, and he settled into happy contemplation of her while he continued to eat, without tasting the food. He felt less isolated now, having someone to focus on.

The effects of his meeting with the children earlier in the day still clouded his mood and squeezed at his insides. In his mind he reran the scene with different dialogue, new directions: the boys wept miserably and ran off to the kitchen to demand answers of Jane. Why was Daddy leaving? What did you say and do to make him go? No, that was puerile. He simply wanted evidence of their caring. It grieved him to think they'd grow up to be the sort of boys he'd always disliked at school, the small-sized stoics and martyrs, the chins upthrust, staunch-hearted little fellows who took the cruelty of the upper-forms boys in stride as merely being their due, and got on with life as best they could despite the loss of their self-respect and dignity. That was the way it was done: it didn't do to buckle, to knuckle under to the pressures. School was preparation, they were all told, for the inevitable blows that would come once they were out in the real world, in society. A history of British passive resistance; Jamie deplored it. It wasn't human for children not to cry, not to seek comfort. For a few seconds, he himself was a little boy again, hurrying to keep up with his father as he strode too quickly along the pavement, the tin of sweets in his pocket drawing Jamie along with their promise. He couldn't ever keep up with his father; the man never slowed down to a reasonable pace.

His thoughts shifting, he saw himself in the kitchen with his mother. She had a Mars bar, a special treat, and with thoughtful precision was cutting the bar in half. Then the two of them sat down at the table and in appreciative silence slowly ate the chocolate. He felt again the dull sorrow that attended thoughts of his mother. Two years, and he still couldn't fully believe she was dead. It was extraordinary, he thought, how difficult it was to accept the death of someone you loved, while the deaths of strangers, or of people about whom you'd been indifferent, were simply statistics you added to the store of information kept in your brain. But someone you'd loved, that was different. It stayed and stayed, and every so often you were tempted to try to turn time around in order to relive the best of the moments the two of you had shared.

He set aside his empty plate, and when he looked over again, the woman's eyes were on him. Mildly flustered, he busied himself lighting a cigarette. When he next looked back, her companion had returned. She was holding a fresh glass of the clear liquid and her eyes were no longer turned in Jamie's direction.

She had a magnificent body for a woman her age, although it was impossible to determine what age she might be—anywhere from her early forties to mid-fifties. The hair and poorly done makeup were misleading. He decided she was forty-four; it seemed a good age. With that settled in his mind, he retrieved his scotch from the top of the piano where he'd left it, and went on inspecting her. She had a long neck, graceful hands, full breasts, narrow waist and hips, lovely slender calves and ankles.

Someone called out his name and he glanced around with a smile, unable to see who'd called him. His eyes returned to the woman in black. He was fascinated by her. Was the man her husband? he wondered. She wore no wedding ring, but nowadays that didn't mean anything. He himself had always refused to wear any sort of ring. His hands weren't good; they were too small, he thought, and rings would only draw attention to this too visible flaw.

His eyes refused to leave her. He'd rarely seen a woman her age so well put together, so appealingly sexual. The black fabric of the dress fell gently over her hips and down to her knees. The fact that the majority of women present were wearing miniskirts made this woman's longer dress seem most sophisticated. Someone touched his arm, and he swiveled with a start to see Jimmy Castro grinning up at him.

"How's it going, eh, Jamie?" Castro asked, giving Jamie's arm a squeeze.

"Oh, fine, fine." Jamie smiled back, as always slightly put off by Castro. Everyone seemed to like him; he got a lot of work. But there were too many things just a little bit wrong with Jimmy: he tried too hard, came on a mite too sincere; he seemed to be everywhere one went, widely smiling, cracking jokes. He'd show up full of bursting energy, asking how things were going—he always knew who was working where and at what—talking away and cracking jokes nonstop. The entire time he was with you his eyes would be scanning the crowd, as if seeking someone more important, more worthy of his considerable attention. Jamie didn't like him and felt somewhat guilty about it.

"So what're you working on?" Jimmy was asking, his mouth stretched into a toothsome grin.

"Some radio scripts," Jamie answered. And there it was: Castro's eyes were drifting away, over the crowd. In a few seconds he'd give Jamie's arm another too hard squeeze, then he'd move on to talk to someone else.

"Radio, eh? Great, great! Keeping the old hand in there! Have you seen Ron? Is Ron here?"

"I haven't. I don't think he's here."

"Man, everybody's here, eh? Have you seen Ron?"

"I don't think he's here," Jamie repeated. Jimmy wasn't listening. His hand had fastened itself to Jamie's upper arm and now gave it a brutal squeeze. Jimmy said, "Catch you later," and pressed on past Jamie to the far end of the room, where he pushed his way into a small group and started talking with frenetic animation. Jamie watched him for a moment, then looked down into his glass. A drop or two of scotch left. He drained the glass, then made his way through the crush, heading for the kitchen and a refill.

He was aware of perfume, a rich, heady scent, and then of his arm inadvertently pressing into a woman's breasts. Raising his eyes, he saw he'd collided with the woman in black, who was now inches away and smiling at him with amused eyes.

"Sorry," he said, trying in vain to put some distance between them. "I didn't spill anything on you, did I?"

"Not a drop," she answered, in mellow American-sounding tones. "I've been watching you watching me," she said disarmingly. "Have I got straps showing or a split seam?"

Jamie laughed, both embarrassed and elated. "Nothing's showing; everything's perfect."

"You wouldn't change anything?" she asked, lifting her glass to her mouth. She held it there, waiting for his answer.

Three scotches gave him courage. "Truthfully?" he asked, starting to enjoy himself.

"Oh, definitely! Be truthful."

"I'd change the hair, do it up, perhaps." He paused, trying to gauge her reactions.

"And?" she prompted, her smile dazzling.

"You're more beautiful than the makeup," he said as tactfully as he could.

"Is that everything?"

"Everything," he stated.

"Where in England are you from?" she asked.

"Cornwall. Where in America are you from?"

"You win that round." She laughed. "Hartford, Connecticut."

"Would you like a refill?" he offered, watching her throat as she swallowed. Her skin looked like cream-colored silk. He felt slightly dizzy from her perfume; it seemed to be in his mouth and at the back of his throat.

"Love one," she said, and gave her glass into his hand.

"Don't go away," he said, prepared to force his way through the crowd.

"I couldn't if I wanted to."

As he was pouring his scotch, it occurred to him that he didn't know what she'd been drinking. He sniffed her empty glass, captivated for a moment by the lipstick traces on the rim. Vodka. He found a bottle, poured some into her glass, then picked up both drinks and pushed his way back through the crowd. Upon seeing her he felt an interior warmth spread pleasantly through his chest and belly. It was an anticipatory rush that had him smiling as he moved toward her, holding out her drink.

She said, "Thank you," and closed her hand around the glass, her eyes on his. "I've seen you perform. You've very good, very talented."

"You have? Where?"

"I saw the revue that just closed, the one with just the three of you. Ron, and a girl."

"Sherrill," Jamie supplied.

"She was very good, too. A haunting singing voice, I thought."

"She's a real triple threat, Sherrill: good singer, good actress, good musician." For the few seconds while he spoke of her, he wondered where Sherrill was and what she might be doing. He couldn't quite imagine her in New York. When he thought of the city, the image he had was of an immense, overpowering place that surrounded fragile Sherrill like a fortress.

"You don't care much for compliments," she observed incisively; her smile thinned out.

He didn't hear her for a moment, then tuned back in and smiled at her again. She seemed more substantial at this close range, yet still very slim. Her rounded breasts under the black dress drew his eyes.

"Do you know the hostess?" she asked.

"I know her boyfriend. Are you with someone?"

She shook her head, pausing with the glass held to her mouth.

"Are you enjoying this?" he asked, glancing around.

"So-so. I'd love to leave."

He tossed down the scotch and waited while she drank half the vodka in one swallow before looking about for someplace to put the glass. He took it from her, placed it on top of the piano, then put his hand under her elbow to direct her out. Halfway to the door she stopped abruptly, turned, and again collided with him.

"I left my bag," she said. "It's on the floor where I was standing."

"I'll get it," he said, and went back, wondering if the collision had been intentional. Whether or not it was didn't matter; he'd relished the brush of her hair against his cheek and the brief touch of her body against his. When he returned she was in the hallway, slipping on a mink jacket. He gave her the small satin bag, then held open the front door. He had no idea where they were going. "Have you eaten?" he asked as they walked down the front path.

"I'm not hungry. Did you eat?"

He nodded. "It wasn't bad. A drink somewhere?"

"Do you have a car?" she asked. "I do."

"Your car, then. Where are you parked?"

"Just across the street, over there." She pointed to a dirty white late-model Mercedes.

Once inside the car, she extended her cold hand to him. "I'm Anne Reynolds," she said. "And you're Jamie. Why don't we go to my place for a drink? Nothing's open now and I'm not in the mood for coffee in a diner."

"Fine," he said and sat back for the ride. He felt as if something had been settled. Without words, without the need for them, his immediate future had just been decided. He turned to look at her. In this light the makeup didn't show and he could admire the pure lines of her profile. Her hair and the mink seemed to be the same color, so that she appeared to be enveloped in a silvery aura. As if sensing his eyes, she smiled over at him.

"Where do you live?" she asked. "Would you mind lighting a cigarette for me? They're in my bag."

He found the cigarettes and lit one. "Walmer Road," he said at last, placing the cigarette between her fingers. The car had warmed up very quickly and he was grateful; it was a bitterly cold night.

"Don't you have a coat?" she asked.

"I don't like them. When it gets colder I'll get out my coat." Why did every woman he met want to know the whys of his coatless state? It had to be some sort of mothering instinct, he decided. The question was beginning to get on his nerves. He didn't like overcoats, or slippers, or gloves, or jewelry. Jane had tried countless times to stop him from going barefoot in the house. He could never see what harm it did, going without slippers. When you were past it and ready for the bathrobe and the striped pajamas, you wore slippers; they were for old men who shuffled from room to room aimlessly, beyond caring about themselves or the future.

"Did *you* know the hostess?" he asked.

"Susan? No. I know her agent."

"Oh?"

"It's a long, boring story. A business acquaintance," she explained.

Jamie looked at the luxurious interior of the car, thinking he'd have to get himself something to drive one of these days. "Are you in the business?" he asked.

"Me?" She laughed. "Never! I'm in research. Free-lance. I've just finished an assignment on politicians' wives and

I'm taking a break over the holidays, until after the first of the year. Are you rehearsing for a new show?"

"I'm working on a radio script at the moment."

"People don't seem to listen to the radio the way they used to," she observed. "I never seem to have it off. CBC?"

"That's right."

They fell into a silence that lasted until they were well up Yonge Street and turning on to Eglinton. Then Jamie asked, "How long have you been here from Hartford?"

"Years and years. How long have you been here?"

"Eight or ten years." He was always vague on dates. It was something that used to annoy Jane; he'd never remembered birthdays or anniversaries, special occasions. Perhaps he hadn't remembered because their life together had a most amorphous form in his mind. "I became a citizen two years ago," he added.

"I'm still American," she said as she directed the car into a paved area at the rear of a large house and turned off the ignition. "Here we are. We go in at the front."

Going through the downstairs door, he asked, "Is this your house? Or do you rent?"

"It's mine. I have a tenant who lives down here." She pointed at the door beside the stairway. "I have the two top floors."

He looked up at her, poised on the stair above him, and thought how nice it would be to take hold of her and kiss her on the mouth. She had a perfectly shaped mouth and he was intrigued by the way her lips moved when she spoke. They continued on up the stairs.

He liked the living room and told her so. She smiled at him as she slipped off the mink jacket. He watched her every movement, more and more attracted to her. She had a natural grace and moved well, long thighs shifting smoothly under the black fabric. He could almost feel the warm, sleek, inner length of her thighs.

"Coffee?" she asked. "Or more of whatever you were drinking?"

"How about both?" he asked. "This really is a super apartment."

"Thank you. Look around. I'll put on the kettle."

He sank down onto the chocolate-brown sofa and gazed contentedly at the room, glad to see shelves filled with books. He never felt quite right with people who didn't read, who didn't have a few books around to give some clue to their personalities. Anne seemed to favor the better class of mystery writers, with a few new novels thrown in, and quite a number of biographies. There were several books he thought he'd like to read, and hoped he might someday be able to ask to borrow them.

She came back after a few minutes and sat down at the far end of the sofa with her legs crossed, one arm extended along the back of the sofa so that her breasts lifted.

"Now," she said with a sigh, "tell me what's wrong with my hair and makeup."

"I've insulted you," he said apologetically.

"No," she disagreed. "I'm honestly interested. Tell me."

Why on earth had he said any of that to her? It was rude as hell. Women were terribly sensitive about that sort of thing, and he'd blurted out the first remarks that had come to mind. Now he felt trapped by his indiscretion. He took his time answering, admiring the shape of her narrow knees. He'd never before been at such close and potentially intimate quarters with a woman so much his senior. Perhaps she had expectations. . . . Looking again at her eyes, and then her mouth, he concluded she hadn't.

"Are you married?" he asked.

"Divorced. And you?"

"Separated." It was the first time he'd put a title to his new status. The word felt heavy and awkward in his mouth.

"Long?"

"No. Not very."

He thought she seemed very composed. Her composure relaxed him, took some of the starch out of his spine.

"I forgot the drinks," she said suddenly. "I'll get them and see how the kettle's doing. Scotch?"

"Lovely."

She got up and went out. How old was she? However old she was, she had more sexuality in her walk alone than Jane had ever displayed in all the years he'd known her: more sexuality, in fact, than the several women half her age he'd made love to in the past few years. She moved like liquid, flowing from one point to the next. He reached to undo his jacket, again with that sense of matters having been settled. She was very beautiful. The apartment was superbly done

up. The events of the past week had been placed at a
bearable distance. He took a deep breath and listened to the
sounds she made in the kitchen, hearing the clink of cups
and glasses, the splash of liquid meeting glass. He did very
much like this woman and her home.

He liked women. It was a fairly recent discovery. During
the early years of his marriage, he'd worked hard to be the
husband and father of Jane's expectations. She, however,
hadn't made any special effort to discover if he had any
expectations, let alone live up to them. That, too, took some
time to learn. He had thought that their sexual involvement
would blossom in time, would become mutually pleasurable.
But Jane grew less interested with each year's passing. He'd
begun to feel subtly rejected, hurt by her consistent lack of
desire. Still, he'd persisted; he'd tried to carry on with a
life-style that daily became more lonely. There'd been less
and less closeness, and finally none at all.

His first short-lived affair left him guilt-filled and miserable. He had returned home to Jane determined to bring out
her latent sexuality. She hadn't, he soon learned, any discernible sexuality: she didn't care for lovemaking. This
realization stunned and shocked him, made him angry. He'd
felt defrauded, and lonelier.

His second, longer-lived, affair had left him somewhat
less guilt-ridden, but miserable only because it ended. In
the course of the three-month relationship, he'd come to
understand that lovemaking was secondary to affection. He
craved the proximity, the warmth of a woman who enjoyed
the sexual activities but who placed a higher premium on
the exchange of thoughts and ideas. He loved the sight and
sound of women, the feel and scent of them. In turn, he felt
rewarded by the gift of their softness in his arms and the
revealing of their awesome vulnerability.

What had drawn him to Sherrill had been, more than
anything else, the combination of vulnerability and ambition. That two such potent qualities could exist side by side
within a small, childlike woman was almost irresistible.

What drew him now to Anne was her womanliness and
innate good taste, her subtle sexuality and sharp intelligence. He was anxious for her to return so that they might
talk more, so that he might go on studying the way the light
fell onto her hair. She seemed to embody all the qualities he

most highly regarded. He wanted to spend time with her, to arrive at a point where they knew each other so well that words were often unnecessary. He wanted to hold her slim soft body and listen, with his eyes closed, to her voice gently breaking the darkness. He wanted someone to relax with, to laugh with, to love.

Chapter 12

Dene returned to the apartment shaken. She made a cup of instant coffee, carried it into the living room, and sat on the floor in the dark staring at the empty fireplace, wishing she could have a fire. She'd have to make arrangements to get some firewood. With her back against the wall, she sat in the reflection from the streetlight outside, reviewing the evening. She could see and hear herself as she'd listened to her mother, could feel again her slow retreat back inside herself as Moira had, with a firm grip on Dene's hand, told about her new husband.

"We met almost four years ago, Dene," her mother had said almost apologetically. "Quite soon after ... Well, we met. You'll like him, I'm sure. At least, I hope you will. He's most kind, most thoughtful. Oh!" She squeezed Dene's hand, then released it, her color still high. "I'm very happy, happier than I thought I ever could be."

"That's wonderful," Dene had said numbly, reaching for some sort of reaction to this news, other than shock. "Tell me all about it. How did you meet? When did you get married?"

"We met through friends actually, and we've been married close to three years. I did try to find you, dear. I hired some people to look for you. But of course no one knew where you'd gone, so it was quite impossible. Right up until the actual wedding ceremony I hoped you'd arrive, that you'd be located or would decide to come home, and then, well ..." She sighed. "Why didn't you write?"

"I couldn't. I . . . couldn't."

"Never mind," Moira said, moistening her lips as she examined Dene's features. "You're here now, and that's all that matters really. Are you going to be staying?"

"I don't know. I think so. I've bought some furniture, things for the apartment."

"But everything's in storage, all your things—"

"Do whatever you like with them," Dene said quickly. "I don't care what you do with them. I don't want to see any of it, ever again."

"If you're completely sure, Anthony's youngest daughter is taking a place on her own and she'd be most grateful . . . After all, they're good quality."

"She can have all of it. Anthony's your husband?" Dene repeated the name in its Anglicized version, as her mother had spoken it: Antony.

Moira nodded.

"Tell me about him!" Dene urged, managing to dredge up a small smile. "What does he do?"

"He's semi-retired these days. He has a law practice, or did. He goes in two or three days a week to the office. We've been traveling quite extensively. In fact, it's lucky you've come when you have. We'll be leaving next week. We go to Palm Beach for the winter."

"Palm Beach," Dene repeated, thinking suddenly, with longing, of expanses of sand, the ocean, a hot sun casting a glaze over drooping palm trees and bougainvillea blossoms. "It sounds great. How long will you be away?"

"We usually go until March. Of course, now that you're back, things are changed—"

"No, no. Don't change anything! I'll be here when you get home." Dene looked around the room, asking, "Where is he now?"

"He had a meeting this evening," Moira answered, glancing at her wristwatch. It was petite and round, set in platinum, with a rim of small diamonds. "He'll be home late, I expect." Raising her eyes, her hand wrapped itself once more around Dene's. "Are you all right?" she asked, her voice, her eyes, her entire manner filled with deep concern. "You look so frightfully thin and frail. And your hair's so long."

"I'm all right," Dene answered automatically, her hand

going to her hair. She wasn't in the least sure of her professed "all rightness" but it seemed important to reassure her mother. It was strange, she thought, that her mother saw her as thin and frail when Dene had always thought of her mother in those terms despite the fact that Moira was a rounded woman of excellent health. "I'm trying to get settled. Things *have* changed and it takes a bit of getting used to. What's your new name, anyway?" she asked, trying for a lighter note and failing. She thought she sounded merely inquisitive, even possibly sarcastic.

"Albright," her mother answered, looking a little guilty. "I'm only just becoming accustomed to it."

"But you're happy," Dene prompted.

"Yes. I am . . . We are. His wife died some time ago, you see. I mean to say, he'd been on his own for a rather long time. Of course, as you know, so had I. We met and got on well. He's so wonderfully *kind*, Dene. Your father was a frightfully insensitive man, always concerned with other matters, things that hadn't anything to do with me, or with you. I thought he loved me; he claimed he did, and I believed him. I think now I was very young and very stupid," she said a little bitterly. "Anthony's made me realize all sorts of things, all sorts. Naturally, we had a period of adjustment, trying to accustom ourselves—after so long, for both of us—to living with someone else. We've managed it, and we're settled now."

They'd talked until the new housekeeper, Mrs. Sanderson, had appeared in the doorway to announce that dinner was laid out in the dining room. Moira had arranged it so that the two of them would serve themselves and could eat without interruption. Dene had been unable to eat. She'd pushed at the cold salmon steak, breaking little bits off with her fork and hiding them under the hollandaise sauce. She'd artfully rearranged her plateful of food without actually consuming any of it. Moira, if she'd noticed, hadn't commented, for which Dene had been grateful. She couldn't seem to control her emotions; they were, at moments, quite violent and left her feeling giddy and faintly ill. She'd wanted to get away from her mother and her mother's new life and proclaimed happiness in order to reexamine her own life in terms of these revelations. Moira's disclosures were, to Dene's mind, like a mirror she felt it vital to hold up to reflect her own existence.

She now saw that she had been expecting everything to remain frozen, fixed, during her years away. Her mother had been a constant—unmarried, unchanging, ever-predictable—in all Dene's thoughts of her former life. But her mother had progressed and altered, had taken someone new into her life. Dene knew she should be happy for her, and indeed did feel something like that, but it was in so remote a region within her that only its echo made itself felt. The overall reaction she had to the evening and to seeing her mother again was shock: more reality she felt unequipped to absorb.

Her eyes fixed on an indefinite point in space, she lifted the mug of coffee to her mouth. It was tepid, and tasted like boiled water flavored with coffee. She set the mug back down on the floor.

She thought about Charlie, the super, and wondered what he'd be doing now. It was too cold for him to have the garden door open. Undoubtedly he'd be seated inside his apartment with a bottle of Chivas, if he'd had the money that week, listening to one of his scratchy Puccini albums, and singing along. She wondered what the inside of his apartment looked like; she'd never seen it. She missed him, and the drunken consistency he'd lent her life. She decided she'd write to him in the morning. She didn't want to lose touch with him. She didn't know why, but thinking about him for these few moments had reduced her shock and lightened her mood. She no longer felt entirely comfortable sitting in the dark and got up to switch on the overhead light. She gazed up at the old globe fixture, thinking she'd have to get some lamps. The globe cast a stark light over the surfaces in the room, sent the walls with their slight cracks and flaws into sharp relief, and brought the Boston fern into almost unbearably clear focus.

On impulse, she went for her sketch pad and pencils and came back to resume her seat on the floor, starting to draw the fern on the mantel. She could, when she was drawing, lose herself entirely to the act of transposing the object of her vision to paper. Her hand lacked the control it once had had, which made her impatient. The only drawing she'd done in years had been the outline sketches for the Families.

Recalling the Families brought her around to the thought of what she was going to do here, now that she'd returned. The apartment would soon be furnished and she'd have nothing more to do to it. There had to be work of some sort for her to do or she might—she could feel herself dangerously close to it—go mad. There were only so many walks on Yonge Street or along Eglinton she could take, only so many shopping expeditions for food-for-one she could go on before her need for a daily routine became vital in order to sustain her, at best, precarious emotional equilibrium.

With a jolt that made her hand with the pencil slide out of control across the page, she remembered Jake's cameras. Suddenly, fiercely, she wanted them. Throwing aside the sketch pad and pencil, she clambered to her feet and ran to the telephone in the kitchen.

A man answered. It took her a second or two to realize that this must be Anthony.

"It's Dene," she explained. "I'm sorry to call so late. Could I please speak to my mother for a moment?"

"Of course," Anthony responded pleasantly. "Just a moment."

He was English. Moira hadn't mentioned that. It made sense that her mother would feel most at ease with someone whose background coincided with hers and whose accent wasn't jarringly North American.

"Dene? Is anything wrong?"

"No, no. I'm sorry. I remembered there's something I do want. Jake's cameras." She spoke his name aloud for the first time since his death and felt her body bend in on itself as if his death were rawly new again. "I'd like to have his cameras," she said breathlessly.

"I didn't put them into storage," her mother said. "They're here, in a box in the attic. You can collect them any time *Are* you all right, darling?"

In a small voice, Dene answered, "No." Then, hearing how she sounded, she added, "I will be. It's harder than I thought it would be, coming back. All the streets have memories. I suddenly remembered the cameras, and I do want them. Nothing else, only the cameras."

"Dene," her mother sighed, "someday you're going to have to talk about it, get it out from inside you and discuss Jake and Mimi."

"I know that. I know! But not yet. I'm not ready yet. I'm sorry to call so late, but I was thinking ... I don't even know why I want the cameras."

"It's all right," her mother said indulgently. "I quite understand."

"Do you?"

"I do, I assure you."

"I'll call and let you know when I'm coming to pick them up."

"Hold on a moment, darling. Anthony's trying to say something." Moira covered the mouthpiece with her hand and Dene listened to the muted murmur of voices before the hand went away and her mother said, "Anthony's said if you'd like to come along with us next week, we'd both be delighted to have you."

It brought tears to Dene's eyes. A stranger, someone she'd never met and hadn't known existed until a few hours earlier, was willing to offer her a holiday. "He *is* kind," she said, choked by the idea of this stranger's magnanimity. "But I couldn't."

"If you change your mind, we'd adore having you along. There's plenty of room. We rent a house, you see, and there's staff, and guest quarters. Why not think about it?"

"I will. I'll think about it. Good night."

She hung up and went unsteadily back to the living room, slumping down onto the floor. What was she doing? Jake's cameras. What would she do with them and why had she asked to have them? She didn't even know how to use a camera. Something urgent inside her insisted she have them. It might be dangerous, she warned that insistent voice. She wasn't at all sure she could cope with the proximity of things that Jake had handled.

She lit a cigarette and sat back against the wall with her eyes closed, hearing the front door open and close. Two sets of footsteps ascended the stairs—Anne and someone else. Maybe Charlie had come back for a nightcap. She opened her eyes, listening. The footsteps were overhead now. They stopped for a moment. Then one pair of feet moved off to the rear of the house, toward the kitchen.

Her eyes fixed on the ceiling, she continued to listen. After a short time the second pair of feet returned from the kitchen. What am I doing? she asked herself. She felt as if she were evolving into some sort of vampire, sucking up night noises and drawing a bizarre kind of strength from them. But Anne had been so very kind to her. She liked Anne even though the woman mystified her with her talk of screams in an empty house, and lovers who'd been but were no more. Anne was a kind person, Dene thought, lowering her eyes. She put out the cigarette, got up and emptied the now cold coffee down the kitchen sink, then went into the bathroom to shower. The idea of owning Jake's cameras had given her a destination. Those cameras would, in some way, determine the future course of her life.

Anne put the kettle on to boil, then stood for a moment by the stove, trying to bring herself into control. She couldn't. She was aware of Jamie in the living room, aware, almost, of his very breathing. Throughout the time she'd been at the party she'd felt his eyes like small flames that had touched against her here, there, there, until her entire attention had been fixed on the silent, attractive man across the room. Even when other people had come between them, blocking the line of vision, she'd sensed his eyes.

She'd recognized him almost at once. He wasn't as tall as she'd thought he'd be, but he was better-looking than he appeared onstage. Up close he had a complicated aura: disappointment, good humor, intelligence, sadness, optimism. When he'd brushed against her on his way out of the room, she'd felt a small shock, almost electric. She wondered if the collision had been entirely accidental; she couldn't be certain. Had she willed it to happen by placing herself in his path, or had he deviated slightly off course in order to approach her? It didn't matter. She liked the look of him, hints of red in his hair, the quality of his smile, the resonant depths of his voice.

He was far younger than she. There couldn't possibly be a future because of the considerable difference in their ages. Yet he seemed so interested. He'd stared and stared at her until she'd felt naked. His eyes had approved her, had heightened her awareness of her body until it seemed as if it were his hands and not merely his eyes that had touched against her, until her concentration on the conversation with that other man—she didn't even know his name—had evaporated. She'd felt transparent, both weakened and emboldened. When she'd first felt Jamie's eyes, she'd wanted to go over to him and say, "Let's stop this right now and go somewhere. It might only be once; it might only be for a week." However long it was to be, she wanted it. She could almost feel the weight of his body on hers, the thrust of pleasure. Her breasts felt heavy, her legs unsteady.

She returned to the living room to find Jamie seated comfortably on the sofa, examining her books. Whatever happened here would happen because she willed it. She wanted him to claim her, to make a definitive gesture that would culminate in their climbing the stairs together to her bedroom. It had been months, closer to a year, since Ken had left. It felt like years. At the end, Ken had removed himself. She'd been expecting it, but there had been habits and appetites that had developed in the course of their two years together. She'd found it difficult to reconcile his absence with her continuing need for him. She had, naturally, sent him on his way with a smile and a small, affectionate kiss. She'd wanted to strike him, to give him a shove that would have sent him flying down the stairs. But she'd kissed him good-bye before returning upstairs to strip the bed and, on some demented impulse, to burn the sheets. She'd cut them into small pieces, then fed them into the fireplace until nothing remained but an unpleasant smell and strange ash formations in the grate. They were still friends.

"How long have you been separated?" she asked.

Jamie turned. His mouth answered, "A week." His eyes spoke of fresh wounds and recently drawn blood. He looked battle-fatigued. She wanted to comfort him and, in the process, comfort herself. "Do you have children?" she asked, and then watched, dismayed, as his eyes clouded and his mouth replied, "Two boys."

"I'm sorry," she said helplessly, not really able to imagine what it could mean to give up your claim to two children you'd made from parts of yourself. "Is it going to be permanent?" she asked.

His eyes widened fractionally and he tilted his head slightly. "You have beautiful features," he said, as if she were a painting he found worthy of praise. "Perfect features."

"I *had* them," she said, without coyness. "Once upon a time, I was young and razor-sharp, and being beautiful was a weapon I used against the Harvard boys with a vengeance."

She laughed, showing her teeth. "I was considered 'fast company.' I'll get the coffee." She stood up. "How do you take it?"

"Black, please."

They each had another drink, and the coffee. He didn't reach out to make any gesture; he didn't stay. She wasn't sure how to react. In recent years she'd grown accustomed to men who felt it mandatory to stake their claims at once, to make known their desires and then leave it to her to fulfill them, as if their statement of desire was all that was required. Jamie pocketed his Gitanes and said, "It's getting late and I've got a script to finish."

She walked down the stairs with him to the front door, only remembering as he opened the door that he didn't have a car.

"Look, I'll run up to get my coat and drive you home."

"I'll get a taxi out on Yonge Street," he said confidently, appearing all at once anxious to get away. "Thank you for the coffee, the drink."

"My pleasure," she said, and waited.

He placed a light kiss on her mouth, then turned and went down the front steps. She closed the door and looked up the stairway, thinking about her days as "fast company." There was almost nothing she hadn't done by the end of her junior year. She'd drawn the line at painful acts; everything else had been a joy and she'd valued her looks because they'd attracted so many young men. Now, suddenly, she felt old and terribly tired at the prospect of climbing two flights of stairs in order to get to bed. Why hadn't anyone ever warned her that there'd be such calamitous changes in the course of her life? Why had she never suspected that Frank might one day find himself another beautiful college girl to fall in love with? Growing old had never entered into any of her plans. She remembered the shock she'd experienced attending her twenty-fifth reunion at Radcliffe, seeing all the middle-aged women who'd once been such splendid young girls. She'd been there too: yet another of the middle-aged brigade. If only she could reconcile herself to being alone, living alone . . . Her hand on the banister, she began to climb the stairs.

Chapter 13

Sherrill went along to her first audition and sat in the reception area looking at the other women. Oddly, she felt, not competitive, but unexpectedly sympathetic. It didn't make sense that all these attractive, talented women were directing their energies toward something so nonsensical as a voice-over for a cat food commercial.

It had to boil down to money, she thought, and to the credit that would be added to a résumé. None of it really meant anything. She couldn't see this audition as a life-or-death issue, something critical to her immediate career and her future.

The other women were well-dressed. One or two appeared fairly relaxed, but all of them betrayed a certain anxiety. Suddenly she knew she was going to get the job because she had no anxiety; she actually didn't care.

When her turn came, she entered the board room with a wide, natural smile and shook hands with everyone present before sitting at the far end of the massive table where the mike and script were set up. She scanned the script, aware of everyone's eyes on her, then asked, "What kind of voice would you like?"

Someone answered, "A kitten."

Wanting to laugh, but suppressing it, she said, "Okay, right," and quickly read through the short script a second time.

"Take your time," one of the men volunteered, as he looked at his watch.

She glanced over at him with a smile, straightened the pages of the script—all the while working up a cat voice inside her head—and said, "I'm ready." It was nuts, she thought, to be there trying to come up with a kitten voice while the seven or eight people collected around the polished expanse of table watched her soberly.

The girl running the tape machine cued her in and Sherrill started off with a cockney cat, just for the hell of it. Everyone cracked up, but they let her go all the way through it.

Grinning like the others, the clock watcher asked, "Could you give us some different accents?"

"Sure," she said, enjoying herself. "Tell me what you want and I'll do it."

"Well, what?" The clock watcher looked around the room.

"French?" Sherrill suggested.

"Great!"

She threw them completely by doing a loose French translation of the script, then went ahead to do German, Russian, and Yiddish kittens, southern belles, Bronx and Brooklyn kittens, Boston Wasps, West Indians, and, finally, a plain old middle-American one. By the end, everyone was laughing and congratulating her. The girl working the tape machine was instructed by the clock watcher to go out and send the remaining women home.

"You've got it," he told Sherrill with a smile.

She returned his smile; he felt like an old friend. "Thank you," she said. "It was fun."

She was given the address of a sound studio on the West Side and told to be there the following Wednesday morning. Elated, she again shook hands with everyone, and left.

Winning the first audition she attended had to signify things would go well; the years put in in Toronto were going to pay off with rewards in New York. John had three more auditions already lined up. She felt better than she had in months, and decided to walk home, hoping to work off some of the churning energy left over from the audition.

It was another sunny day, although on the cold side. She moved at a good pace along Madison Avenue, glancing every so often into shop windows, convinced she could best this city. Today in her mind the place was an enormous, vicious-looking animal with cowardly tendencies. It was only the look of the beast, and its size, that were menacing. When confronted, its challenge met, it lost its bravado and backed down. Michelle was right: if you didn't let people see how much your career mattered to you, if you made a show of independence, suddenly you were desirable.

At Thirty-fourth Street, she turned east toward Third

Avenue and continued on downtown on Third, walking a little more slowly as some of the soaring excitement eased out of her system. She'd done it: she'd landed the first job she'd gone after. Catching sight of her reflection in a store window, she grinned.

She wanted to do something, or buy herself a present to commemorate the occasion, but all the shops she passed seemed to be specialty food shops. She compromised and bought four huge Delicious apples, laughing aloud as she left the store, recalling her Yiddish kitten.

Rae was in the front hall collecting her mail. Impulsively Sherrill told her about the audition.

"I thought you wrote music," Rae said with a knowing smile.

"I do, but I go out for auditions every now and then—"

"Come on," Rae laughed. "You don't think after thirty years in the business I can't spot an actor when I see one?"

Sherrill flushed, knowing she'd been caught out. "I guess you probably can," she conceded. "I just wasn't sure how . . ."

"How the landlady would take it," Rae finished for her. "Me, I don't care. Everybody's got to live somewhere. Long's you come up with the rent, it doesn't make a bit of difference to me. Anyway, I get a kick out of you kids."

"I do compose, though," Sherrill explained. "In fact, I was thinking I might rent a piano after all, if you really don't mind."

"Who minds? Can you play at least?"

"Oh, sure. I studied for six years. I was at the Royal Conservatory, but after a while I got tired of the—seriousness, I guess."

"In England, this was?" Rae asked.

"No, in Toronto."

"Oh! Well, never mind. At least you can play. I can't stand those people who sit and noodle. You know? Scales and stuff. That crap drives me crazy. So, listen. When're your things coming?"

"Not for at least another three weeks."

"What're you sleeping on, then?"

"The floor. I've got a sleeping bag."

"Boy, you kids! I tried sleeping on the floor, I'd wake up

in the morning over at Beth Israel Hospital." She shook her head doubtfully.

"It's not bad. I wouldn't want to do it for the rest of my life, but I don't mind for a few weeks."

"You want to borrow anything, ask me."

"I will. Thank you."

Rae went off down the hall to her apartment at the rear and Sherrill opened her mailbox. Empty: She closed it and went upstairs to let herself into the apartment. The sleeping bag was rolled up under the window; her few cooking utensils were aligned on the small counter beside the sink; she'd hung her clothes in the closet and was using the two suitcases, stacked one atop the other, as a table. The room seemed huge, and she liked its spartan atmosphere.

She placed the apples on the counter, arranging them like a still life. The elation was gone now. She'd come down. Turning, she confronted the three gaping windows, deciding she'd hang plants over the upper halves and cover the lower portions with the curtains when they arrived. It occurred to her that she was becoming daily more bothered by those uncovered windows. Getting as close to them as she could, she looked out. No one could possibly see into the apartment if the bottom halves of the windows were covered. If only her furniture would come. It disturbed her to have to creep about the apartment at night, dressing and undressing in the tiny bathroom for fear of being seen by someone in one of the buildings across the way, or out walking on the far side of the street.

The days were getting shorter. It was almost dark and it wasn't yet four-thirty. Lights were on in the house across the street and she watched a middle-aged man take a book from a wall of shelves, then leave the room. She wanted, all at once, to call her mother, and turned to look at the telephone sitting on the floor, debating whether to call now or wait until after eight when the rates went down.

Now, she thought, and sat cross-legged on the floor to dial. As she waited for her mother to answer at the other end, her excitement flowed back, so that when she heard her mother say hello, she jumped right in.

"Hi, it's me. Guess what?"

"How are you? What?"

"I got a job. The very first audition I've been to, and I got the job! Isn't that terrific?"

"Is it a terrific job?" Josie asked, her voice amused.

"Well, that depends on what's terrific to you. I'm doing a voice-over for a TV commercial, playing a kitten."

Her mother laughed. "I'm glad for you," she said. "How's it going?"

"Oh, pretty good," Sherrill answered, looking over at the windows. "My stuff hasn't arrived yet, but otherwise it's all right. I'm starting to find my way around, but I still get mixed up between what's east and what's west. How're you doing?"

"Same as ever. I was just thinking about you, as a matter of fact. There's a piece in today's *Star* about a new show your friend Jamie's in. It's a very good write-up."

The mention of Jamie deflated Sherrill's mood. "That's really nice," she said lamely, wishing her mother hadn't mentioned it.

"What's the matter, Sherry? Isn't it the way you thought it would be?"

It was uncanny, Sherrill thought, how perceptive her mother could be. "Nothing ever is," she replied thoughtfully. "But I'm coping. I just wanted to let you know the good news."

"I'm glad you did. Listen, don't spend all your money talking on the phone to me. Are you all right?"

"I'm fine. I've got three more auditions lined up. At the rate I'm going, things ought to go really well."

They talked a moment longer, then said good-bye. Sherrill hung up and again looked at the windows. Christ! Why couldn't she stay up? She wished her mother hadn't talked about Jamie. She could feel herself starting to sink and lifted the receiver to dial Michelle's number. Maybe they'd be able to go out for a hamburger, or to a movie. The answering service picked up. Sherrill started to leave a message but the operator peremptorily said, "Hold!" and left Sherrill dangling. She waited almost two minutes before hanging up to return to the window. It had started to rain. The streetlights came on; the street below looked shiny and ominous—a stage set where an accident might occur, or an establishing film shot leading to an act of violence. She shivered, momentarily daunted by her imaginings.

She longed for someone to call, for somewhere to go. Where was Michelle? she wondered. Probably out on a call. There was a movie playing on Twenty-third Street she wanted to see, but she didn't feel like going out alone in the rain. The telephone rang and she jumped, then ran to answer.

Michelle said, "Hi! How did it go?"

"I got it! How about that?"

"Hey, fantastic! What's the job?"

"Voice-over for a cat food commercial."

"You don't exactly sound thrilled about it."

"I was, but I've come down a little. I tried to call you a few minutes ago. I got the service and they left me hanging on hold, so I gave up."

"Let's celebrate," Michelle suggested. "Come on over and I'll cook something delicious and fattening."

Sherrill didn't really hear her. She was thinking about Jamie, picturing his face when he laughed, the dimples in his cheeks.

"Well?" Michelle asked. "Don't you feel like it?"

"Sure. I'd love to. What time?"

"Come now. You can keep me company while I throw something together."

"Okay. Would you like me to bring anything?"

"No. I've got everything. Just come."

For a few minutes after the call Sherrill stood with her head thrown back, gazing at the cracked ceiling. Jamie. He waved good-bye, then turned to walk off down the deserted street. Coatless, hatless, he joked about filthy postcards before leaving. She wanted to write to him, to put into words how much she missed the sight of him and the husky murmur of his voice in her ear.

Slowly, she straightened. An affair that had never begun couldn't now be considered over. Stop thinking about him! she told herself. He was there; she was here. Perhaps she'd been tempted by nothing more here than an illusory promise, but she was going to stick it out. Other people learned to ignore the crumbling brownstones, the shopping-bag ladies, the derelicts, and the young thugs who seemed to ooze menace as they swaggered along the streets. She'd learn, too.

She stepped out through the front door and started toward Third Avenue at a brisk pace, telling herself there was absolutely nothing to be afraid of. No one lurked suspiciously in any of the doorways. Nevertheless, she felt better when she reached Third Avenue. There were plenty of people, and fairly heavy traffic, but no available taxis. It seemed, as Michelle had once observed, that all the taxis in the city put on their "Off Duty" lights the moment the first drop of rain fell. She walked up to Twenty-third to stand at the bus stop. She felt a little sleepy and waited for the bus, dazzled by the lights of the oncoming traffic. The reflection of the lights on the wet pavement struck her as beautiful and she stared, unblinking, down the avenue until the bus arrived and cut off her view.

Michelle had prepared a casserole of ham and broccoli with a Cheddar cheese sauce and bread crumbs and was sliding it into the oven when Sherrill arrived.

"Give me your coat and umbrella," she said. "I'll hang them up in the bathroom."

"Thanks." Sherrill surrendered them. "It's coming down like crazy."

"You're soaking wet. Hang on and I'll get you a towel."

Now that she was no longer living here, Sherrill thought the apartment looked charming, even spacious. Of course, the sofa bed was closed and there were no garments draped over the furniture. In the nonfunctional fireplace, Michelle had set a vase of yellow daisies.

"That looks really lovely," Sherrill complimented her. "I'd never have thought of putting flowers there."

"In this place, I can't afford to waste any space. How about a drink?" Michelle asked, holding a towel in her hands.

"Some coffee?"

"Not a drink drink?"

"No, thanks."

"Okay, coffee," Michelle said, with a little shrug, handing over the towel. "Tell me about the audition. When's the job? I can't believe you, you know. You arrive in town and pull down a job within the first month. It took me almost five months to get my first job, and you know what it was? You'll croak when I tell you."

"What?"

"Standing on Madison Avenue at lunchtime one day handing out pamphlets for a new restaurant that was opening."

"That doesn't sound so bad."

"Are you kidding? D'you know what I had to *wear*?"

"What?"

"I had to wear a pig suit, for Chrissake!"

"A pig suit?" Sherrill laughed.

"A goddamned *pig* suit. It was a pork restaurant that was opening. I made fifty bucks, though." She shrugged again and lifted the coffeepot off the back burner.

Sherrill moved to follow her, then stopped.

"Hey!" Michelle peered at her from around the corner. "What're you doing, dreaming?"

"Listen, Misha," Sherrill said. "Would it be all right if I stayed over? It's a rotten night and I'm getting kind of fed up with the sleeping bag. Would you mind?"

"Hell, no! We'll watch a flick on the tube and play Scrabble. I've got an audition first thing in the morning, but you can sleep in. I won't wake you."

"No, no. I've got to be up early, too. I have to pick up my glossies from the repro place. I just don't feel like hiking all the way back downtown in the rain. To be honest, it's starting to get to me, living in that place like a squatter."

"I know," Michelle sympathized. "But it's only another week or two."

"What can I do to help?" Sherrill offered, feeling better.

"Nothing. There isn't room in here for both of us anyway."

"What's your audition for in the morning?"

"A dubbing job. Italian movie. I think they want my voice for somebody like ... oh, what's her name? I've forgotten. Anyway, it's Italian."

Sherrill leaned against the door watching Michelle measure coffee into the pot. The day after tomorrow she had an audition for the revue replacement. Then, on Friday, she had an audition for a singing yogurt commercial. If she pulled down all these jobs she'd be earning quite a bit of money, but gaining almost no visibility. It was success without glamour. She smiled to herself at the idea. Someone, she thought, ought to write a handbook on how to get ahead in show business without ever setting foot on a stage or film set.

"What're you drinking?" she asked Michelle, who was pouring something into a glass.

"You'd hate it. Cassis."

"What's it like?"

"A little bitter."

"Taste?" Sherrill asked.

"Okay, but you'll hate it." Michelle held out the glass.

Sherrill took a sip, made a face, and handed back the glass. "You're right. I hate it. How can you drink that?"

"Because I'm out of everything else. Say, how many of those jumpers have you got, anyway?"

Sherrill looked down at herself. "Why?"

"I'm curious. I don't think I've ever seen you in anything else."

"I've got three of them, this gray one, a camel-colored one, and a dark green. Don't you like it?"

"It's all right. I mean, for hacking around. But for auditions. Did you wear that today?"

"Sure I did. Why not?"

Michelle started to laugh. "It's probably why you got the job," she said, a hint of admiration in her voice. "I don't know *anyone* in New York who'd dare go to an audition dressed like that."

"There's nothing wrong with it. It's clean, neat, and presentable."

"You look like you're on vacation from a Catholic girl's school."

"That's okay," Sherrill said, unbothered. "I don't mind."

Michelle shook her head, still laughing. After a moment, she said, "It's probably going to work for you. What's different always catches on here. I just had a flash," she said, her voice dropping.

"What kind of flash?"

"You're going to set them on their asses." She sounded awed. "You really are. I think I'm going to be jealous. But," she added, her smile returning, "I'll try to live with it. Let's go sit down. The coffee'll be ready in a couple of minutes." Halfway to the sofa, she stopped and studied Sherrill for a long moment. Then she sat down, saying, "I don't know how, or why, but I've got this feeling you're really going to click."

"Don't," Sherrill said quietly. "It's kind of scary."

"It shouldn't be," Michelle said, surprised. "Isn't that what you came here for?"

"I suppose. But I don't sit around thinking about it all the time. I mean, the kind of people who get fixated on their careers . . . they're boring."

"Don't worry about it," Michelle said confidently, sitting back and crossing her legs. "The one thing you're never going to be is boring."

Chapter 14

Dene apologized to her mother for being in a hurry; she lied about having an appointment, then raced upstairs. It was very cold at the top of the house, and the dimly lit, many-dormered attic seemed far larger than she'd remembered. Everything was very neat: stacks of cartons all carefully labeled, pictures leaning in symmetrical rows against the wall, lampshades piled one atop the other like ice cream cones. She found the carton marked "Cameras—JW" at the rear end of the room, set apart from a group of boxes whose labels indicated they contained china and glassware from the Rosedale house. Looking at them, she had an almost overpowering desire to sit down on the dusty wood floor and open them one by one to examine the articles she and Jake had accumulated during their time together. It was too risky. If she opened any one of the boxes, she'd be even more overpowered by the rush of memories that was bound to attend every single item.

Lifting the flaps to ascertain that the cameras and lenses were actually inside, she picked up the carton. Her mother was hovering at the foot of the stairs, wearing an anxious expression.

"Won't you even stay to have a cup of coffee?" Moira asked. "You've got a smudge on your cheek, dear." She reached out to wipe the dirt from Dene's face.

"I really can't. I've got only fifteen minutes to get downtown."

"Will you come by later? I do so want you to meet Anthony. He's very keen to meet you."

"Let me call you. I will call," Dene promised and kissed her mother's cheek before escaping out the front door.

The carton was heavy. Her arms ached by the time she got to St. Clair and started to look for a taxi. She'd planned this very badly. She should have had the taxi that had brought her wait. It would have validated the lie about her downtown appointment. There wasn't a taxi in sight, but a streetcar was coming. She'd try again for a taxi at Yonge Street, and if there wasn't one, she'd take the subway, then walk the five blocks back to the apartment.

She looked unseeingly out the window, the box heavy on her lap, wondering if Charlie had received her letter yet. She'd mailed it four days ago. Perhaps he had it by now and was sitting down to write a reply. She hoped he'd answer.

On her way up Duplex toward the house, she saw Anne's nephew, Charlie, washing the Mercedes. He had on another plaid sports shirt, in predominantly green tones this time, with the sleeves rolled up. He was holding a hose in one hand, a large soapy sponge in the other. Whistling melodically, he slathered soap over the trunk, then dropped the sponge into a bucket, stepped back, and turned on the hose. He looked very healthy, Dene thought, and very young. She couldn't make herself believe he was actually as old as Anne had said. Of course, the full, bushy beard was deceiving.

She debated saying hello, but she saw her and smiled as he turned off the hose. Wiping his wet hands down the sides of his jeans, he went toward her. "Let me give you a hand with that," he volunteered, holding his arms out.

"No, that's all right," she said, reluctant to allow anyone to touch Jake's things.

"Come on," he persisted. "You look about ready to drop." He lifted the carton out of her arms and she had no choice but to open the back door while he followed behind her to place the carton on the kitchen table.

"What've you got in here, rocks?" he asked. "Weighs a ton."

"Cameras." She felt crowded with him in the room. He seemed to take up too much space, and he smelled slightly musty, as if his clothes needed laundering.

"Cameras, huh. You do photography as well as design toys?"

"No. They ... uh ... they were my husband's." She

wished he'd leave; she willed him to go, but he wanted to stay and talk.

"Is Anne home?" she asked helplessly, remaining by the door. Perhaps he'd sense her desire to be left alone, and go.

"Yeah," he said. "She's making lunch." He grinned again. "Why don't you come up and have some with us?"

How, she wondered, could he extend an invitation without first consulting Anne? Maybe Anne had told him to ask her.

"I'd love to, but I've got an appointment downtown." She looked meaningfully at her watch. "God! I'm running late. Thanks a lot for helping with that. And thank Anne for me. Tell her I'll try to call her later when I get back."

"Sure. Hey, don't let me hold you back. I've got to finish the car before the soap freezes." He went toward the door and she stepped aside to allow him to pass. He said, "Catch you later, eh?" and with a smile he loped off down the back steps. After a moment she heard the sound of water hitting the car.

Letting out her breath, she locked the door, then approached the carton. There were two cameras, both in their cases, and several containers with lenses, three packs of film, all of which had, according to their dates, gone well beyond expiration. Her hands unsteady, she picked up the Canon and snapped open the case. She could, too easily, see Jake with the camera suspended from its wide black strap around his neck. She felt as if she were holding a part of him in her hands, and experienced anew the full impact of her grief. She withdrew the camera from its case to turn it this way and that. The little dial on the upper right-hand corner indicated there was still film in the camera.

"God!" she whispered and hastily put the camera down on the table, trying to remember when Jake had last used it. The day came back with regrettable ease. The week after Christmas. New Year's Day, 1966. They'd gone out into the back garden to build a snowman. Everything had glistened, ice-bound, in the sun of that bitingly cold afternoon. Jake had run back indoors for the camera and returned to take the pictures that were still inside it now. The indicator dial sat at 22. Would the photographs still be good? If they were, would she want to see them? She didn't know. She couldn't decide if she wanted this last piece of evidence of their life

together. She left the Canon on the table to reach for the
Pentax Spotmatic. The film indicator was at zero. Relieved,
she examined the camera, fascinated. She looked through
the lens and saw only black. The lens cap was still on. She
tried to take it off but it didn't seem to want to come.
Frustrated, she began to go through the contents of the
carton, hoping to find an instruction booklet. There were
only wads of newspaper someone had packed around the
cameras to protect them.

Out of breath as if she'd been running, she took several
steps away from the table and stood regarding the array of
cameras and attachments. Hearing sounds outside, she turned
to see that Charlie had rewound the hose and was disconnecting it. She'd told him she had an appointment. If she
didn't go out, he'd know she'd lied. Why hadn't she said she
preferred to be alone, instead of fabricating an excuse?
There was a camera store on Yonge Street; she distinctly
remembered passing a display of cameras and glossy multi-
color come-ons for film processing. They might have an
instruction booklet. She'd need fresh film, too. If she fig-
ured out how to use the cameras, she'd be able to start
taking pictures. Once she knew how to take pictures, she'd
go on to learn how to develop the film, and then to make
prints. Suddenly, she had to know how all of it worked. She
hurried out, walking quickly toward Yonge Street and the
camera store. Once she knew about developing, she might
try her hand at the film left in the Canon. If she could be
the one to reproduce the images she'd somehow feel better,
as if, in a way, she were returning herself and Jake to life.

Anne and Charlie were finishing their coffee after lunch
when the telephone rang. Charlie made a move to answer it,
but Anne said, "Never mind. I'll get it." She picked up the
receiver to hear Jamie's voice, without preamble, say, "Would
you like to see a show and have dinner?"

"I'd love it. How are you?"

"Oh, fine. I'm right in the middle of something but I
thought I'd call."

"I see. What time?"

"Seven. Is that good?"

"That's perfect. I'll see you here at seven. Or would you
like me to meet you downtown?"

"No, I'll come for you there."

"All right."

"Good," he said. "Seven. Bye-bye."

She hung up and turned to look at Charlie, who'd been following her end of the conversation with interest.

"You've got a date," he said with a smile.

"I do."

"Who's the lucky fella?"

"Jamie. We met Saturday night at the party. I told you about it."

"You didn't tell me about any Jamie," he said, still smiling. "From the look of you, I guess you're not too unhappy about the call."

"He's years younger than me. I think he's just being kind."

"Oh, bullshit! *Kind.* I wasn't related to you, I'd be calling you for dates three times a day."

"What did Dene say?" she remembered to ask.

"Said she had an appointment. She went tearing off about ten minutes after she came back."

Anne gazed down at the tabletop, trying to sort through her thoughts. She felt a tremulous kind of expansion inside her chest, as if everything in there had been critically overcrowded and Jamie's call had cleared some of the clutter to let in extra air. She pictured him sitting on the living room sofa looking at her books and felt a spasm of excited optimism. He'd called; he'd asked her out for the evening. He liked her and wanted to see her again. She felt like laughing and crying. He really was sweet, and his smile . . .

"I'm going to clear out," Charlie said, his voice cutting sharply through her daydreams. "The car looks like a car again instead of a delivery truck. And you owe me two pillowcases full of clean laundry. Don't forget to get the snow tires put on. Remember what happens every year: the first big snow comes and everybody goes skiing down all the hills in town. It's a very hilly city, you know," he said, as if the thought were occurring to him for the first time. "Maybe hundreds of years ago that big hill at Davenport was the original shoreline of the lake. I mean, it goes right the way across the city." He got up and leaned forward over the back of the chair with his hands braced on its top. "Listen, d'you think I should ask her out?"

"Who, Dene?"

"Yeah. What d'you think?"

"Leave her be, Charlie," she said quietly, meeting his eyes. "I don't think she's in any condition for dating. She's trying to settle in and having a hard time of it. Something happened there," she said, considering Dene. Her eyes slid off Charlie to fix on the hood over the stove. "She's so . . ." She couldn't think of an appropriate word to describe Dene's defenseless frailty. "I don't know," she said. "Do whatever you feel like doing, sweetie, but don't be disappointed if she says no."

"Okay. Message received." He unhooked his jacket from the doorknob, went back to kiss her on the forehead, then made his way to the door, where he stopped to say, "I think it's dynamite you've got a date. You've been dragging your ass ever since Ken split. Don't go into this whole big number about how you're so old and he's so young and all that crap. Go have a good time and let whatever's going to happen, happen. Jamie who, anyway?"

"Ferrara."

"The guy who does that show on the tube, right? What's it called? You know the one I mean. The variety show he's on every once in a while and he's so goddamned straight-faced funny."

"I know."

"He's the only good thing on it," he said, then waggled his fingers at her and let himself out.

She sat on at the table, inspecting the remains of the lunch. Her heart was beating heavily, slowly, as if it had grown too large for her chest and was having difficulty functioning properly.

She loaded the dishwasher before going upstairs to open the closet, trying to decide what to wear. The evening ahead had all the significance of a special occasion. She knew she'd remember it. Her life was about to change again, and she was both glad, and frightened. She told herself she was being juvenile, reading far too much into what was, after all, nothing more than a casual date. The man had recently separated from his family; he was probably lonely. That didn't quite ring true. After all, he was a well-known actor and undoubtedly had a great number of friends, not to mention women. She tried to reason herself away from this sense of occasion, but couldn't. It *was* momentous, and she wanted the evening to be worthy of remembering.

The black dress was out of the question; she'd worn it Saturday. Nothing else looked right. Becoming overheated and annoyed, she went a second time, more slowly, through the closet, trying to see with some objectivity what might be best. He'd said she didn't need makeup and that she'd look better with her hair up. He'd been critical of her appearance. It was the first time in her life anyone had been. Did that mean that her looks were finally gone? Last week that possibility hadn't unduly alarmed her. This week it frightened her—because of Jamie. Why would a man his age choose to be seen in public with her when there was such patent disparity in their ages, when she was so hopeless with makeup and the only other way she could wear her hair was twisted up in a knot? Why had she gone to that damned party in the first place? She'd been making good progress; her life was pleasantly tolerable. She'd gone to the party, Jamie had been there, and now her single life was completely intolerable.

She got out a pair of white flannel trousers and a white cashmere turtleneck sweater. To hell with it! She'd wear what was comfortable, leave off all makeup but for some mascara and rouge, and put her hair up into a knot. She'd look a thousand years old, but, she reminded herself, she'd never made any pretense of being anything other than who and what she was. The problem was that who and what she was had undergone radical changes over the years and from time to time she was no longer entirely certain of her identity.

As if to reacquaint herself with her own reality she spent quite a while studying herself in the mirror, acknowledging the lines around her mouth and at the corners of her eyes, taking stock of the flesh well beyond its prime.

It would be a pleasant evening with a charming young man. Nothing more.

The store manager said he didn't have an instruction booklet for that particular model of Pentax. "It's seven or eight years old," he told Dene. "Basically, the newer models aren't too different. You could use one of those booklets to figure out the shutter speeds and all that. But your best bet's to buy a book on 35 millimeter cameras and start from scratch."

"Where would I get one?"

"I'm all sold out. But any bookstore would have them."

She purchased three rolls each of black-and-white and color film, then went in search of a bookstore. In the end she got three different guides to 35 millimeter single-lens reflex cameras and two coffee-table editions of collected contemporary photographs, then took a taxi home in order to get to work right away.

She sat on the living room floor and carefully read all the technical information pertaining to the focal-plane shutter, film speed, focusing, depth of field, and polarization. She studied the chapters on control of light, on flash attachments, and on various types of filters and lenses. She got the Pentax and sat with it, examining its features. She worked the lens aperture control and the lens focus control, lining up the Boston fern, then focusing on it. She experimented with the film rewind knob, the shutter release button, the film advance lever, the shutter speed dial. At last, filled with nervous anticipation, she opened one of the containers of color film and, following the directions in the manual, set the spool into place in the left-hand well, pulled the end of the film across the camera, inserted it into one of the slots of the take-up spool, and wound it on until it was secure. Then she closed the camera back and, glancing every so often at the instructions, depressed the shutter release, winding the film forward until the frame counter indicated the camera was cocked to take its first picture.

At this point she gently set the camera on the floor and stood up to stretch. She walked to the window to see that it was already dark. What time was it? After six. She'd spent almost four hours reading and studying. It seemed amazing: the most effortless afternoon she'd spent in more than four years. She had a rare feeling of satisfaction. And she was hungry. Moving her shoulders up and down to ease some of the stiffness, she went to the kitchen to see what was in the refrigerator. She'd have a quick snack, then read the chapter on flash attachments. She might even be able to try taking a few photographs before she went to bed.

She leaned against the kitchen counter while she ate her peanut butter and jam sandwich, and looked around trying to decide what objects might be suitable for a still life. Nothing appealed to her eye. Opening the refrigerator door for an apple, she was arrested by the sight of the various jars on the shelf: jelly, jam, mustard, mayonnaise, ketchup. Moving quickly, she removed the jars from the refrigerator and carried them into the living room, where she arranged them on the floor in front of the fireplace. There were nine jars and bottles in all, each of a different size and color. She spent almost half an hour working out an arrangement. Pleased, she sat down with the instruction book and her apple, to read up on the use of the flash attachment.

At nine-thirty, she was ready to try. Lying on her stomach on the floor, she held the camera to her eye and looked through the lens. It was hard to decide if the light was good enough. She hadn't realized that the camera settings would be more complicated, and different, when using the flash. If she had proper lighting, if she could preset all the lights so that when she looked through the lens what she'd see would be the final image before the actual negative was exposed, then she wouldn't have to guess about the quality of the light.

She returned the jars to the refrigerator, and mopped up the damp rings on the floor near the fireplace. With the lens cover back in place, she set the Pentax on a corner of the kitchen counter and went to prepare for bed. She would, in the morning, try to do the still life with natural light. She'd also go back to the camera store to buy some lighting equipment and more manuals.

Curled up on her side facing the wall, she saw herself walking along a street taking pictures. In her mind everything was viewed through a lens with a tiny light meter arrow on the right-hand side indicating whether or not the subjects were sufficiently well lit to go for an exposure. A central biprism allowed her to slide what she saw in and out of definition. Her eyes, like shutters, blinked and captured scene after scene. Her dreams were still photographs dropping one upon another, endlessly.

Chapter 15

The revue director claimed to like Sherrill very much, but the job never came through. She did land the singing yogurt commercial; then things slowed down, almost to a halt. John said it was the season. "Things are quiet around Christmas. After the new year, it'll pick up. Relax, sweetheart. You're doing just great. Enjoy the holidays and forget it for now."

Michelle corroborated what he'd said. "It *is* deadly right now," she told Sherrill. "Why don't you go Christmas shopping or something?"

She'd ignored Christmas altogether so far. The idea of spending the holidays alone depressed her. She had bought two boxes of Christmas cards at Macy's one afternoon when she'd been over on the West Side for an audition, but she hadn't written them. Now, unless she sent them airmail, or special delivery, they'd arrive around the first of the year. Somehow she'd lost her momentum and couldn't bear being idle, sitting around the apartment with no auditions to attend, no work to do. The cards hadn't seemed important.

She forced herself to sit down and start addressing them. It made her feel even farther away from her friends and the life she'd lived in Toronto. Chewing on the end of her pen, she remembered the idea she'd had about success without glamour. Maybe, when the cards were done, she'd put some ideas down on paper just for the hell of it. At least it would be something to do. The idea of being at work—on anything— gave her a lift.

She was on the last of the cards when John telephoned.

"Listen, I know it's the last minute, but I've got a call to fill and you're my only girl in town who can sight-read. Can you make it for a voice-over at two-thirty?"

"For what?"

"Another commercial. The girl we had lined up came

136

down with some goddamned bug or other. Give me a yes or a no, sweetheart. I have to get someone over there right away. They're paying scale and a half."

"Sure. Okay. Where?"

She wrote down the name and address of the agency, then ran into the bathroom to put on a little makeup. There was no time to change out of her jumper into something dressier. She shoved the finished cards into her bag, grabbed her coat, and raced out. Luckily there was a cab letting out a fare halfway down the block. She tore down the sidewalk just as it was about to pull away, and pounded on the window. The driver, looking aggrieved, stopped. She jumped in, gave the address, then sat back to catch her breath.

There was no one in the reception area and she waited for two or three minutes before approaching the inner office door. She was about to open it when a tall, graying man came hurrying out. Startled, they stared at each other. Then he smiled and ran a hand through his hair. "Sherrill?"

"That's right. John forgot to tell me who I was supposed to see."

"I'm Drew," he said, shaking her hand. "What's the matter?" he asked, seeing her confused expression.

"I thought this was an audition," she said. "I'm wondering where the thirty other women are."

He laughed delightedly and held open the door. "Come on in," he invited. "John should've told you. You've got the job. He played your voice tape for me over the phone. I guess he explained the situation, huh?"

"He didn't," she said, entertained by the novelty of the situation. It was the first time in her career that, sight unseen, she'd landed a job. "You want me to do a voice-over right now?"

"Right. In here." He led her along a corridor and into a sound room, where he gave her a headset, positioned her in front of a mike, handed her a sheet of music, and said, "I'll run the tape while you read this over a time or two. Then we'll go for a take. Okay?"

"It's going to have to be okay, isn't it?" she said with a grin.

"I guess so. You want a coffee?" he asked, prepared to go into the control booth.

"No, that's all right, thanks," she responded, picking up on his urgency. "Let me just take a fast look at this."

He sat down at the console in the adjoining booth while she shrugged off her coat and ran through the music. Nothing complicated, but it was in a slightly lower key than she usually sang.

"How're you doing?" he asked over the mike from the booth.

"Okay." She turned to look at him. He was, she now had the time to see, a well-dressed, quite attractive man in his early forties or so, over six feet tall, with a slim build. He looked both tired and very wide awake. She decided this was because of what were probably premature wrinkles around wide-set blue eyes. He had a warm smile and large, slightly crooked teeth. He seemed to exude competence and control. His voice came over the speakers again, asking, "Ready to hear the sound track?"

She nodded, then listened as he ran the tape. She hummed the melody line, mouthing the lyrics, then looked over at him again as the tape ended. It was another of the world's great romantic beer commercials, she thought, smiling. She felt good, glad to be doing something more constructive than sitting around the apartment worrying about having too much free time on her hands.

"Want to go for a take?" he asked somewhat anxiously.

"Are you the sound engineer?" she asked, adjusting the headset more comfortably.

He laughed again and lit a cigarette. "I wish to hell I was," he answered, tipping his chair back. "I'm the account executive for this fiasco. Listen—what's your name, Sherrill? —get it in one take and I'll buy you dinner. I want to get the hell out of here. I've got to run the finished commercial over to the studio by four-thirty. Think you can do it?"

"Let me sing it to myself once, okay? Then I'll try it with the sound track."

"You want me to run it again?"

"No. I only need a minute or two." She held the music and for a moment saw only meaningless dots and lines. Panic turned her overheated. "C'mon, c'mon," she whispered to herself. The notes clicked into definition and once again represented sounds she could hear inside her head. She wet her lips, cleared her throat, then leaned in to the mike to ask, "What's your name again?"

He righted his chair abruptly. "Drew. You okay?"

"Oh, sure. It's a little on the low side, but I'll give it a try, if you're ready."

"Beautiful. I'll cue you in."

He rewound the tape and she listened to the babble that emerged from the speakers before he started at the beginning and cued her in. She sang the heartwarming Christmasy beer lyrics with as much feeling and meaning as she could muster. When she had finished, she watched Drew play with the dials as the tape ran out. Without looking up, he said, "It sounded great to me. I'll play it back and you tell me what you think."

The headphones looped around her neck, she listened, her eyes on the immense black speaker fastened to the wall in the upper corner of the sound booth. At the end, she looked once more at the man in the booth. His expression one of relief and satisfaction, he made a thumbs-up gesture. "You get dinner," he announced, smiling at her through the glass. "If you want it. The only snag is you've got to come with me while I drop this off. It's due to air tonight."

"All right," she agreed, a little flutter in her chest. She wouldn't have to go home. The apartment was drafty; the wind squealed around the edges of the three windows while heat hissed ineffectually in the radiators. All the ingredients were there for a good bout of depression, and anything that might keep that at bay was more than welcome.

Drew was pulling on his jacket. She picked up her things and walked out to the control room. He was closing down the console with one hand while extinguishing his cigarette in an overfull ashtray with the other.

"You've got a great sound," he complimented her. "I wouldn't have believed a little girl like you could sing with such balls."

"I'm not a little girl," she said quietly, amused by his remark.

"Twenty?"

"Almost twenty-six," she said, opening her handbag. "I've got to mail these." She showed him the Christmas cards.

"No problem. We're done in here." He turned off the lights and took her arm to lead her along a different corridor, through the outer office to the elevators. "I've got to pick up a few things from my office," he explained as they emerged from the elevator to travel along a thickly carpeted corridor. "Two seconds, okay?" He threw open a door, revealing a large corner office with a magnificent view of the end-of-day city. Automatically, she went to stand by the windows while he grabbed a briefcase and started tossing things in.

"Great view, isn't it?" he said, snapping shut the briefcase before pulling his coat from a hanger on the back of the door. "It'd be a lot more sensible if the desks faced the windows instead of the doors. Probably get a lot more work done around here. But then I suppose everybody would get neurotic as hell about people creeping up behind them."

She laughed, imagining it. "Do you live in the city?" she asked.

He nodded. "Where do you live?"

"Gramercy Park."

"Nice area," he said, retrieving his briefcase. He extended his arm to indicate she should precede him out.

Going down in the elevator, he asked, "What kind of food do you like?"

"Oh, anything. I'm easy. Aren't I supposed to sign a contract or something?"

"It's in my bag. I'll get you signed up and taken care of over dinner. Deal?"

"Sure. I don't mind." The casual carelessness of all this bothered her slightly. She wished she could turn off her brain and relax. Here was an attractive man willing to take her out to dinner and, for a moment, all she could think about was Jamie. Compared to Jamie, this man was hopelessly "civilian," and not especially charming or witty. He was pleasant, though, and seemed to have a good sense of humor. Forget it, just forget it! she warned herself.

In the taxi she risked looking over, to find he was staring at her with a half smile.

"What?" she asked, starting to smile. He really was good-looking. She liked the smell of his cologne.

"Now that I stop and look at you," he said, "I can see you're not a kid. I suppose everybody comes on to you that way."

"Close," she replied. "But not all." He had a pleasant

speaking voice, too, and good blue eyes, not the pale, watery kind but a dark, substantial blue.

"Where're you from?" he asked.

"How do you know I'm not from New York?"

"You're too—fresh," he said, "too unsophisticated. Your clothes, I mean. You don't dress the part."

"That's true," she agreed. "I don't believe in type-casting. Where are you from?"

He laughed. "How do *you* know *I'm* not from New York?"

"You don't act like a Madison Avenue account executive. You also don't sound as if you grew up in the Bronx."

He laughed harder, then asked, "Have you met that many of them?"

"Not really. I've done two other commercials and had about six auditions. You don't fit the image. Anyway, most of them wouldn't be able to find the on/off switch on a console."

"That's a point," he said, his eyes shifting away to study the street signs. "On the northwest corner there," he told the driver, then turned back to Sherrill. "Chicago," he told her with a smile. "Hold the cab. I won't be long."

He climbed out and loped along the sidewalk to disappear into a large office building. He'd left his briefcase behind, on the seat beside her. She was tempted to look inside, but didn't. What could possibly be in there, anyway? She sank back, for the first time considering the potential of the situation. She was going out for the evening with a man. Anything might happen. She hadn't given much thought to her sexuality since the closing night of the show in Toronto when she'd battled down her response to Jamie. Now she was highly aware of being a female and looked down at her knee socks and loafers, thinking the man had a lot of courage to invite her out, dressed as she was.

Drew emerged from the building and she took advantage of his approach to study him. He had long limbs that swung with a kind of effortless, simian grace. His clothes were expensive: brown flannel trousers, cream-colored shirt, subtly printed silk tie, tweed jacket in beiges and browns, and a handsome double-breasted fawn trench coat. He slid back into the taxi, bringing with him the scent of cold air and a renewed essence of cologne. She smiled without knowing why, and he took hold of her hand.

* * *

He thought she was exceptionally appealing with her schoolgirl's clothes, her slim youthfulness, her quick wit and sharp brain. In the course of the evening he found he had a steadily growing desire to know what she looked like under the clothes. He watched and listened to her, entranced, while they waited for the food and she told him some of her experiences in the city. The throaty music of her voice washed over him pleasurably, so pleasurably he missed a good deal of what she said. He drank a vodka martini, watching her sip at a glass of red wine.

"You never did tell me where you come from," he said finally, as the waiter set their steaks down on the table.

"Didn't I?" She glanced up at him, then down at the plateful of food in front of her. She was no longer hungry for the filet mignon she'd ordered half an hour earlier. She didn't feel like eating at all. What interested her was the question of how and when he'd make his first move toward her. She had no doubt that he wanted to make love to her. The question she couldn't answer was whether she cared to have him make love to her. "I'm Canadian," she said, "from Toronto."

"You don't sound like one," he observed, picking up his knife and fork, trying to determine if she had any breasts. It was impossible to tell. "You don't say 'oot,' and 'aboot.' "

"I lived in England for two years when I attended the London Academy."

"No kidding! I lived in England for a year," he said happily, pleased by the coincidence. "What's the London Academy and what does it have to do with saying 'oot' and 'aboot'?"

"It's a music and drama school. You *really* don't know what it is?"

"Nope. Does that make me a dunce?"

"No, it makes you a civilian. It's a nice change. After a while, you get tired of talking shoptalk all the time. It gets boring. That's the trouble with performers, you know. They never talk about anything but shows and auditions and who's doing what, and where, and how they just missed out on getting this terrific part in a David Merrick show."

"All shoptalk's boring," he agreed, cutting into his sirloin. "Aren't you hungry?"

"I'm slow, but I'll get to it."

"Then I'll wait for you," he said, replacing his utensils on the table. "We'll have another drink, and you can tell me what you'd rather be doing."

"I didn't say I'd rather be doing something else."

"No. But I've got a sneaking suspicion you would."

She thought about that while he signaled the waiter and ordered a third round of drinks.

He felt very at ease and in control; he thought he knew how the evening would end and was pleased by this unexpected bonus. He'd planned a quiet Christmas, doing the rounds of parties and catching up on new movies. Now he'd have company: bright, pretty company.

"There's nothing else I'd rather be doing," she said after the drinks came.

"Really?" he pursued it.

"Well," she conceded, "I've been playing with the idea of maybe writing something."

"Aha! See! I knew it. What would you like to write?" he asked.

"Oh, I don't know. I can't bear sitting around doing nothing—which was what I was doing when I got the call today—so I was thinking about writing a book."

"What about?"

"It's just silly. Let's forget it. I'm not a writer."

"Okay. It's forgotten."

After her third glass of wine, she realized that the denouement of the evening had already been tacitly settled. The instant this realization struck her, she seized up. She'd have to take off her clothes, or have them taken off by this stranger. He probably had a wife somewhere; if he didn't, he undoubtedly had half a dozen women on a string. Was it possible he was what he appeared to be: a nice man who felt equally as displaced in this city as she, and who hadn't yet met a woman whose interests and life-style were compatible? It was possible. She wasn't particularly aroused by the prospect of being naked, of making love with him. Neither was she completely averse. More than anything else, she was curious. She turned to look at the other people in the restaurant, glad to be out in public with a handsome man who hadn't taken his eyes off her for more than a few seconds in several hours. It was something that had never happened to her before. She couldn't decide if his visual attention was part of a well-practiced technique with women, or if it was sincere.

"What's your last name?" she asked, abandoning her steak halfway through.

"Raymond: Andrew Arthur Raymond. What's yours?"

"Westcott."

"What're you grinning at?"

"Oh, nothing. Just something a friend said to me."

"About what?" he asked.

"About first names being last names."

"Oh! Dessert?"

"I don't think so, thank you."

"Coffee, then." He ordered, and when the waiter had cleared the table, Drew lit Sherrill's cigarette, saying as he did, "You smoke too much. What are your plans for the holidays? Going out of town?"

"I like smoking and I'm not going anywhere. Why?"

"What about Christmas Day? Surely you've been invited to dinner somewhere."

"I don't really know anyone in the city. My friend Michelle has gone home to have Christmas with her family. Aside from her, I only know a couple of women I've met at auditions."

"Okay, we'll have Christmas dinner together," he declared. "How's that?"

"Terrific!" she said readily, dizzy from the wine. "Who gets to cook?"

"Are you any good?"

"My mother's great. She's a vegetarian, makes phenomenal casseroles. At Christmas, though, she usually breaks down and does a turkey."

"What about you?"

"Me, cooking? I'm mediocre." She laughed. "You any good?"

"We'll both cook. That way there'll be equal blame for disasters and equal credit for successes. How about duck? Do you like duck?"

She shook her head. "I'd rather have chicken, a roasted chicken with stuffing."

"Perfect."

She nodded her heavy-feeling head, thinking things were

happening too quickly. But she hadn't any desire to object, or to slow things down. She wondered what his first move would be, and hoped he wouldn't be in a big hurry to push himself at her. She hadn't made love to anyone in three years, not since she'd had too much to drink on the opening night of the first show she'd done for Della and had allowed herself to be taken home to bed by an actor she hadn't seen since. It hadn't been especially pleasant, what she remembered of it, and her only inclination toward lovemaking had come nightly when she'd stood onstage in the dark with Jamie.

She thought of Jamie and felt disloyal, as if Jamie knew of her actions and would be hurt by them. She missed him; it was a sudden pain. She wondered if he'd receive her Christmas card and think about her. Drew tapped on the back of her hand to recapture her attention. She raised her eyes to his and smiled.

Chapter 16

As Jamie approached the house it looked very familiar to him, as if he'd been there dozens of times. Its well-maintained exterior and gleaming windows seemed to beckon him. He smiled in anticipation of a second viewing of that dramatic living room with its inviting rows of books. But he'd forgotten Anne—what she looked like, how appealing he found her—so when she opened the door, his senses were pleasurably heightened.

"You look lovely! That's a great outfit," he complimented her. With her hair pulled back from her face and a hint of makeup she looked exquisite. The smartly cut white flannels and white cashmere sweater flattered her creamy skin and silvery hair.

She thanked him and turned to lead the way upstairs. He followed, drawn by the curve of her hips and lift of her buttocks. She looked younger than he remembered.

"Have we got time for a drink?" she asked, pausing in the living-room doorway.

He pushed back his cuff to look at his watch, debating. "That depends," he said, returning his eyes to her. "If we want to try for the show at the Royal Alex, we don't have time. If you're not all that keen on the play, we can have a drink and see if there's a movie on you'd like to go to."

"Let's go to a movie," she said, with what he thought was engagingly girlish eagerness.

"Fine. Then I'll have a scotch, please, if you have it."

"There's a newspaper on the coffee table."

"Is there anything you especially want to see?" he asked. "You decide."

He felt very much at home as he unbuttoned his jacket and sat back on the sofa, turning to the entertainment section of the *Star*. One after another, brief scenes projected themselves across his mind: he and this lovely soft-looking woman out dining together; out dancing; out walking; up in her bedroom making love. He was tantalized by the idea of positioning her before him and then tenderly taking her out of her clothes, freeing her body for his hands.

She came to sit beside him, setting the drinks on the table. "See anything good?" she asked.

He breathed in her perfume, his senses more sharpened by the second. Putting down the newspaper and glancing perfunctorily at his hands to make sure they were clean of newsprint, he asked, "What are you in the mood to see? There's quite a lot on."

"I don't know. You choose."

"How about *Women in Love*?" he suggested. "It's on nearby."

"Fine." She held the glass of vodka to her mouth, her eyes on him. Suddenly she smiled. "It's really very nice to see you again."

"It's very nice to see *you* again," he said, and reached for his scotch.

She relaxed, turning slightly more toward him so that he was aware of her breasts and their movement under the luxurious sweater. "May I ask you something?"

"Of course," he answered.

"What would you like for your life, your career? I mean, would you like to go to Hollywood, or New York, and be a star, that sort of thing? Or are you happy with the status quo, performing around the city ... ?" She dwindled off, not sure what it was she wanted to ask him. Perhaps, she thought, she was trying to pin him down on his future movements. And that was absurd because he was no more likely to know than she. Yet perhaps, she thought on, what she was really asking was whether or not he would be willing to include her in his future. Like a schoolgirl, she wanted profound commitments to be made.

He laughed, as if amused by the question, and said, "I don't see myself as a star. Even if I did, this wouldn't be the city for it, or the country. Canada doesn't have stars."

"But it does," she disagreed.

"Not living in Canada. We've got expatriate celebrities everywhere, but not more than one or two who actually live and work here."

"I suppose that's true," she said.

"We've got television stars. But after their twenty-six weeks, or their thirty-nine, they're back to square one looking for jobs again. Anyway," he said seriously, "I haven't planned. I enjoy the work, and the writing. I don't know." The issue of his future, like the concern women displayed for his lack of an overcoat, was irksome and not really important.

"What did you do before you got into acting? Or were you always a performer?"

Pulling himself back from his musings, he smiled. "I've only been at it since coming to Canada, about eight years."

"And before? What did you do?"

"I was in medical research. Pathology, actually. Before that, I was one of the distinguished members of the Queen's finest."

"The British Army?"

"In Africa. I was there for three years, in North Africa and East Africa—Libya and Kenya—the Mau-Mau business."

"Really?" Her eyebrows lifted.

"I loved Africa. I'd like to go back there someday." It was impossible to explain to an outsider what it had been like, particularly in Kenya. Before going out there, he'd made the mistake of reading the writings of Jomo Kenyatta. His reading had rendered him far more sympathetic to the Africans than it had to the British Army. Once he'd recovered from

the initial strangeness and the quiet fear all newcomers
invariably had of going beyond the compound, especially in
the dark, he'd begun to love the place. With an inward
smile, he remembered the evening soon after their arrival
when he and Briggs had set off toward the village where
they'd been told they could get a drink. The unrelieved
blackness of the night, punctuated by the cries of animals,
had quickly rendered them both uncertain. Within half a
mile of the compound, they'd found themselves walking
back to back, cracking jokes nonstop, menaced by the sudden startling screech of birds and the imagined presence of
Mau-Mau lurking within inches of them in the enveloping
dark, set to pounce and kill. They hadn't gone more than a
mile—both of them declaring they wished they'd never
embarked on this ridiculous quest for a drink—when they
were suddenly pinned by a spotlight and a deep voice split
the night, booming, "SIMAMA!" Both men froze, convinced
they were about to be killed. When nothing happened, they
took several tentative steps. Again the huge voice shouted,
"SIMAMA!"

Simultaneously, he and Briggs had realized they must be
outside a police compound. Sure enough a corporal askari,
one of the Kenya police, had emerged from the darkness
into the spill of the spotlight to address the men in Swahili.
He and Briggs had looked at each other helplessly. Finally
Jamie had blurted out, "Brown Trout Inn," which was their
destination, and the askari had waved off into the blackness, indicating the pub was farther along in the direction
they'd been headed. The askari had said, "Okay." Both
Jamie and Briggs had stupidly chorused "Okay," and gone
stumbling ahead in the direction the askari had pointed out.
Later, after they'd gone for language training, they'd laughed
over their blundering that night. Both freely admitted that
they'd been terrified.

For a moment now, Jamie wondered whatever had become
of Briggs. Then his attention returned to Anne. He looked at
her, wanting to close his hand gently over her rounded,
cashmere-covered breast. She had a beautiful mouth, and he
thought it would be exciting to kiss her, to ease her down
and feel her breasts cushioning his chest while he tasted
and explored the slick interior of her mouth.

"What did you do in the Army?" she was asking.

"The Army. Oh, I was with the Veterinary Corps."

"Were you a veterinarian?"

He nodded, his eyes on her mouth.

"And you gave it up?" she persisted. Aware of his eyes, she moistened her lips, finding it hard to concentrate on the conversation, all the questions she wanted to ask him. She was curious and could feel herself moving toward him while remaining stationary. Unlike so many men she'd known, he had substance: not in his size, but in his presence, and in the way he looked at her. His eyes held her more completely than another man's arms might have. She found him utterly magnetic. She would have been quite content to sit for hours, locked solidly into his gaze. The way he looked at her made her feel attractive and desirable. There had been very few men she'd known who genuinely liked women and transmitted their liking visually.

He picked up his glass and took a long swallow, unable to stop staring at her. She looked adult, he thought; she seemed ripened and womanly. When compared, say, to Leslie, she looked *completed*, as if she'd arrived at her ultimate destination as a woman. Warm and experienced and welcoming. "I gave it up," he acknowledged finally, noting that the pauses between their words were growing lengthy. He could see she felt it too. He couldn't be misreading the slight parting of her lips, or the way her eyes followed him. Yet she seemed relaxed, ready for whatever might happen, and he liked that quality about her. Was it because she was older than other women he'd known? If it was, there was much to be said for her additional years of life and experience. She would be ardent, he decided, and marvelously pliant. He could see and almost feel the slim abundance of her body in his arms. "If we're going to go," he said, "we'd better go now. The film starts in half an hour."

She didn't say anything but continued to watch him over the rim of her glass. At last she sighed and said, "I'll get my jacket," and leaned over to set her drink down on the coffee table.

His hand, of its own volition, closed around her narrow wrist. He looked at his hand on her arm, momentarily mesmerized by his own act and her acquiescing reaction. Her bones seemed to realign themselves so that she appeared smaller and more fragile. She looked down at his hand around her wrist, then again wet her lips and tried to speak, but couldn't. Her free hand wafted through the air to curve against his cheek. He was so sweet, she thought, so very sweet. There was absolutely nothing about him to suggest any darkness in his character; he was an open and gentle man and it showed.

In a last lucid moment, he realized he was attracted to her seniority, her age. There was an unquestionable challenge here; he wanted to test her accessibility, to know if her advantage in age would be reflected in her appetites, her sexuality, her knowledge and intelligence.

She was briefly frightened. An interior voice warned her that she was embarking on an impossible path and therefore doomed to failure. She and this much younger man couldn't possibly have a future together. In ten years she'd be fifty-seven, while he'd be only forty-three. He would not care, in ten years' time, to be seen with someone so obviously much older. Yet it was flattering to think he could actually desire her. She found herself taking small, shallow breaths as he closed the gap between them. His hand tightening slightly around her wrist, he came forward to touch his lips to the side of her neck. His caress was so gentle, so respectful, that she knew there was no longer any question of making a decision; her body had decided when she'd opened the front door to him and the sight of him had caused her insides to lift expectantly. She gazed at him, willing him to kiss her mouth with that same respectful tenderness.

The flesh of her neck was scented and soft and he breathed in deeply as his lips grazed her skin; then he released her wrist to take his hand slowly over the swell of her breast. She neither withdrew nor objected but remained perfectly still, her eyes slightly widened.

"Are you sure you want to do this?" she asked, in a near whisper.

He stared at the pulse beating in her throat. How was it that she could seem both so young and so adult? Her question had a ring of mature authority to it that impressed him; yet the question itself seemed academic in view of the willingness in her eyes and on her mouth as she allowed his hand to continue its shaping motion on her breast.

"Do *you*?" he asked, watching her mouth.

She slid her hand over the back of his neck and brought

his mouth to hers. Her kiss, they both knew, was the answer. He loved the sweet expertise and appetite of her mouth. Eager for the reward of her bared flesh in his hands, he slipped both his hands under her sweater and reached behind to unhook her brassiere. When he drew his hands up her ribs and around over her breasts, she seemed to dissolve, her nipples shriveling at his touch.

Slowly breaking away, her hand still on the back of his neck, she said, in a deepened voice, "Let's not play this like teenagers in the back seat of a car. Shall we go upstairs?"

He took hold of her hand and stood up. She rose from the sofa, thinking she'd feel better without her clothes. The loose bulk of the brassiere under her sweater was disconcerting, smacking of adolescent fumblings; she felt faintly humiliated. Yet when she looked again at his face all she could think was how very sweet he was, and how unpremeditated all this seemed to be. He hadn't planned this, any more than she had. But she was falling; she could feel herself falling, and knew that he would be her last lover. There was a real and inescapable finality to all this. For however long it lasted, she would be happy. When it ended, as it was bound to do, she couldn't imagine how she would go on living. Terrifyingly, she could predict the end before they'd even begun and she had an appallingly deary view of the solitary, aimless life she'd have after Jamie left. For years she'd played at the game of taking what pleasure she could from a given situation and then being philosophical, but emotionally calm, when the game had to end. The rules no longer held; she'd already fallen in love with this man she knew she could keep only for a short while.

Why think of that now? she asked herself. It would merely spoil the present, and she wanted to enjoy him. She could barely restrain herself from stopping him as they headed toward the stairs and asking him to guarantee he'd never leave her. She knew in advance he'd be an imaginative yet considerate lover.

"Are you all right?" he asked, seeing her change of expression.

"Don't I seem all right?" she asked, further drawn to his sensitivity: he seemed to know how she felt.

"If you want to change your mind," he said, "I'll understand."

"I don't want to. Have you changed yours?"

He smiled and tugged on her hand, drawing her back to kiss her on the mouth. "I think you're very beautiful," he said truthfully.

She smiled tremulously at him. Then her smile became firmer, less uncertain and she kissed him deeply, fiercely so that they nearly toppled from the step upon which they both stood.

Feeling restless, Dene decided to go for a walk. On her way out she picked up the camera and looped the strap over her neck. She had no idea why, but she felt better with the weight of the camera on her neck. In passing she glanced at the door to Anne's apartment, wondering why she'd seen so little of Anne recently. She felt rather disappointed. Earlier she had heard the ring of the doorbell, and then two pairs of feet ascending the stairs. Maybe Charlie had come over for dinner, or perhaps Anne had found a new lover.

As she walked down the slippery sidewalk in the snow, she pictured Anne with a lover. It was a highly plausible picture; Anne was very sexual. In her own view, Dene had never been an overtly sexual woman, certainly not someone with an aura as powerful as Anne's. She'd loved making love to Jake, so much so that she couldn't imagine making love to anyone else.

For months after the accident, she'd gone on wanting Jake. Her craving had felt unseemly, and she'd willed it away. It had taken some time to go. Eventually she'd felt only an interior echo of desire, as if her body had a memory that recalled an activity it was no longer capable of performing.

The snow had started late that afternoon and was now beginning to accumulate thickly. She loved the light, the almost eerie reflections created by the flakes falling past the streetlights. There was little traffic; a few pedestrians were out on Yonge Street, looking elated and not at all bothered by having to trudge through the unplowed streets. The first snowfall of the season was always special, she thought, tracking the progress of an elderly woman as she arrived at the curb, waited for the lights to change, then proceeded rather quickly across the road. She almost made it to the far side of the street, but slipped and fell heavily to the ground. Dene, some thirty feet away, stopped, her heart pounding.

She was about to start forward to help when two young men rushed up to assist the old woman to her feet.

Quickly Dene lifted the camera and snapped open the case. She removed the lens cap and dropped it into her pocket as she looked through the lens. Opening the aperture full, she focused, then made several exposures. Reminding herself not to wind the film forward after the last shot in order to prevent an accidental tripping of the shutter release button, she replaced the lens cover, closed the case, and allowed the camera to hang once more at her side. Why had she done that? she wondered. Observers would surely find her picture-taking of the scene ghoulish. But she'd had to photograph what she'd witnessed. Once she had done it, the old woman and the two young men had become completely real to her; she was able to go nearer to where the young men were dusting the snow from the woman's coat while solicitiously asking if she'd hurt herself. As Dene came up to the trio, she suddenly realized she hadn't anything to say or to contribute, and she stopped, hearing the woman state she was all right. She thanked the two men profusely, and carefully picked her way on down the street.

Heading north on Yonge in the opposite direction to the one the old woman had taken, Dene told herself the pictures probably wouldn't come out. There hadn't been much light, even with the aperture fully open. But she'd had no control at all of her compulsion. It was as if a previously unknown segment of her brain had taken control of her. Oddly, she'd felt a profound gratification during the act, a satisfaction almost sexual.

She walked for two hours, all the way up to Lawrence and Yonge on the west side of the street, and back down again on the east side. She was tempted several more times to photograph snow scenes; her hands went to the camera, but she didn't give in. The composition wasn't quite right, or the subject matter wasn't perfect, or the blowing snow obscured the image.

She stopped in a coffee shop to have a cup of hot chocolate with ersatz whipped cream and an order of whole wheat toast with honey before heading back to the apartment. She thought of the place as "the apartment," not as home. Home had been in Rosedale and would never be anywhere else; home was no more, could never again exist.

She was, she thought, a displaced person, like one of the immigrants seen so often on the city streets after the war. She'd heard people speak of them as "D. P.'s" and had wondered why it sounded like such an insult. After Jake's death, she'd understood exactly how the immigrants had to have felt, all but possessionless and alone, alive in an alien land.

She was going up the steps when the front door opened and Anne emerged with a man. Startled, Dene stood to one side on the porch, studying Anne's beatific expression and the serene smile of the man with her.

"Dene!" Anne exclaimed happily. "How are you? Jamie, I'd like you to meet Dene, my tenant."

Jamie said hello and held out his hand. Dene studied him a moment before shaking hands with him. She managed to say, "Hello," then looked at the drifting snow on the porch floor, wishing they'd continue on their way so she could get inside to her apartment.

"We're just going out for something to eat," Anne said. "Isn't it beautiful?" She held her open hand palm upward to catch some snow. It was a graceful gesture that both Jamie and Dene noted and approved. "Would you like to come with us?" she asked Dene, then glanced at Jamie, as if to say, "You wouldn't mind, would you?" and he nodded, indicating he wouldn't.

"Oh no," Dene said, almost frantically. "Thank you, I've just been out. I mean, I stopped in a restaurant on my way back and had something. But thank you all the same."

"You're welcome to join us," Jamie said, sensing Anne's fondness for the younger woman, who seemed almost ethereal in her shyness contrasted to Anne, who was positively aglow.

"No, honestly." Dene thought Jamie looked familiar. She wondered where she'd seen him before. He was a lot younger than Anne.

"Well, if you're sure," Anne said, moving slightly closer to Jamie.

"Thanks anyway," Dene said, and slipped in through the door. Once inside, she turned to peer through the glass and watch them go off down the street hand in hand.

In the apartment she removed the camera and set it down on the sofa. Still in her overcoat, hat, and boots, she perched on the arm of the sofa. They were lovers, Anne and Jamie. They'd just been upstairs making love. The realization came in a surge of anguish she couldn't understand any more than she'd understood her need to photograph the fallen elderly woman and the two young men helping her to her feet. She had, she now saw, hoped for something from Anne, something that had to do with the warmth and interest she had displayed and Dene had been beginning to trust.

Feeling bereft, she continued to sit, staring sightlessly, thinking she'd simply traded locations: one prison with invisible barriers for another. At least Charlie had made music. Anne could only make love, which had an accompanying theme of sounds Dene didn't care to hear—certainly nothing as lyrically impressive as Puccini. Why did she care? she wondered. What did any of it matter? Unthinkingly, she reached for the camera and sat holding it in her lap with both hands, somewhat comforted by the bulk and feel of it.

Chapter 17

Drew pushed away his empty coffee cup and said, "Let's go back to my place." He spoke, Sherrill thought, as if the two of them were an established couple who'd been together for years, traveling regularly back and forth between their two apartments. Perhaps the wine had fogged her judgment, but it seemed that in just a few hours Drew had covered ground that should have taken weeks. He'd held her hand; he'd asked her preference, then ordered dinner for her; he'd talked about growing up in Illinois and his parents and three sisters; he'd put together plans for how they'd spend not only Christmas but New Year's Eve as well; and he'd elicited from Sherrill a complete rundown on her career as well as her family background. His decisiveness was compelling, and she thought, briefly, that it might be a relief to let someone else take control for a time and

allow himself simply to drift. She looked at him through
slightly narrowed eyes, trying to imagine what sort of lover
he might be. She had no idea. In her limited experience,
she'd discovered that how a man looked rarely had any
significant bearing on his feelings for women or how he
performed with them. Her first lover, a fellow student at
LAMDA, had been a slight, shy-seeming boy. But he'd been
gentle and surprisingly adept. She'd often wished she'd
cared more for Ian than she had, but too many things had
interfered—their individual ambition, his fierce dedication
to the theater, and her plainly stated intention to return to
Canada.

The actor she'd gone home with on the opening night of
Della's first show—she'd forgotten his name—had been handsome, beautifully built, and a technician. While she couldn't
remember all the details of that night, she did recall his
dutifully laboring over her for what had seemed a prescribed
amount of time before he'd moved ahead toward his own,
somehow self-indulgent, satisfaction.

Now Drew was suggesting they go to his place, and he
was as much of a mystery after all the hours of conversation
as he'd been when she'd entered the recording studio.

"Okay," she agreed.

They'd go back to his place and he'd make love to her. She
didn't mind. He was attractive and well dressed; nothing
about him repelled her. He had a decent sense of humor and
apparently enjoyed her, which was certainly good for the
morale. Yet as they left the restaurant and stood on the
sidewalk in the snow looking for a taxi, she felt somehow
naked, and afraid. Her instincts insisted she was prepared
to stake too much on the wrong man. She countered by
telling herself she was an idiot, that nothing had yet been
offered. But it had, and she knew her future, or at least
some portion of it, was already tied up in Drew Raymond.

She watched him scanning the streets for a taxi and felt
faintly contemptuous of him. What had struck her earlier as
his elegant grace now seemed like gangly awkwardness. He
was too tall, and not broad enough in the shoulders. His
features just missed handsomeness, and his teeth were really
quite crooked. His expression was a bit vacant as he returned
to her along the sidewalk, saying, "I guess we'll have to take
the subway."

At once, she stiffened and said, "Could we take a bus? I really don't like the subway." She'd tried the subway one morning on her way to an early audition. She had gone down to Fourteenth Street, to the Union Square station, where she'd waited for the train with quite a large crowd of people. She'd grumbled silently about the stupidity of setting auditions at nine-thirty in the morning when most actors could barely talk coherently, let alone deliver a good cold reading. She'd stood near the front of the crowd, wondering what perversity in her character urged her to keep on subjecting herself to the humiliations of the business.

A train had finally appeared at the far end of the tunnel and approached the platform. Then something strange happened. The people lining the platform had silently backed off. It wasn't until several minutes later that Sherrill realized the conductor had been frantically blowing the train's horn. She saw the man go past in his small compartment, and in the few seconds it took for him to enter and leave her line of vision she noticed that his face was creased with fear. Immediately she'd thought there was a bomb on board. This idea was compounded by the mass of people who erupted backwards out of the carriages as the train finally stopped and the doors opened. There was a tangible panic in the air as the passengers leaped from the cars, stepping to one side of the doors, while on the platform, everyone watched in continued silence. The crowd of people in front of Sherrill had parted and two young black men in brightly patterned Dashikis sauntered from the carriage. Someone shouted, *"They're the ones!"* and Sherrill had turned to see the two men vault the guard rails and go running off up the stairs to street level as a subway policeman reached for his walkie-talkie with one hand and used the other for balance as he, too, vaulted the rail and took off after the two blacks.

All around her, people asked, "What happened?" Sherrill turned to see a man of about forty stagger from the car. Well dressed in a suit and tie—an executive—he was covered with blood from forehead to waist. His once white shirt clung redly wet to his chest. His hand on his face, he stood on the platform looking dazed. For close to a minute he remained alone, gazing at the blood dripping from his hand. Then a number of people rushed forward to assist him, while the murmurs of "What happened?" proliferated.

The doors of the train had remained open and at last people slowly began to enter the cars. Shaken, Sherrill stepped into the car directly in front of her, the one from which both the young blacks and the beaten man had emerged. It was obvious that the incident had occurred here. There were telltale signs of a scuffle—a torn *New York Times* scattered in the aisle, blood spatters on the floor—and opposite Sherrill a young girl of eighteen or so sat quietly crying into her fist. Everyone ignored her; the passengers all seemed once more composed as the train pulled out of the station, heading uptown. Conversation started up; businessmen shook out their newspapers and folded them lengthwise and then in half before settling back to read their way uptown. It was exactly as if nothing had happened and the young girl wasn't openly crying.

Sherrill had stood up and, reaching for the strap to steady herself against the sway of the train, which seemed to be moving very fast—perhaps to make up for lost time?—bent to ask, "Are you all right?"

Looking grateful that anyone had bothered to ask, the girl nodded. "They stepped on my feet," she explained "It was awful."

"What happened?" Sherrill glanced down to see that the girl's feet did look as if they had been trodden upon.

"I don't know." The girl looked down the length of the car. "The guy, you know, he was just sitting there reading the paper. Then these two guys got on. The black ones, you know? They stood over by the doors for a couple of minutes. The next thing anybody knows they start beating up the other guy." She shook her head disbelievingly. "It was really nuts. You know? I mean, the guy was just sitting there and they dragged him up and started hitting him. Nobody did anything," she said softly. "That's what's so horrible. You know? Nobody did anything to stop it or to help him."

For several nights afterward the scene had replayed itself in Sherrill's dreams: the victim stood on the platform touching his hand to his bloodied and beaten face while Sherrill watched, immobilized with fear and sympathy. She hadn't used the subway since.

Drew reached for her hand, and, smiling, said, "You want the bus, we'll take the bus. No problem."

She liked him for going along with her wishes without

feeling any need to question her or to comment negatively. She was so grateful that her throat actually closed and she gazed mutely at his profile, wondering why she'd found him so unappealing only moments before. He *was* a nice man. She told herself she was lucky. Most men were put off by her, one way or another; they always had been. Drew wasn't, she reasoned, because he didn't really know her yet. Once he did, he'd find all kind of things about her to dislike. She looked dreadful without makeup; she hated having to talk to anyone first thing in the morning; plan-making mildly intimidated her, and she'd already allowed him to go ahead and plan for the next ten days. She was undoubtedly establishing dangerous precedents. Surely he'd expect her to go on letting him make plans, or expect her to be pleasant in the morning, or want her to make love all the time. What was she *doing*?

His apartment was located on the twelfth floor of a fairly new building in the East Seventies and furnished with modern furniture of clean, spare lines. The living room was long and rather narrow, its end wall offering a view of the river. There was a pullman kitchen enclosed by louvred doors adjacent to the front door and a bedroom that had been created out of the short end of the L-shaped living room by the installation of a wall of bookcases. A free-standing folding screen acted as the door between the bedroom and living room. She complimented him on his taste. "This is really nice," she said, pushing off her shoes before going to stand by the window. "It doesn't feel like New York at all."

"It doesn't, does it." His eyes remained on her as he hung up his trench coat, then slipped off his sodden shoes. "Let me take your coat. I'll hang it up for you."

"Oh, sure," she said, tearing herself away from the view. Mechanically, she undid the buttons and shrugged off the coat, turning to find him standing close to her, smiling.

"What's funny?" she asked, prepared to share the joke.

"I'm not laughing."

"Well, smiling."

"I was just thinking," he said, accepting her coat. "You're one of the nicest things, if not the nicest, that's happened to me in the three years I've been in the city."

"Why?"

From the closet by the front door he answered, "Not only

do you sing like a baritone angel, but you're bright and funny and pretty, and you've got a brain like a steel trap. People might think I was doing a little cradle-robbing," he said, returning to stand beside her at the window. "But that doesn't particularly bother me. During the day the view's not as good," he said thoughtfully. "All the dirt shows."

"How old are you?" she asked him.

"Forty-one."

"You don't look it."

"No? *I* sure as hell think I do."

"Well, maybe. I don't know. What's forty-one supposed to look like?"

"Like me, probably. You don't look almost twenty-six."

"I know. But inside, I do."

"I take it you're not involved with anyone."

She shook her head. "Are you?"

"Off and on. Off, right now."

"Have you been married?"

"Years ago. It didn't take. Would you like something to drink?"

"Do you have any tea?" She stood now with her back to the window to study the room. Her entire apartment wouldn't have filled the far end of the living room.

"As it happens," he said, dropping his hand onto her shoulder, "I do."

His touch surprised her—she hadn't been expecting it so soon—and she stood waiting to see if he'd do more. He didn't. His hand lingered a moment, then he went off to the kitchen to make the tea. She wandered around the carpeted room in her stocking feet, pausing to look over at the front door where their shoes sat in a heap on a plastic tray. She looked down at the deep burgundy-colored carpet and curled her toes into the velvety pile. The place made her feel impoverished. Either the teak furniture and tastefully underdone rooms were the work of an interior decorator, or Drew had fine taste in furnishings.

From the kitchen doorway she watched him pour boiling water over a teabag in a blue-and-white-striped mug. "Did you do the decorating?"

"It was a company apartment," he explained, "for visiting dignitaries, that kind of thing. They were going to get rid of it, so I offered to take over the lease. It was completely furnished, including pots, pans, and dishes. I didn't have to do a thing except move in and put fresh sheets on the bed. My lease has another year to run, then I'll probably renew. It's worth the rent, which isn't all that high. You should see the new company pad on Park Avenue. It makes this place look like a flophouse. What d'you take in your tea?"

"Have you got any lemon?"

"Lemon." He opened the refrigerator door to look. "I've got one of these squeeze things." He held up a plastic lemon.

"Never mind. Just sugar, please."

"Sugar I've got," he said. "How much?"

"One and a half."

"One and a half," he repeated, measuring sugar into the tea before giving it a good stir. "I," he announced, presenting her with the mug, "shall have a brandy."

She wondered if he was going to get drunk. He'd had three vodkas at dinner and a brandy after; now he was going to have another brandy. She mistrusted people who drank too much. Usually the anger and the grievances of a lifetime came spilling out when someone got drunk.

She sat on the sofa. If she took the chair, he was bound to interpret it at a sign that she wanted to keep her distance. She did want to, but was also interested to know what would happen, and actively fought her nervousness. There had to come a time when she could deal with men with some measure of composure.

He turned on the television set and came to sit beside her on the sofa, undoing the top button of his shirt, loosening his tie. "Okay if we watch the news?" he asked, his eyes on the screen.

"Sure." Nothing was going to happen. Nevertheless, she couldn't relax. She tucked her legs under, sipped at the tea, and watched the Channel 7 news: murders and bomb scares, car crashes and feuds between congressmen; city politics and Richard Nixon. She couldn't understand how the Americans could have such a man as their President. He seemed so hatefully smug and megalomaniacal. She thought Hubert Humphrey would have made a good President; in the 1968 campaign he'd seemed far more human and caring than Nixon had. There was something sinister about Nixon, something in his eyes that hinted of fanaticism, and of a desperate need for personal acclaim. But what did she know?

She'd thought Trudeau was a great guy, a terrific politician, until she'd heard a group of Montrealers verbally assassinate him one night at a party. She didn't know a thing; she was probably typical and voted like everyone else, for the guy with the best costumes, the best song-and-dance act.

Drew had slouched down into the sofa and was cradling the brandy snifter in the palms of his hands, gazing fixedly at the TV screen. She wished he'd do something so she could stop being nervous.

The weatherman appeared on camera and Drew turned to her. "Would you like me to take you home now?"

"All right," she replied, disappointed.

He tossed down the last of the brandy and stood up, wondering why he'd asked to take her home instead of leading her into the bedroom. Maybe because she didn't seem ready for anything like that. She looked so goddamned young. But that was only the clothes. Dressed in something else, she'd look more her age. Still, he reasoned, there was no rush. They'd have Christmas together. It was a refreshing change to be with a woman who didn't expect to be treated in a specific way: the drink somewhere before dinner, the dinner itself and the attendant small talk, the drink after and the conversation riddled with innuendos, the debate over whose place, and, finally, the move into her bedroom or his, where the action was invariably anticlimactic; there was never anything to talk about after. Lastly, there was the middle-of-the-night taxi ride to take the lady home or to return from her place. Inevitably, he wondered why he'd bothered. He'd be hung over in the morning; he'd have a headache and an upset stomach and he'd bitch at his secretary, who'd roll her eyes knowingly and keep him supplied with black coffee until midafternoon, when he'd start to recover.

He was sick of slick women who talked a big game and made a great show of independence but really wanted to find some guy and tie him down just as hard and fast as they could. The dialogue rarely differed from one date to the next. The predictability itself of these evenings had, in the last year or so, slowed him down so that he'd stopped going out so much. Nothing Sherrill had said or done since they'd met that afternoon had been typical or predictable, and he liked the novelty of being with a woman who broke the established patterns and rules.

In the taxi they were both quiet. He was annoyed with himself for so peremptorily putting an end to the evening. She was wondering what it was that had turned him off. When they pulled up outside her place and he asked, "Would you like me to see you up?" she was relieved to discover she hadn't turned him off after all and said, "All right." Then she laughed. "We could spend the night seeing each other home." He laughed too and, doing so, seemed familiar to her.

As they entered the brownstone and climbed the stairs to the second floor, she was overcome by a sense of something wrong. The house seemed too silent, too dark. She was embarrassed at the prospect of having Drew see her place after the sleek opulence of his apartment. There was a smell of cabbage in the hallway; the hallway itself seemed darker than usual. She listened, unable to hear a sound. Rae played her radio until two or three in the morning most nights. Perhaps she'd gone away for the holidays.

The door to the apartment was ajar. Sherrill put her hand out, then at once withdrew it as if contact with the wood might injure her in some nonspecific fashion.

"Wait a minute!" Drew shifted her to one side. "Did you lock up when you left?"

"Of course I did."

"You're sure?"

"I'm positive."

"Okay. You'd better let me go first, just in case they're still inside."

Who could be in there? she wondered, alarmed.

He pushed open the door and she crowded into the doorway beside him, the breath rushing out of her lungs at the sight of the devastation. Her books and papers were strewn about on the floor. Her clothes lay scattered everywhere. What had been a full quart of orange juice was now a small puddle at the bottom of the glass jug that rested on its side atop a white blouse irreparably strained. A narrow window sat propped against the arm of a sofa and she turned to look again at the door, realizing that it was the transom from above the door.

"That's how they got in," she said thinly, pointing with a wildly shaking hand at the transom.

"Jesus!" He took a step into the room. "I guess we'd better call the police. Can you tell what's missing?"

She couldn't make herself accept that what she was seeing was real. Trembling, she stood in the middle of the room and turned slowly, trying to determine what had been taken. The furniture had only arrived the week before and hadn't yet become familiar to her in its new surroundings. "The television set," she said. "And the radio. My sewing machine." Haltingly, she moved into the kitchen, then to the bathroom. Lastly, she climbed up to the sleeping loft, then descended the ladder to stand surveying the mess while Drew talked on the telephone to someone at the police station.

"They're sending a team over right away." He draped his arm protectively around her shoulders.

"They took my iron and my toaster.... I can't stay here!" she cried, feeling more and more threatened. "I can't! I'd be terrified. What am I going to *do*? I'd never be able to sleep here without thinking someone was trying to break in."

"Don't worry about it," he said reassuringly, hugging her to his side. "After we've seen the police, we'll pack up some of your things and you'll come back to my place."

Numbly, thinking only of being rescued from this nightmare, she said, "Okay, thank you. I could *never* stay here! It's . . . I can't believe it! They took my alarm clock, all my jewelry. But they missed this." She held out a small, square gold-colored box.

"What's that?"

"My pierced earrings. Maybe they thought it was a powder compact or something. The earrings are the most valuable things I own." She closed her hand hard around the box and held onto it. "They even took my luggage to carry everything off in." Her voice vibrated with pending tears and she coughed to clear her throat, determined not to cry in front of this man.

"D'you have insurance?"

"No."

"Too bad," he said. "Well, you're going to have a nice tax deduction."

She glared at him, for a moment wanting to kill him. All he could see in the situation was her material loss. He didn't seem to understand, to feel what she did: the violation. Someone had gone through all her personal things, had touched and abused everything that had previously been completely private. They'd even tipped a box of tampons out onto the bathroom floor. She felt soiled, invaded.

As if sensing he'd said the wrong thing, he removed his arm from around her shoulders and took hold of her free hand. "Listen," he said, "I was ripped off three times before I moved into the place I've got now. The first time they hit me, I went out and replaced everything. A week later they hit me again. At that point I thought, to hell with it, and didn't bother to replace anything. I rented a TV set and some other stuff. Three months later they ripped off the rental things. But the first time it happened, I felt like I'd been stripped naked and put up onstage at Radio City. It isn't funny, I know. I'm really sorry. If you hadn't come uptown to do the voice-over, it probably wouldn't have happened."

"They must have been watching and checking when I came in and went out," she whispered, horrified. "My God!"

"It's over now," he said placatingly.

She shook her head. "No, it isn't. It's just happening."

While she gave the two policemen all the information she could, along with an initial list of what was missing, Drew ran down to a deli on Third Avenue and came back with three big cartons.

"We'll take as much as we can now," he said, "and come back for the rest tomorrow. You're right: you can't live here."

She was shaking so badly she couldn't get her cigarette lit. Drew took it from her fingers and lit it for her. She gazed up at him in absolute gratitude. "I've got to live somewhere," she said hoarsely.

"You can stay with me until you find another place."

"But I paid two months' security here."

"Write it off, Sherrill. Forget it."

"I'd be breaking the lease . . ."

"No one's going to come after you."

"But all that money . . ."

"I'll lend you some, if you're short. You're trustworthy, aren't you?" he teased with a smile.

"Why?" she asked flatly.

"Why not?" he said. "If you get to the point where you can't help a friend, you're in big trouble. So why not?"

She couldn't answer that.

Arbitrarily, while standing under the shower in Drew's bathroom, trying to rid herself of the feeling that she'd been physically befouled, she thought about a poem by Edna St. Vincent Millay. The only line she could remember had to do with bittersweet upon a broken wall. It ran annoyingly through her mind like a fragment of music, and she wished it would go, or that she could recall the entire poem. She thought of another line about loving someone less than life, a little less, but wasn't sure it belonged to the same poem. What bothered her most about the fragmented lines of poetry was their connection with Jamie. She felt small and naïve, unequal to the sometime horrors of life; she also felt her presence in this man's apartment was the ultimate betrayal of her love for Jamie.

She pounded her fist against the tiled wall. This was the end, she swore. Jamie was of the past: he'd never been more than a peripheral part of her life and he was going to remain where he belonged. She would not think of him again. The decision didn't make her feel any better.

In the aftermath of her shock, she now found things terribly funny. The sight of Drew sitting on the side of his bed in a bright yellow terry-cloth robe struck her as hilarious, although actually he looked very good. The color was flattering to his tawny complexion. When she sat down beside him and he put his arms around her, she found that funny, too. When they'd finished making love and he fell quickly into a deep sleep, she pushed her face into the pillow and wept over the dismal tangling of arms and legs she'd surrendered herself to. There'd been no grace or lyricism to the encounter. It had contained pleasant moments. He'd been very considerate, and gentle to the point of irritation. She would have preferred something closer to an assault, something more definitive that might have blocked out the subtler yet substantially more real assault that had taken place earlier on her home and possessions. She reminded herself that she owed Drew a lot: not only had he employed her on the commercial, he'd literally rescued her from her ravaged apartment.

Raising her face from the pillow, she stared into the darkness. Next time they made love it was bound to be better. He had cared about her responses, her pleasure. It was just that it took her such a long time to get started, and at the point when she'd begun to enjoy his caresses, Drew had been ready to finish. That didn't matter; they' work things out.

She lay thinking until close to dawn when, at last ready to sleep, she rolled onto her side and fitted herself against Drew's back. He was wonderfully warm. She closed her eyes and breathed deeply.

In the morning, Drew awakened full of cheer and energy, eager to make love. She didn't want to, but couldn't think of any legitimate way to refuse him. To her surprise, it was more pleasurable this time and confirmed her reasoning of the night before that it would improve.

Over breakfast while he outlined his plans for their day, she smiled and listened and drank several cups of coffee, absorbing his words without really hearing them. Once they got used to each other, he'd understand that she was hopeless in the morning and leave her to come to at her own slow pace. She smiled at him over her coffee cup, thinking what a nice man he was. Already she was terribly fond of him.

Six weeks later, at Drew's insistence, they got married.

Part 3
Preoccupations
1971–1979

Chapter 18

Jamie didn't know when the novelty of life with Anne wore off; he was just aware one day that he no longer found her challenging or desirable. His initial interest waned slowly and steadily until he was merely fond of her, as he might have been of a handsome, doting aunt. He still enjoyed her company, her witty and intelligent views, but he'd become restless and a little bored by the predictability of the situation. He felt, too, that he'd been entirely fair in terms of his contributions to the household, and to her. The time was rapidly approaching when he'd have to move on.

It wasn't, however, until he met Lucienne that he realized his time with Anne had run out altogether. Lucienne was young and lush, sharp, exceptionally talented. He was tremendously attracted to her Gallic good looks, her husky, accented voice, her laughter. She was working as an assistant director on a film he'd been hired to do on location outside Montreal. They found themselves taking breaks together and spending evenings when they could, and, finally, nights together.

When it came time for him to return to Toronto, he began to prepare for the confrontation with Anne. He anticipated a tearful scene, although he'd never witnessed Anne in tears; he expected recriminations of one sort or another. All the way back to Toronto on the plane he worked up his arguments for the defense, trying to marshal the words and thoughts he hoped to use to explain his reasons for putting an end to their time together.

They had had three good years. To his way of thinking, time well spent with anyone was a bonus rather than something one ought to expect as one's due. He only wished he knew how to convey this to Anne, who he doubted shared his philosophy. Living with Anne had enabled him to relax in a way he'd never before done. Being with her had been

171

effortless pleasure. She had made no demands, seemed to have no unrealistic expectations.

"As long as you're happy to be here," she'd told him many times, "I'm happy having you here."

He'd taken her at her word and had settled into a lifestyle he doubted could ever again be duplicated. She was warm, interested, witty, and highly demonstrative. She inspired him to speak his thoughts, to express his affections, to surge ahead in his career. With Anne as a cushion for his disappointments, he'd taken bolder steps than he'd risked previously, with the result that his successes multiplied. He'd easily met his monthly financial obligations to Jane and the boys; he'd bought a small car and refurbished his wardrobe. He'd also lavished gifts on Anne, deriving tremendous satisfaction from watching her delighted reactions. For the first time, he actually had some savings. He was being called for more work than he could handle. When he arrived back in the city now, he was due to depart again almost immediately for a ten-week national tour in a revival of the old original revue, minus a few numbers, with Ron and Matthew Salesman. Matt was good, not as accomplished as Sherrill had been, but a solid performer with a fine background. Jamie thought he could legitimately use the tour as an excuse, along with the other statements of fact he was regimenting much in the way he set out a row of lead miniature soldiers prior to painting them with scrupulous exactness and the proper colors.

We've gone as far as we can together.

We've run out of things to say to each other.

You deserve someone who'd be able to spend more time with you.

I love you but not enough to stay. . . .

Diligently, he rehearsed his lines, rejecting some, considering others. He felt guilty. By the time he'd collected his bags from the carrousel at Terminal Two in Toronto and settled in the back of an airport limousine for the ride into the city, he'd worked himself up to a state of full-scale anxiety. He'd have preferred the relationship to come to a natural end. The time no longer existed for that to happen. He couldn't continue on with Anne in view of his feelings for Lucienne. He was in love for the first time. He'd loved Jane, to a degree; he loved Anne, as well. But it simply didn't compare to the tremendous gusting emotions Lucienne aroused in him.

On the practical side, the logistics of this decision were worrying. Leaving Anne meant going out to hunt for an apartment, or moving to Montreal, as Lucienne had suggested. He was quite taken with the idea of Montreal—he liked the flavor of the city, the French enthusiasm for films and theater, not to mention the countless excellent restaurants and the relaxed, Continental attitude to life. He was concerned, though, about what might happen should he one day decide to return from Montreal. The way the business was in Toronto, if you were out of town for two weeks, everyone forgot about you; you had to get your eight-by-tens and résumés together and go downtown making the rounds, knocking on producers', directors', and casting agents' doors obsequiously asking to be remembered for the next show being done: an exercise in humiliation. It was the one aspect of the business that thoroughly demoralized and disenchanted him. Yet it had to be done. The alternative was to get out of the business altogether. What the hell would he do then? Whatever qualifications he'd once possessed were no longer valid, or even useful, after eleven years as an actor and writer. His only credibility lay in those skills. To leave town and relocate in Montreal was exceedingly risky. But there was Lucienne. He wanted to go to Montreal, to be with her. No one else had ever so closely approximated his ideals as she did: she was independent, clever, very exciting in bed; she was a great off-the-cuff cook, able to throw this and that into a cast-iron pot to come up with a magnificently seasoned, superb meal; she was young, only twenty-four, and, he believed, destined for a remarkable future. She'd already been offered several film roles even though she claimed to prefer working on the technical side of film-making. When they'd parted at Dorval airport a few hours earlier, she'd admitted she was considering accepting one of the roles offered.

"You'll come back, eh?" she'd asked with a smile.

"I'll ring you first chance I get," he'd replied evasively. She didn't know about Anne, although it was likely she'd guessed there was someone when she'd asked for his address and he'd given her that of the agency.

"All my mail goes there," he'd explained. "Matt forwards

calls, and holds everything for me. It gives him something to do," he'd joked feebly, hoping to elicit another smile. She had a wonderful crooked grin and a winsome way of tilting her head slightly to one side to regard him quizzically. He thought she could easily be a film star. She had a sort of smoky opacity that would come across well on film. She was also a cultured woman, with a degree in fine arts, and played piano beautifully. She was the first educated French-Canadian woman he'd met who was equally at home both in French and English company. He'd avoided giving her a direct answer, but they both knew he'd go back—if not right away, eventually. His immediate concern was Anne. Was he crazy to be thinking of leaving her? She, too, was a cultured woman. Her degree was not in fine arts but in political science. She was an elegant cook, and exceptionally well read. She was fifty years old. That was irrelevant, he told himself. But it wasn't. She didn't look fifty—certainly not her body—nor did she act it. The hinge in all of this was his feelings: he simply didn't love her enough to want to spend the rest of his life with her.

By the time the limousine pulled up in front of the house, he'd got himself strung taut as a piano wire. He'd have to find the right moment to make his announcement; it wouldn't do to blurt it out. He wished desperately he could somehow bypass the unpleasantness there was bound to be: close his eyes, open them, and find himself released, free of the relationship.

He paid the driver, picked up his two suitcases, and carried them to the front porch, where he had to put them down again in order to search for his house keys. What had he done with them? Probably autosuggestion had been at work on him and he'd intentionally managed to misplace the keys: a bit of symbolism he could well have done without. He rang the bell and waited, hoping Anne would be home. She wasn't. In somewhat of a quandary, he searched his pockets a second time, with no results, and finally rang Dene's bell, anxious to get in off the porch, where he felt embarrassingly exposed, as if his duplicity were a luminous coating to his skin clearly visible to all passersby.

Through the glass of the front door he saw the door to Dene's apartment open a crack, and Dene peered around the corner. He smiled and waved. She emerged into the hallway. As always, she had a camera slung about her neck. She looked even thinner and more wraithlike than she had three years earlier when he'd first seen her standing on this porch in the snow looking utterly discomfited while Anne introduced them. He was very fond of Dene. There was something otherworldly about her, and about her photographs. Most of the walls of the apartment were obscured by overlapping prints and blowups. She was an outstanding photographer, and he wondered, not for the first time, why she never bothered to do anything more with her work than simply add it to the daily growing montage that spread, like history, over her walls.

"I've lost my keys," he told her with a smile, leaning in to kiss her cheek.

"I think Anne's gone to the hairdresser," she said, nervously fingering the Pentax. "She didn't know what time you'd be getting in. Did you have a good trip? How was the filming?"

"Oh, good, good," he said dismissingly, bringing his suitcases into the hall. It was never easy for him to talk about his work—to anyone. He didn't know why. It might be tempting the wrath of the Fates, like whistling in a dressing room, or wishing someone good luck on opening night. "How have you been?" he asked interestedly. "Got a lot of new photographs?"

"Some. I've started on faces. You wouldn't consider letting me do you, would you? I mean, someday when you've got time." She made this request in a self-effacing fashion, as if asking him to indulge her obvious ineptitude. Could she actually believe she lacked talent as a photographer? It seemed incredible to him that she might.

"Sure. If you'll let me have a few to use. I wouldn't mind having some new eight-by-tens. I'm still using the old ones and they're a bit past it." .

Her features clouding, she said doubtfully, "I don't know. I've never let anybody have any of them. But maybe. I guess it couldn't do any harm, could it?"

"I don't see how." He was puzzled by her apparent fetish about allowing people to see her work. He conjectured, accurately, that he and Anne and Charlie were probably the only people who'd ever been privileged to see it.

Almost a year earlier, Dene had invited Jamie and Anne

down to dinner one night. They'd gone downstairs to discover that Dene had sold the sofa and chairs and replaced
them with four square white armchairs. Her explanation
had been that the other furniture had "conflicted with the
photographs." Now nothing in the apartment conflicted with
the photographs: the photographs *were* the apartment. She'd
transformed the place into an astonishing gallery of street
scenes, still lifes, studies, all of which imparted to the
viewer a sense of tragedy and loss, despite the superficially
happy content. Life in its starkest form was pinpointed on
the living and dining room walls. That same evening, after
they'd returned upstairs, Jamie had confessed to Anne that
he was curious to know what sort of things Dene had on the
walls of her bedroom. Anne had looked at him sharply, to
detect any sexual innuendo contained in the remark. Satisfied there hadn't been any, her expression had softened and
she'd commented, "If they're as tortured and beautiful as
the others, I don't think I could stand it. It's as if she's
re-created the world as she sees it, in microcosm."

He and Anne had all along been aware of Dene's increasingly antisocial behavior. Initially, she'd seemed shy and
frail; now she seemed withdrawn and ethereal. The only
people she appeared willing to talk to were Anne and Charlie. She was friendly toward Jamie but he knew she mistrusted him. He was sorry she didn't feel secure enough to
include him among her friends. He genuinely liked her; he
was impressed by her work and the strong intelligence it
conveyed. She was a woman of intellect for whom something had gone drastically wrong. He and Anne agreed that
there had to be quite a story behind Dene. In the three years
she'd lived in the house, however, she'd yet to volunteer
any but the most commonplace details of her former life.
She had a mother who came infrequently for lunch or a cup
of tea, and to whom Dene regularly spoke on the telephone.
Aside from her and an elderly couple who'd come one afternoon and never again returned, Dene seemed to see no one.
Whenever Jamie encountered her, she was on her way out—
with the camera around her neck and her pockets bulging
with spare containers of film, a telephoto lens in her
handbag—to walk the streets taking pictures.

Once, coming out of CBC on Jarvis Street, Jamie had
spotted her at the corner of Carlton, photographing a group

of old rubby-dubs through her telephoto lens. The resulting print, which appeared on the dining room wall some weeks later, was an arresting study of four aging drunks passing around a bottle in a brown paper bag, grinning wildly as if at some joke. It was a sordid yet sympathetic rendering so sharply defined that the very texture of the paper upon which it was printed was itself an integral part of the image. Dene had a uniquely personal statement to make. Her work brought to Jamie's mind the 1930s and early 40s studies by Walker Evans and Ben Shahn and those other photographers who'd captured the human condition at its low ebb during the Depression. Dene evidently was living through a depression of her own and perhaps, like the world, would emerge from it into emotional prosperity. He hoped so. It was a great pity for her not to share her overwhelming talent with others.

"Would you like me to help you with your bags?" she offered.

"That's all right, love. I can handle them. See you later." He started off up the stairs, then stopped midway, realizing he couldn't get into the apartment. He was behaving like an idiot, he thought. "You can't get in," Dene said from her doorway. "Why don't you wait here until Anne gets back? Would you like some coffee?" She looked somewhat uneasy.

"I'd love a cup." He carried the suitcases back down the stairs to park them to one side of the front door. "It's very good of you."

"Come in," she said, moving into the living room. "I'll put on the pot."

He entered, his eyes going at once to the far wall where he saw quite a number of new shots. "You've got new pictures up," he called out to her in the kitchen. "They're fantastic, Dene!" She made some reply he failed to hear, and he moved closer to the wall, gazing at a huge blowup of a child sitting in the dirt outside what looked to be a typical corner store, say, in Cabbagetown—a once impoverished east end area where people were now buying and restoring the Victorian houses with an eye to future real estate inflation. With grimy hands and bare, filthy feet, a dirt-streaked face and eyes as luminous as a cat's, the child of five or six was playing with two lidless tin cans and a stick. The resignation on her face was of someone old, beyond hope.

Jamie turned from the photograph. It was too upsetting. He felt restless. He'd hoped to see Anne at once; seeing her, he'd have been able to gauge her mood and his own feelings. He wished life were less complicated. He wanted to keep Anne as a friend; he did care deeply for her. Why wasn't it possible to move from one place to the next without someone's being hurt? He despaired at the idea of causing Anne any unhappiness. She didn't deserve that. But the time had come for them to separate.

He sat down in one of the armchairs, recalling his stay in New Brunswick the previous year. He'd accepted a job with Theatre New Brunswick, to play Jaques in *As You Like It*. It was one of his favorite roles, and the three weeks of rehearsal had gone well. A number of old friends had been in the company, notably Herbie Chapman, a fellow Englishman from Sussex. Jamie had known Herbie for a good seven or eight years and had liked the small, wiry man from the start.

They'd sat in the hotel bar in the evenings, swapping war stories and show-biz gossip. Sometimes a group went to the all-night chicken joint for barbecued sandwiches. Everyone always ate too much on out-of-town jobs; aside from rehearsing, there was little to do in the evenings once you'd run through the two or three movies playing in town. Then Anne had arrived, as arranged, to spend a week.

Without saying so, it had been plain that she'd disliked not only the hotel but Jamie's sixth-floor room in the old upper reaches of the Lord Beaverbrook Hotel. It was located directly across the street from the theater and most of the cast stayed there. She'd been disappointed by the hotel food, again without expressing it, and Fredericton itself. Even the river view at the rear of the hotel failed to impress her. With the exception of Herbie, all the kids in the company had been many years younger than Anne and had treated her with excruciating politeness, the way all "civilians" were handled: with distance, good manners, and a modicum of polite interest. Jamie knew the kids in the company had made an effort, were prepared to like Anne. But she hadn't fit in. She was older, and innately elegant, and very out of place. Jamie couldn't help but see how out of place and uncomfortable Anne felt. He didn't want to suggest she might feel happier returning home for fear she might misinterpret his motives. But she'd sensed the change in the atmosphere and had the grace to cut short her visit voluntarily. She'd stayed for the opening night and afterward remained unobtrusively in the background while Jamie and the cast proceeded to get happily blasted to celebrate the night's success.

When they'd finally returned to the room Jamie had tried to cheer her up—she'd looked so distracted that he felt guilty. He'd made love to her, savoring the softness of her body, for a long time, until she'd been herself again, laughing and responsive. She left for Toronto on the afternoon flight the following day. Once she'd gone, Jamie had been able to relax again. Yet the very fact that he could relax in her absence bothered him. It wasn't quite right. Nothing was.

Herbie, who had ten years' seniority and the wisdom of the ages, had quietly commented, "You seem on edge, Jamie. I take it things got a bit sticky."

"A bit," Jamie had admitted, reluctant ever to discuss his private life with anyone, even as old a friend as Herbie.

"Perhaps it's winding down," Herbie had observed before deftly rerouting the conversation with an anecdote concerning a bout of malaria he'd had during the war when he'd been stationed in the Far East.

Herbie's observation had triggered Jamie's thinking on the differences between himself and Anne. This consideration had been building steadily, into a veritable fund of guilty resentment, until he'd met Lucienne. Being with her had illustrated all too clearly that he and Anne had gone past the point where they should have remained together. They'd evolved into a habit, and that smacked too strongly of his marriage to Jane.

He believed Anne should have kept on with her career. She'd said she preferred to be at home when he was there, since he was so often hired for out-of-town jobs. It was a bad move. Had she kept working, it would have allowed them to maintain a little distance, which, in turn, might have kept them closer. Maybe. He wasn't sure of anything. What he most wanted was to put things into their proper perspective so that they could part, if it did come to that, and still remain friends. It was possible that Lucienne had been nothing more than a delightful diversion. Yet when he exam-

ined his reaction to this idea the response that swept through
him at once negated that possibility. He was in love with
her; he wanted to spend every possible moment with her.
His head was starting to ache.

He paced the near-empty living room, aligning, then
realigning his thoughts, the things he wanted to say to
Anne: his work was taking him farther and farther afield; it
wasn't fair to her to expect that she'd stay home and wait
for him to return from ever-longer trips away. Now was a
perfect example. In a week's time he'd be going off for ten
weeks. It simply wasn't realistic that she should remain
home alone, killing time until he came back. When he was
home they didn't have very much to say to one another. He
felt guilty—right down the line. He felt bad that she'd given
up her work for him; he hadn't asked her to do that. He
hadn't asked her to do anything. All her decisions had been
entirely her own. Yet they'd affected him.

He thought of Mark and Stephen. Initially, after he'd left,
he'd tried to see them regularly. By the third month the
boys seemed to become uninterested in their outings, and
the exchange of visits became more and more irregular until
they'd ceased altogether. He telephoned less and less often
with time, reasoning that he hadn't anything to contribute.
If he couldn't be there to help actively, on a day-to-day
basis, as a part-time, too often absent father he was of no
use to them. It was the only reasoning he could apply to a
situation that grieved him more deeply than anything ever
had.

. It had been almost two years since he'd seen the boys.
There was rarely a day when he didn't think about them,
missing them. But they were better off with Jane. She had
her legal separation and would undoubtedly go after a divorce
someday. He paid her a sum of money every month; the
idea of being unable to pay that money haunted him and
drove him to accept jobs he wouldn't have ordinarily. As
long as he could provide the four hundred and fifty dollars
a month he was honoring some part of his obligation to his
sons.

Dene returned carrying two mugs of coffee. He was fascinated by her angular beauty. Her carroty hair hung almost
to her waist, a glossy slide of silk. Her pale, freckled skin
was so clear it seemed poreless. Her long, bare arms looked

surprisingly strong, as did her feet in their heavy clogs. She was, he knew, thirty-seven, but had the appearance of a much younger woman—except for her eyes and the slight inward curve of her body. The curve spoke of pain, and a soul that had bent itself protectively inward around it.

"You take it black, don't you?" She held the mug out to him.

"That's right, I do. Thank you."

She sat on the edge of one of the white Parsons's chairs, holding her mug with both hands. "I'll photograph you whenever you like." She looked up at him from beneath slightly lowered lids. "Let me know when you've got some free time. Okay?"

"I will." He raised his mug and took a swallow. "Good coffee," he said, and smiled at her. He wondered about the pictures she'd take of him. Would she depict him as tragically, as sadly, as the other subjects she chose? He was about to express his curiosity when there was the sound of the front door opening. At once he tensed. Anne was back.

"That's Anne," Dene said softly, unnecessarily, and got up to go to the door. She turned, her eyes held Jamie's for a moment, then she opened her apartment door. "Jamie's here," she told Anne. "He's lost his keys. We were just having coffee while he waited for you. I'll get you some."

Leaving the door ajar, Dene went back to the kitchen for another cup. For several seconds Anne remained outside in the hallway, beyond Jamie's line of vision. Then she stepped into the doorway, and during the second or two she stood there it was as if he'd never seen her before. She was a startlingly beautiful woman, but faded. The hairdresser had done her hair unbecomingly, in stiff-looking curls and waves. He wanted to fetch a brush and have a go at her hair, smoothing and softening it. The welcoming smile on her face dimmed slightly as Jamie stood up, obediently coming over to take her hand and give her a light kiss on the lips. Strangely, his lips brushing hers, he felt desire for her dart through him. But he'd been unfaithful to her and it nagged at him.

"How was it?" she asked, allowing him to lead her into the room. "Did the job go well?" Something had changed. He wasn't the same as he'd been when he left.

"Oh, fine," he said airily, retrieving his coffee. "We

wrapped on time. Everything went well. And you? What've you been up to?"

"This and that. Nothing's new. Montreal obviously agreed with you. You look very well. Have you gained a little weight?"

He'd been gaining steadily for the past three years. Why did she choose to comment on it now? he wondered. Perhaps just as he'd noticed the changes in her, she was seeing those in him. They were, he thought, like polite strangers, sizing each other up as potential opponents. They had everything, and nothing, to say to one another. He suddenly, shatteringly, realized that he hadn't bought her a present. He'd never before returned home without some gift for her, a piece of pretty jewelry, or an article of clothing. This time he had nothing. He'd completely forgotten. It wasn't right. He wished he'd run over to Yonge Street and bought her something instead of idling away the minutes staring at Dene's photographs.

They sat down and silently waited for Dene to return with Anne's coffee. The conversation consisted of their approving comments of Dene's newest work, and the glorious September weather. Jamie dreaded going upstairs. He felt disloyal, guilty, miserable. He studied Anne's legs, then looked again at her dreadful, stiff hairdo. Lucienne had long, straight blond hair, slippery to the touch. He wanted to yell at Anne, to shout accusations at her. Ridiculous. He was the guilty party; he knew it and hated it. He wished he had some idea of how to handle the situation.

Chapter 19

For the first three months, Sherrill enjoyed being married. She and Drew entertained his friends, and were entertained by them. They went to the theater, to movies, to Central Park on Sunday afternoons for long walks. They managed to fill their off-time with an almost ceaseless round of activities. Through Drew, she managed to get more and more voice-over and commercial work until she'd established a good reputation and was making a substantial income. Occasionally she did on-camera work, the odd commercial, two or three lines in a TV show or film, but mainly her career hinged on her many voices and accents. She no longer felt the need to wear her old jumpers and knee socks; she believed she'd outgrown them and gradually built up a wardrobe of designer dresses and plain but well-tailored pant suits. John continued to represent her, but this was a formality; the majority of her work came direct.

Drew evolved, for her, into what she could only think of as a habit. He was there; they made love now and then when she'd had a glass or two of wine and felt sufficiently relaxed to enjoy it; but it wouldn't have upset her if he hadn't been there. She liked married life best when Drew had to go away on business trips, leaving her home alone. At those times she felt protected by her married status, yet marvelously free and independent. She was always a little disappointed when he returned home, and felt remorseful as a result. They'd be affectionate toward one another for the first few days after his return—then they'd settle back into companionable silence.

It was during one of his longer absences that Sherrill sat down to play with her "success without glamour" idea. It amused her. She wrote about how to attend auditions, what attitude to maintain to get the job; she described how it felt to hear oneself on the radio or TV chirpily endorsing this product or that; an entire chapter was devoted to "being different" and what sort of clothes and makeup would accomplish this.

She so relished putting her ideas on paper that the activity very quickly overcame her. By the time Drew returned from his three-week business trip, she'd written over a hundred pages and was anxious to do more.

"What're you doing, Sher?" he asked in passing several nights after his return.

"Just fooling around," she answered.

He smiled. "Could you maybe fool around with it after dinner? I'm starving."

Mildly angry, she put her work away and went to the kitchen to slam two steaks on the broiler and throw a salad together. She wasn't even hungry. After dinner, when she'd cleared the table and loaded the dishwasher, she immediately went back to work.

"More fooling around?" he asked, playing with the remote-control box for the television set.

"That's right," she said, looking over at him. "You don't object, do you?"

"Hell, no. Why should I object? What're you writing, anyway?"

"Nothing important." She turned her attention back to the chapter she was doing on how to win over commercial people by always going for a novel approach to the script. She suggested, instead of simply reading the lines, trying singing them, or doing them in a foreign accent. It struck her as very funny and she laughed aloud, then looked across the room to see if Drew had heard. He hadn't. She went back to work.

In between jobs, in the evenings, on weekends, she sat at the dining table with the manuscript. She'd never had more fun in her life and felt a real sense of loss when she arrived at the end of all she'd wanted to say.

"I finished it," she announced one evening near the end of their first year together. "Two hundred and seventy-eight pages."

"What're you going to do with it?" he asked, his eyes on Walter Cronkite.

"I don't know. Have it typed up, I guess."

"What for?"

"I thought I'd try to sell it, get it published."

He didn't respond for a moment. Then he said, "Could I read it?"

"Sure, if you want to. Do you know anybody at the office who'd be willing to type it up?"

"Probably. Let's have a look."

Somewhat reluctantly she gave him the sizable stack of handwritten pages and sat down to watch him read. Every time he smiled or laughed, she stopped him to ask what he'd found funny.

"It's good stuff," he said. "Leave me alone so I can read." He patted her on the knee like an indulgent uncle and went back to the manuscript.

Unable to bear the suspense, she got up, put on her coat, and went out for a walk. She walked across town to Madison, then continued uptown looking in the windows of galleries and antiques stores, trying to get her mind off the book. What if he didn't like it? That wouldn't matter, she told herself. She believed it was good. Drew didn't read much at the best of times, and when he did buy a book it was usually a full-color collection of photographs about underwater explorations or tropical islands. Occasionally he read something on the best-seller list—a thriller involving some clever con man who bilked a group of thoroughly nasty people out of a million in diamonds, or something that told how to make a fortune investing in real estate. His interests and hers failed to coincide. She adored novels and spent upwards of a hundred dollars a month at Brentano's and Doubleday's and Classic. She'd managed to fill four of the shelves of the bookcase dividing the living room from the bedroom, and Drew had started to complain about the lack of shelf space.

She walked, trying to imagine if publishers would be interested in a book like hers. Why wouldn't they be? Some of the stuff that got published was absolute garbage, yet it managed to sell thousands, maybe millions of copies. Whether Drew liked it or not, she decided she'd have the manuscript typed up and try to sell it. She had nothing to lose.

At the corner of Eighty-fifth she crossed Madison and began walking downtown on the opposite side, glancing into shop windows without actually seeing anything. She wanted to sell *Success Without Glamour*. It had become an obsession. By the time she arrived back at the apartment she was determined to publish the book; she was also geared up to defend it against any possible attack Drew might make. She was so geared up, his praise came as a shock.

"It's really good, Sher." He grabbed her and swung her around. "You've got real talent."

"You think so?"

"Listen, I'll ask around the office tomorrow and see if one of the girls in interested in typing it up for you."

"You really like it?"

"It's a funny little book. I don't see why you shouldn't be able to sell it."

"I can't believe it! You *like* it." Still in her coat, she sat on the sofa, stunned. "How do you publish a book?" she asked.

"Beats me," he said, checking the time. "The news is on." He reached for the remote control and ran through the channels, settling for the Eyewitness News Team on Channel 7.

Slowly, she got up to hang away her coat. She'd get a literary agent, she decided, and went for the Yellow Pages. She'd send the book to every agent listed until one of them thought it was good enough to submit to publishers.

She was so excited she couldn't get to sleep. She lay in the dark beside Drew thinking how it would be to see her book in print, to have it in the stores. Don't get carried away, she warned herself. Take it one step at a time and see what happens. And don't go turning down any jobs until it happens.

For three months the manuscript traveled from one agency to the next, until Drew got the name of an agent who was an old schoolmate of a friend of a friend at work. Sherrill called up, spoke to the man, explained the situation, and was told to drop the manuscript in at the office as soon as she could.

On a hunch that something good was about to happen, she hopped into a cab and delivered the manuscript within the hour.

"You're in luck," Hank Converse told her. "I'm between secretaries right now, so I've been answering my own phone. I have a reputation," he confessed with an engaging, dimpled grin, "for being hard to get on the telephone."

"The timing must be right." She laughed.

"Is this any good?" he asked, tapping the top of the manuscript.

"I don't know," she replied truthfully. "I only wrote it."

He chuckled, shook his head and said, "I'll read it tonight. If it's no good, I won't waste anybody's time. If it's good, I'll get it right out."

She instinctively trusted him. He was a tall, boyish-looking man in his mid-thirties. There was an aura of success about him, and about his suite of offices. She liked the subdued reception area and the waiting room/library that housed books on three walls and was furnished with comfortably worn leather armchairs and framed letters from old, established authors. The overall atmosphere was one of slightly seedy gentility—unobtrusive and comfortable. She went home to wait out Hank's answer.

She waited three weeks. Finally she tried to reach him on the telephone. Impossible. His secretary, who'd been hired the same afternoon Sherrill took in her manuscript, was sympathetic. "I know," she said. "He's really awful. I've left half a dozen messages on his desk. Hold on and I'll slip in, see if I can get him to pick up. I think he's got someone with him." Sherrill held on for close to five minutes. At the end of that time, the secretary returned to say, "He said he's given the manuscript to one of the other agents in the office. He wants a second opinion."

Infuriated, Sherrill thanked her and hung up. She snatched up some stationery, sat down at the dining table and dashed off an enraged letter to Hank telling him that if he couldn't rely upon his own judgment as to whether or not a book was good, she certainly didn't want someone so indecisive representing her. She slapped a stamp on the envelope and went right out to mail it.

Three days later, Hank telephoned. "I've decided to take the book on," he said, "I'm sending it out this afternoon. I'll keep you posted." They talked for several minutes; he stated his enthusiasm for the book but never once mentioned her letter. She knew she'd made her point.

Less than a month later, Hank telephoned again. "I've got an offer on *Success Without Glamour*. It's not very good, so don't get too excited."

"What's the offer?" she asked breathlessly, her spirits rocketing. She didn't care how much it was. Someone wanted to buy the book.

"They're offering thirty-five hundred for hard and soft rights. I've told them they're crazy, but it's my job to pass along offers to you. We could get more somewhere else."

"Will they go higher?" she asked.

"I can probably get them up to five," he said, sounding slightly more enthusiastic. "They are crazy about the book. It's up to you."

"Try for five," she said giddily. "The money's not as important as getting the book published."

"That's true," he conceded. "I'll get back to you."

Within an hour the deal was closed. She was to get five thousand dollars' advance. The hardcover and paperback rights were, Hank told her, to be cross-collateralized—whatever that meant. She'd receive twenty-five hundred on signing the contract, the balance when the revised manuscript was accepted. He ran down all the terms. She scarcely listened. She was desperate to get off the telephone so she could call her mother and tell her.

"I'll go over the contract with you when it comes in," Hank said. "It'll take three or four weeks. Congratulations!"

Her mother was in a meeting with a client, Sherrill was informed.

"Have her call me as soon as she's free, will you? It's very important."

She paced the living room, so full of energy she didn't know what to do with herself. She wanted Drew to get home so they could go out and celebrate. She checked her watch, waiting. Unable to contain herself, she ran to the phone to call Michelle. The service picked up. More disappointed by the moment at being unable to share the good news, she left her number and hung up, then slouched on the sofa. The telephone rang; she bolted across the room to answer it.

"Hi, Sherrill? This is Jean Diamond. I'm going to be your editor. I wanted to call and tell you how excited we all are about your book. Everybody here's talking about it."

"That's terrific! I can hardly believe this is happening."

"I've got a few revisions I'd like you to do. Could you make it for lunch next Friday? I'd like to introduce you to everyone, then we can sit down and go over the revisions."

"Sure. Oh, wait a minute." Quickly, Sherrill flipped through the diary beside the telephone. "I can't make it Friday. I'm doing a voice-over. Is Thursday any good?"

It was Jean's turn to check her diary. "Thursday's out. Monday we have an editorial meeting. Tuesday I've got lunch with an author. Let's make it Wednesday."

"Great!"

"I'm really looking forward to meeting you," Jean said. "It's a sensational book. See you next week."

Sherrill put down the receiver and looked at what she'd written in the diary: lunch, publisher, 11 A.M.

My God! she thought. I did it!

The revisions were far more extensive than she'd imagined they'd be. She sat down at the dining table with the manuscript and went to work. Drew, initially proud and congratulatory, began to grumble.

"Do you realize we've been eating out every night?" he complained. "When I come home from a hard day's work it'd be nice to relax with a drink and a decent meal."

"I'll send out for a pizza," she offered.

"Shit, Sherrill! I do *not* want a pizza."

"All right. Tomorrow I'll go over to Gristede's and do some grocery shopping. But let me finish what I'm doing right now."

She bent her head over her work and he glared at her for a long moment, then sighed and went to take a shower. He was thoroughly confused. Sure, he thought the book wasn't bad, and that she was pretty damned clever to have come up with it. But did she have to spend every goddamned waking hour at it? She'd even turned down three jobs in the previous two weeks in order to go on with her writing. Any one of those jobs would've paid more in the long run than the trifling advance the publishers were paying her.

"You're throwing money away!" he accused, emerging from the bathroom. "You've turned down three jobs that would've made you five times, ten times the money that thing's going to earn." He pointed one long finger at the offending manuscript.

"I don't care," she said without looking up, her hand moving steadily over the ruled pad on which she was making notes. "I'd rather be doing this." She finished the sentence, replaced the cap on her felt-tipped pen, and turned to look at him. "I'll be finished with it in another couple of weeks and then things'll be back to normal. Two weeks is hardly a lifetime."

"Two weeks? You've been at this for *months!* What about me? You're up half the night, and asleep in the morning when I leave. We never talk anymore, let alone eat or have sex. Two weeks better be the end of it," he warned. "I'm getting fed up."

She despised the expression "have sex," but thought better of commenting at that moment. "Two weeks," she promised, giving him a hug. "You ought to be happy for me. Not everybody sells the first book they write."

"Not everybody gets married as one thing and turns into something else. I mean, if you'd told me you were a writer, I'd have been prepared for all this. As far as I knew, you were a singer, an actress."

"That's not true. I *told* you I wanted to write. I told you that the very first time we ever had dinner together."

"I don't remember your saying anything."

"Well, I'm sorry if you don't remember, but I definitely did tell you. Anyway, what difference does it make whether I'm an actress or a writer? It's a career either way."

"I'm beginning to think that's all you care about."

"Don't be silly. Of course it isn't."

"It sure looks that way," he pouted unbecomingly.

"It's not that way," she insisted, giving him a kiss on the chin. "Let me finish this last bit and we'll go out for something to eat."

"Tomorrow we eat in," he reminded her.

"My treat tonight. I got a residual check today." She smiled at him coaxingly. "Your choice of restaurant."

The revisions got done; she delivered the typed pages to Jean, then telephoned John to say she was ready to go out on calls again. Drew stopped complaining and life returned to its previous pattern. The book had gone into production, which meant, Jean explained, that it was being copy-edited before going off for typesetting. In a few months Sherrill would receive galley proofs to correct; a few months after that, it would be a finished book, ready to be shipped to the stores. All at once, the idea of six months without writing struck Sherrill as depressingly empty. When Drew next left for a two-week trip to San Francisco, she got out her ruled pads, her felt-tipped pens, and sat down to start a new book, a novel. Her writing habit had evolved into a full-scale compulsion; she simply could not stop. She kept her work hidden from Drew, told him nothing about it. It was wiser, she thought, not to tell him.

Two months before publication of the book Jean called up to ask Sherrill to attend the spring sales conference and meet the sales force. "We're going to do a major ad campaign," she explained. "The first step is getting you introduced to the salespeople. The second step involves the sales people getting the booksellers worked up. And the third step is an author tour on publication. Would you be willing to tour?"

"What would it involve?"

"Three weeks, probably fourteen or fifteen cities—all the major markets; radio and TV, newspaper interviews, booksigning sessions. We'll tell you all about it at the conference. The book's gathering a lot of steam. We're going for a fifty thousand first printing, major media advertising, maybe even some fifteen- or thirty-second spot ads on television."

"Tell me where and what time and I'll be there."

She couldn't quite believe the enthusiasm was genuine, but it seemed to be. She met the salespeople, who warmly shook her hand and complimented her. She was asked to talk about the book and gave an impromptu ten-minute speech, was heartily applauded, and then sat down to try to eat the chicken à la king lunch. She wasn't able, she felt too nauseated. She put her nausea down to overexcitement and forgot about it until several days later when, in the middle of a dubbing session, she had to excuse herself and run to the women's room, where she was violently ill.

She was pregnant and had strongly mixed feelings about it.

"I'm not willing to raise a child in Manhattan," she told Drew. "If we decide we want this baby, I think we're going to have to move out of town."

"Sure," he said. "No problem. We can move wherever you want. I'd like to have a child, Sher," he said quietly. "But if we move away, what about your work? Are you going to commute into town for auditions?"

"I'll handle it," she responded, thinking she wouldn't miss going out to auditions. She'd be free to spend all day every day writing. Drew wouldn't have to know a thing about it.

"Does that mean you want to go ahead and have a baby?" he asked cautiously.

"I guess it does." She couldn't imagine getting rid of the baby. The child taking form inside her was very real. How could she possibly end its life? Just considering an abortion,

she felt a terrible sadness, and knew she'd have the baby.
She wanted to see what it would look like, how it would feel
as it grew inside her.

"Well," he sighed, "I guess that's it for your tour."

"*What?*"

"You're not going to go off on a jaunt around the country
in your condition."

"Of course I am," she declared. "What made you think I
wouldn't?"

"You'll damage the baby."

She laughed disbelievingly, her eyes wide. "What century
are you living in?" she asked lightly. "It's not going to hurt
the *baby*. It might make *me* a little tired, but that's all."

"You're crazy," he said flatly. "You're completely crazy."

"I'm not in the least crazy," she argued. "I'm a perfectly
healthy twenty-seven-year-old woman, who's going to have
a baby. I'm also going to have a best seller, if what Jean and
the salespeople say is true."

"You're crazy," he repeated, looking injured. "First you
don't want the baby, then you do. First you tell me we'll
never give up this apartment, then you want to move out of
town. You want to keep all the balls in the air like some
demented goddamned juggler. Who the hell d'you think you
are, anyway?"

Flabbergasted, she could only smile. "I'm Wonder Woman,"
she said, laughing, thinking of her mother. "For God's sake,
Drew. I don't *think* I'm anyone. I'm just me. I've got a
publishing house that thinks a book I've written is dynamite; they're counting on me to help sell the book. I'd *be*
crazy if I didn't go along with it. It's the chance of a lifetime. And as far as the baby is concerned, I'll be away for
three weeks. I'll just be starting my fourth month by then.
Nothing's going to happen to the baby; everything's going to
be just fine. Will you please relax and stop acting like
somebody's maiden aunt?"

"If you drank, you'd be an alcoholic. You've got a compul-
sive nature."

"Well, then"—she laughed again—"it's a good thing I
don't drink, isn't it?"

He failed to see the humor. For a solid week he went
about wearing a reproachful expression. Then he seemed to
forget and things were quiet again.

Chapter 20

Anne followed Jamie into the bedroom and watched him start to unpack. She stood quietly on the far side of the bed as he threw open the first of the bags to lift out an armful of shirts. Her eyes remained on him so intently he could feel them, like small surgical probes, against his flesh. She watched, and she guessed.

"You're going to leave me, aren't you?" she said in a neutral voice. "Something happened in Montreal."

At once he stopped and slowly straightened, trying to put some sensible words together. "We don't seem to be going anywhere," he said inadequately.

"I see," she said, pulling back her shoulders. "Well, if that's the case, there's certainly no point to our being together, is there?" She reached for a cigarette from the package on the bedside table and took her time lighting it, reminding herself that she'd known from the beginning that they had no future. She'd always known, but still she wasn't prepared to have it end. Her brain seemed to be racing around inside her skull like a small furry gray animal and she couldn't slow her reactions down sufficiently to assemble her thoughts. "When will you be going?" she asked.

He looked around the room, feeling sadly bewildered. He could leave the two suitcases packed, throw the rest of his things into the back of the car and go. She was giving him a chance at a departure as close to painless as he could ever hope to have. But it wasn't as he'd imagined things would be; he felt transparent and ashamed, and wondered for a moment why he was leaving her at all. She didn't go in for scenes or for unwarranted confrontations; she had discretion and a sense of timing. He doubted he could say the same for Lucienne; he imagined she had quite a temper and that she'd display it soon enough. He was surrendering the tranquil sameness of life with Anne for the lusty and heated uncertainty of existence with a much younger woman. It was his turn to have the edge in years, and he believed he knew at that moment how Anne had to have felt all along. The shoe was about to be placed firmly on the other foot and he wasn't sure he'd be able to handle the situation with anything near Anne's dignity. He wished she'd go out of character, throw a scene, break down and weep. Perhaps if she did, he'd see her differently, and stay.

"Well." She took a deep breath. "If you're going, you might as well do it now as later." She felt as if she'd been run over by a truck; she'd been flattened, crushed; it was difficult to remain upright. She looked longingly at the floor, wishing she could lie down and go to sleep until all this was over. Everything was happening as she'd always known it would, and the feeling was like death. Her emotions had become a dense black bag that gaped open, threatening to enclose and suffocate her. She wanted to cry, to scream, to offer all sorts of arguments against his leaving; she wanted to fall to her knees, sobbing out her love for him. Instead, she remained in the room a few seconds longer, then went slowly downstairs to the living room, where, with external calm, she moved about the room collecting things of his and placing them on the sofa. There were quite a few books, and small items—birthday gifts from his friends and from her, souvenirs of the trips they'd taken to Bermuda and to Mexico, keepsakes exchanged between cast members on opening nights. She found a shopping bag and filled it, then went for a second and a third, filled those as well. She remembered to add several pots of his and some pieces of crockery he'd bought. Finally she lifted down his two Eskimo paintings from the hallway wall.

He descended the stairs from the bedroom carrying the two suitcases just as she finished placing the last of his things on the landing.

"I think that's everything," she said, closely examining her dusty hands. "If anything else turns up, I'll let you know. Better still, I'll drop it off at Matt's office for you."

He stared at her, dry-mouthed, filled with respect for her. She seemed self-possessed and as unflappable as always. That, too, was one of her appealing qualities. Her near-violent responses in bed had always seemed to him an astonishingly rewarding view of the opposite side of her nature. Again, desire for her flickered in his belly. He couldn't think of anything intelligent to say. When he opened his mouth to speak, she saved him by saying, "I'll give you a hand with those thing, if you like."

"No, that's all right. I can manage."

She remained at the top of the staircase watching as he made several trips down to the car. Then he came back up the stairs and stopped on the landing in front of her.

"We'll stay in touch," he said. "If there's anything you ever need, please call me. I'll let you know where to reach me."

She shook her head and managed a small smile. "I won't call you," she said softly, holding her hand out to him. "Good luck, Jamie. If there are calls, I'll refer them to Matt."

Ignoring her outstretched hand, he embraced her, dismayed to find her rigidly resistant. It was obvious she was suffering through the gesture, so he broke it short. "Take care of yourself," he said, wondering why neither of them had more significant things to say.

"Oh, I will." She held her shoulders back and her chin up, the smile still applied to her mouth like lipstick put on in the dark. "And you, too."

He stood waiting, hoping for something more to be said. When she failed to speak, he said, "I do love you. It's just not . . ." He gave up, turned, and went down the stairs.

Once in the car, he tried to think about where to go, but couldn't concentrate. He was too upset. He turned on the radio, threw the shift into reverse, and backed out into the street, heading downtown. There was a song playing on the radio, sung by a woman with a young, haunting voice. His eyes filled with tears. He knew, as he listened to the melancholy lyrics, that there were things—neat vodka, long slim legs, and certain songs—that would always remind him of Anne.

Halfway to the Windsor Arms, he pulled the car over to the curb, debating going back to the house. His chest heaved with unshed tears; he lit a Gitane and choked down the smoke, then pulled back into the stream of traffic.

Anne remained at the top of the stairs staring down their empty length until it occurred to her that she felt brittle

and achy. She needed a drink. It took considerable effort to
move down the hall to the kitchen. She opened the cupboard, got down the vodka bottle, and placed it firmly on
the counter in front of her. She wouldn't, she thought bitterly, have to burn the sheets this time. They were still fresh,
stainless; they bore no evidence whatsoever of Jamie's existence in her life. Pristine sheets, they could bear her body
between their cool folds; she would emerge in the morning,
leaving the bed to look as if she'd merely reclined on it for a
brief nap. No twisted, mangled sheet to attest to heated
nighttime activities, simply the slight indentation on the
pillow where her head had lain: an old maid's bed, a nun's
pallet. That bed and its clean sheets was her future. She
didn't think she could bear it. Her hand trembled as she
poured a tumbler full to the brim of the vodka before carefully replacing the cap and returning the bottle to the
cupboard.

Nothing new, no surprises, just pain—immediate and complete. Gazing down at the glass of vodka, she entertained an
image of herself kneeling on the bathroom floor beside the
tub, her arm outheld beneath warm running water. One
clean, deep incision down the length of a vein, a few seconds of pain, then numbness and, finally, a sleep from
which she needn't ever awaken. The image held her attention; her mind kept coming back to it again and again. She
had no desire to live beyond this moment; she was going to
have to give the issue of her life careful consideration.

Drink in hand, she went to sit down in the living room
and automatically lit a cigarette. The six weeks of Jamie's
absence had been intolerably lonely. He'd telephoned regularly, but the calls had been too brief, and unrewarding.
He'd sounded hurried and dutiful, like someone reporting in
to a fretful mother; he certainly hadn't sounded anything
like a lover. Compared to calls he'd made from location
during the first year they'd been together, they had made it
all too apparent that his interest had diminished. She could
so easily remember waiting each evening that first year for
his calls: the sound of his voice, the warmth of closeness
she'd felt as his words filled her, refreshing his reality for
her. Now there'd be no more telephone calls, ever.

She'd been expecting this. Why, then, did she feel so

devastated, so destroyed? Not knowing when, she'd failed to arm herself properly. How did one acclimate oneself to pain? She considered hostages and their pain of separation from everything routine to their lives, their fear of imminent death. That was different, though, because there was no question of choice in the matter when one was taken hostage. She had had a choice; she made it three years earlier when she'd allowed Jamie into her life, disregarding her interior voice that had cautioned against it.

She lifted the glass, then set it down again. The vodka didn't appeal to her; she had no desire whatever to drink it. In fact, the idea of drinking made her feel ill. Getting drunk wouldn't solve anything or make her feel less bereft. She needed some fresh air, she thought suddenly, and crushed out her cigarette in the ashtray as she got to her feet. Dinner out somewhere, that would be good. Someplace expensive. Perhaps Dene would like to go with her.

Grabbing up her handbag and keys, she ran down the stairs to knock at Dene's door. Dene came to open it immediately, as if she'd been waiting, and said, "Hi! Come in."

"I thought I'd like to go out to dinner," Anne said, feeling herself smiling widely, stupidly, unnaturally. "Why don't you come with me? We'll go somewhere nice and have a good dinner." Why was Dene just standing there, not saying anything? It was infuriating, the way Dene remained in one spot, simply gazing at Anne's face. "Have you got something on? If you're free, why don't you come? My treat," she added, feeling the words hurling out of her mouth like minute pebbles. *Come on!* she silently insisted. *Say something; do something; don't keep standing there like a goddamned statue!*

Dene was riveted to the light in Anne's eyes, and to the sight of the woman whose body seemed to want to go in six different directions at once. It was as if a fire had been started somewhere on Anne's body and, although she wasn't yet conscious of it, her body had commenced an independent reaction to the flames. Dene wondered if she herself had appeared this way to people after the accident. It was more than likely that she had.

Sensing Anne's tremendous impatience, Dene said, "I'll have to change. Why don't you come in and wait for me? It

won't take me more than a couple of minutes. Come in," she
coaxed, as if addressing a reluctant child.

Anne smoked furiously, oblivious to the ashes that fell to
the floor, thinking that everyone was acting strangely today.
First Jamie, coming in that way and starting to unpack as if
he'd intended to stay when he'd known he wouldn't. Why
had he bothered to come back at all? Why hadn't he gone
directly to a hotel and spared her that little scene? But he
wouldn't have done that; it wasn't his style to avoid matters. He had such decency and courage; he was so sweet. . . .
Her throat was starting to close; her eyes stung with the
need to cry. She coughed, blinked several times, then drew
hard on the cigarette. To hell with him! He was gone and
that was the end of it. Gone. It was done, ended. She was
alone. Again. Alone. "Oh, God," she whispered, wrapping
her arms around herself, shifting her weight from foot to
foot. "God!' she whispered, her eyes raking the photographs
on the walls as if the faces there constituted a silently
condemning audience who found her as wanting as she
herself did. His smile, and those moments when his laughter burst into the air like rare, rediscovered music, and the
mellow murmur of his voice breaking the dark menace of
night . . . How could she possibly survive this return to a
solitary existence? It had been all right before Jamie; she
hadn't been unhappy. Now there was no one; she'd even
given up her free-lance work in order to be there for him
when he was between jobs. His absence would come as a
daily reminder of all she'd had and lost. What am I going to
do? she wondered, fear, like ice, creeping over her body so
that she shivered and tightened the bands of her arms
around her treacherous, ever-aging body. Why did she have
to be so much older than he? If she'd been younger . . . She
was lying, trying to delude herself into believing that a
younger version of herself might have proved more enticing.
The reality was that no version of her, at any age, could
have kept him longer.

"What's the matter?" Dene asked, reappearing in the
living room.

"Just chilly," Anne said, with another forced smile and a
voice that sounded like a stick struck on a small tin drum:
hollow and flattened. "Ready?"

"I've just got to get my bag. You're sure you're all right?"

"What are you in the mood for?" Anne asked, extinguishing the cigarette. "Chinese? French, or Italian? My treat, your choice."

Anne was so distraught that Dene thought it would be best to state her preference in order to relieve Anne of the necessity of making a decision. Her movements were uncoordinated and jerky as if she'd lost some vital part connecting her motor abilities to her brain. Jamie wasn't coming with them, Dene realized. She'd heard him come in and then go out several times. He'd left. They'd split up. That had to be why Anne was behaving so oddly.

"Italian," Dene said. "I'm all set."

"Good! Let's go!"

Anne shot to the door, threw it open, and raced out onto the front porch, where she stopped, turned to make sure Dene was following, then turned again and flew down the steps so quickly, with such a near-palsied lack of coordination, that Dene gasped, fearful Anne would fall. Incredibly, she didn't, and continued on her way around to the rear of the house and the car. Dene was afraid to have Anne drive in her present condition. She wondered for a moment if Anne mightn't be drunk, but at once rejected the idea. She'd seen Anne drink too much on several occasions and she'd never behaved even remotely like this.

"Why don't I drive?" Dene suggested, running to keep up.

"You drive?" Anne had to pause and think about this. Dene's assumption of any measure of control in the situation seemed all at once to lend her added dimension. A few minutes earlier, Anne had found her irritatingly slow-witted and leaden. Now Dene seemed to be by far the more rational of the two of them. "Yes, all right," Anne consented and went on past the Mercedes to stand at the passenger door of Dene's Toyota, agitatedly tapping her foot while she waited for Dene to climb into the car and reach across to unlock the door. Once inside the car, Anne fastened her safety belt, then immediately lit another cigarette. She felt frustrated by the restraining belt and had to force herself not to unfasten it. The small gray furry animal had increased the speed of its movements and was racing about inside her skull cavity as if trying to dash itself to pieces against the inpenetrable bone walls. Her eyes smarted; it was becoming increasingly difficult to stop her throat from working; her desire to scream was overwhelming.

Dene backed out into the road, shifted into first, and headed down Duplex toward Eglinton. She tried to think of which Italian restaurant they could go to. There was George's Spaghetti House or Old Angelo's, or La Scala. "How about La Scala?" Dene said, deciding that the serene elegance of the restaurant in the converted house downtown on Bay Street would be the right place for Anne in her present state. The quiet atmosphere might help to calm her down.

Anne didn't hear. She was mentally backtracking over the brief scene in the bedroom with Jamie. She'd said too little. So had he. Why hadn't she reminded him of ... of what? He needed no reminding of the time they'd spent together. He'd said they'd shared three good years, and they had. There was nothing more she could have said, yet it felt as if there should have been. She wished she'd thought to point out to him how she'd regularly had to clean the bathroom after he'd used it; how she'd made a point of getting up before him in order to fix his favorite breakfasts; how she'd managed to keep track of the socks he discarded here and there; how she'd laundered his underwear—and taken a proprietary joy in these small domestic acts.

"I keep thinking of things I should have said," she spoke aloud, forgetting that Dene knew nothing of what had happened.

"When?" Dene asked.

"This afternoon. When he left. If he hadn't been gone ... I mean, he was away for six weeks. Naturally, I cleaned the apartment and changed the sheets. I even picked up his shirts from the laundry and had all his summer clothes dry-cleaned, ready for storage. It felt so odd going into the bathroom and finding it clean. He made such puddles everywhere, splashes all over the mirror. . . . It's already getting cold at nights." She turned to stare at Dene's profile, fascinated by the red spill of hair cascading over her shoulder. "You do have the most beautiful hair," she said distractedly. "I thought I'd sit down and get drunk. It's what people always seem to do in situations like this. But I wasn't in the mood for it. I'd like to be drunk without having to do the drinking."

"I know," Dene said, spotting a parking lot on Charles Street across the road from the restaurant. "I know exactly what you mean. I carried a fifth of scotch around with me everywhere for a month after the accident. I thought eventually I'd stop somewhere and drink the whole bottle. But I never did. In the end, I stuck it away at the back of a shelf and didn't find it again until I started packing to come back here. I gave it to Charlie, the super. He preferred Chivas, but he was just as happy with Dewar's."

"What happened?" Anne asked bluntly, hoping to be diverted from the pain.

"Here we are," Dene said and switched off the ignition. "Would you lock the door, please?"

Feeling dizzy, Anne got herself out of the car and onto the sidewalk. Dene came around to lock the passenger door before going to pay the parking lot attendant. Finally she returned, to link her arm through Anne's.

"What happened?" Anne asked again after they'd been shown to a table and given menus.

"Would you like to have a drink?" Dene asked solicitously, as if offering medicine. "I'll join you."

"Why not?" She gave Dene a smile so distorted that she actually succeeded in looking ugly. Fortunately the smile only lasted a second or two, then dissolved abruptly and she looked, if not beautiful, at least recognizably herself.

Dene ordered the drinks and offered Anne a cigarette. Somehow, seeing Anne in this condition was having a positive effect on Dene. For the first time in seven years she could think about Jake and Mimi and experience no pain. Its absence was a bit shocking. She felt quite unlike herself, and wondered if she seemed as altered to Anne as Anne seemed to her. "I take it," she said gently, "that you and Jamie have split up."

Mutely, Anne nodded, her eyes fixed on Dene's.

"It's terrible, isn't it," Dene commiserated, glancing down at Anne's tightly laced fingers. "Nothing feels the way that does," she went on, intrigued by the waxen whiteness of Anne's hands. "You think you can't live past the moment.

You do, though. That's the worst part of it: you do live."
Raising her eyes to look at Anne, she said, "I can't believe it
now, but it's taken me all these years to get to the point of
believing, of accepting it. I never wanted to before. Now it
seems as if all of it happened to someone else, someone I
used to know very well but haven't seen in years."

"What *did* happen?" Anne asked in a hushed voice, realizing she was about to learn who Dene was, and why.

"Jake and I were together for eight years. We met when I
was twenty-two and got married two years later. I suppose I
was young for my age, and very naïve. Perhaps I wasn't.
Anyway, that doesn't matter. He was my *life*," she said
passionately. "I adored him. If we were apart for more than
a few hours, I couldn't get anything done. If he was more
than a few minutes late getting home, I was convinced that
he'd died, that I'd lost him forever. I think," she said soberly, "that I was obsessed with him. He was the only man I'd
ever been interested in, the only one I'd ever loved. I'd had
boyfriends before Jake; I'd slept with several other men.
But I hadn't really wanted any of them. So it seemed positively miraculous that he felt about me the way I did about
him." She paused, then said, "I thought we were very happy.
Oh, we had arguments from time to time, the way couples
do when they're getting to know each other. But we were
... we seemed to be so happy." Her voice rose on the last
syllable so that the word ended on a questioning note. "Evidently, *I* was the happy one. And Jake was ... I don't know
what he was.

"One afternoon when I was supposed to be downtown
shopping, I decided not to shop after all but to get back
home because there was a big snowstorm forecast and I was
afraid I'd get stuck with the car on one of the hills, or have
an accident. It wasn't that I couldn't handle driving in the
snow. After all, I'd lived in Toronto most of my life and was
accustomed to driving in all kinds of weather. But Jake used
to enjoy treating me like a little girl. To be honest, I think I
enjoyed playing that role for him. When I stop and think
about it, I can almost feel myself shrinking to get back
inside that little-girl feeling. It's quite odd.

"So anyway," she sighed, "I got home a good two hours
before I was supposed to. I noticed that Jake's car was in the

driveway and thought it was a little strange, but nothing to be alarmed about. He'd probably heard the forecast, too, and come home early. I let myself into the house to find my sister Mimi sitting in the living room. I can still see her. She had on a red dress and she was sitting in the wing chair with her legs crossed, smoking a cigarette. She saw me and jumped up as if I'd pointed a gun at her. I remember smiling and saying hi, getting ready to ask her what she was doing there, to tell her what a nice surprise it was to see her. But the look on her face was so peculiar that I didn't say anything. Then Jake came down the stairs carrying several suitcases. I watched him come all the way down the stairs and put the bags down in the hallway, wondering what was going on.

"I was stupid," she said flatly, without rancor. "I've never had a suspicious mind, so even with the evidence right in front of me, I still couldn't put two and two together and come up with a remotely correct answer. I think I said something absurd like 'What's in the suitcases?' and Jake stared at me the way Mimi was staring—in a way that made me feel so dumb that it was only through their considerable tolerance and affection I'd been allowed to live as long as I had. Because obviously, without their indulgence, I'd never have lasted a week on my own. I felt positively ashamed, as if I'd soiled myself or said something obscene.

"He said, 'I was going to leave you this letter,' and I asked, 'What letter? What do you mean?' I kept looking at Mimi, then at Jake, then back at Mimi. I *still* couldn't figure it out. She was my little sister, my baby sister, not even two years younger than I. My mother had been pregnant with Mimi when my father left her. It's why she could never forgive him. I worshiped Mimi, just as I did Jake. I thought then that life was all sunshine, and love, and perfection. I lived in a celluloid dreamworld, and they'd all actively helped me create it—Jake, Mimi, and my mother.

"Well." She cleared her throat and wrapped her hand around the glass in front of her. "It seemed that Jake and Mimi had been having an affair for almost two years and the letter they'd intended to leave for me said all this. And more. A lot more. I was so stunned I couldn't think of anything to say. I kept gaping at Mimi, saying her name

over and over as if that would somehow remind her of the
loyalty I believed she owed me, or maybe that I'd always
understood that blood was supposed to be thicker than water,
and how could she have done this to me. I don't know what
I was trying to get her to do: Just get her to stop, I think. Her
expression was filled with contempt and she went to stand
beside Jake—like a sentry, I thought, as if I were watching
all this happen from a great distance. He talked about being
sorry and about how the letter would explain everything.
Then he stuffed the letter into my fist, opened the door,
picked up the suitcases, and he and Mimi left. They didn't
look back, either of them. They made me feel as if I didn't
exist. But if I didn't exist, how could I be standing there in
the doorway, watching them drive away together? I couldn't
move. After they'd gone, I stood and watched the snow fill
in the tire tracks in the road. Then I remembered the letter
and read what he'd had to say about our 'perfect marriage.' "

She picked up the glass, looked at it, then replaced it on
the table. "I'd bored him," she said sadly. "He found me
dull, and predictable, and asexual. It was like reading about
someone else. None of what he said seemed to apply to me
as I knew myself. Who was this person he was writing
about? I wondered. It couldn't be me. It didn't sound like
me. But it was. Now I know it was *all* about me. I couldn't
comprehend any of it then. I'd been the person he'd wanted
me to be. And that was what I couldn't understand: I
molded myself into the Dene he said he loved, into the
woman he claimed to want, and he'd despised that woman's
mealy-mouthed complacency and smugness. It was a terrible letter, cruel. So cruel. I think I could have taken it if
he'd *said* what he had, but somehow the fact that he'd
written it all down made everything irrevocable. He'd pronounced sentence on me. And I was guilty, if not more, for
having encouraged me to be the way I was." She sighed and
waited while the waiter took their orders. When he'd moved
off, she picked up again at once. "The big storm came after
all, just as forecast. There was an accident. They both died.
The irony of it was that they didn't get thirty miles; they
didn't even make it to Hamilton. Apparently he lost control
of the car. There was a huge pileup involving something
like thirteen cars. Six people died—Jake and Mimi were

two of them—and nine were badly injured. And that was the end of it." She picked up her glass and took a long swallow of the scotch. Anne was staring at her unblinking. "It's my first drink since the accident," Dene said, shuddering. "It burns going down."

"My God!" Anne said at last. "Your own sister."

"My mother sided with me, of course. She acted as if Mimi had never existed and she's only mentioned her name once since I came back here. But I remember Mimi. She was lovely—very alive, very ambitious, very opinionated, very beautiful. I'm not surprised Jake fell in love with her. Every man she ever met was a little in love with her, including all her teachers at school. She was everything I wasn't. I dream about them," she confided. "I dream it's me in the car with Jake and we're running away from our lives. We always collide with a mountain, a steel mountain. And just before the impact, I turn every time to look at Jake and he looks exactly like my father."

Chapter 21

In the weeks before she left to go on tour, Sherrill and Drew bought the Sunday *Times* and scoured the ads. Drew confessed he wouldn't mind Westchester; Sherrill preferred Connecticut. They finally found a house on the Stamford-Darien line in Connecticut, and Sherrill began to order baby furniture and clothes, as well as the appliances and additional furniture needed to fill the three bedrooms, living and dining rooms, and kitchen. She felt more alive than ever before. She loved being pregnant and kept a close watch on her slowly changing body. The obstetrician's warning that she'd probably have to have a cesarian delivery didn't disturb her; it didn't really register.

Drew was more affectionate than ever and she responded with new feeling for him. They made love more often, and for the first time she began to experience intense orgasmic pleasure. She couldn't help wondering if being pregnant had heightened her sexuality. If that were the case, Drew might end up being totally disillusioned once the baby was born and she returned to her previous lack of interest in lovemaking. For the present, she simply went along, discovering new appetites and capacities.

She was convinced Drew had come to terms with her imminent departure, her new career, so it came as a surprise to find him withdrawn on the evening before she was to leave for Boston.

"What's the matter?" she asked him, pausing in her packing.

"Nothing," he said curtly, fumbling with a pack of cigarettes.

"Tell me," she urged. "What's the matter?"

"Nothing," he repeated. He held a match to his cigarette, then cursed loudly and tossed the cigarette into the ashtray; he'd lit the wrong end. "Fuck it!" he muttered and lit a fresh cigarette.

"Something's bothering you. Why don't you tell me what it is?"

"You're leaving me to make this whole goddamned move on my own," he accused.

"I'm not," she protested. "We're not moving until two weeks after I get back."

"Sure. And I suppose the packing's going to get done by magic."

"We've got two whole weeks to pack in," she said reasonably, suspecting he had more on his mind. "What else?"

"I've already told you how I feel about your going off on this jaunt around the country. It's irresponsible. You're pregnant."

She sighed and continued placing clothes in the garment bag. "I thought we'd settled all this," she said quietly. "Are you going to start it up again?"

"Who the hell cares, anyway, if you're on 'The Tonight Show' or not?"

She straightened and slowly turned to stare at him. "*I* care," she said evenly. "My publishers care. It's a fantastic break, getting on that show. *What* is the *matter* with you?"

"Nothing's the matter with *me*. You're the one."

"I'm the one what, for God's sake? Will you please say what you're trying to say and stop all this dancing around? You're starting to drive me crazy."

His eyes sparred with hers for several seconds, then he looked away. "We've been getting along so well lately," he said miserably.

"That's not going to change."

"It will."

"I know what it is," she said, breaking into a smile. "You're going to miss me, aren't you? You're usually the one going off on 'jaunts' around the country. But this time it's me, and that's different, isn't it? C'mon, Drew," she coaxed, putting her arms around him. "Everything's perfect. We're having a baby; I'm having a best seller; you just got a promotion and that whopping raise; we've got a gorgeous house in Connecticut. Things couldn't be better. Will you please relax? I'll be back in three weeks."

"Yeah, well . . ." His mood dissolved and he held her, stroking her hair. "I guess you're right," he said. "I'm going to miss you."

Christ! she thought. Was she going to have to spend the rest of her life dragging Drew out of his moods? The prospect exhausted her.

After a time, she unwound his arms from around her and returned to her packing. She tried to put the conversation behind her, but it niggled. Something was wrong; she couldn't pinpoint what it was. It had to do with Drew's attitude, the deprecating references he made to her writing and to the tour. It continued to bother her all the way to Boston. Once there, however, she was too busy to give him further thought.

She'd imagined the tour would be swanky, with everything laid on. It was, but she hadn't the time or energy to enjoy it. She arrived in Boston in the early morning, was interviewed by one of the newspapers at the airport. Then the local sales representative rushed her into the city, where she did three more interviews that morning—two on the radio, one for another newspaper—and two in the afternoon. After the second of the television shows, the rep drove her to Logan airport, saw her off at the gate with a handshake, and she was on her way to D.C. There she was met by another rep, taken to her hotel, and told she'd be picked up at eight the next morning. She had a room service dinner, telephoned Drew, who sounded decidedly disgruntled, washed her underwear, took a shower, and fell into an exhausted sleep.

After the tenth or eleventh interview it occurred to her she was being asked the same questions over and over. It was an effort to think up variations on her answers, to treat the questions as if it were the first time she was hearing them. Most of the interviewers hadn't read the book, but had only glanced at the biographical material and book jacket copy; an alarming number commenced the interviews by asking, "What's your book about?" She came to dread the question because she felt like a fool trying to answer without sounding smug. But she answered, and the interviews went on.

Day after day it was the same—in Atlanta, Philadelphia, Cleveland, Detroit, Chicago, Minneapolis—until she arrived in California, where she had a free weekend. She was so fatigued she could do no more than sit in a lounge chair at the Beverly Hills Hotel and watch, fascinated, the goings-on at poolside. People moved constantly around the perimeters of the pool, and in the background could be heard the nonstop thunk, thunk of tennis balls hitting rackets. Everyone was tanned an impossible golden brown; the women were all thin and clad in miniscule bikinis; half a dozen men who looked preoccupied dashed in and out of the poolside cabanas making and taking calls, while the PA system gave forth with a steady stream of names. It was, Sherrill thought, like watching a plotless movie. Few people used the pool, and the waiters did a booming business in drinks. Eight-thirty Monday morning, she climbed back on the merry-go-round.

She was so nervous doing "The Tonight Show" she had no idea afterward of what had been said. Her seven-minute segment went so quickly she felt she'd only just sat down when there was a commercial break, and the next guest was introduced. She sat with what she was sure was a glazed expression until the show ended, then was driven to the airport by the L.A. rep, who congratulated her profusely and assured her she'd cracked everyone up. How? she wondered. She couldn't remember a word of the interview.

The days evolved into a mechanical routine: she arrived in a city in the evening, got out her clothes for the next day, left a wake-up call with the switchboard and set her traveling alarm to be on the safe side, then she plunged into a twitching unsatisfactory sleep, to awaken when the telephone and alarm went off simultaneously. Then she washed, made up, repacked the overnight bag; in the lobby she turned her bags over to the rep, checked out, and the day began. After "The Tonight Show" she was recognized several times in airports; it gave her a lift. The San Francisco rep said the sales on the book had shot up overnight and there was talk of going back to press for a second printing.

"You were terrific," he told her. "Did you see the show?"

"I was too tired. I went to sleep."

"I loved that story you told about the cat food audition you did in French. Was that true?"

"Yup." She didn't feel like talking. One of the things she'd quickly learned was to conserve her strength, and her answers, for the interviews. She liked the signing sessions best. Reality was meeting ordinary people who shyly approached to buy the book and have her sign it. After "The Tonight Show" large numbers of people began to appear at the bookstores. It elated her. The warmth and interest, the conversations of these people made the whole lunatic trip worthwhile. She vowed she'd never again do a promotion tour. They'd been designed, she was positive, to kill off authors.

At last she flew home from Seattle. Drew wasn't at the airport. She looked for him, waited fifteen minutes, then took a limo to the apartment. He wasn't home. She called the office. His secretary said, "He's in Connecticut today, Mrs. Raymond. He said if you called to tell you he'd be back before six."

Annoyed, Sherrill carried her bags to the bedroom. What the hell was he doing in Connecticut when he'd promised to pick her up at the airport? Perhaps something had gone wrong on the deal with the house. What, though? The contracts had been signed, and the 10 percent paid. The closing was to take place in two weeks' time. Maybe some of the furniture was being delivered. Was that possible?

She took a shower, then lay down. The idea of starting to

pack up the apartment first thing in the morning defeated her. The smart thing to do would be to call a moving company and have them do the work.

When he arrived home, Drew was outraged by the idea.

"You're going to pay *six* or *seven hundred dollars* to have somebody *else* do our packing?"

"I'll pay for it," she said calmly. "It's worth it. I'm too wiped out even to think about it."

"I knew it!" he declared. "All your talk about how maybe the tour was just going to make you a *little tired,* and how you'd do all the packing when you got back. Look at you! If you weigh a hundred pounds, I'll eat my hat. You're probably *killing* that baby!"

"Melodrama," she sighed. "My bloody life's turned into a melodrama. I worked my ass off for the last three weeks and I'm *tired.* I've got the money to pay the movers, so why shouldn't we do it? The baby's just fine, happy as Larry in here." She patted her still-flat belly. "And what were you doing in Connecticut when you were supposed to be picking me up at the airport?"

"*Somebody* had to be there for the delivery men while you were off gallivanting around the country playing superstar," he snapped.

She chose to ignore the insult. "What delivery men?"

"From the appliance store. The washer, the dryer, the dishwasher, the new stove, the refrigerator. You remember ordering all those expensive things, don't you? You remember getting permission to move things in before the closing, don't you?"

"Stop talking to me in that tone of voice, Drew. We agreed on the appliances, and if you don't want to pay for them, I will. I'm sure if you'd called her, the real estate broker would have been happy to let the delivery men into the house."

He opened his mouth, then shut it.

"That hadn't occurred to you, had it?" she asked. "You've decided, for some reason, to start playing the martyr."

"And you've decided to start throwing your money in my face!"

She laughed loudly. "That's horseshit! I'd like all this to stop now, please. I'm hungry; I'd like to eat."

"I ate in Connecticut."

"That's swell." She walked past him to the kitchen to open the refrigerator. Aside from some moldy cheese and half a container of orange juice, there was no food. "What've you been living on?" she asked.

"I certainly wasn't going to stock up on food for myself."

"Why not? Don't you need to eat?" She was becoming angrier by the moment. "You knew I was coming home today. Couldn't you at least have bought some bread, some cold cuts? There's a deli at the corner, for God's sake."

"I didn't have time."

"Beautiful." She pushed past him and went to stand by the dining table, leafing through three weeks' accumulation of mail. She wasn't in the mood to open letters, or to argue. It was bad enough she'd had to clean the bathroom thoroughly before she was able to use it, but no food was going too far. "Damn it!" she said. "I'm hungry. I'm going out for something to eat."

"That's just great!" he said aggrievedly. "You're not home two hours and already you're going out."

"I'm *hungry*! What the hell am I supposed to do, eat toilet paper? Speaking of which, when did you run out? Was it the first or second week after I left? And when did you give up cleaning the sink after you've shaved in it, or rinsing the toilet bowl? The whole goddamned place is a mess!"

"That's your job!"

"*My* job? Whoever told you that? It was your idea to fire the cleaning lady, not mine. This is stupid. We're just going to go round and round. I'm going out. Are you coming with me, or not?"

He looked at his watch. "The news is on."

"Fine! Watch the news!" She picked up her bag and slammed out of the apartment. As she marched up to Third Avenue, she wondered why she was living with this man. He was behaving like a spoiled, petulant child, punishing her for her absence by allowing dirt to accumulate everywhere in the apartment and by making ludicrous accusations about her failure to do her housewifely duties. It would have been different if she'd ever, at any time, been solely responsible for those duties, but they'd always shared the chores after Drew fired the cleaning lady. Why, she

asked herself, did she have to be the one to do all the
patching up, the soothing and calming? She'd just returned
from a backbreaking tour of fifteen cities. Did he imagine
that was glamorous? Maybe he did. My God! she thought.
Was it possible he thought she'd been out having a whoopy
time for three weeks, being wined and dined and generally
feted while he'd been left to his own devices? From all the
signs, it certainly looked that way. He undoubtedly equated
the tour with one of his business trips. He had no idea what
she'd been through. He saw the tour as an ego-inflating
experience, instead of the very real drudgery it had been.
She was going to have to set him straight. No. Maybe it was
best to let it blow over. There weren't going to be any more
tours, at least not in the immediate future. Forget it, she
told herself.

At the Blimpie Base she ordered a ham and cheese with
the works and watched the boy behind the counter pile on
the sliced tomatoes, the shredded lettuce, the olive oil and
vinegar, the sprinkling of oregano. She couldn't remember
being hungrier. She ordered a coffee, then headed back to
the apartment. Either Drew was going to start behaving like
a rational adult, or he could just get the hell out. She liked
the idea of moving into the Connecticut house alone; she
liked it so well she felt guilty. For the first time, that
evening, she began projecting herself and the baby into the
future, without Drew.

Michelle came up to visit one weekend soon after they'd
moved in. Drew stayed out of the way. He disliked Misha,
found her "too show-biz for my weak stomach," and played
golf for most of the weekend in order to avoid her.

Michelle walked from room to room, exclaiming over the
spaciousness of the house, and its charm. "It's fabulous. I
love it. Anytime you want to take off for a weekend and
need someone to come stay with the baby once it's born, call
me. Anytime."

Michelle had progressed on to her second married lover,
having abandoned the first with much stormy weeping. The
change of lovers had taken its toll. She no longer dressed
with her former flamboyance. If she cared to summon up
what she called her "stage presence" she could still get

double takes on Fifth Avenue, but she said she couldn't be bothered. She preferred to save her energies for work. She'd landed an ongoing part in a midday soap and had a grueling work schedule. Sherrill watched the show from time to time, out of curiosity, and thought Michelle was very good. The program was, of course, high-gloss melodrama from start to finish, but the cast was excellent, and even convincing. People often recognized Misha on the street and she was alternately annoyed and pleased by this. "One of these days," she told Sherrill, "I'm going to have enough money in the bank to buy myself a farm somewhere, maybe in Pennsylvania. Then I'll let them kill me off the show. I'll move to the sticks, find some nice unsuspecting rube, let him marry me, and I'll forget I ever lived here and had a career. I'm sick to death of it. You were smart to marry Drew. He's a sweetheart, and so easygoing."

Sherrill chose not to say anything. Michelle was not, Sherrill had discovered, the most perceptive of people. She simply didn't see how strongly Drew disliked her, or how foolish much of what she had to say might appear to "civilians." As far as Drew went and Michelle's opinion of Sherrill's smartness in marrying him, objectively there were times when Sherrill thought she had been lucky in finding him. But as the months passed and *Success Without Glamour* hit the *Times* and *Publishers Weekly* best-seller lists, he seemed to become daily more morose. He was positively gloomy when the movie rights were optioned by a California company, for which Sherrill was to be paid ten thousand dollars. He was depressed when, well after publication, the Literary Guild decided to pick up the book and paid eight thousand dollars for the privilege. His moods seemed to decline in direct proportion to the ascendance of the book. When she drove into New York to appear on local TV shows, or to do a signing session at Scribner's, he was livid.

"You shouldn't be running around in your condition!" he barked at her.

She ignored him. It was the safest thing to do. She began to fear that if she ever opened up and went for him, there'd be nothing left of him but a handful of bones and a few strands of hair. She bought a new Mercedes 250 with her first royalty check. Drew didn't talk to her for three days. As long as conversation kept safely away from her writing, things went tolerably well between them. He was solicitous, maddeningly overprotective of her as she grew larger and larger with the baby. Every so often she'd wander upstairs to find him sitting in the rocker in the nursery, staring into space. She'd continue on down the hall, reluctant to disturb whatever reverie he was having.

He seemed to understand, at best, one out of four things she said; her goals confused him. He assumed that with the publication of *Success Without Glamour* her writing career had come to an end. She thought it wiser not to enlighten him. The novel was almost completed and she had every intention of submitting it to Jean when it was. She felt guilty, almost evil, as if she'd relentlessly used him for her own purposes and, now that she'd attained some success, no longer required him. The truth was he resented her success; he saw it as he might have seen another man: something . . . someone who was taking her away from him. She constantly thought that if he'd only displayed some support, some enthusiasm, they would have been having a truly wonderful life together. As it was, his love for her seemed to grow heavier every day. She wanted to end the marriage, but dreaded hurting him and so kept putting off proposing they break up. She believed any suggestion in that direction would be interpreted by Drew as a choice she was making between him and her career. It was nowhere near that simple. He was forcing her to choose because of his steadfast refusal to accept her success. Many times he commented on her soaring income. "I guess you'll want to start wearing my suits next," he said, with an expression that made him ugly. She ignored these comments; the more she did, the more critical he became—of her continued efforts to publicize the book, of the telephone calls from Jean or Hank, of the small tide of fan mail forwarded from the publishing house, of anything pertaining to her career. She hoped the child would be the glue that held them together. She was wrong.

Delivering Perry was far more complicated and painful than either she or Drew had imagined it might be. The complications were so many and so diverse that she ended up staying in hospital for almost two weeks while a distraught, angry-looking Drew came nightly to pace her room for an hour before leaving abruptly. She felt sorry for him for having to witness her pain, for having had to be there through an entire night in the labor room. The doctor had tried, at six in the morning, to put together a surgical team. Neither she nor Drew could understand why, when the doctor—like his predecessor in New York—had warned them from the outset that a cesarian would be likely, he hadn't bothered to prepare for that eventuality.

During the long hours of the night when the two of them were alone together in the narrow labor room, Sherrill felt very close to Drew. The feeling held right through the night, on into the next day. The same evening of Perry's birth, she lay in her room eagerly awaiting Drew's arrival, anxious to tell him how much she loved him. When he arrived, he stopped in the doorway to stare at the masses of flowers, his face slowly suffusing with color.

"Who died?" he joked, trying for a smile that emerged as a grimace.

"Aren't they fantastic? *Everybody* sent them."

"I don't suppose you noticed any from me," he said, standing by the foot of her bed glaring at the exotic arrangements clustered on every surface.

"Of course I did. They're right here." She pointed to the vase of roses on the bedside table. "They're lovely."

He was so discomfited and even embarrassed when she tried to speak of her emotions, that she all at once lost the desire to give voice to them, and the emotions themselves. The sprouting of love that had commenced so unexpectedly failed to survive the evening. By the time Drew departed for home, Sherrill no longer cared for him in any but the most negligible fashion.

She put the tragicomic aspects of Perry's birth out of her mind. The infant was so terribly tiny and vulnerable it was painful to see. She went down to the nursery many times a day to stand watching the baby's spasmodic movements inside the incubator, the fragile shell of his chest as he labored to breathe the purified air being fed into his enclosed environment.

Within a month, though, he had gained several pounds and seemed anything but fragile as he screamed his demands—to be picked up, to be nursed, to be changed. She lost her awe of him and got on with learning how to live with him. She was not the natural-born mother she'd thought

she'd be, and so was profoundly grateful to her mother
when Josie took a month away from her office to come down
and help out with the three-month-old baby.

Josie took immediate stock of the situation. Within half an
hour of her arrival she knew that what she was in the midst
of was not a family but two distinctly separate individuals
with diametrically opposed views who'd had a child together
but were otherwise unrelated. She thought Drew was a
decent man with kind impulses who hadn't any real comprehension of the woman he'd married. Josie several times
saw him staring at Sherrill in bewilderment, as if the things
she said and did were so far beyond the bounds of his
experience and understanding that she might have come
from another planet. Sherrill tried, but couldn't quite conceal her unhappiness. She burst into tears after waving
Drew off one morning, and returned to stand in the doorway watching her mother feed Perry applesauce. Josie said,
"You'd better sit down and tell me all about it."

Sherrill mopped her eyes on her sleeve. "He's driving me
crazy."

"How?"

"He patronizes me, writes off what I have to say because
I'm in a 'mood,' or I'm just "temperamental.' I knew the day
we were getting ready to go down to City Hall I was making
a mistake."

"I don't see that it makes any difference how you came to
be married. People have been known to make a go of it on a
lot less than the two of you have."

"That's not it," Sherrill said, watching as her mother
adeptly laid Perry across her knees and tenderly stroked
the length of his back until he emitted a watery burp. "It
sounds crazy, but he's jealous. He's constantly making references to my car, to my income—snide references—as if
I'm nothing more than some kind of high-class hooker.

"At first I didn't want to believe it. It's incredible to me
that he'd resent my success. I think he thinks it makes him
look bad. Which is ridiculous. How could being married to
someone successful make *him* look bad?"

"Let me put Perry down for his nap and then we'll talk."
Her mother rose to carry the baby upstairs to his room.

Sherrill paced the kitchen until her mother returned.
Josie took her time pouring two cups of coffee, adding cream

and sugar to her own before carrying the cups to the table. Then she had to clean, rinse, and dry an ashtray and find her cigarettes.

After a sip of coffee and her first puff on a cigarette, Josie exhaled and said, "I'm not going to tell you what to do with your life. I've never done that and I never will. If you're unhappy, change things. I wouldn't dream of making this decision for you, Sherrill. You'd hold it against me for the rest of my life. Even if you were mature enough not to do that, I'd hate myself for having interfered. I will listen, though. It's what I'm here for. And I'll help in any concrete way I can. You know that. I just won't tell you what to do to solve this problem. You're going to have to work it out for yourself."

"I don't see why I should have to *hide* my work from this man!" Sherrill exploded. "And I can't cope with *two* children. I don't care enough for Drew to dote on him. I didn't mind pampering him before Perry was born, but I sure as hell mind now. Especially when anytime anyone so much as mentions the book, Drew goes berserk. The thing is, I don't want to hurt him."

"You know what they say about omelettes," Josie observed with a slight smile. "You've got to break eggs."

"Clichés. Are you going to sit there and give me clichés when my bloody life's coming apart?"

"Calm down a bit and try to think sensibly. What would you do, given all the options?"

"Do? I'd get out of here. No, I wouldn't. I love this house. I'd like him to get out. But I can't ask him to do that. It's his house. That's not fair."

"Who ever told you life was fair?" Josie laughed. "You're too old to be talking that kind of garbage. Don't you think your work in the marriage is worth anything? Sure you do. Look, Sherry. You know exactly what you want to do and how to do it. I don't really know why you're getting yourself so exercised."

"Nobody *likes* to fail. I thought I could make this marriage work. It's scary to decide to give it up. But I can't stand it anymore. It's idiotic that I should have to hide my work when Drew's home. I'd like to write on the weekends, if I feel like it. Or at night. I can't. As far as he knows, my writing career's over. Except for the calls I get to do shows

here and there. I've even stopped telling him about them
The last couple of times I've had interviews, I lied and told
Drew I was going shopping in town with Michelle. Christ!
It's insane. I want to enjoy this; I worked for it."

"You know what to do," Josie repeated.

"Yeah," Sherrill sighed. "I guess I just wanted to hear
myself say it out loud."

By the end of her mother's stay, Sherrill had decided to
face the possible consequences and have a talk with Drew.
She sat down with him in the living room one evening after
Perry had finally gone to sleep and said, "I don't think we
can keep going, Drew."

"What d'you mean?" He stared at her, baffled.

"Look, I'm not happy. You should be with someone who
wants to be a housewife and a mother. That's not me. I
thought I could do it, but it doesn't fit. I feel like I'm
playing a part here, and playing it so badly that if there was
an audience watching they'd boo me off the stage."

After a time, he said, "You're not happy?"

"I might as well be truthful," she said. "I'm a writer. I
want to write. I'm tired of arguing with you about every
little thing that has to do with my book. I had a career when
we met. I don't understand why my changing careers bothers
you so much."

He sat looking at his hands. "I love you!" he declared, as
if the statement gave him certain rights and privileges that
had been denied him. "All this time I thought we were
happy."

"*You* were happy," she corrected. "I've been rolling over
and playing 'good dog' for you, pretending I don't mind your
cracks about my work, about everything I've done that pleases
me and just seems to make you angry. What the hell difference does it make who earns how much? I don't care. But
you do. I've been going crazy trying to convince myself I
could be happy with you. I can't do it. Surely you don't
want to live with someone who isn't in love with you?"

"I thought we were *happy*," he repeated, wounded.

"I'm sorry," she said helplessly. "I know you probably
won't believe it, but I really did try, and I'm terribly sorry."

A week later, he moved out.

Chapter 22

Anne was away for three weeks. Dene had no idea where she'd gone, but assumed Anne had decided to take a vacation. While she was away, Dene watered Anne's plants and stacked her mail on the kitchen table. The night before Anne was due to return home, Dene went out to buy milk and cream, a dozen eggs, a pound of bacon, a loaf of bread, and, as an afterthought, a bunch of yellow baby mums. She put the food in the refrigerator, left the flowers in a vase on the coffee table in the living room, then hurried downstairs to change. She was having dinner with her mother and Anthony.

She still found it strange to see her mother with Anthony and kept wanting, foolishly, to smile at the sight of the two of them. They fussed over each other in small ways that were touching to witness. Anthony was an amiable, witty man with a generous nature. It was obvious to Dene from their first meeting that he adored Moira, and often he'd say to Dene, "Isn't she lovely? I find it extraordinary that someone like your mother would marry an old codger like me."

"You're not an old codger, and she finds you equally extraordinary," Dene disagreed fondly. He was effortlessly good company, wonderfully easy to talk to. They'd fallen into the habit of taking Sunday afternoon walks together, chatting as they strolled arm in arm along the rolling downhill expanses of Churchill Park. He was fatherly, and gave sound advice whenever Dene asked his opinion. Saturday afternoons he donned his whites and went to his club for lawn bowling. Periodically Dene would accompany her mother; the two of them would sit on a bench on the sidelines quietly watching and commenting on the game.

She could see why her mother loved him. He wasn't a particularly handsome man—about five foot ten, with a fringe of silver-white hair, hooded brown eyes, a brushy white moustache, and an undistinguished nose—but he exuded goodness and caring. He was precisely the father Dene would have chosen for herself, the perfect husband for her mother. Moira had grown younger since their marriage, and more active than she'd ever been. She regularly telephoned Dene to say, "We've got tickets for the O'Keefe [or the St. Lawrence, or the Royal Alex, or some other theatre] for Saturday. We'll collect you sixish, darling. Anthony's made reservations at Fenton's [or Winston's, or Fernando's, or half a dozen other superb restaurants] for six-thirty. Do wear something pretty, won't you, darling? You look so lovely when you make a bit of an effort."

Rather than being offended, as she might once have been, by her mother's admonitions to dress up and be pretty, Dene was amused. When she saw that their outings were going to become routine, she relented and bought several new outfits to wear. Her reward was a stream of plays, musicals, ballets, and operas she'd never otherwise have seen. She was disinclined to attend shows alone, and until Jamie left, Anne had been too busy.

With her mother and Anthony due to leave soon for Palm Beach for the winter, Dene anticipated spending the majority of her evenings at home. It was becoming more of a wrench each year to wave them off at the airport, knowing it would be five months before she saw them again.

"You're always more than welcome to join us, you know," Moira said, as Dene was leaving. "You're really so stubborn. There's no reason why you couldn't spend a fortnight. Some sun and fresh air would do you a world of good."

"There's ample material to photograph," Anthony contributed. "Do think about it. You could come anytime, anytime at all."

She returned to the apartment toying with the idea of taking two weeks off to join her mother and Anthony in Palm Beach. She was about to get ready for bed when the doorbell rang. Looking out the front window, she saw Charlie on the porch and went out to let him in.

"I've got a pizza," he said. "Hungry?"

"I had dinner with my mother. Come in, if you like. You can eat your pizza here."

"You're sure?"

"Come in," she said with a smile.

He hung his plaid jacket over the doorknob and settled himself cross-legged on the floor with the pizza on his lap. "I took this babe to the movies," he explained. "I had this whole format lined up, right? Movie, something to eat after, maybe a drink somewhere, a little boogie. She was such a pain in the ass, I walked out and left her in the movie. Remind me never to get involved again with a customer. Especially one on the make." He shook his head and opened the box to remove a slice of the pizza. His mouth full, he asked, "You don't have any beer, do you?"

"I've got some Cokes," she answered, fascinated by the sight of him on her living room floor. He seemed very at home.

"A Coke'd be great." He grinned at her, his cheeks bulging, then swallowed and said, "You don't really mind, do you? I didn't feel like going straight home. That chick really depressed me. You know what she did?"

"What?"

"She sat there through the first half of the flick explaining every goddamned thing to me like I was some kind of moron. I can't stand it, people talking all the way through a movie. Anyway, I didn't say anything, you know, thinking she'd get the hint and shut up. No way. Drove me nuts, so I split, left her sitting there talking to herself."

"I'll get your Coke."

"You look sensational," he said, suddenly noticing her dress. "I've never seen you all dolled up before. You ought to do it more often. That's a really dynamite dress."

"Thank you." Smiling, she went out to the kitchen for his Coke. She had trouble accepting the fact that Charlie was older than she was. He seemed so young, except for his middle, which had begun to thicken perceptibly, and his hair, which had started graying here and there.

"Sure you don't want a piece?" he asked, holding a wedge in the air.

"Honestly." She sat down on the floor with her back against one of the Parson's chairs, watching him eat.

"You got some new stuff up, I see," he observed, pointing with the pizza at the wall over the fireplace, then shook his head. "Goddamned great stuff. You're nuts not to sell it."

"No one would buy it."

"They'd stand in line to buy it and pay top dollar. You know what your problem is, Dene?"

"What?"

"No confidence."

"You think so?" She smiled at him again.

"I mean it," he said seriously. "I had your talent, I wouldn't waste my time sitting home nights staring at my master-pieces. I'd be selling my stuff and out having one helluva good time."

"What's your idea of a good time?" she asked, curious.

"Going out, maybe to a movie, a disco, maybe a concert at Massey Hall. I don't know. Not sitting around, that's for sure. How come you don't have a TV set?"

"I don't know," she said, looking around the room, feeling swamped by Charlie's tremendous energy.

"They're good company, you know."

"I suppose they are. I've never thought about it."

"Think of all the old people, shut-ins. All they've got is the tube. The tube's like a friend. You know?"

"You're probably right."

"We should go out one night," he said, starting on his third slice.

"All right," she said quietly.

"Yeah?" He beamed at her. "For sure?"

"If you like. Why not?"

"Hey, terrific! How about next Saturday?"

"It's my last night with my mother and Anthony before they leave for Florida."

"Okay. Friday."

"All right."

"I can't believe it!" he said, closing the lid on the box and making a face. "Man, that is rank pizza! Don't ever go to that place over on Yonge. It's the pits." He leaned on one hip to pull a handkerchief out of his pocket and wiped his hands, all the while shaking his head. "I really can't believe it. Three years later, you're finally willing to go out with me."

"You never asked me before, Charlie."

"You weren't in the right place."

"What d'you mean?"

"I mean your head wasn't in the right place."

"Maybe it wasn't," she agreed thoughtfully.

He picked up the can of Coke and drank it down in two long swallows, mopped his mouth and beard with the handkerchief, then crushed the empty container with his hand and plonked it down on top of the pizza box before getting to his feet. "I'm gonna split. Where's your garbage?"

"That's all right. Leave it."

"You're sure?"

"Just leave it."

"Well, okay. I'll call you during the week, we'll figure out the time for Friday."

"Fine," she said, rather relieved he was going. She needed time now to reconcile herself to the fact that she'd just accepted a date.

"My aunt gets back tomorrow, eh?" he said, pulling on his jacket. "Where'd she go, anyway?"

"I don't know. I thought maybe you did."

"Nope. Didn't say word one to me. Well, listen, thanks for letting me come barging in. You don't mind I came by, do you?"

"Not at all."

"Thanks. I'm crazy for your hair," he said, touching her hair briefly before opening the door. "Greatest hair I ever saw. Talk to you later, eh?" He let himself out.

She sighed, bent to pick up the Coke can and pizza box, and carried them to the kitchen. She was just going into the bathroom when she heard a noise overhead and stopped, wondering if Charlie had come back and gone up to Anne's apartment for some reason. She stood listening, hearing faint footsteps. After a moment, there was silence again. She waited, but heard nothing more. If it was Charlie, he was either staying the night upstairs or looking for something. If it wasn't Charlie, who could it be? Anne wasn't due back yet.

She went for the keys and walked upstairs to try the door. Locked. She knocked but got no answer, so used her key. The lights were off on the second floor but, looking up the darkened staircase, she could see a glow from Anne's bedroom. Apprehensive, she started slowly up the stairs, and came to an abrupt halt in the doorway, startled.

In the pale light from the bedside lamp Anne was stand
ing nude in front of the full-length mirror, her robe hanging
down over her arms. She stood in profile to the mirror, with
her head turned toward it, intently studying herself. Dene
remained in the doorway, unable to speak, riveted by the
sight of Anne drawing her hands up the length of her body,
then cupping her breasts. Her body, Dene thought, was
exquisite, silvery in the thin light.

"I'm still a little bruised and swollen," Anne said, without moving, "but I'm happy with it." She kept her hands
cupped around her breasts for a moment longer, then placed
one hand flat on her belly.

"Pleased with what?" Dene asked, dry-mouthed. She had
an overpowering desire to run back downstairs for her camera so that she might photograph what she was seeing.
Anne's body was flawless, perfect, her breasts shapely and
full, her waist narrow, her hips slim, her legs long and
graceful. As Dene watched, Anne's hands continued to travel
slowly over her body.

"The face," Anne said. "I wouldn't have done it if I'd
known how painful it would be, far more painful than they
led me to expect." She held her breast in one hand; with
the fingertips of the other hand she touched the nipple.
"They make slits under the lower lids and pull up the loose
flesh there. Then they make other slits here and there, in
the hairline, tighten everything up." Her hands left her
breast and settled at the points of her hips, curved in over
her lower belly. "I've got yellow circles under my eyes, but
they'll fade in a day or two, and there's still some swelling.
Otherwise, I'm happy with it. What do you think?" She
turned her head without moving her body.

"You had a face-lift?" Dene asked stupidly, her eyes
fixed on Anne's hands. They were side by side on her belly
now, pointing into her groin.

"What do you think?" Anne repeated.

"Why?"

"Why?" Anne turned back to the mirror, her hands once
more gliding the length of her body before coming to rest at
her sides. She drew her shoulders back so that her breasts
lifted. "Because I've got this body that didn't look right
with a fifty-year-old head on top of it. I considered dyeing

my hair but I've decided not to. *Tell* me," she invited, presenting Dene with a second viewing of her face.

"You're beautiful. But you were beautiful before."

Anne shook her head. "Why shouldn't I," she said reasonably, "do something to improve myself? I couldn't see any reason not to."

"What are you going to do?" Dene asked, almost able to feel the camera in her hands, to see the prints of the pictures she'd take.

"I'm not going to *do* anything. Well, that's not strictly true. I'm going to see men, treat them on their own terms: have fun and forget it. I'm fed up sitting around here with nothing to do. I'm bored," she said. "I'm lonely. You get used to a man after three years. You get used to *feeling*."

"You could always go back to research."

"It was more boring than sitting around here, if you want to know the truth. Politicians' wives are just a notch above engineers' wives; they're all just wives." Her head slowly moved until she was once again contemplating her reflection. "Were you visiting your mother? You're all dressed up."

Dene looked down at herself, then at Anne. "We had dinner. They're leaving next week. Do you like what you see there?" she asked.

Anne nodded. "How old do you think I look now?"

"I can't answer that."

"Why not?"

"Different people look different ages."

"But I look younger," Anne prompted.

"You look younger."

"Good. That's all I wanted." She reached to pull one side of the robe up over her shoulder so that her breasts were now framed by the satiny fabric. "They use black thread," she said. "I looked unimaginably grotesque when I came down from the recovery room." She shuddered and drew the robe closed. "I had all kinds of time to think while I was at the hotel."

"What hotel?"

"I spent the last two and a half weeks at the Royal York. It's a wonderful place to remain anonymous. I didn't want to come home looking the way I did. I watched television, read the papers, and thought about my life. It didn't add up to much. It was actually depressing. So I've decided to put an end to that life and start a new one—new face, new clothes, the whole shooting match." She belted the robe and came across the room to look into Dene's eyes. "Do you know what they used to call me, the Radcliffe girls, the Harvard boys? Fast company. I made love with a boy for the first time when I was seventeen. I *loved* it. I was discriminating, of course. But I was—easy. Easy was a terrible thing to be in those days when all the other girls were saving up their virginity like dowries. I managed to live with it. The funny thing is, when I married I lost my interest. Or maybe he stopped interesting me. I don't know. It doesn't matter. I got my interest back after he left me. I like skin," she said softly, "the feel of someone's skin next to mine. You think I'm a fool, don't you? I can see it in your eyes."

"I don't think that. If it's what you wanted, the surgery, I mean, why shouldn't you do it?"

"Exactly!" Anne smiled for the first time, then at once relaxed her face. "I was told not to do that for another week or two."

"Does it hurt?"

"It pulls a little. You have the face of a child," she said, touching her hand to Dene's cheek. "Innocent. I'm shocking you."

"No." Dene straightened and unhooked her hands which she belatedly realized she'd been holding clasped in front of her. "If you're all right, I guess I'll go back down. I came up because I thought maybe Charlie was here. Or a prowler. I did knock."

"I know. I heard you."

"How did you know it was me?"

"I know your footsteps. It's all right," Anne said softly. "I'm not losing my mind, or making a pass at you. I'm just trying to get a few years' more mileage out of the equipment."

Dene didn't know what to say.

"I'm going to have a drink. Would you like one?" Anne invited.

"Uh, no, thanks. I'll be going now."

"You wanted to photograph me, didn't you?" Anne said

surprisingly. Without waiting for an answer, she said. "Wait until the swelling and the bruises are gone."

The moment Anne expressed her willingness, Dene lost any desire to photograph her. "I've had a long day," she said evasively. "I'm glad you're all right. I'll see you in the morning. We could have lunch if you like."

"Tomorrow," Anne said vaguely.

Dene turned and started down the stairs.

"Thank you for the flowers," Anne said. "You're very sweet."

Downstairs, Dene undressed and climbed under the shower, thinking about Anne, those strange minutes upstairs and the way Anne's hands had traveled back and forth over her body. She wondered what Charlie's reaction would be to this news; she wondered what Anne thought she'd accomplished by her face-lift. It did make her look slightly younger. What Dene couldn't understand was why she'd subjected herself to pain for such small gains.

After her shower, she looked at herself critically in the mirror on the back of the bedroom door, the image of Anne's silvery body superimposing itself upon her own. There was utterly no similarity. Dene was larger-boned, taller, more angular. Anne, although quite tall, gave the impression of being small, magnificently formed, totally female. Dene put on her nightgown and went to the kitchen to make a cup of tea. Seeing Anne had triggered her thinking about Charlie. Could she make love with him? "I couldn't," she whispered aloud, hoping that wasn't what he had in mind. While she could readily see Anne's sexuality, and found the sight of the woman nude before her mirror somehow very appropriate, she couldn't even consider the subject of her own sexuality. She wasn't ready for that yet, didn't know if she ever would be. The only man with whom she felt comfortable was Anthony, because he was elderly and kind and safely married to her mother.

Sitting at the kitchen table with her tea, she replayed the incident upstairs. She knew she'd never forget stepping into the doorway to see Anne standing before the mirror, the light casting a silvery glow over her slender body. If only she'd had her camera. . . .

Chapter 23

It was surprising how quickly their situations became reversed. When Jamie first met Lucienne, she looked up to him as someone well established in the business. She was an assistant director—which translated into a glorified fetch-and-carry girl. Within a year of their moving in together, it was Lucienne who was well established, and Jamie's status, while remaining fixed, had altered in view of her ascendancy. By comparison she'd surpassed him, and he felt decidedly uncomfortable at times because of it. When they were among their French-speaking friends, it was Lucienne who was lauded, recognized, exclaimed over. When they were among the English-speaking, Jamie was greeted with excitement and eagerness, and Lucienne was obliged to take a back seat. Initially, both were delighted with this consistent shifting of acclaim; it added a certain delicious flavor to their being together.

When they were at home, life was quite ordinary. They had rented a farmhouse in the country. Jamie tended the sizable vegetable garden he'd carefully laid out, then planted, weeded, and generally nurtured. Lucienne prepared their evening meals with her typically effortless panache. They spent the evenings listening to music, or watching rerun films on television, or making love in whatever place they happened to be when the impulse took them. One of Lucienne's greatest attractions was her willingness, even her insistence, on making love in unusual settings—to be within feet of other people, yet well hidden from unwelcome eyes while they coupled frenetically behind some bushes in a public park, or even in a football stadium, added a further splash of excitement to what was already a highly pleasurable pastime.

From time to time he thought about Anne, and even sent her a Christmas card the first year he lived in Montreal, as he did Sherrill. Sherrill had either moved or simply not bothered to respond; they'd lost touch. Anne didn't reply either, but it didn't upset him. He'd made the effort to maintain contact; if she didn't keep it up, that was the end of it. For some reason, he kept the only two Christmas cards he ever received from Sherrill. He knew she'd been married because her second card bore both hers and her husband's names. He wondered what sort of man she'd married.

The rest of his Toronto friends kept in touch and some even came to visit at the farm when they were working in Montreal, or passing through on their way to the Charlottetown Festival, or to The Neptune in Halifax, or Theatre New Brunswick.

All in all, he felt happy. Yet as Lucienne became more and more in demand, and he continued to do what he'd done before without really progressing, he couldn't help feeling he'd arrived at the dead-end level of success in Canada: steady employment, a minimum of acclaim, and a future of alarmingly foreseeable sameness.

During their second year together, Lucienne subtly changed. She was more temperamental than before, less openly respectful of his accomplishments and his work. Small comments were made when they were out together; when he lay sprawled on the living room floor of an evening, working out a radio or television script, she moved noisily around the house as if he were engaged in a purely self-indulgent hobby that required him to clutter up the place, rather than being involved in a serious effort to continue his employment. He couldn't understand her attitude. He was supportive of her efforts, and truthful when she asked him what he thought of this role, or that one, she'd played in a film. He was silently amazed at how quickly Lucienne's success overtook their lives and transformed them. In just over a year she went from being someone who might have potential all the way to stardom. She and Jamie actually worked together on several films and he observed, proud of her and pleased by her instinctive professionalism. She was far more than another pretty face with a pair of decent-looking breasts, attached to assist where her talent failed. She had character, insight, a natural ability to understate that was vital to a screen performer.

After her fifth film, she began to talk avidly of the possibility of becoming a director: she'd been critically bitten by a film virus and wanted to write, star in, and direct a film of her own; she wanted to make statements. He couldn't, nor had he any desire to, minimize her ambition. A woman of perception who'd undoubtedly make an intelligent film statement, she was traveling away from him at a giddying speed. It saddened and frightened him.

From the beginning he'd understood that their chance of a future together was negligible at best, but hoped they would create something more durable than they had. Their futures seemed to have been prewritten somewhere—like a script with pages withheld until the final day of filming. By the end of the second year he began, unable to help himself, to display his unhappiness in their decreasing free time together.

He missed Toronto and his friends there. He began mentally preparing himself for the end, for his probable return to Toronto. A little irritable, and nervous, he was drinking more than he ever had; he'd gained more weight since leaving Anne. He'd made the transition from young, comedic roles to middle-aged comedic and serious roles. Fearful of losing his talent, he fretted more over his work than he ever had. His hair was thinner and graying; his belly had thickened. Where once he'd found his reflection in the mirror tolerable, he now tried to avoid mirrors altogether. They seemed to reflect far more than just his physical image; they were depicting a quasi-successful, aging man without roots. He spent more and more time on the garden, turning the earth to ready it for the next spring's planting. He carried weeds and vegetable matter to the compost heap he'd created at the bottom of the field nearest the farmhouse. He studied seed catalogs, trying to lose himself in planning next year's harvest. He spent hours painstakingly painting the miniature lead soldiers he'd ordered from England. The once companionable silences between himself and Lucienne turned uncomfortable, fraught with all sorts of unspoken arguments. Both of them recognized the signs of disintegration but chose to say nothing.

Lucienne went off for three months' location work on an American film. When she returned home, Jamie knew at once she'd become involved with someone else. She couldn't quite look him in the eye. When she shied away from his caress, he blew up.

"You went off for three bloody months and you've found yourself someone else!" he declared. "Why the hell don't you just admit it? Who was it? The producer, the director, the cameraman? It was someone. I know how it works. I've *been* there, remember?"

"All right," she said evenly. "I did. Does that satisfy you?"

"Who was it?"

"You have no need to know that."

"I've got a bloody need. Who?"

She named the producer of the film. He wanted to hit her. Instead he raged about the living room, kicking the furniture and knocking things off tables. "You bloody slut! You've got no fucking *loyalty*." Even as he raged, he knew he hadn't the right to become as upset and angry as he was, but he couldn't help himself. He was wounded and had nowhere to direct his hurt but at its source.

"I am not going to lie to you," she said quietly. "I have no need to defend myself, either. I am not obligated to do those things. You know how it is with a film company; you know these things."

"I know *all* about it!" he shouted. "I know all about you, and how you operate! You've got the morals of a bloody alley cat!"

"I will not listen to this," she insisted.

"You'll bloody listen!"

"I will not!" She turned and slammed out of the house to walk away up the road.

He stood on the porch and watched her disappear into the distance. She'd be back, he knew, but it no longer mattered. They were doomed; their allotted time had run out before he was ready. His anger and hurt grew, proliferating. By the time she returned to the house two hours later, he was ready to sail into her again with bitter accusations about her gross disloyalty, her breaking of all the small promises they'd made to one another.

"We talked about getting *married*!" he ranted. "I wanted to *marry* you!"

"I have never said we would marry."

"You bloody little *liar*! We talked about it."

"We talked about it," she conceded. "But we did not agree."

Ultimately, they did agree, shouting, to part.

Once this agreement was reached, they were both miserably contrite.

"I did not intend it to be this way, eh," Lucienne claimed, truthfully.

"I believe you," he admitted, and went on to apologize for the months of aggrieved behavior he'd subjected her to. She apologized for failing to honor him with the honesty he deserved. They made love sadly, sweetly, and then Jamie commenced the long-delayed preparations for his withdrawal from her life. Nearly three years of a fine relationship had come to a close. He felt ill with the sudden loss both of his justified anger and of the only woman he'd deeply cared for.

There were commitments remaining to be fulfilled in Montreal, so he moved back into the city. For the first time, he felt the advancing dilemma of the second half of his life. At almost forty he was compelled to acknowledge that if he didn't devote himself with some dedication to his career he might very well end up with nothing. He felt he had little enough as it was, without Lucienne. For months, when he went to bed at night, he ached, missing her. He felt incomplete. His only remaining alternative was to concentrate on his career.

In a business where simply keeping afloat from month to month was a major accomplishment, he couldn't afford to be cavalier. He would attend to his career and make a name for himself. Having made this decision, he felt better and seemed able to breathe more deeply; the ache diminished. He slowly relaxed. As the months passed, he felt more and more like himself, now that his deplorable behavior with Lucienne had been placed at a distance. He'd acted badly and, to make up for it, stayed in touch with her to applaud her continued success. Bearing him no malice, she reciprocated by keeping him current with her movements here and there via witty little notes. Finally, gratifyingly, they'd managed to come past their grievances with each other to evolve as friends.

His frame of mind lighter, and reasonably well directed, he began socializing once again. He met Julie at a party. They began dating. He found her warm, even motherly.

When she invited him to move in with her and her two sons, he accepted. He liked her; she was good company, pleasant to be with and undemanding. Her two boys came as a bonus. With them he was able to enjoy much of what he believed he'd missed with Mark and Stephen, who now seemed to him like complete strangers. He'd seen them only once in the previous four years and the meeting had been an utter failure. They'd had nothing to say to one another. After that, he'd reconciled himself to their absence from his life. Yet there was rarely a day when he didn't think longingly of them.

His time with Julie lasted six months. They parted amicably, as friends, and Jamie returned to Toronto. Once settled back in Toronto, he found himself missing Julie's boys. He often confused them in his mind with Mark and Stephen; the faces of the two sets of boys became frighteningly interchangeable. He thought constantly of telephoning to talk to his sons but was intimidated by his memory of their last awkward meeting. Dozens of times he went to the telephone to call them. He couldn't. He was afraid.

He rented an apartment on St. George Street, in the Annex—originally the wealthy residential area of the city some hundred odd years before and now considered the "inner core"—moved in, bought some furniture, and set about renewing old contacts. He liked to walk the tree-lined streets of the district, streets busy day and night with the traffic of university students and the upwardly mobile families who'd bought the large old homes of the area and were busily restoring them with a vengeance. Every other house was having its façade sand-blasted or its attic renovated. Plastic-domed skylights graced almost every roof. Shutters and thriving plants were de rigueur, as were coach lamps and large mod numerals beside the front doors. The city had changed during his years away; to the good, he thought, noting the several small new theaters that had sprung up around town, as well as the ongoing good plays produced at the St. Lawrence Centre. Theater appeared to be not only alive here, but flourishing. He went out to reestablish his contacts with hope for his own career.

It was purely by accident that he ran into Dene one afternoon downtown on Yonge Street where she was engaged, typically, in photographing the sleazy Yonge Street "strip" between Dundas and Queen streets in glaring, unrelenting daylight.

He called out to her. She turned to stare blankly at him for a few seconds before her mouth relaxed into a delighted smile and, replacing the lens cover on her Pentax, she came hurrying toward him, exclaiming, "Are you back in the city now?"

She seemed quite altered, more open and less attenuated. In fact she looked altogether healthy. She even submitted to his hug with some degree of willingness, which came as a complete surprise in view of the painful shyness and discomfort she'd previously exhibited toward him.

"It's great to see you! Have you got time for a coffee?"

"Sure," she agreed readily, taken off guard by her excitement at seeing him again. She'd always liked him. Of course she'd felt bad for Anne when they'd split up, primarily because of the broken-spirited way in which Anne had taken the breakup, but that hadn't altered her fondness for Jamie. "Are you living here now?" she asked as he directed her into the nearest coffee shop.

"Just got back," he answered, settling them into a booth. "How are you? You look wonderful. Still taking pictures, I see. Are you still keeping them all to yourself?"

"I wouldn't have the nerve to show them to anyone. We never," she remembered, "did your photographs."

"Why don't we do them now that I'm back?"

"All right. I'd like that. Are you in a show here?"

"I will be. I've got a radio drama lined up, and I'm working on a few other things. How," he asked tentatively, "is Anne? I take it you haven't moved."

"She's all right," she said carefully. "I haven't moved. Charlie's still around, too, and the same as ever. He comes over with pizza sometimes, when his dates don't turn out the way he hopes they will. His store on Queen Street's really doing well: He's expanded, knocked down the wall to the place next door, jazzed it all up, and he's doing record business. Have you been down to Queen Street yet?" she asked eagerly.

"Not yet, no." He smiled at her, scarcely able to believe this was the same woman he'd known before.

"You should," she said. "It's wonderful. There's a lot of

renovation, some very good specialty stores and nice little restaurants. The city's changed."

"So have you."

"Oh, me. I'm the same as ever," she said dismissingly. It wasn't quite the truth. Some mornings being forty came as a shock. She didn't feel that old and couldn't honestly believe she looked it. But there were times when she felt that old, and older. It seemed then as if she'd lived forever. Her toy-designing days were so far in the past that occasionally she wondered if she'd actually done that. At moments, she felt newborn and weak at the knees.

"You have changed," he disagreed. "A lot. You look better than I've ever seen you."

"I've come to terms with . . . my past, I suppose. It was hard to do."

"I know," he sympathized. "It's never easy. Tell me, how is Anne?"

"Such a lot has happened," she said, biting on her finger. "I'm not sure I should tell you this. I don't know how I feel about telling you."

"Has something happened to her?" he asked.

She looked off into space. "Some time back," she said, "she went away for a few weeks. No one knew where she'd gone. Charlie and I assumed she'd taken a vacation. Anyway, when she came back she'd had a face-lift." She turned to look again at Jamie. "I couldn't see that it made any difference. She looked somewhat younger, but it wasn't a startling change. Well, she had it done. Then she went out and bought herself an entirely new wardrobe of simply fabulous clothes. She looked . . ." She shook her head unable to describe how Anne had been transformed. "She looked *stunning*. She let her hair grow long and wore it in a loose knot on top of her head. Just the faintest bit of makeup. She didn't even resemble the woman who sat beside me on the plane. That's how we met. Did you know that?"

"I think I did."

"Oh. Well, she started going out. I didn't find out about all this until much later. She'd go downtown to the hotels, the Windsor Arms or the Park Plaza, sit discreetly at a table in the bar and get herself picked up. Not every night, but maybe two or three times a month. She'd wear an exquisite dress, fix her hair, put on some makeup, and take off.

Sometimes she'd date the men she met half a dozen times; sometimes she saw them only once. Some she brought home, with others she went to their rooms. She was having a great time, she told me, getting a lot of phone calls, invitations out. She spent all her free time shopping the boutiques on Yorkville, buying clothes. Every so often, I went with her. We'd have lunch in the Hazelton Lanes or at the Coffee Mill, then Anne would buy something—a two-hundred dollar pair of shoes, or a five-hundred-dollar dress. She seemed to have a limitless supply of money. When I asked her about it, in as roundabout way as I could, she said, 'It's been invested for years. It's about time I spent some of it.'

"I couldn't argue with that," she said, searching Jamie's eyes. "After all, it was her life, her money. And she seemed so happy. Really happy. As I said, I had no idea about the hotel business. I guess I assumed she was going to a lot of parties, or something . . . meeting people.

"Well." She paused to take a deep breath. "One night about two years ago, I heard her come in with someone. It was about ten o'clock. I was watching TV—Charlie talked me into buying one—and heard them go upstairs. About two hours later—the late show was on—I heard a noise, a sound I can't describe. I turned down the volume on the set and went to stand near the door, listening. There was a thud, a heavy thud like something falling. I opened my door and stood in the hallway. I didn't like the sound of it. You know?"

"Christ!" Jamie murmured. "Go on. What happened?"

"I felt scared. I don't know why; I just had this feeling that something wrong was going on up there. Then I heard her scream, this terrible high scream. I couldn't think what to do. I ran back into my apartment to call the police, then grabbed the first thing I saw, the poker from the fireplace. I found the spare set of keys Anne used to keep at my place and let myself into her apartment.

"I went racing up the stairs to her bedroom." She shook her head and covered her mouth with her hand, then lit a cigarette. "I didn't even think. I just saw him and hit him across the shoulders with the poker. He whirled around and I hit him in the arm, then across the knee. I didn't want him to get away; I wanted him to be there when the police arrived.

"It was horrible," she said in a near-whisper. "Anne was lying on the floor. There was blood all over the place. I thought he'd killed her. I was terrified."

"*Christ!*" Jamie repeated, paling.

"When the police came, she refused to press charges. So I lied, Jamie. I said I'd heard her screaming, and when I came up to find out what was going on, he'd tried to attack me, too. I didn't want him to get away with what he'd done. And I was afraid he might come back to do it again. So he was arrested. I said the poker was Anne's, that I'd picked it up in her living room. I *lied*. I testified against him and he went to prison."

"What about Anne?"

"It wasn't as bad as I'd first thought. But it was pretty bad. She was in the hospital for a week. She's never been the same since. She won't go out. It's all I can do to get her to go for a walk, or a meal, or to a movie. I honestly think that if it wasn't for me and Charlie, she'd lie down and let herself die. She goes up and down. Some days are better than others. Most of the time she just stays upstairs reading or watching television."

"It's a dangerous game," Jamie said somberly. "I've met a few women who've picked up some bad numbers. A woman I knew in Montreal had almost the same thing happen to her. She met this guy at a party. He offered to take her home. When they got there, he beat the shit out of her. I'm sorry to hear that happened to Anne, really sorry."

"She's better now," Dene said lamely. "Not the same as she was, but better." She put out her cigarette. "Let's change the subject. Okay?"

"Sure."

"Where are you living now?" she asked.

"On St. George. I've got an apartment in one of the hold-out houses that hasn't been done over yet. It has a fireplace and I've got the use of the garden." While he talked, knowing Dene wanted to be distracted, he couldn't help feeling he was at last seeing the real Dene, and the woman was very appealing. She had courage and loyalty; she'd also softened with time. Her hair had grown very long; silvery streaks showed through the red. Her face was still angular but not so fleshless, and her eyes were bolder than before. She seemed to be on the verge of something; perhaps it was

to be her emergence into the public eye. He felt a sudden
surge of protectiveness toward her and knew, in that moment,
that they were going to be lovers. He knew it intuitively,
and could almost feel her long, narrow body against his; he
also knew she'd be shy and unpracticed. This insight heightened her appeal for him. There was something about Dene
that he could only describe in his own mind as "lovely." It
had to do with the purity of her thoughts and actions, and
with the way in which she sought to protect her friend—her
loyalty to Anne, and her discretion. "You're beautiful," he
said recklessly, and watched the color rise from her neck to
her face, to the very tips of her ears. "You really are," he
insisted, as if she'd disagreed.

She had no idea what to say or do. For the first time in
more than ten years a man she found attractive was claim-
ing to find her desirable. Her inner response was so profoundly receptive she found it all at once impossible to meet
his eyes. It was as if he'd read her thoughts and presented
them back to her in perfect sequence. After a moment, she
shook her head and then, for want of anything better, looked
at her wristwatch. "I could take your picture this afternoon,
if you've got time."

"Perfect. Where?"

"I don't know. We could go to Allen Gardens. The park's
nice at this time of the year, with the leaves starting to
turn. The light's very good in the late afternoon. Have you
ever noticed that?" she asked him, momentarily distracted.
"It only happens in the late spring and early fall. There's a
fullness to the light after three or four o'clock, so that everything seems to be very—real. Realer than real, somehow."

"I think I know what you mean," he said, smiling again.
He, too, then checked his watch. "Why don't we walk over
to the park and do it?"

They went to Jamie's apartment. She was so nervous she
could scarcely talk. They both knew why she was there. Yet
he applied no pressure at all. He opened a bottle of wine
and they sat down to talk.

"It's upsetting," he told her, "that business with Anne. I
can't stop thinking about it."

"I know," she agreed. "Sometimes I have nightmares about
going up there and finding her on the floor, covered with

blood. He hurt her so terribly, Jamie. No one had ever hurt her, in any way. Of course, she was wounded when her husband left. But that was different. No one's ever hurt me, for that matter. Somehow, though, I think I could—handle it. I'm not sure I can explain that."

"I know what you mean. What you're saying is that you wouldn't close yourself off from the world the way she's done."

"No, no. I did that. I did it when I ran away to New York and became someone else for four years. I just think I'd find a way to *absorb* it. Oh, I don't know." She sank back against the sofa cushions and stared at him. He kissed her, then drew away to sit holding her hand.

When they progressed from exploratory kisses on the sofa into his bedroom, she was so tense she couldn't unbend her limbs. He was gentle and considerate. "I'm happy just holding you," he murmured, stroking her slowly, lovingly.

Gradually she unbent sufficiently to begin to feel a little pleasure. The turbulence of her reactions, once released, shook her. She was plunged into a state of blind, almost insatiable need that he seemed eager to try to satisfy. "You're lovely, lovely," he said repeatedly, and she could feel herself flowering in the warmth of his munificent approval.

They talked for hours, lying naked side by side in his bed, exploring each other's thoughts and pasts with a freedom engendered by their lack of any permanent attachment. She was able to tell about Jake and Mimi, and then listened avidly to his interpretation of what she'd revealed. His analyses and comments were valid and intelligent. He helped her make sense of what had, for too long, been thoroughly incomprehensible.

"It didn't have anything to do with you," he told her. "I think we all want to feel guilty when something like that happens, when someone we love chooses someone else to fall in love with. We think it has to be some fault of ours. But it isn't. It's simply the way things happen. People's feelings change."

He told her about Lucienne, and of his feeling of failure with Mark and Stephen. "It's the one great failure of my life," he admitted. "I spent entire days thinking about them but I can't make myself telephone. I'm afraid to try, and fail again with them."

He talked of Julie and her two boys, and of his sometime
fears for his future. She listened closely, aware of the trust
he'd placed in her, and tried to offer well-considered replies.

From the outset the relationship distressed her. She hated
having to lie to Anne about where she was going on those
evenings when she went out to meet Jamie. She felt treacherous being involved with someone who'd caused her friend
pain. Yet from that first afternoon they met again, Dene
guessed that Jamie represented another step she had to take
in her own evolutionary process. She wasn't in love with
him, but she loved him and was profoundly glad of his
interest in her. She wished she were in love with him, but
she also knew he was simply fond of her. Neither of them
could push fondness past its limitations into love.

She assisted him over the transitional period of his return
to the city. She went with him to several parties and tried
not to mind when he touted her proudly as a photographer
of exceptional abilities, bringing her forward into the lime-
light where he was determined she belonged. The result of
all this was a number of calls from actors wanting glossies
comparable to those she'd done for Jamie. She did the jobs
but refused to take credit for the pictures. She felt vaguely
threatened by the idea of people she didn't know requesting
her to work for them. She had no strenuous objection to
photographing Jamie's friends, but when Jamie recommended
her for the job of still photographer on a film that was
scheduled to be shot in Toronto that winter, she flatly
refused.

"It's a great chance," he argued. "It'll do your career a lot
of good."

"I don't *want* a career. I'm someone who *takes* photographs.
I'm *not* a photographer. There's a lot of difference."

"You *are* a photographer," he told her. "Everything you do
is a photograph, whether you think it, say it, or actually
photograph it. Some people write and other people are writers. There's a real distinction and you happen to fit into the
being category rather than the *working at* one. Take the job,
Dene. You need to do it; you need to get those photographs
off the walls and into the world where people can see them.
You're too talented to be such an unrelenting purist."

"I'm not a purist. I'm a coward. There's a distinction
too."

He laughed and put his arms around her—a gentling gesture. "You're not a coward. Cowards don't return to the scene of the crime and then spend years trying to make sense of the crime. They just run like hell."

"I ran."

"But you came back; you've stayed to work it out."

She began to smile.

She took the job and loved it. She could maintain her feeling of invisibility on the set while actively participating in the process of filming. The director was ecstatic with her efforts and began recommending her for jobs with directors on other films. Whether she wanted it or not, she had a functioning career. Jamie had been right: she did need an audience for her work. In astonishingly short order, she had one. She had to hire an answering service to keep up with the flood of telephone calls; she had to have stationery printed, and a rubber copyright stamp made up with her name on it; she had to hire a part-time bookkeeper, and to open a business bank account. She was a professional, with far too much work being offered, and a lover who represented a potentially fatal threat to her one important friendship—that with Anne.

At last, she knew she had to make a decision. It wasn't easy. In the six months they'd been seeing each other, she and Jamie had become more than lovers; they were friends, and she was reluctant to lose him. She felt circumstances were forcing her to give up one good friend in order to keep another. It struck her as horribly unfair.

"We're going to be friends," Jamie said one evening, as if again having read her thoughts. "Why don't we break it off now and wish each other luck. I know it's got to be rough for you where Anne's concerned. I know how much you care about her."

"But what about you?" She had vague fears for him that had to do with the lack of interest he took in his own well-being. He seemed to live from day to day without concern for how the way in which he lived might affect his health or his future. She glimpsed hints of defeat in his attitude, and feared he thought himself unworthy of a future.

"Don't you worry about me," he said with a grin that was so typically, heart-warmingly Jamie she could only put her arms around him and rest her head on his shoulder, wishing there were some way she could repay all he'd done for her. An offer of friendship was too insubstantial a reward for the infusion of hope he'd given her. Even her offer of friendship had to include, of necessity, certain conditions in order to protect Anne.

"If only I could invite you to drop by sometime," she said sadly, "or to come for dinner. I'll miss you." She raised her head to look at him. "I wish you could find someone to really love, someone who'd really love you. It's what you need, you know. You deserve that, Jamie."

"So do you," he said, moved. "It's what we all need, if we had the courage to admit it."

"I'll never marry again," she said solemnly. "I couldn't risk it. I'd be afraid. I've gone past the point where I'd ever be willing to place so much of myself in someone else. I don't think I want it. I'm happy as I am. And I owe you more than I can ever say for that."

"You don't owe me anything," he said firmly. "Send me an invitation to your first gallery showing. I'll come with champagne and roses."

She sniffed and smiled, collected the few things she'd kept at his apartment, and went on her way. He watched the door close after her, thinking it was a great pity he hadn't been able to love her. They might have had a damned good life together.

Dene went home—she actually thought of the apartment as home these days—and went directly upstairs to knock at Anne's door. "We're going out to dinner together," she stated.

Anne, clad in a once-smart gray skirt, a nondescript shirt, and a baggy red cardigan, flatly refused. "I'm not in the mood."

"We'll put you in the mood," Dene insisted, and took her by the arm to lead her upstairs. "You spend too much time alone here. If it wasn't for me and Charlie you'd never go out."

Anne pulled her arm free and looked accusingly at her friend. "You've come one hundred and eighty degrees, haven't you?" she said, her eyes narrowed. "You've gone from being the pathetic waif to playing the aggressive career woman. I'm not sure it suits you."

"Don't!" Dene said softly, stung. "You know I'm not that way at all. We're friends. I care about you. It's unhealthy living the way you do. Why don't you go back to your free-lance work and get out more? It'd be good for you. Won't you please change your clothes so we can go out?"

"Why?" Anne wanted to know.

"Because I love you. And I think I've made a mistake. I've gone along believing the best thing I could do for you was simply to leave you be. I also think," she said carefully, treading on dangerous territory, "that you've gone on blaming that insane man for too long."

"You think that's what I've done, that I've used him as an excuse?"

"Haven't you?"

"What difference would it make if I had?" Anne countered.

"It makes a lot of difference. Blaming someone else for your problems isn't ... worthy of you. If you like, I'll call Charlie and ask him to join us."

"I haven't said I'd go."

"Now you're being childish, playing games," Dene said wearily.

Anne started to snap back a reply but thought better of it. Her anger seeped away and she ran her hand over her hair, saying, "The only thing I'm too young for is a bed in the home. All right," she sighed. "Let's get the hell out of here. I'll find something decent to wear and buy *you* dinner."

Impulsively, sadly, Dene embraced the older woman, murmuring, "Don't talk about yourself that way. Don't *think* about yourself that way. You're important—to me, and to Charlie, to lots of people. If you could be important to yourself again, you'd see you've got plenty to live for."

"Don't ask for everything in one go," Anne said sagely, disengaging herself. "Be satisfied with the little steps I can take. It's not a game of 'Red Rover,' Dene. I can't ask, 'May I?' and have all my requests granted. I wish to Christ I could, but I am old enough to know better." She went off up the stairs to the bedroom and Dene remained on the landing wondering what it would take to return Anne to her formerly vital self. Perhaps, she thought, she was indulging in fantasies; perhaps the former Anne was gone forever.

Chapter 24

Drew found himself an apartment in the city and, almost overnight, turned into someone Sherrill no longer recognized. He hired a lawyer. She hired a lawyer. Bitter negotiations commenced. The things Drew's lawyer had to say didn't sound as if they could possibly have originated with Drew. In despair, she telephoned him at the office. He was cold. "You wanted this. I'm not going to give up my son without a fight."

"I'm not *fighting* you," she said, near to tears and struggling for self-control. "But be reasonable, Drew. How could you look after the baby? You'd have to hire someone. And why should I give you my *car*? I bought it with my own money. You're just not *thinking!* You're forcing me to defend myself."

"Let the lawyers handle it, Sherrill. Please don't call me here again. You've got my number at the apartment. If there's an emergency, you know where to reach me."

She was in the middle of a legalistic nightmare. Her lawyer advised her to go to the bank and withdraw half the money from the joint savings and checking accounts. When she got there, she discovered Drew had cleaned out both accounts. Panicked, she withdrew some money from her old, pre-marriage account, had Drew's name struck from the checking account, and deposited enough to cover checks she'd written in the past few days. This move by Drew frightened her. It was premeditatedly cruel. He knew she had only a few thousand dollars of her own, and that money wouldn't last very long. What would she do when she ran out? Her royalties weren't due for four months; even then, they usually arrived weeks late.

Unnerved after six months of fighting, she called her mother to explain the situation. "For God's sake, please don't tell me to make my own decisions now! I need help; I need good legal advice. Those two lawyers aren't going to be happy until blood's drawn. You should hear them talking to each other on the telephone. They practically smack their lips over all the offers, counteroffers, counter-counteroffers. Drew wants full custody of the baby. I want to pack everything right now and come home."

"Let me make some calls and I'll get back to you."

"When?"

"In a couple of hours. Go have a drink and try to calm down. I'll call you back."

Close to three hours later, the telephone rang. Flatly, Josie said, "You're in trouble. Either you stay put and fight it out or you stand a good chance of losing Perry. Fighting it out means staying home and showing what a model mother you are until this thing comes to a hearing. I've talked to a friend of my old friend Larry, a lawyer in New York. He says that unless Drew can prove negligence or moral turpitude on your part, the court usually decides in favor of the mother. If you go out of state with the baby, you'll be guilty of kidnapping. So whatever you do, stay right where you are."

"Kidnapping? We're talking about my own child, not somebody else's."

"I know that."

"I'm scheduled to tour with the new book on publication. I've got all kinds of commercials lined up in the city. Can't I even *work*?"

"Cancel the tour, but do the commercials and take the baby with you," Josie said encouragingly. "If you need to talk, call me anytime. Why don't you give Michelle a call and get her to come give you some moral support?"

"I think I will. That's a good idea. My God!" she exclaimed. "I can't believe this. He's turned into someone I don't know. He won't even *talk* to me."

"Did you expect him to quietly surrender and just walk away?" Josie said reasonably. "He thought he had a home, a wife, a family. Now he doesn't have one damned thing he thought he had. I feel sorry for him. You should, too. He doesn't have the resources you've got, or the resilience. You'll get over this eventually. I'm not sure he ever will."

"Fuck him! He didn't have to do it this way. I wasn't

going to ask him for anything. I was even willing to buy out his share of the house when I got my royalties. I'll tell you one thing, though: he'll have to *kill* me before he ever gets Perry."

"It won't come to that, sweetheart. I promise you it won't."

Michelle listened, then asked, "How long do you want me to come for?"

"I don't know. For as long as it takes, if you can stand it. I'll let you use the car so you can get back and forth into the city to work."

"That's okay. I've still got the trusty old Bug. I'll be there in a couple of hours. Put the coffee on."

Jean Diamond said, "Listen, it's all right. We can redirect the tour money into an advertising blitz. Don't worry about it. I know how rough it is. Start a new book," she suggested. "That'll keep your mind off it."

After Michelle had been living in the house close to six months, she said, "I think I'll start looking for a house up here. I'm getting a little fed up paying for a place I don't live in anymore."

"Listen, Misha," Sherrill said carefully. "I have to tell you I'm not going to stay. Once this business with Drew's settled, I'm going back to Canada."

"I'd still like to live out here. It's a pity you can't sell me this place. I'd buy it in a minute."

"I'll tell you what. I'm asking for the house as part of the settlement. If I get it, I'll sell it to you."

"Deal." They shook hands. Within weeks Michelle was permanently installed in the house. Her furniture filled a lot of the gaps left by what Drew had taken with him.

Sherrill went back to her writing; it became a way to block out the world. She'd always had a strong respect for words; now she felt something akin to reverence for them. Setting words on paper was an important commitment and she immersed herself in the process with renewed passion. The reality inside her head, the places and people she could move from her thoughts onto paper, satisfied her more fully than life ever had. And aside from the pleasure inherent in the process, writing allowed her to ignore her daily-growing impatience with Michelle.

She had hoped that life with Misha wouldn't be a depressing repeat of her first experience living with her in Manhattan. But Michelle hadn't changed much. She was still in the habit of dropping her clothes wherever she happened to be when she removed them; she still wore tatty, graying underwear; she still encouraged the latest of her married lovers—she was on her fourth now—and came away from her rendezvous with them to subject Sherrill to late-night, nonstop recitations of her grievances. She claimed she wanted to meet a single man who'd want, to marry her. As far as Sherrill could see, Misha did nothing to put herself into a position where she might meet a man like that.

With Drew's departure, the invitations from neighbors and couples in town dropped off sharply. As a separated woman, she represented some sort of undeclared threat to the married community. Even her novelty as a resident celebrity quickly wore off. She was tolerated because of Perry but not openly wooed as before. As a mother, she was a notch above the divorced women in town without children. Those women, she noticed, soon left to move up to Westport, or back into Manhattan where they'd be able to live with some hope of meeting and making friends.

Her novel, *Friendly Lovers,* received mixed reviews in both the trades and the media. But on the strength of *Success Without Glamour* it was optioned for the movies, picked up by the Literary Guild, presold to a paperback house, excerpted into a women's magazine, and sold in half a dozen countries. Fortunately Hank had insisted on a "pass-through" payment clause in her contract which stipulated that any income over and above the advance would be passed along to her within eight weeks of its receipt by the publishers. The money began to come in and she felt far less pressured, yet no less anxious.

Every so often she'd find herself standing—in her bedroom, or the kitchen or living room—staring into space, carefully examining the inner landscape of her mind. At these moments, depression sidled menacingly close and she had to take herself out of doors in order to escape the temptation to give up and succumb to all the ludicrous demands Drew and his lawyer continued to make. She fled from the glimpses of reality that seemed like warnings signposted along that inner landscape. She feared a settlement would never be reached and she'd spend the rest of her life imprisoned in the house with Michelle.

Michelle seemed oblivious to Sherrill's growing discontent. She bemoaned her fate with hateful regularity, and was uninterested in Sherrill's writing or her, by now, old-hat problems.

Periodically, when Misha was off for a weekend in the city with the latest of her progressively older married lovers, Sherrill crept thief-like into Misha's room and relentlessly cleaned it. She scoured the bathroom as if the place were contaminated, which it might certainly have been in view of the condition Misha allowed it to get into. Incredibly, Michelle never minded. She'd emerge from her newly immaculate room with a beaming smile to thank Sherrill profusely. "I never can seem to keep up with it," she'd say, then sweep back inside, proceeding with manic determination to reduce it once more to a cluttered magpie's nest— with crumpled, used tissues strewn everywhere, candy and panty-hose wrappers under the bed or on the floor beside the wastebasket Sherrill so faithfully emptied. Stacks of long-overdue library books accumulated on the floor; clothes destined to be dry-cleaned piled up over the backs of chairs; soiled underwear lay in slithery piles atop the hamper; the window shades remained drawn day and night; the room smelled of sleep, of deodorant and perfume. In the course of each day, Sherrill would stop at least once to glare at the closed door to Michelle's room, for a moment filled with hate for the carelessly beautiful woman whose freedom had never been challenged. To save herself from the corrosive effects of this feeling, Sherrill hired a cleaning woman to come twice a week.

After three and a half years of wrangling, the settlement was agreed upon and signed. The court date would be, her lawyer assured her, easy to set up. "Go out, enjoy yourself. We'll see you in court."

Go out, enjoy herself. Where, how? Michelle arranged a blind date. Sherrill met the man, found him pleasant enough, chatted with him over dinner, then spent two hours at the movies plucking his hands from wherever they happened to alight upon her.

The men she met in the next months had all, without exception, been previously married and were desperately anxious to do it again. Their conversations revolved around their ex-wives, the settlements they'd had to make, their feelings of abuse and bewilderment. They were also, without exception, determined to march in a direct line to someone's bedroom—their own or the newest woman's—after the barest minimum of acquaintanceship. The most attractive men she met were married, either to women they adored, or to women to whom they had all sorts of complicated emotional and financial obligations.

She accepted dates until the pattern began to offend her. She grew weary in advance of a date, knowing she'd be taken to dinner somewhere; she and the man would present their credentials and state their personal philosophies, then they might go to see a movie, or even up to the Long Wharf Theatre in New Haven to see a play. After the movie or play, there'd be a drink somewhere, and while the drink was being consumed, the sexual invitation would be made. When she arrived at the point of wondering if her name hadn't somehow managed to find its way onto a bizarre mailing list, she decided to take herself out of the marketplace and off the block. Dating had evolved into a demoralizing practice with results so predictable there was no point even to pretending to be surprised. She'd encountered men who claimed to want to take care of her, men who believed that once they'd taken her to bed they were just a step away from moving in and availing themselves of her money, men who had nonstop tales of woe they wished to tell. She went back to her writing.

In her free time, she went to the supermarket, did the laundry, cooked the meals, and occasionally insisted that Misha baby-sit to she could get out for a movie. She felt stifled, as if she'd traded Drew in for another husband of a different gender. Michelle arrived home each evening with precisely the same expectations: a hot meal, a comfortable place to collapse and watch TV, a well-organized household in which she was required to take no active part beyond romping with Perry when she was in a good mood, or baby-sitting with him on those evening when Sherrill announced she was going out. Sherrill prayed for the court date to be set.

She played the piano for relief and distraction and tried
to sing one afternoon to Perry, who at first smiled uncertainly, then started to laugh. She never again sang for him
but would gladly play the piano while he danced and cavorted
around the living room like a stocky marionette. He had a
fine sense of music and rhythm, and she encouraged him to
sing and dance.

Perry was her focus, her anchor; she loved him as she'd
never loved anyone other than her mother. And one didn't,
she knew now, love a parent in the same way one loved a
child. Even at his most hateful, when he threw tantrums
and shouted back at her, she felt a kind of helpless love for
him. Just as marriage hadn't been what she'd been led to
expect, neither was motherhood. When Perry was openly
defiant and stubbornly disobedient, she wished she'd never
had him. When he was fresh from the bath, or soundly
asleep, she gazed at him and felt love, like pain, crushing
her lungs. Overall, she was glad of his existence. Without
him, she might simply have surrendered and let Drew march
all over her. Because of the divorce, she had to remain in
the house in Connecticut; because of Perry, she had to
examine her motives, her ambitions, and try to live with the
limitations that had been set on her life. Perry slowed her
down, rendered her more thoughtful, and analytical of his
actions as well as her own. She'd been forced to grow. It
wasn't easy to accept that this period of enforced growth
was a result of Drew's meanness of spirit. She'd been compelled to remain in a town that had begun to seem to her
like an extended prison yard where she might take a limited
amount of exercise but where she could never attain true
freedom. She had daydreams about piling Perry and their
essential belongings into the car and taking off. The daydreams brought depression dangerously close so that she
flew to her novel for solace, hiding from reality in the
accumulation of handwritten pages that lived in a box on
her dresser.

After six more months the hearing date was set. Michelle
agreed to stay home and wait for Perry to get home from
school while Sherrill went to the Superior Court in downtown Stamford, where she was to meet her lawyer. There
were four other cases slated ahead of hers, and she sat in

the last row of the courtroom beside her lawyer, wondering where Drew was and if, after all the palaver, he didn't intend to show up for the final round.

He appeared just as their case was being called. She watched him take a seat near the front with his lawyer. He looked well, but he'd aged. Pointedly he ignored her until it came time for her to take the stand. Then his eyes never left her. At one point, while she prepared her answer to a question the judge had asked, their eyes met and she wondered why he'd taken the case as far as he had when she now understood that he'd always known he couldn't possibly win. She'd raised Perry from infancy. He was a happy, boisterous boy almost five years old who had no memory of his father. Drew had set himself up to lose. His sole aim in these four years of chaotic infighting had been to penalize her in the most painful way possible for having hurt him, for having succeeded in her career despite all the sizable obstacles he'd tried to place in her path.

The case was settled in less than fifteen minutes. The judge awarded her custody of Perry and she raised her hand, to the judge's evident consternation, to say, "May I ask you something?"

Interestedly, the judge leaned on his elbows. "Certainly."

"Is there any reason his father and I couldn't have joint custody of Perry? I know Drew would like to be able to see him. And someday a time may come when Perry might prefer to live with his father."

She glanced over at Drew to see that he'd covered his eyes with his hands. His shoulders shook and she knew he was crying. She'd never felt sorrier for anyone in her life. All this could have been accomplished painlessly, quickly. But he'd chosen the most difficult route possible. The judge addressed the issue to Drew's lawyer, who turned to whisper to his client. Without taking his hands from his eyes, Drew whispered his response. The lawyer stood up to say, "That would be acceptable, Your Honor."

The judge instructed the court clerk to include this provision in the final document, then went on to cover the rest of the points in Sherrill's petition. She was awarded the house, a substantial amount of alimony, and child support. Again she raised her hand. This time the judge chuckled. "Now what?" he asked.

"I'd like to waive the alimony," she said. "I really don't need it."

Her own lawyer looked apoplectic by now and had fastened his hand to the judge's bench as if fearful of falling down. The judge again presented the issue to Drew and his attorney. After a second whispered consultation, Drew's attorney said, "That is also acceptable to my client, Your Honor."

The balance of the hearing went quickly. Sherrill shook hands with the judge, then descended the steps from the witness stand to pause near Drew, hoping he'd speak to her, that they might, at this last moment, salvage some measure of friendship for each other. He gazed at her with an unreadable expression, then turned and walked out of the courtroom. Sherrill's lawyer put his hand on the small of her back to direct her out, and she went. In the parking lot he advised her when she could expect to receive the final decree. She listened without really hearing. She was watching Drew unlock his car, then stop and look over at her. She said good-bye to the lawyer and walked back across the lot toward Drew.

"If you were trying to make me feel like a louse," he said dully, "you succeeded."

"I don't need the money, and he is your child, too. Why did we have to go through all this, Drew? Why?"

He looked down at the ground, then directed his eyes back to her. "I can't talk to you," he said. "I never knew how to talk to you. I've got to go. I've got a meeting in the city."

He climbed into the car and drove away. It was over; he was gone. It was unlikely they'd ever see one another again. She sighed, exhausted and relieved. She had a future that suddenly stretched unendingly in front of her like a 3 A.M. freeway. She could go anywhere she chose. She just had to resolve the problem of Michelle.

Perry hadn't yet arrived home from school. Michelle was in the living room, ensconced on the sofa, her feet propped on the coffee table, the TV remote control in her hand, a bag of Fritos corn chips in her lap.

"How'd it go?" she asked, glancing over at Sherrill.

"Fine, fine." Sherrill went through to the kitchen to put

on a pot of coffee, then leaned against the counter to wait while it percolated. With trembling hands she lit a cigarette, thinking about Michelle. In the past few months, for reasons known only to herself, Misha had decided to take on the role of Sherrill's household adviser. She knew a better way to do practically everything, although in reality she didn't contribute at all to the running of the house. Sherrill doubted she'd ever had to do so much as make her bed when she was growing up. Misha was patently the product of a family that had been so intimidated by her beauty that all they'd ever expected her to do was enhance the atmosphere of the family home by gracing it with her presence. Nevertheless, she knew better, faster, more efficient ways to do everything.

Sherrill had been cleaning the sink one evening after dinner and Misha happened to pass through. She paused to offer a suggestion that Sherrill might clean it more effectively with Comet. Everyone knew Ajax wasn't nearly as good.

Sherrill had been shrieking at Perry one afternoon for tracking mud all over the kitchen. Misha thought Sherrill might deal with the boy more wisely. "He'll only grow up to resent you if all you do is yell at him," she said placidly.

Michelle had wanted to know, upon finding Sherrill doing a load of laundry, if she'd discovered this marvelous new bleach.

Had Sherrill considered buying such and such a cut of pork?

It had progressed from suggestions to statements of dislike: Misha gave up onions and garlic, declaring categorically that she would no longer eat any food containing either. Misha went off beef and wouldn't touch it; she insisted the very smell of it was enough to make her sick. She went on a crusade against sugar, and gave it up. "It has no nutritional value whatsoever. None!" she declared knowledgeably.

Suddenly the meals Sherrill served up were tasteless and boring, all in order to satisfy Michelle. Now she wondered why the hell she'd gone on pandering to the ever-changing dictates of this woman who had evolved into a minor-league tyrant. She stubbed out her cigarette and walked back to the living room. "This isn't working out," she said quietly. "It

feels as if we're married, with you sitting in here watching
television and me out in the kitchen because it's the last
private place I've got left to go. You've got all kinds of
demands and suggestions, Misha, and you're driving me
absolutely nuts. It's been more than four years since you
moved in here and I've never once criticized you for being
sloppy or for never offering even to take out the garbage, let
alone clean that pigpen of a room. You've never even *mentioned* chipping in to pay Ruby for braving her way into
your room twice a week."

Michelle removed her feet from the coffee table and sat
up. "What brought *this* on? Didn't you get everything you
wanted from Drew?"

Her tone of voice and her snide remark enraged Sherrill,
but she refused to give in to it. "You've never contributed
anything," she said, still quietly, sitting down at the far end
of the sofa, wondering why she felt so guilty about speaking
the truth when she knew she was right. "You think that
paying me two hundred dollars a month toward the mort-
gage covers all your obligations here. It doesn't. You've done
nothing but *create* work for me. Not only have I got Perry's
laundry to do, and my own, but you cheerfully leave me
yours. There's no reason why you couldn't do your own
laundry, or take the garbage out once in a while, or offer to
cook dinner for a change, or show up with some groceries
every so often."

"I don't make the kind of money you do. And I happen to
work all day—" Michelle began in her own defense.

Sherrill's rage took over. "What the *fuck* do you think *I* do
here all day? You've got this idea that I'm just a dumb little
suburban housewife who's being subsidized by a publishing
company. I happen to take my writing very seriously,
Michelle! It's important to me, and I *work* at it. How much I
earn is absolutely no concern of yours."

Michelle jumped to her feet, her face bright red. "You
can go to hell! If that's what you think of all I've done for
you, you can go straight to hell! I'll move back to the city."

"You were here when I needed you," Sherrill allowed.
"But you've been capitalizing on the situation ever since.
You've never given any consideration to my problems or the
pressures I've had to live with. You just go charging in full

steam ahead, issuing orders about how there's to be no more onions and garlic, no more sugar, no beef. You've given up this, that, and the other goddamned thing and Perry and I are supposed to give it all up with you. Well, I'm sorry, but Perry's favorite food in the world happens to be hamburgers. And I love steak, smothered in onions. Pack up your trash and your disgusting underwear and go back to New York! I'm going to live the way I want, without having you hanging over my shoulder like a Rhodes scholar with a degree in household sciences telling me you know a better way." She stalked to the doorway to the kitchen, then stopped and turned back. "To make it easier, I think I'll take Perry up to Toronto for the weekend to see his grandmother. That'll give you a chance to clear out without an audience. And you can forget about any offer I ever made to let you buy this house."

"*Oh, fuck you!*" Michelle screamed. "*Fuck you!*"

The following morning Sherrill and Perry took a Connecticut Limousine out to Kennedy to catch the midday flight to Toronto. Josie was waiting at the airport. Perry let out a yell when he caught sight of her and flew into her arms at a speed that nearly sent her toppling backwards. She wrapped her arms around the boy and reached past him to kiss Sherrill. Then the three of them went out to the car.

Sherrill gazed out the car window at the new buildings lining both sides of Highway 401. She breathed deeply, feeling disencumbered for the first time in almost seven years. She'd be able to sell the house and bring Perry home to Canada.

"I think," she told her mother, "we're going to come back. Not right away, but eventually."

"Good," Josie approved. "That's a wise idea."

"You think so?" Sherrill smiled.

"For purely selfish reasons, of course." Josie smiled back. "I don't get to see this guy often enough." She squeezed Perry against her side so that he yelped and then laughed. "Or you, for that matter. There's nothing down there you can't find here."

"That's certainly true," Sherrill agreed.

"Why don't you think about renting an apartment here for a year?" Josie suggested. "Until you decide which area of the city you prefer."

"Good idea."

"You've changed," her mother said appraisingly.

Sherrill nodded.

"I've never liked you better," Josie said.

"I've never liked myself better. I think facing Michelle was the last hurdle. I don't know why, but I was afraid of her. It was nonsense. There wasn't a damned thing to be afraid of. Not a thing."

When they returned to Connecticut, Michelle was gone. She'd helped herself to a number of items that hadn't been hers and had left her room destroyed. Sherrill hired two college boys to repaint the bedroom and the living room, then settled down to life alone with Perry. She thought often of moving back to Canada but didn't yet feel ready to make the move. She wanted first to savor the novelty of her freedom. She also wanted to give Perry time to get used to the idea that they would, ultimately, be going to live in what was, for him, an entirely new world. He'd enjoyed his visit to Toronto but had, throughout the time they'd been there, talked about "... going home." They needed, Sherrill thought, to accustom themselves to one another before tackling city life.

At last, almost two years to the day Michelle moved out, Sherrill called Rose, the real estate broker who'd sold Sherrill and Drew the house. Rose came right over to have a look around and decide on a price. The figure she mentioned was thirty thousand above what Sherrill had thought she could ask. Rose went off to have the listing prepared and came back a day later to have Sherrill sign it. The following Tuesday there was an open house. Every real estate agent in the area came through within a two-hour period. There were an astonishing number of them, and by the time the last of the women had gone off up the road, gunning the engine of her Ford Fairlane, Sherrill had a pounding headache. She wished she'd never started any of this. Rose assured her the worst of it was over and Sherrill allowed herself to be pacified.

The day after the open house, a nonstop parade commenced. Prospective buyers trouped through the house. They looked in the closets, they opened the oven and refrigerator doors, some of them even went so far as to read parts of the manuscript Sherrill had inadvertently left on the kitchen table. Sherrill thought she might very well go mad. Every time she closed herself into the bathroom the telephone rang or some broker arrived unannounced to show another couple through the house.

In self-defense, Sherrill boldly sat down at the kitchen table to work, and let the agents show their clients through the house with no assistance from her. Her sudden lack of interest resulted in three offers in one day. She accepted the highest just to put a stop to the traffic.

With the binder signed and only the termite and building inspections pending, Sherrill was once more able to enjoy her daytime hours alone in the house. Perry was away from eight-thirty in the morning until four-fifteen when the school bus delivered him home. She worked during the days, then devoted the late afternoons and evenings to her son. She accompanied him when he rode his bike down the side of the road; she took him into New York City for Saturday matinees; she went with him to the park to toss a football back and forth. Perry gradually blossomed under his mother's attention. His tantrums took place less frequently; there seemed fewer occasions when she had to scold him. He had turned from a diffident, unruly little boy into a fun-loving, easygoing person whose company was enchanting.

With the manuscript of her third book completed and off being typed, she turned her attention to the house. Room by room she decided what would be kept, what could be sold, what would simply be discarded. Daily she made trips to the dump to dispose of more trash. She came across old glossies from her revue days, and the program for the last show she'd done for Della, with her and Jamie's and Ron's photographs on the front. She had to smile at how young, how innocent they all looked. She'd forgotten Jamie's dimples, his dark hair and brown eyes. She no longer looked years younger than her age. She'd managed to catch up with herself and felt comfortable. In many ways it was a relief to know who she was. She had Perry, and a career; they felt like everything she needed.

She was anxious to get back home to look up all her old friends and renew ties. She'd miss this house, and the Connecticut beaches, the incomparable beauty of the state

with its splendid old clapboard house and the dogwoods
blossoming pink and white in the spring. But she had no
real friends here.

She felt, and knew she looked, older; she was no longer
the tiny gamine creature whose baritone voice was so startling. She was a thirty-five-year-old divorcée with a child,
someone who'd found herself in the beds of too many strangers before she'd decided to give up making love to men she
didn't want in a doomed effort to find herself accurately
reflected in their eyes. She'd evolved from a performer into
an author. It was time to move on.

Yet it was a little frightening to give up everything that
had become familiar after ten years in this country. Connecticut had become very much like home, but no matter
how much interest she took in American politics, or how
actively she involved herself in school affairs, no matter
how accustomed she was to saying "bathroom" and not
"washroom," and "boiled ham" instead of "cooked ham,"
and "huh" instead of "eh," she was a foreigner. Despite the
fact that she sounded fairly much like all the other women
around town, and dressed like them in jeans, Shetland pull-
overs, and long-sleeved shirts, with Bass loafers, it was only
in appearance that her similarities existed. She didn't belong.
She wanted to go home where, even after ten years away,
there were speech patterns that were as comfortable and
comforting as an old flannel nightgown; there was a Canadian quality of reserve, even smugness, she understood. She
was a part of all that, and missed it. She'd attained her
credibility, and a success that wasn't what she'd had in
mind when she'd started, but it was undeniable success.
She had her child and her portable talent and she was
taking them home.

Chapter 25

Jamie at once recognized Jane's voice on the telephone. It was a surprise that after all these years her intonation should still be so familiar. She sounded tense. Her voice, even in the brief "Hello, Jamie?" conveyed the signal that he was about to hear bad news. In quick mental reflex, he went down a list of possible reasons why she might be calling: increased alimony; a pending visit from the boys, who had perhaps been asking to see him; a declaration of her intention to take the boys and return to England.

He said, "Hello, Jane. How are you?"

There was a slight pause. He could hear her draw in her breath before she began to speak in a voice he could only think of as leaden. "I've had a lot of trouble reaching you," she began. "I tried the office on Friday evening, but it was closed. Then I tried ringing Matt at home, but I couldn't get to him until today. There's been an accident," she said, and paused again. Jamie realized that his grip on the receiver had become fierce, so intense his entire arm was aching.

"What's happened?" he asked.

"It's Mark." She drew in another, more ragged-sounding breath. "I *tried* to reach you," she repeated, her voice going higher.

"What's happened to Mark?" he asked, and then knew, with sudden horrifying intuition, that his younger son was dead. She confirmed it. He listened as she described how Mark had been riding his ten-speed home from school when a hit-and-run driver had sent the boy and the bicycle hurtling through space; he listened as she explained that Mark had been dead before he hit the pavement. The police, she said disconsolately, were attempting to find the driver. She went on listlessly, defeatedly, to give him the details of the funeral. In a voice he failed to recognize as his own, he replied, "I'll be there." The conversation ended. He replaced

259

the receiver, feeling he'd been catapulted out of a world where everything was familiar into a place where nothing, not even the sight of his own shaking hands, was identifiable.

Shoulders hunched, head bowed, he stood beside the telephone trying to absorb the impact. He tried to picture Mark but could see him only as the little gap-toothed boy who'd sat beside his older brother on the sofa at the High Park house listening as his father tried to explain why he had to leave them. Had he never left them, Mark might still be alive. No. He shook his head and went to sit on the sofa where he lit a Gitane, gratefully drawing the acrid smoke deep into his lungs. Mark was dead; he no longer breathed or spoke or had gaps in his mouth new teeth would fill. He would never reach adulthood and seek to reestablish communication with his father.

Jamie felt old, so old he didn't know if he'd be able to rise from the sofa to go to the bathroom and clean himself up, shave the stubble from his face before putting on a suit and going down to the car to drive out to the suburbs where he'd make an all but useless attempt to console his former wife at the loss of their child. He smoked the Gitane and stared into space, wondering what the hell it was all about. What in God's name was the point of going through a lifetime of ups and downs, successes and disappointments, when lives could be taken away in just a few seconds? It made no sense. It hadn't made any sense years ago in Africa when he'd watched black and white men die inches away from him, or when he himself had sustained shrapnel injuries he couldn't convince himself might have been lethal had they struck other parts of his body than the ones they had. A leg wound and a minor belly wound hadn't really been threats to his mortality. What had been a real threat had been his inability to rationalize or justify the senseless-seeming fragility of human life.

He looked down at himself and was filled with disgust by his body. The sight of his bulging belly repelled and dismayed him. The telephone began to ring. He ignored it. He didn't want to talk to anyone; he couldn't trust himself to speak. He had the arbitrary notion that if he so much as picked up the receiver and held it against his ear, what would emerge from his throat wouldn't be a hello but an uncontrollable scream that might loosen the bricks from their mortar and cause the entire building to collapse inward. After the sixth ring the telephone was silent. He smoked the cigarette down until he could no longer hold it, then dropped the stub into the crowded ashtray on the floor and, exhausted, got to his feet. At once he forgot his intention in standing up and turned to look at the sofa, debating whether or not to sit down again. No, better not to sit down. He might never get up. Dust might settle on him; cobwebs would appear; he'd turn to rock on the spot. Commanding his body to move, he went slowly down the short hall to the bathroom, where he switched on the light and confronted his face in the mirror as his hand automatically turned the hot water faucet. *You ugly bastard,* he thought. *You bloody ugly bastard. You didn't even have the courage to see those boys when you had the chance.*

While he shaved, ignoring the repellent full image and concentrating on only those parts of his face he was involved with, he thought about the women he'd known. Of them all he could think of only one he wanted to call to come be with him for a few hours. Only one.

He'd given up his right to be a father to those boys. They'd grown up without him. It had been his choice, not theirs. He'd entertained a vague but persistent hope of one day getting to know them and allowing them to know him— all of them men, finally, with certain experiences in common. Now that could never be. His estrangement was total. He was readying himself to attend the funeral of a fourteen-year-old boy he'd known once upon a time but whose features had become hopelessly mixed up with those of another little boy he'd once known. He risked another look at his reflection in the mirror. A mistake. His hands clenched. He had to resist an impulse to put his fists through the mirror. There was no way he could get through this alone. After rinsing the soap from his face, he towelled dry and returned to the living room to stand near the telephone, trying to pull himself together sufficiently to call. Only one person would understand exactly how he felt, wouldn't try to inflict synthetic sympathy upon him. He reached for the receiver and dialed Dene's number.

The answering service picked up and he felt despair welling inside him. He was about to say never mind when Dene came on the line saying, "I've got it. Hello?"

Using the bare minimum of words, Jamie asked her to come to the apartment right away.

She said, "I'll be there in half an hour," and hung up.

He loved her for the immediacy of her response. Eased somewhat now, he returned to the bathroom to shower. Then he dressed in his best custom-made suit and shirt, sober silk tie, and English boots. He felt like a mechanical windup toy. Fully dressed, he sat again on the sofa and waited for Dene.

She arrived without her camera. Its absence struck him as highly symbolic, but he couldn't comment. He let her in and went to stand by the window, speaking with his back to her. "I've got to go to a funeral," he said hoarsely, wondering how it was possible to sound so everyday when it was his dead child he was talking about. "My son was killed in a road accident on Friday morning."

"Oh, Jamie," she said softly. She gazed at his broad back and longed to comfort him. In that moment she believed she finally understood how inadequate everyone must have felt when they'd attempted to console her after the deaths of Jake and Mimi. Nothing anyone could say would penetrate the thickly enclosing walls of sorrow. She went to stand beside him at the window and held his hand while both of them gazed, in their separate silences, at the street outside.

As they were on their way to the funeral parlor in Jamie's car, Dene said, "I had a roll of film. It was in the camera for years. I knew one day I'd have to develop it, but I was terrified of the happy images there were bound to be. I think subconsciously I knew that if I waited long enough the images would simply dissolve, disappear or something." She looked over to see that he was listening intently. "About two years ago," she went on, "I gathered my courage, took the film out of the camera, and put it through the process. I was so scared I was actually crying. Like a little kid," she said, with a small regretful smile. "The negatives were ruined. There were only dark shadows and gray spaces, no discernible images. I threw the whole mess in the trash and sold the camera."

"Someday," he said, "I'll be able to appreciate that."

Something inside him changed that day. He went on with his life much as before, but without his prior capacity for pleasure. He moved in briefly with a young singer he met and liked. Her youth overwhelmed him after a few weeks, and he moved out again. He decided he preferred to live alone. He had women to stay overnight occasionally, but discovered that once the night and its feverish activities had passed he couldn't wait to be away from them. He took to creating elaborate, well-thought-out excuses in order to get rid of his guests first thing in the morning: he had an appointment; he had no food for breakfast; he had work to do; his ex-wife was coming over to collect an alimony check. He had excuses for every possible occasion, and he used them all. He wasn't entirely aware of the direction he was headed until Mary spent a night with him.

Mary was a young redheaded dancer he'd dated from time to time and whose company he'd enjoyed in the past. He invited her to spend the weekend the last week in October—a year to the day Mark died. He tidied up the apartment in anticipation of her arrival, changed the bed linens, laid in a supply of his favorite foods, including a jar of imported English ginger marmalade; he vacuumed the rugs and cleaned the bathroom; he washed and put away a substantial accumulation of dirty dishes; he cleaned the ashtrays, dusted the furniture, wiped clean the TV screen and the windows, put out new candles in the living room and on the dining table, and finally opened all the windows for a few hours to air the place out. He stood back to survey the effects of his work, satisfied that everything looked and felt right.

Mary arrived with a small overnight bag and an eager smile. From the moment she walked through the door, he knew he'd made a mistake. First of all, she smoked. Instead of using just one ashtray, she went from room to room scattering ash in every available receptacle. He told himself it was ridiculous to get annoyed. After all, he himself smoked. But her smoking irritated him inordinately. Next, he made dinner, and not only did she not offer to help, she busied herself in the living room taking one after the other of his record albums from their covers, then failed to replace them. She played his least favorite sort of music on the radio, then turned on the television set without bothering to switch off the radio. He stifled his growing irritation and served the meal—curried chicken with rice and half a dozen small

bowls of condiments only to sit in fascinated repulsion
watching her eat. There was a napkin, a new cloth one right
beside her plate, but she ignored it and ate greedily, with
bits of food adhering to her mouth and chin. He wanted to
put out his hand and roughly clean her face.

They went to bed together. She was a tour director, an
instructor. He lost both his interest and his erection, kissed
her good night, turned on his side, and tried to go to sleep.
He couldn't. Mary's slim dancer's legs kept finding their
way over to his side of the bed, where, with muscular
obstinacy, they refused to be moved. She whuffled in her
sleep, made noises that kept him awake. At last he gave up
and went to sit on the sofa, watching TV with the sound
turned fairly high, not giving a damn, even hoping it might
wake her. It didn't. She slept soundly right through "The
Late Show." He had several scotches with beer chasers,
smoked half a pack of Gitanes, and ultimately fell asleep on
the sofa under an old mohair blanket.

In the morning, with no valid reason or premeditated lie
with which to rid himself of her, he went about making an
elaborate breakfast. At the very least, he'd be able to eat a
bang-up meal. He boiled water and brewed a full pot of
Melitta coffee; he poached eggs and fried bacon; he grilled
tomatoes and mushrooms; he toasted bread, and set butter
and the ginger marmalade, in a small crystal bowl, out on
the meticulously laid table. Then he roused Mary, who,
bleary-eyed, smiled and staggered after him to the table.

With a circle of bread crumbs rimming her mouth, a bit of
egg yolk on her chin, and a lit cigarette in an ashtray on the
corner of the table, she reached for the marmalade and
dropped it. The bowl caught the edge of her coffee cup and
sent its contents spilling over Jamie's new tablecloth. The
cigarette rolled from the lip of the ashtray and sizzled out
on the wet cloth. The fragile crystal bowl shattered upon
impact with the coffee cup, and glass and marmalade
swamped the already destroyed table.

In a state close to rage, Jamie hustled the girl off to the
bedroom, where he said, "Get dressed and I'll run you
home." He returned to stand at the dining table, furiously
regarding the ruins. It was the last goddamned time he'd
have a woman stay over. Not only had Mary soiled every
ashtray in the apartment, she'd destroyed the entire week-

end. He hadn't even had so much as a spoonful of the expensively delicious marmalade. He had a purely irrational impulse to murder the girl. Instead, he threw on an old too-tight pair of jeans and a sweat shirt and drove her home. The perplexed girl began to thank him for the weekend but, presented with his rigidly set features, simply said, "Goodbye," and leaped out of the car. Jamie headed back to the apartment at a speed of well over fifty miles an hour. He was stopped by a uniformed policeman who stepped from the sidewalk and, with a languid gesture, waved Jamie over to the curb.

With the speeding ticket sitting on the dashboard, Jamie continued home, his outrage complete. After clearing away the debris and regretfully consigning the remains of the marmalade and the crystal bowl to the trash, he sat down at the table with a cup of coffee, a pad and a pencil, and began to outline new resolutions for his life. He would, for a minimum of a year, take all the stage work he could get. If he was going to be an actor, then he'd damned well learn his craft. There was no better place to do that than on a stage in front of a live audience. He'd spent a lot of years getting by in the business without training. He wasn't too old to start taking a few lessons. Something else he needed to do was get his body back into some sort of decent condition. So he'd take up tennis again, or work with weights; he'd enroll in some dance classes, and maybe take a few theater arts courses at the university. He'd made the choice to become an actor; now he was going to have to turn himself into a bona fide performer with qualifications. He didn't altogether disallow his previous experience, or the several awards he'd won for his radio and television work. But an actor's place was on the stage, and that was where he intended to spend the next year. If he didn't make it, he'd get the hell out of the business altogether, cash in his ACTRA retirement plan, and use the money to go into some other business.

Next he decided there would be no more women making themselves at home—for one night or more—in his apartment. If they cared to invite him to spend a night with, them, fine. But no woman was going to come to his place and scatter her bloody cigarette ashes everywhere, move things and fail to replace them properly, and destroy an entire jar of imported marmalade he'd gone to a lot of trouble to buy.

He sat back from the table and examined the list, then leaned forward to add, in a firm hand, "No more involvements." Having written this, he again sat back and wondered what he meant by that. Well, he knew, didn't he? For the last eight years he'd gone from one woman to the next, from one place to the next, like some physical and emotional nomad. He had no desire or intention ever to marry again. Yet, perversely, in the back of his mind lingered the remote idea that somewhere out there, walking the streets of the world, was a woman he could love. Perhaps that was a young man's notion, a youthful, leftover ideal. It was best not to think about it. He was settled; he liked the apartment and the furniture he'd bought. He liked the neighborhood, situated as it was just on the fringes of Yorkville, although he still thought about and missed the St. George Street apartment.

He'd grown heartily tired of fabricating excuses in order to free himself of the presence of some woman he had, in a moment of lonely weakness, invited home with him. These women only disrupted his routines. The majority of them were looking for husbands, and he was the last man on earth fit for that role. He freely admitted it. Yet, acknowledging this, he felt suddenly lost. All he had was his career; he was planning to focus entirely on it. What sort of future would that give him? At the end of a year's time, if he'd succeeded in working steadily in the theater, he'd plan his next step. He was almost forty-two years old. Either he formulated plans now and followed them through, or he gave up altogether and went to work parking cars or waiting tables. He groaned aloud, an odd sound rending the still air of the apartment, then listened to the echo, his eyes on the page of writing on the table. As when Mark had died, he felt old.

If anyone noticed his change of attitude, they didn't comment. He received as many invitations as ever: to parties, from women. He went along, aware that he was becoming a little shabby in his dress and that he'd taken to drinking rather heavily on social occasions. What the hell did it matter? He knew he wasn't an unpleasant drunk, one of those repressed, angry men who after a few drinks let their venom spew over anyone who happened to be nearby. He was a relatively happy drunk, content to remain in the corner of one room or another, quietly downing one glass of scotch after another until the edges of reality had been pleasingly blurred out of definition. There were beautiful women he dated from time to time, some he made love to, others he kissed and left on the doorstep. He had friends around to dinner, and there were Sunday night poker parties that moved around the city and took place at his apartment every six weeks or so. When he had a rare free night, he went out for a good dinner, and picked up a ticket to the opera, or the ballet, or to one of the plays in town where a friend was appearing. He sent opening-night telegrams to his colleagues, faithfully attended every audition Matt sent him on, and luckily managed, between theater jobs, to land half a dozen commercials. The residuals ensured his alimony payments—they were literally alimony payments now. Jane had finalized divorce proceedings several months after Mark's death. He was content, in a fashion, and went about nailing down more and more work. By March of 1978, he had jobs lined up well into the fall of '79. His working future was secure. The fact that some of the jobs overlapped so that he'd be rehearsing one show during the days while playing in another evenings didn't bother him in the least. He was accomplishing what he'd set out to do.

Occasionally he ran into Dene. They'd have coffee somewhere and talk philosophically of the directions their lives were taking. While still basically a shy woman, she'd managed to attain some degree of confidence in her work now that she was becoming fairly well known not only in the city but in film circles. She regularly showed up on film sets as still photographer, and twice she and Jamie discovered they'd be working together. On the second of these occasions Dene admitted that Anne wasn't well.

"She's all right physically," Dene said, gazing into the depths of an empty paper container that had held black coffee. "But I'm worried about her emotional state. She's allowed herself to get *old*, Jamie. She's only fifty-six, but she looks a hundred. Even Charlie, who's usually oblivious to everything, is really worried about her. Last winter she flatly refused to go out of the house. She said she was afraid of the ice, afraid she'd fall down and hurt herself. Nothing either of us said could convince her to go as far as the corner to get some fresh air.

"And she smokes in bed," she went on. "She burned up the mattress and luckily happened to wake up. She came downstairs screaming. Charlie was with me," she admitted, looking a little embarrassed. "We've been ... seeing each other, off and on. Anyway, it was a good thing he was there because I couldn't have controlled her. She was absolutely hysterical. He hit her," she said, shame-faced. "It was horrible. But it really was the only thing he could do under the circumstances. He knocked her cold. We put her to bed in my apartment while the fire department got the fire put out. We had to buy her a new mattress and Charlie repainted the entire third floor, including the outside of the house. I'm afraid for her," she said, her intent gaze now directed at him. "There's something I want to say to you, Jamie. I know all this started after you left Anne, but I want you to know I've never blamed you for any of it. I don't believe it had anything to do with you. It had to do with how Anne's always thought of herself. She believed that the only thing she had to capitalize on was her looks. It's pathetic," she said, with some anger. "She's still a very good-looking woman, with a fine brain. I only wish there were some way to snap her out of this."

"You can't change her," Jamie said thoughtfully. "No one can force anyone else to change. You've got to want to do it for yourself."

"I know that," she agreed solemnly. "I needed to talk about it, get it off my chest. She *worries* me."

"If there was something I could do to help, I would. I don't think it would be fair to Anne to ... build up her expectations, I suppose."

"I honestly wasn't trying to suggest anything," Dene said quickly. "I really did need to talk about it. I had kind of an upsetting letter this morning. Do you ever remember my mentioning Charlie, the super of the place where I lived in New York?"

"The one who drank and then cemented the bottles to the top of the wall?"

"That's right. He died. I got a letter from the lawyer handling his estate. I wouldn't have believed Charlie could have *had* an estate. Obviously he did. He left me a small bequest, which is why they got in touch with me. Otherwise, I'd probably never have known. He died at some fancy drying-out spa in Connecticut called Silver Hill. God," she said sadly, shaking her head. "All these years we've been writing back and forth. Not regularly, you know, but at Christmas and other times. I admired him. He had the courage to admit what he was and not pretend to be anything more or less than that. It does take courage, you know."

"I know." Then, surprising both of them, he said, "I miss you."

She took hold of his hand. "I miss you, too. Maybe someday we can get all this straightened out and be friends without having to feel guilty. I feel so *conspiratorial* every time I run into you, then have to go home and keep it a secret. I love Anne, you know, Jamie. I don't know what would have become of me if I hadn't happened to sit beside her on the plane when I decided to come back here from New York."

There was nothing to say. They sat holding hands, thinking their own somber thoughts, until Jamie was called to the set to shoot his scene. He looked back at Dene to smile and wave. She watched him enter into conversation with the director, wondering what would become of Jamie. Like Anne, he seemed to be aging prematurely. How, she wondered, did you stop the people you loved from committing slow, private suicide?

Part 4
Destinations 1980

Chapter 26

Sherrill found apartment life novel after so long in a house. The underground garage was a luxury, especially when it rained. She did miss being able to walk out the back door into the garden, but the balcony provided an illusion of the outdoors. Perry had taken the move well enough, although he was suffering some small anxiety about starting at a new school in September, in a new country where he had no friends. She had her own anxieties for him, but kept silent and hoped that once school started he'd fall into the routines as readily as he had in Connecticut.

Within a week of their arrival, the telephone calls began. Her old friends had received her change-of-address cards, had noted the dates, and were now calling to welcome her back and invite her to lunch, to dinner, to a party. Calls also began to come in from the local newspapers and TV and radio stations, requesting interviews. She assumed that either Hank or her publishers had put out the word of her return, but it was Della who, having given up producing and gone into public relations, had notified the media.

The interviews were, for the most part, far more interesting than those she'd done in the States. The interviewers had read up on her background; the majority of them had even read one or more of her books. They wanted to know why she'd come back to Canada, did it seem different to her after nearly ten years away, why she had given up performing for writing. She answered all the questions, then went out to buy the papers to see if what she'd said would be misquoted. One of the articles was captioned "Author Returns to Canada: Big Fish in Little Pond," and went on to quote her accurately: ". . . she says this is her home and that she always intended to return." The caption, however, irked her; it made her sound pompous, even arrogant.

The Canadian distributors of her books telephoned to arrange a signing session.

"Why don't we wait," she suggested, "until the new book comes out in May?"

"May? That's *ten* months away!"

"Do you think you'll get any kind of a turnout for a signing session now?" she asked. "I mean, the last book came out ages ago."

"We'll get the turnout," the marketing director said confidently. "You give us a couple of hours of your time. We'll set up something."

She shrugged and said, "Sure, all right. Let me know where and when."

A substantial number of her friends thought she was completely crazy to come back. Angie, an old high school friend, said, "I got your change-of-address card, eh. I couldn't believe you'd actually come back to old Toronto the Good. It's so goddamned boring."

Sherrill found it anything but boring after her years in Connecticut and said so in her interviews, some of which read, she thought, like shopping guides.

Perry took himself off to ride up and down in the elevator.

"Don't press all the buttons, sweetheart," she cautioned. "It drives people crazy."

"I'm just gonna go have a look around."

Ten minutes later he was back. "There's this kid who lives downstairs. I met him in the elevator. We're going out to play. Okay Mom?"

"Play where?"

"I don't know. *Okay*, Mom?"

"Okay. But check in every few weeks and let me know where you are. All right?"

"Sure. And listen! When do I get my own keys? Josh has *his* own keys."

"Who's Josh?"

"The kid who lives downstairs."

"Where downstairs?"

"Oh, wow!" Perry said impatiently. "In 202, okay?"

"Okay."

He bolted out and slammed the door.

Within a week he knew every kid in the building. The telephone rang regularly, chirpy little voices asking if Perry was there. When he wasn't out playing with his friends, he was plonked down on the living room floor in front of the television set, playing with the channel selector box for the cable TV, punching the buttons and changing stations until he found something he wanted to watch. The allure of so many channels was very potent, and when Perry gave up the box to go out to play, Sherrill had trouble resisting the impulse to pick up the thing and start punching buttons herself.

In the evenings, after Perry had been put to bed, she collapsed in the living room, too tired to write, and watched television. By the end of the first month, with the last of the cartons gone and everything put away, she finally started to rework the new novel. She had considerably less time here than she'd had in Connecticut and began to feel guilty about the days when she did no writing at all—because she had an interview downtown on some radio station, or because a photographer was coming from the *Star* to photograph the apartment for the family section. She could easily see how, with her current schedule, she might never have the time to write another book. Her friends, when they phoned, commented about this or that article they'd read in the papers.

Perry was watching television in the living room one evening. Sherrill came in to tell him dinner was ready, then stopped, staring at the screen where a middle-aged man was doing a margarine commercial.

"My God!" she exclaimed with a surprised laugh. "That's Jamie!"

"Who, that guy?"

"I know him! That's Jamie! I don't believe it. I didn't think he'd still be here. I'll have to get in touch with him." She felt odd, seeing him.

"Wow, Mom!" Perry said excitedly. "You really *know* that guy? He's famous, for Pete's sake!"

'Famous?"

"He's on a zillion commercials. I see him all the time. There's this camera one, and a bread one, and one where he sells this cereal. A whole *bunch* of them. You *really* know him?"

"We used to work together," she said, watching the screen although the commercial had ended. "Dinner's ready. C'mon, sport, before it gets cold." She'd check the telephone book after dinner and call Jamie.

His number was listed. She stared at his name, examining her reactions. It was ten years later, but she still reacted to the sight of him on television, to his name in the directory. With a mounting sense of excitement, she tried his number. No answer. She promised herself she'd try again in the morning. It was suddenly important to reestablish contact. There were things she wanted to tell him, things she understood now that she hadn't been able to make sense of ten years earlier. In her memory, Jamie stood in surprisingly sharp definition: a gentleman of exceptional talent, humor, and kindness.

Rather than slacking off, as she'd hoped might happen, the media interest seemed to grow. She was giving interviews on an average of three times a week, and she'd been approached by three different Canadian publishing houses wanting to buy the Canadian rights to her new book. She called Hank and turned the matter over to him.

"Not on this contract," Hank said. "North American rights are held by Grand. But maybe next time around, we'll cut out the Canadian and have an auction. The interest's that big, huh?"

"Well, I've had three calls so far. I'm just referring everyone to you. I can barely keep up with the media people. I can't handle the publishers, too. Are you answering your phones these days, or still playing hard-to-get?"

"Don't worry, Sher. I'll take the calls."

"I don't altogether trust you," she said lightly, meaning it. "How are you going to know who's calling and why?"

"I'll take care of it."

She didn't care for his tone. Perhaps, she thought, she'd give some consideration to the possibility of agenting herself. She could hire a personal secretary who'd probably be more effective in the long run than Hank. She'd have to give it serious thought. She disliked the hinting impatience she heard in his voice each time she talked to him about something pertaining to her books and he assured her he was looking after everything. Too often calls came back to her, people saying they'd been unable to reach Hank, he hadn't returned their calls.

At irregular times for several weeks she tried Jamie's number. Then she turned her attention to work. When the telephone became too much of a distraction, she hired an answering service and let it take the calls while she was working. It helped. She got the changes made on the manuscript. When she was at the post office to mail it back to New York, the man behind the counter said, "Didn't I see you in the paper last week?"

"You may have." She smiled.

"Yeah, sure. You're the writer, eh? What's this, another book?"

"That's right."

"That was a good picture they had in the *Globe*. That'll be five ninety-seven."

The girl at the cleaners also recognized her, so did the pharmacist. She felt good, complete, and productive.

With a clear slate, she decided to give Jamie's number one last try. For all she knew, he'd moved and the directory listing was out of date. On the third ring, he answered. She'd have known his voice anywhere. With a laugh, she said, "I bet you'll never guess who this is."

Willing to play out the game, he mentioned several names.

"It's Sherrill," she told him. "Sherrill Raymond—used to be Westcott."

"Sherrill! I've been reading about you in the papers. You're back in town."

"I've been back a couple of months. You're impossible to get hold of. Do you know that?"

"I'm working," he explained. "I'm in a show at the St. Lawrence Centre. We close next Saturday night. What about you? Are you writing a new book?"

"I've just finished the rewrites."

"No kidding! No more singing?"

"I haven't really done any since I left. I tried singing for Perry one afternoon a while back. He laughed, and I decided I'd better not try again."

"Who's Perry?"

"My son. He's almost eight.

"And what about your husband? Is he here with you?"

"I'm divorced. What about you?"

"Me too."

"Great!" she declared, thinking she sounded like a complete idiot, overeager and giddy. "Listen, Jamie, come over for a coffee or a drink. I'd love to see you."

"I'd like that. I hate to be rude and cut you short, but I'm on my way out. I've got to get downtown to the CBC to do a radio show."

"Oh! Let me give you my number."

"Right. Hold on."

She gave him the number, then they said good-bye.

She poured herself a cup of coffee, feeling somewhat let down. She had no idea what she'd been hoping for—perhaps a bit more enthusiasm than he'd displayed. Well, never mind. It had been nice to hear his voice again. She wandered down the hall to her bedroom and stood in the doorway admiring the room. She did very much like this apartment, but at moments she felt rather claustrophobic, even lonely. After several seconds she moved toward her desk and got a ruled pad and a felt-tipped pen, carried them and her coffee back to the living room. She sat down at the dining table and, chewing on the end of the pen, gazed into space. Then she began to make notes.

Jamie hurried down to the car feeling curiously energized. The sound of Sherrill's voice had given him a big lift. As he drove downtown, he resurrected her from memory. She had lovely curling hair, and those large, haunted eyes. Her image returned readily to him and he could see her onstage, seated at the piano; he could hear the throaty depths of her voice. When he'd first seen the article in the newspaper, he hadn't recognized her. For one thing, her name had changed. For another, he hadn't known her as a writer. Perhaps, if he had time this afternoon, he'd stop by the library and pick up one of her books. Then he'd call when he had some free time, and go see her. She was divorced and had a son. He couldn't picture her as a mother. In his mind, he saw her as she'd been. He very much wanted to see her again. As soon as he had a spare minute he'd ring her, go round to see her.

A week went by and she didn't hear from him. She wrote it off. He probably wasn't interested, or didn't have the time to renew old friendships. Undoubtedly he'd changed. If the television commercial was anything to go by, he'd aged quite a lot. She considered going down to see him at the St. Lawrence but wasn't yet at a point where she felt sufficiently confident to go to the theater alone. Then a cousin she hadn't seen in years telephoned to say, "Hey, superstar! I've been reading about you in the papers. And every time I turn on the radio, there's your sexy little voice. I'm dying to see you. How about dinner on Saturday?"

"Would you be interested in seeing the play at the St. Lawrence?"

"Sure," Kate agreed.

"Okay. I'll try to get a baby-sitter and call you back."

Both teenage boys who lived down the hall were willing to stay with Perry for the evening. After making arrangements with the older one, she hurried back to book tickets for the play before calling Kate.

She sat beside Kate in the audience, chatting until the lights dimmed. Then she turned her attention to the stage, waiting for Jamie's entrance. He came on, radiating energy and charm as the middle-aged husband in an English farce. The entire time he was onstage, Sherrill was fascinated by the sight of him, filled with a strange pride. He was wonderfully droll; his voice was deeper, more melodious than ever. By the end of the performance, she felt very full, satisfied as if she'd eaten a sumptuous meal. In fact they hadn't yet had dinner.

"Lousy play," Kate observed. "But Jamie's always good."

"Do you know him?"

"I've seen him a lot, but I've never met him."

"We used to work together," Sherrill said.

"That's right!" Kate smiled eagerly. "I forgot that. Where should we eat?"

"You decide. I still don't know the restaurants."

Kate mentioned several places. Sherrill was barely listening; she was going over her reactions to seeing Jamie again.

"So how does it feel," Kate asked, "being back, being a big celebrity?"

"Sometimes it feels like some weird kind of PR job. I don't take it all that seriously. It's just work that sells books. You know?"

"You certainly seem in control of it," Kate said. "You haven't gone power-crazy or anything."

Sherrill laughed. "I don't have any power, I only write books. The publishers have the power. Anyway, it doesn't interest me. It never has. What about you? Do you feel powerful being a shrink?"

"A little," Kate admitted consideringly. "It depends on your interpretation. I feel good being able to help."

"I feel good being able to divert people, to keep them entertained for a while. That's all writing is: storytelling, diversion. I don't see myself as a great literary figure. How do you see yourself?" she asked, looking at her cousin.

Kate tossed her long, frizzy blond hair back over her shoulders. "About the way you see yourself, I guess. You're happy, aren't you?" She glanced over, smiling, then returned her attention to the traffic.

"Very. I'm happy writing. They could take away all the interviews, the signing sessions, and the rest of it and I'd still be happy."

"It's good to see you again," Kate said seriously. "I'm pretty proud of you you know? My cousin, the author."

"I'm pretty proud of you, too. My cousin, the shrink. It's handy to have help right in the family if I happen to need it." They laughed together. Sherrill's thoughts slid back to Jamie.

She began to invite people over to dinner, three or four at a time, and relished the luxurious feeling of being able to relax in the company of friends without feeling pressured to have a man in evidence, or to be out actively looking for one. Her married friends mingled well with her single ones. The single women she knew—like Kate and Della and Angie— expressed some interest in men but had clearly made life arrangements based on their absence. None of them seemed especially unhappy. And everyone made a fuss over Perry, who seemed to be having the best time of his life.

The weekend before school was to start she took him down to Ontario Place on the lakeshore, where he went wild at the Children's Village, climbing in and out of log constructions, sliding down wires, whomping against the walls of a rubber room. He threw a tantrum when she announced it was time to go home. It was his first temper display in quite some time and she took it personally, as if the tantrum signified his displeasure with more than just the end of the outing. Perhaps he would have genuine difficulty adjusting to the city; perhaps he'd arrived at an age where he needed male company and input; perhaps, perhaps ... Her concern for Perry led her into thoughts of Jamie. She told herself he simply wasn't interested and that was all there was to it. Nevertheless, she couldn't stop thinking about him.

Jamie had never been busier. He had two commercials lined up and three radio scripts to do, as well as the play at nights. Every so often he reminded himself to call Sherrill, but there never seemed to be a free moment. He'd been given notice to move; his apartment building had been sold and was going to be renovated. The other tenants had already begun to move out. He needed to find a new apartment but hadn't had time to do any looking. On Sunday, his one free day, he followed up on some newspaper ads. A waste of time. He saw nothing he liked. As he was preparing for bed that night he thought of Sherrill and his spirits soared as they had on the morning she'd telephoned. Fool! he thought. He should've gone to see her instead of wasting his time looking at overpriced, undersized apartments. He'd make a point of going round to see her—just as soon as his schedule cleared a bit. He was beginning to remember more and more about her: the clothes she'd worn, her gray-blue eyes, her music.

Chapter 27

Dene pulled the telephones from their jacks, locked the front and back doors, then sat down in the living room to think. She felt inundated by other people's expectations, by their requests for her time and efforts. Somewhere along the line she'd stopped taking the pictures she wanted and had started filling her days with appointments to work for other people. It had been months, years, since she'd had a day entirely to herself, to roam the city streets with her camera. She missed it badly. Now she felt very much as she had one day ten years earlier, awakening to reality in front of a drugstore on Third Avenue. She wanted to get away for a while, to put some distance between those people with requests for her work and her own desires. Her mother and Anthony would be leaving in a few weeks for Palm Beach. Perhaps this time she'd go with them for a week or two. They'd been inviting her to come along for years, but she'd refused. The time had come for a break, some new space in which to move and think. She went to the bedroom to get one of the telephones from the closet, carried it back to the living room, and reconnected it.

"Darling, we'd adore to have you!" Moira exclaimed happily. "Anthony will be so pleased."

"You're sure I wouldn't be putting you out?"

"Don't be silly. I've told you any number of times there's tons of room. I'll have Anthony ring the airlines straightaway to book you a seat. I *am* glad you've decided to come with us. You've been looking a bit seedy these past few months, darling. You really do work far too hard."

"I know that. I've been thinking about cutting back, maybe stopping altogether."

"You wouldn't give up your photography, would you?" Moira sounded alarmed at the prospect. "You're really frightfully good, you know."

"Not that," Dene clarified. "I'd like to stop taking assignments. I've only got two I can't get out of. The rest . . . it's all expendable. Anyway we can talk about that later. I'll be glad to book my own ticket. . . ."

Moira wouldn't hear of it. "Nonsense!" she said peremptorily. "Anthony will ring his travel agent and make all the arrangements." Lowering her voice, she added, "He does so enjoy that sort of thing. It wouldn't be fair to deprive him of the pleasure, would it?"

"No, it wouldn't."

"We'll see you Sunday, then?"

"Sunday." Dene hung up, once more disconnected the telephone and returned it to the bedroom closet. She felt a bit better, but still beleaguered by the diary full of appointments. With a cup of tea, she sat at the kitchen table looking through the diary. She'd cancel everything but the two commitments she'd made for film stills. They were the sort of jobs she really didn't object to; she was free to wander among the thick lighting cables and what seemed to be acres of equipment, at random photographing the action.

She wanted to turn the studio back into a dining room, to dispense with the bulky rolls of backdrop paper, the lights, the tripods, to make the place feel like an apartment again.

For two days she roamed the apartment, pausing every so often to look at the walls, the floor, the windows, putting her preliminary ideas in order. On the evening of the second day she was startled by pounding at her door. She opened it to find Charlie standing in the corridor.

"*Jesus!*" he said, wild-eyed. "I thought maybe you were dead or something. Why the hell haven't you been answering your phone?"

"Come on in, Charlie," she said calmly. "Would you like a cup of tea, or some beer?"

"A beer, please. Listen, what's up? I've been trying to call you for *days*. I was starting to get very *worried*."

"Were you?" She looked at him closely; he did appear upset. "Why would you worry about me?" she asked, opening the refrigerator for a bottle of the Carlsberg she kept there for him.

"Of course I'd worry about you! I mean, someone doesn't answer the phone for days on end, you start to think something's happened."

"I'm sorry you were worried." She was intrigued by this new view of him. He'd always seemed quite unconcerned about people except for being mildly upset by the dates that never seemed to go quite the way he hoped. "Let's go sit down." She led the way back to the living room and lowered herself into one of the Parson's chairs. Charlie sat opposite, glowering at her. He held the bottle to his mouth, took a healthy swallow, then said, "So, what's up? How come the recluse routine?"

"I've been thinking." She gazed steadily at him, wondering why she'd never thought to take his photograph. He had a wonderful, never-changing face. The only outward signs of his age were the graying of his hair and beard, the outcropping of small creases around his eyes. He was still solid, trim, youthful, in one of his perennial plaid shirts and Levi's.

"About what?" he asked. His huge hand obscured all but
the neck of the beer bottle. Her eyes shifted to his hands.

"I want to go back to where I was before," she said.

"You mean split to New York?"

She smiled. "No, I mean back to the beginning, when I
took photographs for my own pleasure, not for money.
I don't need the money; I never have. I'm not doing what
I want."

"Then close the show," he said simply.

"You agree?"

"Sure, why not, if you don't need the bread? I sure as hell
wouldn't bust my nuts at a job I didn't get off on."

"No?"

"Hell, no. Why should you?"

"I let myself fall into it." Her eyes left him; she gazed at
the floor. "I'm forty-four years old, Charlie. Maybe I've got
twenty-five or thirty years left. I want to spend them doing
what I enjoy, not feeling harassed by a schedule I can barely
keep up with."

"You're kicking a dead horse. I told you I agree with you."

"I know. It's just that it feels—irresponsible."

"People drop out all the time. One of these days I probably will, too."

"Really?" Her eyes returned to him.

"D'you seriously think I want to spend the rest of my life
selling old comics and memorabilia?"

"What would you like to do?"

"I don't know. Have a house in Maine, maybe, or upstate
Vermont. Do some fishing summers, ski winters, a little
farming. Who knows? I haven't thought that far. I've got
ideas in the back of my head. I could probably quit now, if
I really wanted to; sell the business for ten times what it
cost me to start it up. Twenty times. What with inflation,
though, the profit wouldn't last five years and I'd be out
looking for something else to do. The thing is, I'd be bored
out of my head in a week all by myself in some house in
Maine or Vermont. And who'd keep an eye on Anne?"

"I would."

This seemed to make him angry. "You planning to spend
the rest of your life baby-sitting for my aunt? Me, it's my
responsibility. But you're not obligated."

"I don't see it that way. I do have a responsibility: I'm her friend."

"You're wrong," he disagreed. "The sooner we leave off coddling her, the sooner I think she's going to decide to look out for herself. I'm not saying I don't care, nothing like that. I just think maybe we've gone too far with this whole business of fetching and carrying for her, not leaving her to do for herself."

"When did that occur to you?"

"I've been thinking about it."

"You might be right."

"Ah, shit!" he sighed. "I don't know. I'm not trying to do a number on her, or on you. I just think she's going batshit sitting up there playing the crazy lady. She's doing such a good job, one of these days she'll really *be* the crazy lady. Maybe we ought to bag it and let her deal with reality for a little while. It'd snap her out of it fast."

"I agree with you."

He finished the beer and set the bottle on the floor, then sat back gazing at her assessingly. "I was just figuring it out."

"What?"

"You've been living here—what—ten years?"

"Almost."

"Ten years we've known each other. Got another beer?"

"I'll get you one."

"Just you sit there. I can get it myself. See that! It's what you do for Anne, too. Relax, I'll get it myself." He got up and went for the beer. When he came back he sat with his arms propped on the sides of the chair, again gazing at her. At last he said, "Four years, I'll be fifty. I've been married twice. I ever tell you that?"

"I knew. Anne told me a long time ago."

"I was too young," he said, "had all these foolish ideas about women, about marriage."

"I did, too."

"I used to think it had to do with all that jumping up and down, fetching and carrying *you* think you've got to do all the time. Women wait on men, eh? I don't think that anymore."

"No, neither do I," she concurred.

"Let's get married, Dene."

She stared at him for a moment, then laughed. "We don't even know each other," she protested.

"Sure we do. We've known each other for ten years."

"Not to get married. My God, Charlie . . .!"

"I've been doing some heavy thinking of my own," he said comfortably, crossing his extended legs at the ankles. "I mean, the past few years, every time another date bites the dust, where do I go? Here. I come over with my pizza, or my Swiss Chalet chicken, we watch the tube for a couple of hours, you cheer me up, and I go home. We understand each other, you and me. That's a lot, you know."

"That's friendship."

"What else is a marriage?" he asked. "You tell me! You've been married; you should have some idea."

"I wasn't married. I was obsessed. That's something else."

"I think you're beautiful," he said. "You know that? All those times I'd come over here, I'd think how goddamn beautiful you are; I'd see how scared you were—at the beginning, that was—and I'd wonder what the hell ever happened to turn you that way. I scare you?"

"No."

"I turn you off?"

"Uh . . . no."

"So, let's get married." He grinned at her.

"You're teasing me."

"The hell I am! I'd marry you in a minute. Tomorrow. We wouldn't even have to live together, you didn't like the idea. I've got a pretty nice place."

"You want to make love to me, Charlie."

"Damn right!"

There was a silence. Slowly she inspected the man sitting opposite: his long, relaxed limbs, his broad chest, his round blue eyes and bushy beard. Her eyes came to rest finally on his immense, powerful-looking hands. Something inside her responded to his hands; it uncoiled, loosening her chest which, until that moment, had felt tightly constricted.

"I'm going to Florida with my mother and Anthony," she said finally.

Charlie put the second empty bottle on the floor and leaned forward with his elbows on his knees. "When! For how long?"

She wet her lips before answering. "We leave at the end

of the month. I think I'll stay for two or three weeks, maybe a month. I need to get away for a while."

"I'll come with you," he offered, sitting now on the edge of the chair.

She shook her head. He sat back in the chair. "Perhaps another time," she said. "I have to be by myself."

His expression plainly told her he interpreted her remarks as a rejection. He was getting ready to pull himself up from the chair and leave.

"I'm not very good at this," she said uncertainly.

"No problem. You want me to split, I'm off, and no hard feelings."

She got up from her chair and bent close to him, looking intently into his eyes. As always, he seemed very young to her. Despite his forty-six years, Charlie would be forever young. She liked the idea of that: a man who, despite the changes all around him, remained constant. She touched her lips to his, then reached for his hand. "Don't be disappointed," she said.

He eased her down on his lap and they sat for several minutes saying nothing. After a time, he asked, "Why do you talk that way?"

"What way?"

"Everything you say is about letting people down, about disappointing somebody. Far as I can see, you never do any of that."

"You don't understand."

"The hell I don't. I only *look* dumb. You've never once let *me* down. That's where it counts for me. Never let Anne down, either. I'll even bet you never let any of those clients of yours down."

"Charlie, all I've ever done for you is be here. That's not *doing* for someone."

"You don't think so?"

"No."

"Just shows how much you know." He began undoing the buttons on her blouse. She stiffened. "Ssshhh," he murmured. He got the buttons undone, then lifted open the blouse, baring her breasts. She closed her eyes as his huge hand gently touched her. "You're so pretty," he said wonderingly, "got the body of a young girl." He drew his hand through her hair, lifting a handful to his lips. "Smell so good."

She sat on his lap watching as if from a distance as he caressed her and put his mouth to her breasts. Gradually the stiffness eased out of her body and she lay against his chest feeling boneless, dizzy. Instinctively, she rested her head on his shoulder, trusting him. She wanted to be completely passive, to allow him to do with her whatever he chose. He seemed not to mind. She kept her eyes closed as his hand stroked up the length of her thigh; she helped, shifting, so he could have access.

"Christ!" he whispered, his arm tightening around her as his fingers struck lightly against her, probing.

It was hopeless. She had no talent for passivity. With both hands she turned his head toward her and kissed him. Then she broke away, stood up and removed her clothes. He watched, a stunned expression on his face, then he held out his arms and brought her close, pressing his face into her belly.

"There's nothing to you," he said softly. "Tiny little thing." He circled her waist with his hands. "Look at that!"

"I'm too old for chairs or the floor, Charlie. Come into the bedroom."

She walked away from him, feeling chilled. What was she doing? Don't stop to think about it! she told herself as she pulled back the bedclothes and turned to watch Charlie undress. Hurry up! she silently urged him. Hurry, before I have a chance to change my mind, before I lose my courage!

The instant his arms came around her she was able to put her thoughts, if not her fears, aside.

"You're trembling. Are you cold?" he asked caringly, trying to warm her with his body.

"It's been a long time," she admitted. "Years."

"That makes two of us." He smiled, stretched out at her side, his hands pleasurably distracting her. "I meant it, you know."

"What?"

"I'd marry you."

"I can't do that. Come here. Lie on top of me."

"I'm too heavy."

"No you're not. Lie on me."

Beneath his welcome weight she felt peaceful, and smiled. "You have lovely soft skin, Charlie."

"So do you." He grinned down at her. "You feel wonderful."

"My husband left me for my younger sister."

"Those things happen," he said philosophically.

"I guess they do. You're amazing."

"No. Merely fantastic." He kissed her shoulder. "I want to look at you," he said, slipping away. "Look at you! Built like a teenager."

"An elderly teenager," she scoffed.

"Beautiful pink nipples and nice small breasts, slim hips, great legs."

"Shut up," she whispered. "You're embarrassing me."

"You can't take a compliment," he accused. "You'll have to get used to it."

"Don't plan on me," she cautioned. "I can't promise anything."

"I don't need any promises, don't want any."

"I'll wake up in the morning and wish I'd never done this."

"No you won't," he said confidently. "I'll wake up right here and I won't let you do that."

"I haven't slept in the same bed with anyone in more than fifteen years."

"So I'll sleep on the floor. Don't complicate things," he said quietly. "Just go with it."

All the while they talked, his hands and mouth caressed her. She wanted to catch hold of him, stop him so that she might think about what was happening, but he was too elusive, too determined not to allow her to think. She closed her eyes again and bent herself open to hold him. As his body merged with hers, she suddenly saw this act as a series of photographs: black and white, an amalgamation of limbs, images of passion. He'd managed to return to her her through-the-lens viewing of life. It felt like a gift. She received him gladly into her thoughts, her body feeling freed at last of the pressures that had accumulated so cumbersomely.

Chapter 28

Sherrill had finally finished the outline and started work on another novel. Perry was well ensconced in the local public school and had made even more new friends there. He was busy and happy, the tantrums had subsided. He enjoyed coming home for lunch midday, letting himself in and out of the building with his own set of keys, which he pocketed importantly every time he went out.

Relieved by his adaptability, Sherrill was working hard and making good progress. She was disturbed one afternoon by the ringing of the telephone and debated answering. Thinking it might be important, she got up from her desk.

"If the invitation's still good," Jamie said. "I thought I'd come for tea this afternoon."

"This afternoon?" Caught up in the fog of her paper world, she looked at the clock. It was just after one.

"Is it a bad time?" he asked.

"No, no. What time this afternoon?"

"About two thirty?"

"That'd be fine, fine."

"You're sure it's not a bad time? If you're working we can always make it another day."

"No, honestly. Come!"

"Good. I'll see you later."

She hung up and for a moment could see his impending visit only as an interruption in the flow of her work. Then she became excited. After all these years, she'd meet Jamie again. She returned to the typewriter, stopping at two o'clock to remove her old T-shirt and put on a long-sleeved, cranberry-colored shirt and some makeup. She sat back down to get a little more work done before Jamie arrived.

The sharp burring noise of the intercom startled her. She jumped up and ran to buzz Jamie in, then opened the hall door to wait for him. The apartment numbers were hard to see, engraved as they were on the actual handles of the doors. Without exception, everyone who'd come to see her had wandered up and down the hall for several minutes before locating the apartment numbers. She found it saved a lot of time and confusion if she simply opened the door and leaned out into the corridor to greet guests.

He came off the elevator and she smiled. He looked older, wider in the chest and shoulders than he'd seemed onstage, but it was unquestionably Jamie. She stood back from the door and he stepped over the threshold saying, "You haven't changed. You look exactly the same."

"So do you." There was a moment of awkwardness as they stared at each other. Then he gave her the green paper-wrapped cone of flowers he carried and kissed her on both cheeks in the French fashion. A little flustered, she accepted the flowers and asked, "Do you really want tea? Or would you like a drink, a glass of wine?"

"Wine would be lovely," he said, looking into the living room. "This is beautiful."

"Sit down," she said, on her way to the kitchen. "I'll be right there." She unwrapped the flowers—lavender chrysanthemums—and put them into the first thing that came to hand, a large water jug. "They're gorgeous flowers," she said, bringing his glass of wine and her coffee into the living room. He'd seated himself in the center of the sofa and looked, she thought, the slightest bit uneasy. She felt rather nervous herself, and wondered why.

"You look wonderful," he said. "You haven't changed a bit."

"Oh, I have. I've aged, grown up. And I'm glad. It's a relief not to be young anymore. I did come down to see the show, you know."

"How did you like it?"

"I thought you were terrific. I didn't care much for the play."

He laughed, nodding. "Not the world's greatest piece of writing. It got very mixed reviews."

"Have you been living here all this time?" she asked, filled with curiosity about him.

"I've been back a few years. I lived in Montreal for a time." He lifted the glass of wine, unable to take his eyes off

her. It was strange, but the moment he'd come off the
elevator to see her leaning out into the hallway he'd had a
powerful sense of recognition. It was something that went
far beyond the fact of their previous acquaintanceship, something almost intuitive. There was such intelligence in her
eyes and she was very pretty. It was hard to believe she was
... How old was she? He couldn't remember. She didn't
look more than twenty-seven or -eight but that, he knew,
was impossible. She'd been in her twenties when they'd
worked together. "Tell me all about your writing. I tried to
get your books at the library, but they were out. The librar-
ian said they're very popular."

"That's good to hear. Remind me before you go and I'll
give you copies."

"When did you start?" he asked. "I don't recall you were
interested in writing."

"I started quite soon after I left, actually. It was just a
whim."

As she spoke, he watched her, captivated. He found her
bright, alive, refreshingly open. His interest in her was
immediate. She was totally different from the women he'd
kept company with in recent years, and despite her youthful
appearance, she exuded a kind of hard-won wisdom that
showed in small, self-deprecating smiles, an ease of manner,
and a reluctance to discuss her success.

"You should be very proud of yourself," he said, meaning
it.

"I just feel lucky that I'm paid to do something I enjoy so
much. Anyway, *you* should feel pretty proud. You were far
and away the best thing in that show."

"You used to have such haunted eyes."

"I wasn't particularly happy. It's amazing how you can
decide to be happy by comparison: what went before was
awful, therefore what goes now is pretty good. It was an
ugly divorce, complete with little squibs in the *National
Enquirer.* I don't know where they got some of the stuff they
printed. Friends in town used to call me up to read me the
latest piece. I finally had to ask them to stop. It was like
hearing about someone else, those pieces about 'Author and
Mad. Ave. Exec.' " She shook her head. "It was all fuel for
Drew's fire. He took my success personally, as if it were a

weapon I held over his head. I *never* did that. Anyway—"
she brightened, pushing back her sleeve to check the time—
"Perry's going to come bouncing in here any minute. If
we're lucky, he'll stand still long enough to say hello and
then go tearing out again." She smiled.

He thought her smile was extraordinary, as engagingly
unpremeditated as a child's. "How old's your son again?"
he asked.

"Seven, almost eight. He's really a little old man disguised as a small boy. You'll see. How's your wine? Would
you like some more?"

"I'd rather have some coffee, if you've got any more."

She took his wineglass out to the kitchen and returned
with a cup of coffee. "When did you get divorced?" she
asked, sitting again in the pine and canvas armchair angled
by the sofa.

"I left Jane soon after you moved to the States. The
actual divorce went through a couple of years back. Where
did you live in Connecticut? Why did you decide to come
back?"

She laughed. "This sounds like an interview. I lived in
Stamford, about thirty-five miles from New York. It was
very beautiful there. I miss the beaches more than anything.
There was so much *space*. That's the hardest thing to get
used to here: the houses being so close together. We had an
acre of land with the house. And that was fairly average.
I've never lived in a proper apartment building. My place
up the road was part of a huge old house that had been
broken up into apartments."

"I was there. You invited me for tea once."

"I *did*?"

"As I recall you watched the tag end of a Bette Davis
movie."

"I didn't!" She laughed. "My God! How rude!"

"It wasn't at all."

"What did you do while I watched the movie?"

"I watched it with you. It was a very pleasant afternoon.
You made tea, we talked for a bit, and that was the end of
it."

"I don't remember. Isn't that something?"

"You had a lovely place with a big stone fireplace."

"That's right. You really were there."

He laughed, enjoying himself.

"What about you?" she asked. "Tell me what you've been doing."

"The past two years I've been concentrating on the theater."

"Didn't you work in the theater before?"

"I never did. Ron and I started out with the revue. I went from there into television and radio. Actually, I began by writing revue material. But I had no background in the theater. I thought it was about time I got some."

"You were always very good," she said. "I've still got the programs, you know."

"You haven't!"

"I do."

"I don't believe it."

"I'll get them." She went to the bedroom, found her scrapbook, removed the two old programs, and brought them back to hand to him.

"You really do have them." Shaking his head, he laughed softly. "Isn't this a giggle?" he said, reading the cast biographies. "Ron wrote his best material for the program notes."

He spent far more time studying the programs than she'd expected he would. He read them from cover to cover before placing them carefully on the coffee table. "I never saved any of these things."

"I save everything. Would you like some crackers and cheese, or a biscuit?"

"No, thank you. When I'm working I usually have an early dinner." He glanced at his wristwatch and she hoped he wasn't going to announce that the visit was over. She looked at him, finding him still very handsome. There was a lot of red in his hair. She wondered why she hadn't remembered that, or the fact that his eyes were hazel and not brown, or that he'd come to her apartment once for tea. She could vaguely recall his visit, but the details refused to come clear.

The front door flew open, Perry marched in, saw Jamie, stopped, and near-shouted, "Wow, Mom, you really do know him!"

"Come and say hi to Jamie. This is Perry."

Jamie shook the boy's hand, able to see no resemblance between mother and son except for the eyes. They both had large, clear, gray-blue eyes, with long, thick lashes.

Perry shook hands, all the while repeating, "Wow! Oh, wow! None of the kids believed it when I said my mom knew you. Boy, they'll have to believe me now!"

Jamie reached into his back pocket to bring out a small package. "I thought you might like this," he said to Perry.

Perry tore off the wrapping. "Oh wow! It's a model soldier."

Jamie was inordinately pleased that the boy called it a model rather than a toy. It was in fact a model, and that this child should be aware of the difference was foolishly gratifying.

"What's the uniform?" Perry asked, going to stand by Jamie's knee, turning the soldier over in his hands.

"It's a Royal Scots Fusilier. Are you interested in models?"

"Only a little," Perry replied. "I don't know much about them. Do you?"

"Some. I like to paint them. I have quite a few books on history, uniforms, that sort of thing."

"Did you paint this one?"

"Uh huh."

"Boy! That's really neat."

Sherrill followed this exchange with interest. Jamie's entire demeanor had altered with Perry's arrival; he'd relaxed visibly. "Perry, say thank you," she prompted.

"Thank you," he parroted. "I can't wait to show this to Josh." He started toward the door, but turned back. "Hey! C'n I see you paint one of them sometime?"

"Sure," Jamie said.

"Wow! Far out! See ya."

"Hold on!" Sherrill called. "I'd like you back here by five, for dinner. Jamie, would you like to have dinner with us? I was going to take Perry out. Five," she repeated to the boy, then released him.

Jamie looked all at once discomfited. "I wasn't planning to eat out and I'm afraid I don't have enough cash . . ."

"That's all right." She smiled. "We'll take you to dinner. Stay! You can't rush off when I haven't seen you for so long. You'll have your early dinner and be downtown in time for the show. I promise."

"All right. I'd like that. Next time will be my treat."

"It was sweet of you to bring that soldier for Perry. I haven't seen him so excited in ages. I didn't even know he was interested in them."

The door flew open again and Perry slouched in, grim-faced, muttering, "Josh had to go to the *dentist*." He went to sit beside Jamie on the sofa, asking, "What is this, coffee? C'n I have some?"

Jamie glanced over at Sherrill to see if it was all right. She nodded. "If you like," he told the boy. Perry picked up the mug, drank half the coffee, then set the mug down, saying, "Hey, I know! Want to play Clue? D'you know how to play? I'll teach you. C'mon, let's play. I'll go get the game."

"Perry! Maybe Jamie's not interested in playing a game right now."

"I wouldn't mind," Jamie said unexpectedly.

"Really?"

"I like games. Clue's very good."

Perry went off again to get the game and Sherrill looked again at Jamie. "Your children must be quite grown up now."

"The younger boy died several years ago."

"I'm sorry. That's awful. I have nightmares sometimes about something happening to Perry. Look, you really don't have to play this game, you know."

"I know, but I'd like to. He's a lovely kid."

"You think so? It's amazing how much nicer other people's kids seem than your own. I think he's pretty nice, but then I'm prejudiced. You're sure you'd like to play?"

"I would, yes."

"Okay." She got up to clear the dining table. Jamie watched, intrigued by the economy of her movements and her slim grace, the length of her neck. She had small, perfect ears that lay flat against her skull; the line of her jaw was firm and well defined. It seemed astonishing that this was the Sherrill who used to wear gray pinafore dresses and knee socks. There were hints of that younger Sherrill about her, but this woman appeared to be far less fearful than that girl had been. This woman seemed to have a quiet, underlying strength; she was purposeful, yet self-effacing. Based on what he'd read in the newspapers, he'd come half-expecting she'd be rigged out with expensive clothes and filled with self-importance. It proved, once again, that one simply couldn't take at face value what appeared in print. There was always a certain editorial slant to the reporting. Nothing he'd read or remembered seemed valid in view of Sherrill's reality. She seemed very small with her short hair, lightly made-up face, sports shirt, and blue jeans. It hardly seemed possible that this motherly, unaffected woman could be the success she was. Obviously, she was successful. Everything about the apartment bespoke it: the stereo components housed in an oak stand; the comfortable, clean-lined furniture; the entire wall of hardcover books; the wall of paintings; the brass curios here and there. Even the sports shirt and jeans, now that he looked at them, were exquisitely cut and of top quality. He'd met other successful women, but none of them had handled their accomplishments with quite Sherrill's effortless grace.

They played the game, with Perry instructing both adults in the rules. Every so often Sherrill looked over at Jamie to see that, true to his word, he was having fun. Their eyes met and he said, "This really is very nice." He looked appreciatively around the room, then at her again. "It's good to be with a family."

"Civilians," she contributed. "I know what you mean. I had some trouble adjusting at first. Now, most of the time, I forget how odd it was looking at civilians from the outside. From the inside, I have to wonder why I ever lived the way I did, spending all my time with people in the business and heartily condemning everyone outside it. It does take some getting used to."

"I could get used to it very easily, I'm afraid." These few hours he'd spent with her and the boy had made him very aware of how fatigued he usually felt these days with his friends in the business. The atmosphere was wholesome and healthy here; no one was "on," no one was promoting anything. He was able to take deep breaths and forget about auditions, cold readings, sullen producers, untalented directors, twenty-year-old casting agents who'd never heard of Jamie Ferrara but who understood he had an impressive list of credits.

Over dinner at a pleasant French restaurant nearby, it was apparent to Sherrill that Jamie was growing increasingly distracted. She thought initially it might be because she'd offered to treat him and felt embarrassed, but she dismissed that idea when the bill arrived and, with a healthy show of equanimity, he continued to chat with Perry while Sherrill paid for the meal. She realized, when he checked his watch for the third time in half an hour, that he was nervous. He had a show to do. She'd forgotten the anxiety that came with being a performer.

When they came out of the restaurant it had started to rain. In high spirits, the three of them hurried through the light mist toward the apartment.

"Where did you park?" she asked Jamie as they approached the building.

"I'm in the guest parking lot at the rear."

"I know you're anxious to get to the theater, so I won't hold you up." She gave him a kiss on the cheek, said good-bye, and steered Perry in out of the rain. Jamie, surprised by her display of tolerant understanding, stood a moment watching her and the boy enter the elevator in the lobby, before he ran up the driveway to the back of the building.

She got Perry bathed and into bed, then went back to her new outline, happy to have seen Jamie again. He'd aged rather shockingly, she thought. He was only forty-three but he looked and acted far older. There was a sadness about him, and she wondered if that was due in part to the death of his son. Undoubtedly some of it was the accumulated *angst* of years in the business. He still dressed well, she noted, reviewing their time together. He'd always had good taste in clothes.

At eleven-thirty the telephone rang.

"Do you really play tennis?" Jamie asked.

She laughed, recalling the mention of tennis over dinner. "I really do."

"Would you like to play tomorrow?"

"I'd love it. Where and when?"

"One-thirty?"

"Perfect."

He named a tennis club downtown, then thought to ask, "Do you know your way?"

She laughed. "I remember the streets. I just don't know which ones are one-way these days. But I'll find it."

As she was getting ready for bed she realized that he must have called her within minutes of coming offstage. The realization warmed her. It meant he'd been thinking about her.

Both of them were out of condition and played a sloppy game, but she played better than average with a strong forehand and narrowly won both sets. Afterward, as they sat in the club restaurant, he studied her, deciding she was the most interesting woman he'd met in years. She wasted no time on inconsequential chitchat, nor did she make any particular effort to impress him or flatter him. He could feel himself moving closer and closer to her. All his adult life he'd had in mind an ideal woman he could live with and love. Sherrill came closer to that image than any other woman he'd met. Yet it was such a potentially dangerous ideal, this image of the perfect woman for Jamie Ferrara, that he was reluctant to give in to what might be only an illusion, created by his need to believe. Without something to look forward to, without someone to hope for, what was the point of his life, his work, his getting through the days? Despite his reluctance, every time he looked at her, saw her smile, or heard her laughter, something that had been cold and hard inside him for a long time seemed to thaw a bit more.

He ordered tea and a cheeseburger. She ordered tea. They found themselves temporarily lost for something to say. It wasn't an awkward silence, but rather a comfortable, companionable one. He felt no pressing need to fill the gap with idle chat, but took advantage of the time to admire, yet again, her pretty features. There was something so ineffably sane and calm and reasonable about her that he felt he could sit at her side for hours, content to bask in her aura. Yet combined with this was her comprehension of the grinding inhumanity of the business in which he made his living. Nothing had ever appealed to him quite so strongly as this combination of qualities. "Are you very disciplined about your writing?" he asked, finally, eager to know all about her.

"I'm disciplined about everything. It's not easy to live with. I drive poor Perry crazy, chasing after him all the time to clean up and put things away. But it's really the only way I can function. I can't live with disorder. I know it drove Drew crazy."

She spoke of her former husband. To his surprise, Jamie found himself suddenly jealous. It was an entirely new emotion, one that made him sit back and consider the implications. Why on earth should he be jealous of a man she'd once been married to? He had no idea; he simply disliked the thought of her with anyone else. He had become, he discovered, possessive of her. It was like having a snake in your hand, one with its teeth well embedded in your flesh: you wanted to shake it off, but couldn't.

"When does your show close?" she asked, noticing the change of expression. "Something wrong?"

"No, no. We close in two weeks."

"And then what?"

"Then I go into rehearsals for a new show. After that, I've got a week off before I do a film."

"A film? That's terrific. Have you got a good part?"

"So-so. A supporting role."

"Where's it being done?"

"Nova Scotia."

"Oh! How long will you be away?"

"Six weeks. After that, I'm clear for a while. I booked all these things ages ago. It was part of my plan: I made a deal with myself that I'd take anything and everything that was offered. I overdid it, I think." As on the evening before, he checked his wristwatch, then seemed to slide into a preoccupied state.

"I've got to be getting home," she said, discovering she was beginning to be able to read his mood changes. "Perry will be out of school soon."

They left the club and stood by the front door. "Thank you for the game," she said. "I'll be happy to play again anytime. I need the exercise."

"One day next week. Where's your car?" he asked.

"Just over there." She pointed out the Mercedes. She prayed he wouldn't make some silly comment about the car. A dozen times since she'd got back one or another of her friends had, upon seeing the Mercedes, made remarks about the size of her income.

"I'll walk you over."

After she'd climbed into the front seat and rolled down the window, he bent to look in at her. "How do you like it?" he asked.

"The car? I love it. It's my four-door, automatic totem: a gift I bought myself."

"Handle well? What sort of mileage do you get?"

"Very good on both counts."

"Well, maybe one day next week I'll come by and cook a meal for you and Perry."

"I'd love it." She would have liked to kiss him good-bye but couldn't think of any way to accomplish it. He straightened and stood back from the car as she put it into Drive. She waved, then watched in the rearview mirror as he stood a moment longer before turning to open the door to a bright blue BMW. She laughed aloud, relieved. Why was she so skeptical, so afraid to trust appearances? she wondered. Jamie was very successful in his own right. He would never, as Drew had done, try to pit his success against hers.

Something was happening between them, and she was glad. How long it might last didn't matter. Her feelings for Jamie were intact, had survived ten years' separation. If anything, they'd flourished and grown without her awareness. He moved her, made something in her yearn toward him. When he grew distracted and gazed off into the distance she wanted to put her arms around him and gently direct him back. There were moments when he seemed like someone poised on the roof of a building, ready either to step out into space or to climb down to safety. She wanted to represent safety, to have him choose to be with her.

Chapter 29

Slowly, seductively, Anne began to remove her clothes. She unzipped her dress and let it slither to her feet, then stood a moment, aware of the effect she was having on the man across the room in the shadows. His eyes were fixed unblinking on her. She dropped the straps of her slip, then eased the garment down her body, allowing it to pool at her feet. Clad now in black lace brassiere and garter belt, she again paused, her eyes connecting with the young man's.

"Go on!" he whispered urgently, drawing hard on the cigarette he held.

She knew the black lace was a flattering contrast to the whiteness of her skin and hair, and looked down at herself, at the tops of her breasts barely contained by the skimpy brassiere. The sight of her own body aroused her and, again looking at him, she drew her fingertips across the exposed areas of her breasts. He remained motionless, his eyes following her every movement. Reaching back, she unhooked the brassiere, slid it off, and presented him with a full viewing of her breasts. He moved a step closer, his face remaining in shadow. He was a tall, broad presence whose features were obscured by the concentration of light behind him. She ran her hands over her breasts as their eyes sparred, then, her lips curving into a slight smile, she stepped out of the black suede high heels—nothing more than a fragile, expensive assembly of thin straps—and sat on the end of the bed to take off the old-fashioned, center-seamed nylons. At last, clad only in the garter belt—the garters dangling not unpleasantly against her thighs and buttocks—she stood again. She dropped the belt to the floor and stood nude before him.

He turned to extinguish the cigarette in the ashtray on the bedside table. As he turned back, he was unknotting his tie, pulling it from around his neck and stuffing it into his jacket pocket. In silence, he closed his hand over her breast, his thumb grazing her nipple. She sighed and came closer, weaving her fingers through his soft, curling hair. He was so young, no more than twenty-five or -six. He smelled sweet, fresh, like a baby; the flesh of his face and neck was firm, smooth. She kissed his ear, licking his downy lobe, her fingertips now tracing the line of his jaw as his mouth touched against her shoulder, then her neck, his tongue darting against her skin. She could feel his hand searching in her hair. He found the combs, removed them, and her hair tumbled down. He was lovely, she thought, adept and sensitive to sensation. His hands skimmed down the length of her body, closing over her buttocks to bring the lower half of her body up against him. He was hard; it pleased her. She turned her head to kiss him, but he released her to fondle her breasts, teasing her nipples. She was very wet, very aroused as he directed her to the edge of the bed, his hands on her shoulders easing her down. He knelt on the floor between her legs, caressing her inner thighs. She felt a sudden sharp pinch at the top of her thigh and moved to sit up, but he whispered, "Stay still," and she lay back thinking perhaps in his eagerness he'd bitten her. The top of her thigh stung, but after a moment she forgot about it. He spread her legs wide, the fingers of both hands moving over her belly and thighs. Again she felt a quick stabbing sensation, this time at the base of her belly, but his mouth and tongue pushed at her, displacing the sudden small pain.

He was very good. One hand fastened itself to her breast while the other, in league with his mouth, played over her insistently until, too soon, she was peaking. She motioned to him to stop, wanting him to come inside of her now, but he ignored her. Once more her flesh was nipped. She cried out in pain, then in pleasure.

While she lay trying to catch her breath, he stood up and removed his clothes. Then he spread himself heavily on her body and thrust into her. She gasped, unprepared, and had to tell herself to relax. He stopped. "Stay as you are," he whispered, and continued thrusting into her. She sought to kiss his mouth, but he averted his head, sinking his teeth deep into the flesh of her upper arm. His hands held hers pinned to her sides. When she tried to free herself, one hand left hers to insert itself between their two free bodies and again she felt the quick pinching, this time at her breast.

"What are you *doing?*" she demanded, trying to get away from him.

He didn't respond but plunged on brutally, his pace increasing. She decided she'd remain inert until he finished. Then she'd insist that he leave. Her body was stinging in the several places where he'd nipped her. Her thighs were dripping from their exertions and she longed, all at once, to be rid of this man. She'd shower and go to sleep. She'd made a mistake this time. He was not so gentle and sensitive as she'd thought.

He went on for a long time, his hips grinding hurtfully against hers until, with something like a snarl, he released himself in her. As he did, pain shot from her armpit to her thigh as he dragged what felt like one long fingernail along her flesh. She cried out, a thin, high scream, and tried again to move away from him but he lay gasping upon her, effectively immobilizing her.

When at last he lifted himself, she stared at him, frightened by his narrow hate-filled eyes. There was blood on his arms and belly. He sat astride her, one hand forcibly holding her clamped to the bed, as he slowly opened the fingers of the other hand to reveal a single-edged razor blade.

Oh, God! she thought. It was her blood on him. He'd been cutting her with the razor. She heaved herself up, toppling him to one side of the bed, and raced to the door, aware now of the blood dripping down her side, running down her belly and thighs. Almost lazily, he fell upon her and brought her down hard on the floor, where, again pinning her, he drew the razor down the center of her chest. Blood bubbled to the surface of her skin, and, terrorized, she struggled to force him off her. His hand shot out and collided with the side of her head, stunning her for a second or two. The razor darted across her breasts; more beads of blood popped to the surface. Then he was on his feet, dragging her upright. She fought, crazed with fear, as he tried to pull her toward the bathroom. She knew if he got her into the bathroom he'd kill her. With all her strength, she brought her knee up into his groin, but he danced aside and she connected with the hard bone of his hip. Smiling now, as if he approved of her efforts to battle him, he struck her several times in the face, then wrapped his arm crushingly around her body, bringing her chest to chest with him.

"You disgusting old slut," he hissed, his arms steel bands crushing the air out of her lungs. "You pathetic old whore! What're you, forty, fifty?"

"*Let me go!*" she gasped, twisting frantically in his grip.

Suddenly he opened his arms. She staggered toward the door, her arms numbed from the pressure he'd applied. He threw out his hand, kicked at her legs, and again she crashed to the floor. She curled instinctively into a self-protecting knot, her arms crossed over her head as he began kicking her. The blows fell on her legs, in the small of her back, her arms. *Kill me,* she thought. *Please, let me die.* She curled further into herself as the heel of his foot connected with her elbow. Then all at once there was someone else in the room. She could hear the sickening dull thud of something striking naked flesh. Then again, again. She kept her eyes squeezed shut, praying for unconsciousness, her body shuddering with pain. Silence. Her heart was beating too fast, too fast. Her arms were paralyzed from the strain of holding them protectively over her head. The police would come next; they'd crowd into the room to gape at her, along with the ambulance attendants. Wake up! I want to wake up now!

She shoved away the stifling comforter and groped on the bedside table for the lamp, found the switch, and turned it on. She was perspiring heavily, the hair at the back of her neck saturated. Her head was pounding, her arms felt deadened. Trembling, she reached for her cigarettes and lit one, then sat against the headboard staring into the room. She'd left the door to the deck open. The cool air gusting in quickly dried her, turning her cold. She pulled the comforter back from the foot of the bed, tucked it around herself, wrapped her arms around her bent knees as she drew hard on the cigarette, waiting for her heartbeat to slow, for the nightmare to recede.

When, she wondered, was it going to end? She longed for sleep but feared a return of the nightmare, so she kept herself awake, immediately lighting another cigarette when the first one burned down. There were a number of scars on the carpet from cigarettes she'd lit on other nights when she'd awakened from reliving what had been a reality and now existed in her tortured dreams. The scorched areas on the carpet were reminders of her inability to get past the experience. She thought if she could just get through one night without waking up in terror the whole thing would be behind her; she'd be able to begin forgetting. She'd thought this for the last five years, but the nightmare showed no signs of departing

Maybe, she thought, she should go into the bathrooom and take every pill she could find in there: she'd be able to sleep her way right past the nightmare and out of life altogether. It was tempting. The idea of pure sleep, unsullied by the rekindled horror of her past, had more appeal than almost anything else she could conceive of.

The second cigarette burned down. She put it in the ashtray and got up, feeling about on the floor with her foot for her slippers. In her robe, she went to stand out on the deck, looking down the 2 A.M. street. A yellow police car drove slowly past, down Duplex. The wind was strong, pushing against her as she stood gripping the rough wood guardrail, sending her hair into wild disorder. She could feel winter in the wind, and shivered. Her head ached and the feeling still hadn't properly returned to her arms and hands. Something had to happen, she told herself. She couldn't keep living this way indefinitely; there was no point to it.

Turning, she leaned against the rail, looking into the bedroom. It looked inviting, but it felt like a trap. She yawned, wrapping her arms around herself for additional warmth. As she stared into the room, her fingers pressed exploringly into her ribs. Her bones were very prominent. She turned again toward the street. A car approached up Duplex and, as she watched, it pulled into the parking area at the rear of the house. Charlie climbed out from the passenger side; Dene appeared from the other. They walked to the back door and let themselves in. Light spilled over the parked cars as someone pushed a switch in the kitchen.

Was Charlie having an affair with Dene? She waited, and

after a few minutes the kitchen light went off; the light in the bedroom went on. After a short time, it too, went off. The house was silent. When had this started? she wondered unhappily, feeling betrayed, lonely.

Chilled, she returned into the bedroom, sat on the side of the bed, and lit another cigarette. She wanted a cup of tea, perhaps some toast to go with it, but was cowed by the darkness beyond the bedroom door. She got up and went into the bathroom to start the water running in the tub. A hot bath would warm her, help her get back to sleep. If only they'd thought to confide in her. Why should they have, though? They weren't teenagers but middle-aged people who had the right to do whatever they chose. In truth, she was happy for them. They'd be good for each other. There was, she thought, an appropriate symmetry to Dene and Charlie's being together. She smiled at the thought as she climbed into the tub.

"Did you see her?" Charlie asked, stretching mightily so that his bones cracked.

"Who?"

"Anne."

"Anne? Where was she?"

"Up on the back deck watching when we came in."

"Why would she have been watching? That doesn't make sense."

"Well, maybe not watching. But she was up there, and she saw us."

Dene leaned on her elbow to look at him. "She probably just couldn't sleep. She has those nightmares all the time. She sleeps no more than two or three hours a night. I don't think she's very well at all."

"She still saw us. We'll be in for a big scene tomorrow."

"Why do you say that?"

"I don't know. Just a hunch." He yawned, then stretched again. "I'm whacked. What time is it?"

"Almost two-thirty."

"I've gotta be up in a couple of hours." He gathered a handful of her hair, and let it slide through his fingers. "Beautiful." He kissed her, then they settled down to sleep.

* * *

In the morning Dene went up to knock at Anne's door. When there was no answer, she let herself in with the spare key. Alarm crept along her nerve endings. The apartment was too quiet, didn't feel right. She climbed the stairs to the third floor, holding her breath, a little fearful of what she might find at the top. There was an acrid smell to the air as she approached the bedroom. She knocked. No answer. She opened the door to discover the burned smell was even stronger.

"Anne?" She moved into the room to see that the bathroom door was closed. The smell was strongest near the bed, and as she got closer she could see a gaping black hole in the side of the mattress.

"Anne?" She rapped on the bathroom door, then tried the handle. It turned. She opened the door to see Anne sitting motionless in the tub, a cigarette burning in an ashtray on the rim. "Did you go to sleep with a cigarette?" Dene asked.

"Evidently, I did," Anne said without looking at her.

Dene exhaled slowly and lowered the lid on the toilet to sit down. "You're lucky," she said quietly. "It could have been a lot worse. I guess we'll have to buy you a new mattress."

"The keepers will buy the inmate a new pallet." Anne spoke sourly as she reached for the cigarette. "Why didn't you tell me about you and Charlie?" Finally she looked at Dene.

"I didn't think you needed to be told."

Anne nodded and returned the cigarette to the lip of the ashtray. "It's a pity," she said.

"What is?"

"I might have burned up with the bed. I wouldn't have minded."

"You're making me angry." Dene took the ashtray and put out the cigarette. "How long have you been sitting in here?"

"Don't be condescending," Anne said sharply. "I haven't lost all my faculties yet. I've been *sitting* in *here* for about fifteen minutes. If you're interested in a full rundown of my night, this is my *second* bath. I had the first one at about two-thirty."

"Why didn't you answer when I called?"

"I didn't feel like it."

"What's the matter?" Dene asked softly. "What can I do to help?"

Anne looked at her and shook her head.

"You're still having the nightmares," Dene guessed. "Maybe an analyst could help," she said gently.

"Maybe a *hypnotist* could."

"Look, I'll be going out to Halifax soon. Why don't you come with me? It'd do you good to get some fresh air, meet some new people. If you don't get out of here soon, you really will go crazy."

"What the hell am I going to do in Nova Scotia?"

"I don't know. It's got to be better than this."

"Maybe," Anne conceded.

"*Are* you all right?"

"I'm just tired. I didn't mean to snap at you. I'm so damned *tired.*"

"Finish up in here and come down. You can sleep at my place while I go get you a new mattress. Will you at least think about coming with me on the trip?"

"I certainly will think about it." Anne stood up.

"God, you're so thin!" Dene said, shocked by Anne's appearance. "While I'm out I'll get some steak and feed you."

Anne climbed out of the tub to wrap herself in a bath sheet. "Get out of here now, would you?" she said shakily.

"You make it hard for people to care," Dene said from the doorway.

"Did I ever ask you to care about me?"

"No one asks. People just care. It wasn't your fault, what happened; you didn't deserve any of that. If you could accept that as the truth, you'd probably stop having the nightmares. The man was *insane!*"

"I was equally insane, tempting fate."

"You were only trying to live. It's allowed. It's also allowed that you rejoin the living."

"We'll see," Anne said, clutching the towel to her. "Please, leave me alone now."

"I care," Dene said.

Anne nodded, then whispered, "Go on, get out of here!"

Dene went.

Chapter 30

Saturday afternoon, between shows, Jamie telephoned. "Do you think Perry might like to go out somewhere tomorrow?"

"I'm sure he would. What did you have in mind?"

"I hadn't thought. A show perhaps. I'll come by around noon and we'll decide. How does that sound?"

"Fine," she agreed.

Sunday at noon, Jamie arrived with a chicken. Instead of taking Perry out, the three of them played several games of Clue, then sat down to watch a film on television. Jamie cooked the chicken in butter and white wine, with Sherrill standing by to tell him where to find whatever he needed. Once the chicken was underway, they returned to the living room to catch the tag end of the movie. Sherrill felt wonderfully relaxed. Jamie's presence seemed very appropriate. She had no expectations of him, but was content to have him there. It was evident that he wanted to be with her and Perry, and she had no objections. She was simply waiting, curious, to see what would happen.

For his part, Jamie found Sherrill and the boy becoming daily more magnetic. Each time he left he thought he'd probably get back in touch with her in a few days' or a week's time, but within hours of returning home he was anxious to ring her up to hear the husky music of her voice, her laughter. He couldn't seem to stay away, and wondered why he entertained any desire to try to stay away. She expressed a continuing pleasure in having him around, so he kept returning. She fascinated him: her opinions, her experiences, her writing career, her good taste, her lack of pretension, her civilian life-style were like a long novel he hungrily absorbed in small chunks. There was so much he liked about her, and about the boy, that she seemed almost too good to be true. He admired the way she dressed, and the way in which she'd decorated the apartment. In part, he kept going back on the off chance that the façade might slip and she'd reveal herself to be less than she'd projected and he'd perceived.

Midmorning Monday when Jamie telephoned, Sherrill said, "Come to dinner tonight. I'll make spaghetti."

"I don't care much for pasta," he said, secure enough with her to be truthful.

"You'll like mine. I buy fresh pasta from a shop up north on Yonge Street and I make my own sauce from scratch. If you don't like it, I'll cook you another dinner."

"All right," he said with a laugh. "You drive a hard bargain."

He came. She served the dinner. He loved it.

"This isn't spaghetti!" he protested.

"Oh yes it is!"

"Well, it's certainly not that slimy wet stuff I've always been served in restaurants."

"Of course not," she agreed calmly. "That's slimy wet stuff. *This* is *pasta*."

He ate two full plates of it, along with several glasses of red wine, and patiently taught Perry how to use a soup spoon to aid in winding the noodles around his fork. Jamie was having a splendid time, one of the best ever. It made him doubtful. He'd given up believing his life was going to work its way to a happy ending. But here was Sherrill, who was making no apparently special effort to convince him of anything. Because of it, he found her increasingly more desirable.

She thought he looked and acted as if he badly needed someone to take care of him in small, but important, ways: to see that his clothes got to the cleaners, that he bought himself a few new things; to remind him to have his hair trimmed; to suggest, with kindness, that he might go on a diet and lose a bit of weight; to hold him and tell him how absolutely lovable he was with his marvelous sense of humor and his quality of reserve. She couldn't help but think that taking care of him might be a worthwhile endeavor.

She wondered what sort of women he'd known and lived with in the past. He'd spoken briefly of the French girl, Lucienne, who was now acting in films, and of his wife. It

was clear he disliked discussing the women in his past. He
was very loyal. She thought this, too, was an endearing
quality.

Monday late afternoon, before he left her to go to the
theater, he invited her to play tennis the next afternoon.
She accepted and they stood at the front door to say good-
bye. She wanted to kiss him and waited for him to take the
initiative. When he didn't, she laughed aloud, threw her
arms around him, and kissed him lightly on the mouth.
Releasing him, she smiled and said, "I'll see you tomorrow."
He left looking dazed.

Tuesday was tennis and lunch afterward at his club.

Wednesday morning they kept Perry out of school and
went downtown to see *The Empire Strikes Back.* Perry insisted
on sitting next to Jamie. The three of them watched the
film, eating buttered popcorn and Kerr's toffees for breakfast. Perry exclaimed aloud over the action, as did all the
other children who'd been allowed to skip school for this
occasion. After the film, they ran laughing through a down-
pour to Jamie's car. Back at the apartment, Sherrill gave
them both lunch. Perry went off to school, but not before
flinging his arms around Jamie's middle, saying, "Thanks a
lot. It was really terrific! See you later, okay, Jamie?" Then
he unwound his arms, grabbed his keys and dashed out: a
small figure in a yellow Snoopy slicker. Jamie watched the
boy go, grateful Sherrill chose to remain silent just then.
Perry's embrace had left him choked up. It took several
minutes for the lump in his throat to dissolve.

Thursday morning Sherrill telephoned her mother at the
office to ask if she'd have Perry for the day on Sunday. Josie
said, "I'd love it. Larry and I will take him to the zoo."
Sherrill promised to deliver him by eleven, then hung up to
stand smiling.

Thursday afternoon, Jamie telephoned to ask, "What are
your plans today?"

"Nothing much. What are your plans?"

"Are you home this afternoon?"

"I'm home," she answered. "Would you like to come
over?"

"I don't want to interrupt you if you're working."

"Come interrupt me."

They ordered chicken from the Swiss Chalet. The three of them sat around the dining table sucking their sticky fingers and laughing for no particular reason. Perry pronounced it "the best chicken I ever had" and went on to ask, "How come we didn't have this in Connecticut, Mom?"

"Because it's a Canadian company."

"Did you know," Jamie said, "that chicken is the most popular food in Canada?" He turned to Sherrill. "That's a statistic. And this," he told Perry, "is some of the best chicken you can get."

"It sure is," Perry agreed enthusiastically. "Boy! You know everything, don't you? You like little kids too. I can tell. Listen, will you sign these for me?" he asked, placing a small stack of paper on the table.

"Perry, what are you *doing?*" Sherrill laughed.

"None of my friends believe I really know him. If I've got his autograph to give them, they'll have to believe me."

Without a word, Jamie took the papers and began to sign them. After completing half a dozen or so, he asked Perry, "How many children are there in your class?"

Perry screwed up his face, thinking. "Let's see. Thirty-two. But you don't have to sign that many. Just for the grade twos. There're twelve of us."

Jamie went on signing.

On Friday morning, Jamie telephoned just after Perry had left for school. Sherrill invited him to come over.

"I've got a lot of errands to do," she said. "You can come keep me company while I do them."

She and Jamie were returning from the cleaners as Perry's school let out for recess. As they walked down the road hand in hand an entire classroom of children all began to wave and shout and pound Perry on the back, congratulating him on not being a liar after all. Horribly embarrassed yet pleased, a red-faced Perry hunched his shoulders and waggled his fingers at his mother and Jamie. Sherrill laughed, and Jamie smiled contentedly as they continued down the street toward the apartment.

That afternoon before Jamie left, they found themselves alone together in the small foyer by the front door. Perry had gone down to 202 to play with Josh. Sherrill had arrived at the point of wondering if Jamie might not be sexually interested in her. But his embrace and the kiss he gave her satisfied the question. He seemed so familiar, as if they'd known each other forever. She breathed deeply, relishing the scent of his cologne, the smooth soft skin of his cheek beneath her fingers. His hand stroked the back of her neck and her hair. She sighed, then whispered, "You're so sweet. I always thought you were."

He shook his head, scenes of his well-practiced exits sliding through his mind. "I don't behave with you the way I do with most people."

"Well, good. I'd hate to think you did. We've all got public faces we have to wear."

He didn't think she fully understood his meaning. "I'll call you," he said, "between shows tomorrow."

"Will I see you on Sunday?"

"Would you like to?" Why, he wondered, did she want to spend her time with him? It seemed almost unbelievable that someone so youthful and bright, of such talent and accomplishment, should actually express not only fondness for him but such overt eagerness. Was it possible she saw him precisely as he was and still managed to like him?

"Of course I would," she replied. "We can go out to a movie and have dinner somewhere. How does that sound? I'd like to see the Cineplex in the Eaton Centre. Have you ever been there?"

"No."

"They have eighteen minitheaters. It's supposed to be fantastic. I'd really like to see *A Clockwork Orange*. Have you seen it? I never have, but I've always wanted to."

"Sounds good to me."

"Okay, then. We'll go Sunday."

He went back to his apartment after the show that night and stood in the middle of the living room, dismayed by the condition of the place, its shabbiness, after the orderly cleanliness of Sherrill's apartment. He really didn't want to live alone any longer. That frightened him, because what he wanted was to live with Sherrill. It was an old pattern, one dangerous to his equilibrium. He was being lured back into his old nomadic ways, and he was getting too old to keep moving, going wherever romance happened to take him. If he allowed himself to become involved with Sherrill, he might lose her as a friend. He didn't want to risk that. He wanted to love her, to make love to her, to lay her down and take a slow tour of her slim, supple limbs before committing himself to the sweet welcome of her body.

He wanted her but was afraid even to think about it. There was bound to be another disappointment in store for him and he didn't feel he could handle any more. But, Christ! He liked her so much, more than liked her. He couldn't think about that either. Why the hell did the situation seem so suddenly dangerous? What's happened to me? he asked himself, turning to look backward down the years, trying to see if he could pinpoint the precise moment when the instinct for self-preservation had become stronger than his desire to love, and to be loved. No more women scattering ashes, dropping jars of marmalade, rearranging the furniture to their satisfaction, adding little feminine touches to his apartment, and leaving records minus their jackets strewn about on the floor. Yet even in the absence of women the place might as well have been subjected to traveling bands of them. There were dishes stacked all over the counters and in the sink. The stove hadn't been properly cleaned in months. The kitchen floor was tacky with dirt and grime. The toilet had been broken for weeks, but he hadn't managed to find the time to fix it. The tub was clean, but the handbasin was covered with a film of dried soap and shaved bristles. The living room was dusty, the glass-topped coffee table needed cleaning, as did the windows. The sheets on the bed should have been changed at least a week ago. The whole place had an abandoned, almost desperate look to it, as if a fugitive had holed up for a month before leaving suddenly, without warning, in the middle of the night.

He switched off the lights, got undressed, and lay down to thrash his way through another night. He knew he threw himself about while he slept and wondered if he mightn't one day harm some woman with his heavy, flailing limbs. He thought of Sherrill, small and vulnerable, saw himself throwing out a hand or a foot only to collide with some pale, hurtable part of her anatomy. He winced and turned over onto his stomach, bunching the pillows under his head. She'd have small perfect breasts, and a tiny waist, with smooth, satiny skin. If she risked spending a night in his bed, she might have bruises to mar the perfection of her body. Jesus! He turned toward the wall, dragging the bedclothes around him. She'd be warm, pliant, and eager. He thought of their kiss in the hallway and groaned softly, then sat up, turned on the bedside light, and reached for a cigarette.

Saturday night Sherrill watched "The Late Show," but couldn't concentrate. Her thoughts kept opening to consider Jamie. Every so often it hit her, in déjà vu fashion, that this was *Jamie*, the man she'd known ten years ago; someone who'd seemed completely inaccessible and mystifying, uninterested. She knew now that what she'd interpreted as lack of interest had, in reality, been the evidence of his shy reserve. She could also see that he'd been unhappy then, perhaps even as lonely as she herself had been. They could never have had any sort of a relationship at that time. She wouldn't have been able to deal with him; she wouldn't have known how. At most they would have made love a few times and then separated. Things were different now. Time, distance, and experience had brought her to an understanding of what she could cope with and what she couldn't; she'd also learned to distinguish between the application of someone else's sexual pressures and the push of her own. She no longer felt any obligation to make love as return payment for a dinner received, or for an evening out. She wanted to make love to Jamie; she wanted to hold him, to make him feel loved and valued. He seemed in need of loving attention, and she wanted to supply it. She could visualize herself body to body with him, could almost feel in advance the tender evidence of his caring. Despite the many small ways in which he'd indicated that he cared, it was plain he wasn't going to make the first move. She knew it. Did it matter if she made the move, took the initiative? She couldn't see that it did.

She turned off the movie halfway through and went to stand outside on the balcony watching cars go past on St. Clair. The traffic was fairly thin at this time of night, but even so, by Connecticut standards, it was substantial.

It was absolutely incredible that she'd had to go away for ten years, to change careers, be married and divorced, have a child and learn how to become a mother, had to travel in and out of half a dozen unsuccessful and brief-lived affairs with men who'd barely managed to arouse her curiosity let alone her desire, all in order to return home and find herself in love again with Jamie.

She leaned against the balcony railing and watched a streetcar come swaying along the tracks. It was sleekly modern, unlike the old, rounded ones. She liked its trim lines, the starkness of its red and black paint. For a moment she longed to see a stream of huge old gas-guzzling fifties cars zooming along the street, and girls in saddle shoes and sweater sets. She wanted to feel again the opulence of naïveté that both a changing world and her own evolution had taken away. Nothing ever again could be simple and uncomplicated. She'd adapted the life of a public figure, with all the attendant invasions of her time and privacy, and not even her thoughts could flow in direct lines. She was surrounded by the trappings of her success, and feared Jamie might either be intimidated by them or grow competitive because of them. She hoped he'd retain his equanimity. After all, she reminded herself, in his own right he was equally successful. But then, so had Drew been.

She returned inside to shower, then got into bed. Her body felt young and lean under her hands. What would she do if she made an overt move toward Jamie and he didn't want her? Nothing. They'd continue on as friends. There were no alternatives. Why, then did it feel as if there should have been?

Sunday morning Jamie got up early after a poor night's sleep. He stripped the bed and put on clean sheets. Then he went to the kitchen, and while he waited for the kettle to boil for coffee he attacked the mass of greasy dishes that had accumulated. While the water dripped through the coffee in the Melitta filter, he got out the Hoover and vacuumed the apartment. He took all the pillows off the sofa and pounded them, sending gray puffs of dust into the air. He polished the glass coffee table, threw open the windows to air the place out. With his cup of coffee sitting on the bathroom windowsill, he set to work with a sponge and a can of Ajax and scoured first the hand basin, then the bathtub, and finally the toilet. He tried to fix the flushing mechanism, but only succeeded in causing the tank to overflow even more copiously than usual. Cursing, he got down on his hands and knees to turn off the inflow valve to the tank, flushed to drain the tank, then painstakingly fixed the armature and stopcock. At last he turned the inflow valve back on, waited until the tank filled, flushed experimentally, and, satisfied, retrieved his now cold coffee and went back to the kitchen for a fresh cup.

He waxed the antique pine dining table—one of his few prized possessions—and the little antique pine bench that sat beside the sofa. He set out fresh candles and lit a stick of incense to rid the place of its musty smell. He considered cleaning the oven, but after staring into its caked, greasy depths for a moment, decided not to; there wasn't time. He went to the bathroom to soak in a hot tub for half an hour. Anticipating a visit from Sherrill, he didn't want her to know how far he'd allowed himself to slide. He wanted her to see how tidy and in control he could be when he cared to make the effort.

The telephone rang while he was dressing. Clad only in his shirt he went to answer.

"Hi, it's Sherrill. I thought I'd come down and pick you up."

"When?" he asked nervously, looking around to see that there were all sorts of things he'd missed during his cleaning spree. The windows were opaque with dirt, the ashtrays needed to be emptied. Christ! he thought, suddenly overheated.

"Now, if you're awake. Are you? You sound a little strange."

"No, I'm awake. All right," he said, knowing it would require days of cleaning to create the kind of impression he'd foolishly thought he could make with a couple of hours' effort. "Do you know how to get here?"

"I think so."

"There's parking at the rear of the building."

"I'll find it," she said cheerfully, and hung up.

He drew all the curtains, sending the apartment into near-night-time darkness. He lit the candles, studied the effect, and put them out again. Instead, he turned on the small light in the dining room and ran to finish dressing. By the time she knocked at the door he'd worked himself into a state of anxious dread. He had the record player on very loud and hadn't enough time to turn it down before going to the door, so they had to shout greetings at each other in the doorway.

"Come in!" he told her. "I'll just turn down the music."

It was a charming old apartment, she thought, and he'd furnished it nicely. There was a chocolate-brown velour sofa, a glass and chrome coffee table, some plants here and there, an oriental robe hung from a bamboo pole on one wall, paintings and graphics on all the other walls, a rough-woven rug on the floor in front of the sofa. The smell of incense was wafted back and forth by the breeze crosscutting the room.

"It's really nice," she said as he straightened from adjusting the volume on the record player. Beethoven's *Eroica* emerged at a more bearable level from the speakers on either side of the sofa.

"Sit down," he invited. "Would you like something to drink? Some coffee?"

"Coffee would be great." She sat on the sofa and continued to look around. Heavy red curtains were drawn over the windows, and there was a bed set in the alcove off the living room. The alcove was barely large enough to accommodate the bed and a small table beside it. He came back with two mugs of coffee and set them down carefully on the coffee table before joining her on the sofa. She hadn't planned what she'd do once she got there, but her inclination was to go ahead and do whatever was required in order to satisfy her curiosity and her appetite. He had evolved into the most desirable man, on the most levels, she'd ever met. They were both unattached, free to become involved, should they care to. She cared to. The fact that he'd make the effort to tidy the place up and change the sheets on the bed, that he'd light incense and attempt to create a mood with lighting and music, moved her. As she sat watching him sip thoughtfully, distractedly at his coffee, she found herself smiling. "You're adorable," she said and leaned over to kiss him on the cheek. She rearranged herself on the sofa with her back against the arm and her legs across his lap. "Let's not go to the movies," she said.

He looked somewhat startled and she had a moment's doubt, wondering if she wasn't making a fool of herself. But then he lifted her feet one at a time and slipped off her loafers, saying, "I'll give you a foot massage. I give," he said seriously, glancing sidelong at her, "very good massages."

She laughed—a rich, happy sound—and he glanced at her again to discover her eyes on him.

"It sounds like a California line," she explained. "Like wow, man, I'm heavily into massage, you know." She did her best flat-out nasal California space-age voice for him. He laughed appreciatively. "Like, you know," she repeated, glad of his laughter as he pulled her socks off. "Like I can really relate, you know, to people who are, like, into massage. I mean, it's where I'm at. You know? Like I remember this one time. I was in the hot tub, right? And this friend of mine, he, like, dropped by after a heavy session with the Orgone box, and we got into some massage. But, like, we didn't invade each other's space. We just really tuned in to where we were at. It was dynamite, man. Like really."

He was laughing hard, his hands expertly kneading her feet. Encouraged, she continued. "You're very good, man. I mean, like really. You know? I could tell at once, like right away, that you were really well centered, really at one with your cosmic energies, *really!*"

Laughter exploded out of his mouth and he closed his eyes for a moment, hearing, like an echo, the last flattened words she'd spoken. He liked her so much, enjoyed her so fully, it felt like an ache in his chest. He wanted to pray, to beg God or someone that this one would turn out right because he didn't think he could go through any more let-downs. He thought of Lucienne, how much in love with her he'd been, how deeply it had hurt when it ended. He was afraid to have this begin, afraid because it might end, leaving him shattered. When he opened his eyes, she was sitting away from the arm of the sofa, very close to him. There was a mischievous light to her eyes as she hooked her arm around his neck to give him a brief, soft kiss on the mouth. "Sweetcakes," she whispered. "Delicious." She sat back and undid the top button on her shirt. The gesture galvanized him, but his hands kept working, now on her calves.

"You *are* very good at it," she said in her normal, throaty voice. She undid the buttons on her cuffs.

"I'll do your hands now," he said, and reached for her right hand. She gave it to him while with her left she unbuttoned his shirt, then laid her hand flat against his chest.

"Don't expect this every time," she said half-seriously, as she got to the last of her own shirt buttons.

He met her eyes but didn't know what to say, and reached for her left hand.

"I'll be so relaxed in a minute or two," she said, "I'll probably go comatose. I don't suppose you'd like to move over there?" she asked, pointing to the bed.

"Are you sure?" His voice came out thick with apprehension.

"Quite sure."

"I'd hate to spoil the friendship," he said tentatively, unable to voice his many fears.

"We won't spoil it," she said with what he thought was enviable confidence. "We'll make it better. I want to make love to you."

"I'll be right back." He lifted her feet off his lap before standing up to hurry down the hall to the bathroom, where he threw off his clothes and pulled on the terry-cloth caftan an old girl friend had made. It was pale green and voluminous and felt good when he moved. When he got back, Sherrill was standing beside the bed. He'd hoped she might undress but realized now that she was someone who'd never go that far. At some point it had to fall to him to make the decisive gesture. The point had arrived. With quick, efficient hands he managed to undress her without actually seeing her body. Then he sat cross-legged in the center of the bed and instructed her to lie on her stomach with her head in his lap.

"I'll do your neck now," he said, and gazed down the length of her naked back feeling oddly as if he were going to cry. She had, as he'd known she would, an exquisite body, with a tapering back and rounded hips. His hands worked on the nape of her neck and her shoulders, his fingers absorbing—like repeated small shocks—the exorbitant pleasure of making contact with her flesh.

She lay not altogether comfortably with her head in his lap wondering how he'd managed to take her out of her clothes without once looking at her. She found the situation terribly funny and wanted to laugh, but thought he might misunderstand and be hurt. She never wanted to hurt him,

nor ever. Everything he said and did touched her more and
more deeply. She knew him intuitively as well as she'd
come to know herself. It would be too easy to hurt someone
who cared as much as Jamie did.

At last she wriggled out from beneath his massaging hands,
saying, "You'll rub me away. Are you ever going to take that
thing off?" She sat back on her heels and smiled at him
encouragingly. "Come on," she coaxed. "Take off your toga.
I want to see you."

Christ! he thought. How could she possibly want to see
him? He was thirty pounds overweight and white as a slug.
All the weights he'd lifted, all the tennis he'd played hadn't
helped a bit because what he really needed to do was practice pushing himself away from the table half a dozen times
a day. He grasped the robe by its hem and in one motion
pulled it off over his head and dropped it to the floor. It was
almost over; he'd take her in his arms now, he'd hold her,
and he'd be lost. For six months or a year, perhaps as long as
two or three years, he'd be in love with her. Then one day
her mask would slip a bit, or her attitude toward him would
change, and there he'd be, moving on again. He felt tired in
advance. But she did have the loveliest body, the most delicious sense of humor, such a captivating intelligence. How
could he possibly resist? He knew categorically that he and
this woman would have more to talk about after they'd
made love than they had right then. That, in itself, constituted the major portion of the pleasure he anticipated.
There'd be no need to frantically fabricate stories in order
to get rid of her; no need to lie about having no food in the
apartment, or the expected visit of his ex-wife to collect an
alimony check. He could simply be himself and relax; they'd
talk and become even closer. He opened his arms, and closed
them around her, and she lay down with him, sighing
contentedly.

"You are," she declared, stroking his chest, "perfectly
beautiful. I like you just the way you are. Do you know who
Mr. Rogers is?"

"No."

"He has a children's show on Channel 13, the New York
public network. The show's out of Boston. Anyway, Perry
used to watch the show when he was little, and I watched
with him sometimes. At the end of every single show, Mr.

Rogers says, 'I like you just the way you are.' The first time I heard him say it, face on, right into the camera, I burst into tears. I felt as if he were talking directly to me. It was the first time in my entire life anybody had ever said that to me. We've all got so many things we hate about ourselves, and other people only seem to compound the hatred. But I do like you just the way you are."

Her hand continued to move lovingly over his chest and arm and shoulder, and he wanted, as he'd never wanted anything in his life, to believe her. What convinced him of her sincerity wasn't so much what she said as the love transmitted through her hand. She seemed to be telling him through his nerve endings that she was trustworthy and could be taken at her word. He didn't think anyone had ever touched him so caringly.

He eased her down a bit so he could kiss her. Her mouth opened and her body suddenly seemed degrees warmer. He loved the way she kissed, the shape and feel of her mouth, the impossible softness of her breasts, which were, as he'd imagined, beautifully formed—small and round with full, very pink nipples. He lowered his head to kiss her breast, closing his mouth over her nipple, and she shivered, her fingers weaving through his hair. Then she'd slipped away and was urging him over onto his back, murmuring, "Let me . . . I want to see you," as her hands swooped down over his belly to close around him. He shut his eyes and felt the breath rush from his lungs in one sharp exhalation as she caressed him with her mouth, her hand skimming down the length of his inner thigh.

She felt incredibly happy, unbelievably happy. Everything about him pleased her: his so-gentle hands, the soap-and-water freshness of his body, the rich mellow throb of his voice. The control passed easily back and forth between them and she acquiesced one moment, he the next. His hand stroked higher on her thighs and she parted her legs to have him touch her meaningfully, importantly, knowledgeably. His touch, she thought, could have been her own. He'd known a lot of women but it hadn't blunted him. If anything, it had heightened his sensitivity. She was glad of the ten years of experience each of them had had with other people. Without that, neither of them would have been ready for this meeting, or able to value it.

He gazed at her for a long moment, adoring the sight of her face, before covering her breasts with his hands, and, with a small, pleased sound, dropped his head between her thighs. She sighed shudderingly and went very still, holding his hands in place over her breasts. It was perfect. She closed her eyes and examined the sensations, feeling herself starting to build. After a time, she squeezed his hands, whispering, "Come up here. Come."

His features looked cleansed, purified as if this act had erased twenty years from his life, rendering him young again and as potent as he'd been in his earlier years. Her body was small and tight around him. She whispered, "Slowly, slowly," and he could feel her muscles relaxing in order to bring him in. He rested, gazing into her luminous eyes, and knew then that it wasn't going to be one year, or three, but forever. She *was* the one he'd always believed existed somewhere out there. Astonishingly, she was no longer a vague "someone out there" but Sherrill right here.

"I think I'm falling in love with you," he murmured, feeling his carefully built defenses and control systems going.

"I know I love you," she said clearly. "I was in love with you ten years ago, but I was too stupid and too scared to do anything about it. I have to tell you something, Jamie," she said, her voice dropping.

"What, love?"

"I don't use pills, or a diaphragm."

"I don't have anything. Do you want me to stop?"

"No," she said firmly, "I do not want you to stop."

In the lull, before they made love a second time, he leaned on his elbow studying her.

"What?" she asked, smiling at him.

"I'll have a vasectomy if you like."

"My God, Jamie!" Her smile disintegrated. "Nobody's ever given me . . . I think I'm going to cry. *Why* would you do that?"

"To protect you."

She rolled over against him, holding him tightly. "I do love you," she said, her lips moving on his shoulder.

He wanted to tell her how much he loved her, but couldn't.

"I *love* you," she said again.

He looked at her, trying to formulate his thoughts; sud-

denly he couldn't think at all. He was too overwhelmed by
caring. "Someone should look after you," he said incisively.
"You can't carry the load by yourself all the time. And I'd
like a second chance . . . I mean . . . I failed with my boys."

She stared at him. "That's not true, Jamie."

"It is. I convinced myself that if I couldn't be there full-
time I shouldn't be there at all. It didn't have to be that
way. I don't know." He pushed the hair back from his
forehead and gazed into space. How did people ever close
the gaps between them? One moment the two of them were
as close as it was humanly possible to come. The next
moment they were trying, with their two different sets of
experiences, to understand something that perhaps defied
all understanding.

"Hey!" she said quietly, smoothing his arm. "It doesn't
matter. It really doesn't. We've got time; we'll get everything straight eventually. There's just one thing. I want you
to listen and not interrupt. Okay?"

"Okay, sure."

"I'm *very* successful, Jamie. I mean, I make a lot of money.
A lot. If you don't think you can handle it, say so now. I
don't want money to become an issue between us. I'm obses-
sive about my work; it's not just a hobby or something it's
likely I'm ever going to give up. I know what acting's like,
how you have to scramble sometimes to come up with the
next rent money. I've been through it all. If we're going to
be together, I want it to be because we *want* to be together,
pure and simple. It doesn't make a bit of difference to me
who pays for what. It's only money and I've got a pretty
good sense of what it's worth. I have to be sure you do."

"I can handle it," he said truthfully.

"Be sure," she cautioned. "How would you feel if one
month you can't make your alimony payment and I offer to
pay it for you? Are you going to be able to handle that?"

"Now, wait a minute. I've always worked and I've never
missed a month—"

"I'm just offering you a hypothetical instance."

"Why should *you* pay *my* alimony?"

"Jamie, if our positions were reversed and I was the one
paying alimony, if I couldn't get it together one month,
wouldn't you help me out?"

"Of course I would."

"Then what's the difference if I help you?"

He sighed. "It'll never happen. But if it does, I'll deal with it. It doesn't make any difference to me how much you earn."

"How will you feel when I go off on tour, appearing on television and giving newspaper interviews? How will you feel about that if you happen to be between jobs and not working?"

"That doesn't have anything to do with me," he argued. "That's your career. Isn't that what you've worked for?"

She smiled, relieved. "Damn right it is."

A week later, after his show closed, at Sherrill's invitation Jamie moved in. Perry was ecstatic. Jamie still felt tentative but tried not to let it show. Sherrill had the sense to leave him plenty of room to move about in.

Chapter 31

There were few tensions. The few there were, were Jamie's, and Perry's. After Jamie had been living with them for less than a month, Perry threw a tantrum.

"You love Jamie more than you love me!" he cried, presenting Sherrill with a full view of his reddened, angry little face.

"That's not true," Sherrill argued. "I love both of you."

"You're always hugging and kissing *him,* and you never hug and kiss me anymore. I want to go live with my dad!"

"Perry, you wouldn't know your dad if you tripped over him in the doorway."

"I would too! I don't care. I don't want to live here anymore. You'd rather be with *him* than with me."

"I thought you liked Jamie."

"He's okay."

"That's not what you *told* me," she said with a smile, kneeling on the floor to put her arms around him. "You told me you thought he was neat. Remember? Just the other

night when I was tucking you in you said you were glad
Jamie was here, because he was a really neat guy. You
just want a cuddle. Isn't that it? Isn't it?" She hugged him
hard, tickling him behind the ears so that he giggled. "What
you need," she announced, scooping him up and carrying
him into the living room, "is a good family cuddle. Come on,
Jamie. It's time for a close encounter."

The three of them rolled around on the living room floor,
laughing. Perry climbed onto Jamie's chest, hooking his
arms around the man's neck, and Jamie held the solid young
boy, feeling happiness flood his system. For a moment he
was seized by such a wealth of caring that he came perilously close to tears. He held Perry, breathing in his little-
boy smell, feeling the fine softness of his hair against his
face, and thought he had everything he could ever possibly
want. Perry wriggled away and knee-walked over to Sherrill, who proceeded to wrestle and roughhouse with the boy,
the two of them howling with laughter. Jamie's chest felt
curiously light as he caught his breath, watching them—the
slim young woman in blue jeans and a sweat shirt, and her
stocky, red-cheeked, tow-headed child.

Sherrill made a point to include Perry as much as possible, and by the time Jamie was gearing himself up to leave
for the East Coast, he'd settled back into himself. With
Jamie's departure only a week away, Sherrill became mildly
panicky.

"It's too soon," she protested quietly.

"It's only for six weeks and then I'll be home." He said
"home" and marvelled at how this place and these two
people had become that for him.

"Maybe I could work out some way to come join you for a
few days or a week."

"That'd be great."

"I'll talk to my mother, see what I can put together."

Jamie had several auditions downtown that week. After
one of them, he encountered Dene coming into the building
just as he was leaving. As always, he was pleased to see her.
After checking his watch, he asked, "Have you got time for
a coffee?"

"I'd love it. I've got half an hour before my next session."

They went into the coffee shop off the lobby and sat down

at the counter. Dene looked better every time he saw her.
She'd started to take more of an interest in her clothes.
Today she was wearing a calf-length black corduroy jumper
with a gray turtleneck sweater and knee-high gray suede
boots.

"You look super," he complimented her.

"Work clothes," she said dismissingly. "How are you?
You look better than I've seen you in ages."

"I've met someone," he said carefully. "Actually we're
living together."

"Jamie! That's wonderful! Who is she? What's she like?
She's good for you; I can tell just by looking at you."

"We met ten years ago," he explained, wanting to stop
and think about Sherrill, to turn her around in his mind,
examining all her aspects. "She moved back here a few
months ago, and we got together."

Dene leaned over and kissed his cheek. "I'm happy for
you." She smiled, then blushed and looked down at her
coffee.

"I love the way you blush," he said with a grin, "as if
every thought and gesture's outrageous."

She laughed. "What are you doing now?" she asked.

"I'm off on Sunday morning to Nova Scotia. Film location."

"You are? So am I. Which film?"

"The Chris Talbert one, outside Halifax."

"My God!" She laughed. "I'm doing the stills. I'm leaving
tomorrow."

"That's great! Maybe you'll get to meet Sherrill, I think
you two would get on well."

"I'm sure we would."

"How is Anne?" he asked.

"Oh," she sighed, "about the same, if not worse. You
wouldn't recognize her. I've actually managed to talk her
into coming along on location with me. A last-ditch thing,
you know? I'm hoping a change of scene will snap her out of
her depression. What's really frustrating is that every so
often she's herself again, sharp and witty. I get my hopes
up, thinking maybe this time she's going to come out for
good. Then it's as if she shrinks, and back she goes into the
old routines. She smokes nonstop, day and night. I'm always
nervous about that. She's up half the night. I hear her

walking around, or the TV set going. Her only outside expeditions are to the library a couple of blocks down. She goes twice a week to get a fresh load of books. That's about it. Charlie or I do her shopping. He brings her cigarettes and the odd bottle of vodka. Thank God she doesn't drink much. Anyway, she's about the same," she wound down. "If she could will herself to die in her sleep she'd do it in a minute. But she doesn't want to be responsible for assuming an active role in putting an end to herself."

"Maybe the trip will be good for her," he said consideringly. "It's lovely at this time of the year, with the trees turning."

"You've been East before?"

"I played the Neptune Theatre in Halifax a few years back. I love the coast. Not Halifax especially, but the countryside and the ocean. They get fabulous big seas there. I like to see the waves crashing in to shore." His face had lit up and Dene looked closely at him, seeing the changes. His accelerated aging process seemed to have stopped; he was holding steady now. Perhaps, she thought, his new love would help him reverse the process.

"What does she do, your lady?"

"She used to be a singer, but she writes now. She's just sold her third book and she's starting a fourth." He picked up his coffee cup and took a sip. "She has a son, Perry. He's almost eight. Lovely kid."

"That should be good for you."

"Umm," he agreed, reaching for his cigarettes.

"What are those?" Dene asked.

"Oh! These? Low-tars."

"You've given up Gitanes?"

"Sherrill," he said with another smile. "She's also cut me down on my drinking"—he patted his stomach—"and all the eating."

"I'm so happy for you, Jamie," she said sincerely. "It's what you deserve."

"What about you?"

"I'll go on as before. I'm happy the way I am."

"Well, as long as you are. There's a good chance Sherrill will be coming out. If so, you two will get to meet."

"I'll look forward to that."

*   *   *

Sherrill arranged for Perry to spend Saturday night with his grandmother so that she'd be free to take Jamie to the airport early Sunday morning. She and Jamie consciously ignored making the final preparations for his departure—as if, in delaying, something might magically happen to prevent his going.

Finally, late Saturday afternoon, they got down to the business of unearthing his luggage and deciding what he'd need to take. In silence, they packed his things. By the end, when the bags contained everything but his toiletries, which would go in first thing in the morning, Sherrill was already feeling his absence. In only weeks he'd become so integral a part of her life that she simply couldn't imagine how she was going to fill the days without him. Where once she'd begrudged all the labor she'd been compelled to do on Drew's behalf, she now took an active pleasure in cleaning the bathroom after Jamie had been in there, doing his laundry, or going out with the idea of buying some small thing with which to surprise him. His presence in her life had given her a sense of purpose quite unlike anything she'd experienced before. With him gone, she feared she might lose not only her sense of purpose but her momentum. Everything would come to a halt and she'd sit suspended for six weeks until he returned. It wasn't, she reasoned, that she'd become dependent upon him so much as that her independence didn't seem quite so significant without him; she treasured the moments they shared, very aware that the sharing itself was a major part of the joy in the relationship.

Jamie simply didn't want to go. He'd spent years hoping to find someone he could live with harmoniously. Now that he'd found her it seemed altogether wrong that he should have to leave, especially when, with each day's passing, he found himself more at ease, more trusting, more than ever fascinated by each new view of Sherrill. She was completely unpredictable; he could never sit back and assure himself that she'd react in a prescribed fashion to any given situation. He had no idea which way she'd go. He'd already discovered that when he expected her to react with anger, she sometimes chose to laugh. When he anticipated her laughter, she sometimes reacted with solemnity. He adored her. At some moments he didn't feel large enough to contain the wealth of emotions she inspired in him; it seemed as if he might swell beyond his capacities and burst. He was happy, and that was still somewhat suspect. He told himself this enforced separation would be good; it would allow them a bit of distance in which to reestablish their perspectives. But even as he told himself this, he didn't accept it.

"It's too soon," Sherrill said again. He agreed completely.

"Perhaps you'll be able to come out."

"I'm going to work on it. If my mother can't stay with Perry, I'll call one of those sitting services. I'll never," she said, looking around the living room, "be able to make it through six weeks here without you."

They tried to make Saturday last as long as possible. They went out to dinner, then walked home at a leisurely pace, to watch the CBC network news, then a late show. Jamie sat with a glass of scotch and a beer chaser, his feet propped on the coffee table, trying to make himself pay attention to the movie. Sherrill sat and watched Jamie, telling herself it was only six weeks, it would pass very quickly. But the time seemed to spread itself like a dark curtain behind her thoughts.

The film ended and they went down the hall to prepare for bed. They made love; they talked. Suddenly it was three in the morning and they both were hungry.

"I'll make you a special going-away breakfast," she announced, and got up to prepare a four-egg mushroom omelette, a pot of fresh coffee, toasted English muffins with Jamie's favorite marmalade, and grilled tomatoes. Then, in their robes, the two of them sat down at the small kitchen table to eat.

After two hours' sleep, they dressed and carried the bags down to the garage to Sherrill's car. There was almost no traffic as they drove out to the airport.

Jamie picked up his ticket, checked his bags, then returned. It was time to say good-bye. She felt peculiarly dislocated, as if she'd somehow been taken out of herself and could neither feel nor speak of the sensations his departure was creating inside her. But he seemed to know. They walked to the far end of the near-deserted terminal, where he put his arms around her. She held him, sensing a dreadful finality to their actions.

"I'll call you tonight," he promised. How could one small person represent so much to him? His feelings for her seemed disproportionate. Yet daily he accepted them with less reluctance. He kissed her good-bye and said, "I'd better get going." Hand in hand, they walked slowly toward the gate. She kissed him a final time, then watched him go, thinking it was a little bizarre that of all the people in the world it was Jamie Ferrara, her lover, who was leaving her. Her mouth curved into a small smile at the strangeness of it. Jamie. Life was ridiculous, absurd. He was gone. She turned to make her way across the ramp back to the indoor parking garage. The car hadn't even had time to cool down.

She felt exhausted and had to chew a piece of gum to keep herself awake driving home. As she headed down the Allen Expressway to Eglinton, it suddenly hit her that he was really gone; she'd left him there. He was flying off to Nova Scotia. For six weeks she'd be returned to the state she'd lived in before Jamie's entrance into her life. Her throat closed, her eyes filled with tears. It was too soon, far too soon for them to be separated.

The apartment was frighteningly silent and empty with both Perry and Jamie absent. She hung away her jacket and went slowly down the hall to the bedroom, where she stopped, gazing at the rumpled bed—the tangled sheets evidence of the hectic lovemaking that had taken place a few hours earlier. With a sigh, she straightened the bedclothes, undressed and slipped into the now cold bed.

At eleven the alarm went off. She remade the bed, showered, dressed, and left the apartment to walk over to her mother's place on Avenue Road. The day was gray and cold, filled with hints of winter. Leaves swirled across the sidewalks, the exhaust fumes from passing cars were plumes of gray-white condensation riding the air. She hunched down inside her pea jacket, recalling her childhood winters in the city, with snow banked several feet high in the gutters and the roofs of the streetcars carrying smooth, unblemished blankets of snow. By the time Jamie came home there'd be snow on the ground and the familiar whine of cars racing their engines as the drivers tried to get their cars out of icy ruts without the benefit of snow tires, which they'd delayed putting on until the last possible moment. She'd have to buy snow tires; she wondered if Jamie had them. He probably did. Although externally his car looked as if it had spent its life in a farmyard, he took great pains with the engine and had it looked at regularly by an East Indian mechanic who doted on Jamie, having seen him several times on TV commercials. He considered Jamie a star of the first magnitude.

Perry was sitting in the middle of his grandmother's bed watching cartoons on TV. Josie was in the kitchen reading the Sunday *Times*, which she had delivered, and drinking her third cup of coffee.

"You look wretched," she observed as Sherrill sat down opposite with a cup of coffee.

"I feel wretched," Sherrill acknowledged, viewing her mother carefully. "I'll never make it through six weeks without him."

"Of course you will," Josie scoffed.

"You know," Sherrill said, continuing her scrutiny of Josie, "you're really a very good-looking woman. Maybe there's some hope for me."

"We don't look a bit alike."

"I know that. But we've got the same genes. Maybe I'll age well. I'd like to be one of those women who reaches her peak at fifty, with a kind of glow."

"Is that supposed to be me?" Her mother laughed.

"If I look as good as you do when I'm fifty-five, I'll be very happy."

"You'll look better. I want to tell you something, Sherry."

"What?"

"If you laugh, I'll break your arm."

"If you tell me not to laugh, it's guaranteed I will. You can't tell people things like that; it always has the reverse effect."

"Were you always this difficult?" Josie wondered aloud.

"I'm not. I just know that every time somebody asks me not to laugh at something, inevitably I do. I'll try not to. What's the exciting news?"

"You remember Larry, don't you?"

"Of course I remember Larry. He's only been around for thirty years. Wait a minute! Don't tell me! You're going to marry him!"

"You must think I'm completely crazy. Why the hell would I spoil a perfectly wonderful relationship by getting married at my age? No," she said, "we're going to go to Florida for a couple of weeks at the end of the month."

"What's so funny about that?"

"I was wondering if you'd mind if we took Perry with us."

"I wouldn't mind a bit. Why would that be funny?"

"Nothing, I guess. I thought you might think so. I mean, you'll have to take him out of school. But I thought he might enjoy Disney World."

"He'd love it. I'd love it. That means I'll be able to go out and see Jamie. Oh!" she said, suddenly seeing the humor. "I get it. You're so cute." She smiled. "Very, very cute. A little motherly push to help things along."

"Six weeks is a long time," Josie said. "And Larry loves the idea of having Perry along. He likes children."

"I guess so, considering the prodigious number of them he's had."

"Five is not a prodigious number."

"It is in this day and age. Anyway, I think you're both cute, and thank you very much. Have you told Perry yet?"

"I was waiting. I didn't see any point to getting him all worked up if you thought it was a bad idea to take him out of school."

"You always liked him, didn't you?" Sherrill asked.

"Who, Larry?"

"Jamie. I remember you telling me once that he liked me. I thought you were crazy."

"Obviously I wasn't so crazy. He's a yummy man and he adores you."

"Yummy?" Sherrill laughed.

"Never mind. You'll get married," her mother said with certainty.

"I don't know about that. We've talked about marriage in general and we agree it's not all that great. It scares me to think about being married again."

"It all depends on whether you're prepared to work at it. Everything worthwhile takes some effort, you know. One of the reasons there are so many divorces nowadays is because it's so damned easy to walk away. Something goes wrong, and that's it. Why stick around and try to fix it? Walk away; it's much less effort."

"I tried marriage once, and I hated it."

"That wasn't Jamie," Josie said sagely. "And you were ten years younger."

"Nine and a half."

"Whatever. I'll drop the subject. Clearly you're not in the mood to discuss it."

"I'm happy the way we are. It's a little rough trying to work, but I'll manage. Right now it's more important to be with Jamie than it is to start the new book. I'll get back to it."

"Make sure you do. Nothing's more appealing than a woman who's got her own interests."

"This sounds like a lecture; it sounds like games-playing, and I despise games."

"It's just common sense. I think," Josie said, getting up, "I'll go tell Perry about the trip." She went off to the bedroom.

Sherrill could hear the murmur of her mother's voice and the raucous background noises from the television set. Then Perry let out a whoop and started talking in a high, giddy voice. Sherrill looked at the wall clock, trying to guess what time Jamie would phone.

Chapter 32

For the next three weeks Jamie's nightly calls became the focus of Sherrill's life. She filled the days with work, plotted her way through the novel, did the shopping and household chores. All the while she anticipated the ringing of the telephone at nine or nine-thirty, and the sound of Jamie's voice. Each morning she went out to send another greeting card or letter off to him via special delivery; each evening he commented on the arrival of the cards and letters.

He chose not to tell her about Dene, or Anne, whom he'd yet to see. He thought it best to allow the women to meet without background knowledge. That way, if they liked or disliked each other, his responsibility would extend only to his having introduced them. He did not see that his previous relationship with Dene, or with Anne for that matter, bore any relevance to his present relationship with Sherrill. He wasn't altogether sure Sherrill would comprehend the importance of his friendship with Dene if she knew all the details; she might choose only to see that he'd remained close to a former love.

The calls were a focal point for him, too, and throughout the days he planned what he'd say to her. While he waited to be called to the set he continued the lengthy letter he'd started writing on the plane. He found it far easier to set his thoughts and feelings down on paper than to try to articulate them in the course of a long-distance call. Each day's absence cast Sherrill into ever clearer definition, causing him to miss her company more and more. His idea of the separation being a good thing was completely misguided; it *was* too soon for them to have been separated. He'd never felt so deprived in his life. He missed her, missed the sight and sound and feel of her. It was as if one of his limbs had been amputated, yet he still had sensation in the empty air where the limb should have been. He tried to convince himself he was setting too much store in her, developing too great a dependency upon her.

He wasn't enjoying his work. He found sitting around most of the day, killing time until he was called to the set, painfully boring. He read books borrowed from the library in town; he played poker with three or four of the other actors; he sat for hours talking to Dene; he got through the days in order to arrive at the nights and the sound of Sherrill's voice. He'd never especially liked filming—there was too much hurry-up-and-wait about it—but he thoroughly disliked it now, and wanted the six weeks to be ended so he could go home. He wanted to be with his lady and his boy, sheltered in the warmth of their interest and affection. He did not want to be out in the cold, bundled up against the frigid offshore winds, waiting, fully made-up, for his chance to go on camera and speak his next half-dozen lines.

"You seem a little edgy," Dene observed at the end of the third week.

"Filming's a pain in the ass."

"You miss Sherrill," Dene guessed. "Is she coming out?"

"Monday afternoon. I thought you said Anne was going to be with you."

"I did. She's here. She hasn't left the room once. She sits up there watching television, or eating meals from room service. She's furious with me because, one, it's colder than I'd said it would be and, two, I didn't tell her you'd be here. She won't take a chance on leaving the room to run into you in the corridor."

"That's absurd," he said without thinking. The cast and crew were all staying on the same floor of the ratty old Grand National Hotel in downtown Halifax. Dene's room was two doors down from Jamie's. He'd encountered her in the hallway a number of times and had assumed Anne must have changed her mind about making the trip. "Maybe," he said, upon reconsideration, "it isn't so absurd. Why don't I see if I can convince her to join us for dinner, or a drink?"

"You're welcome to try," Dene said tiredly. "I'm starting to feel like her keeper, having to remind her to put out her cigarettes, or to go to bed."

"I'll see her when we wrap this afternoon and ask her to come out for dinner," he said decisively.

"Good. Maybe it'll shock her out of her paranoia." Dene sat shivering inside her sheepskin jacket, her hands, purpled from the cold, gripped the Canon hanging from her neck. "I'm afraid for her," she said after a moment. "She's letting go of the string. If she does, the only thing left will be for Charlie to have her committed somewhere. I don't want that to happen to her." She searched Jamie's eyes. "There's *nothing* wrong with her." She placed one of her cold hands over Jamie's. "Please ask her to dinner. It might help, and I'm running out of ideas."

"Tonight," he repeated, chafing her hand between his, trying to warm her. "Are you all right?"

"I'm just cold. This is the coldest damned place I think I've ever been. What happened to all those changing leaves you talked about?"

"You told her about Sherrill?" he asked.

"Not naming names. Just that you were living with someone. It didn't seem to faze her. It's great to see you so happy," she said, abruptly changing subjects. "I know you're a little down right now, but you've found someone who's good for you and it shows. Everybody loves you, you know,

Jamie. It's true," she went on, as if he'd disagreed. "I've never met anyone who didn't have something nice to say about you, or some funny story to tell."

"I haven't been very nice the past few years. I've been busy turning into an old woman. Sherrill's put a stop to that."

"No," she said. "Caring about her has stopped it. You said yourself we all need someone to care about. I exclude myself from that argument because my needs aren't the same as other people's. All I need is the camera, and my life to continue as it is. I worry about Anne because I think if you don't have someone—a husband or wife, a partner—then you really need your friends. They give you—ballast, I guess."

He laughed. "Taking up sailing, are you?"

"Not quite." She laughed with him. "But friends are important. Anne and Charlie, you and one or two other friends I've made, they fill the gaps. I can be affectionate with them, get the warmth and contact I need, even the sex. Charlie's glad to supply that," she said with a little shrug. "Being truthful, I guess I'm happy enough to have him supply it. Sometimes I think it's a little obscene to be forty-four and still interested in sex. Then I think why the hell shouldn't I be. I'd better get to work." She freed her now-warm hand from his. "Wait for me after the wrap and we'll go back into town together." She bent down with her hands on his shoulders so that their noses were almost touching. "You're one of my most important friends, Jamie. I think," she said carefully, "that you're one of the last of a dying breed: an honorable man. In a most dishonorable profession. But then, so are we all honorable men." She smiled, kissed him on the nose, and went off, her arms folded across her chest and her hands tucked up into her sleeves for warmth.

Anne came to the door with her purse, expecting Jamie to be a room service waiter. When she saw who it was she put her hand first to her mouth, then to her hair, and finally to her breast, her eyes wide with surprise and dismay.

She still bore traces of her former beauty, but at fifty-seven she looked at least ten years older with her pure white hair and the cross-hatching of wrinkles around her eyes and mouth. She was, Jamie thought, alarmingly gaunt.

"I've come to ask you to dinner," he said, "and you are *not* to say no." He smiled and kissed her cheek and held her for a moment, further alarmed by her lack of substance. She seemed like nothing more than a skin package containing an assemblage of bones. "It's good to see you again," he said warmly, meaning it.

"You've changed," she said, recovering slightly from her surprise to take in his thinning hair, his substantially increased girth, his gray sideburns, the tired pouches under his eyes.

"*You* haven't," he lied, and saw at once the pleasure this lie gave her. "You're still beautiful." He hoped the gods would forgive him and understand the need for kindness just now. "I'm off to shower and change. Why don't I meet up with you and Dene in the dining room in forty-five minutes?"

"I hear you're living with someone," she said, trying to absorb his reality. It contrasted sharply to her memories.

"That's right. Sherrill. Do you remember her? We worked together years ago, in that revue with Ron."

"The triple threat. I remember. She was very good. Is she still good?"

"She's a writer now. She's not in the business anymore."

"A writer. Wait a minute! What name does she write under?"

"Sherrill Raymond."

Her face again lit up. "I've read her books!" she exclaimed. "I loved *Success Without Glamour*. It was damned funny. Well, I'm impressed. I have to admit it. I didn't want to see you, you know."

"Why not?"

She laughed, revealing teeth that were still strong and white. "I'll be damned if I know. Give me an hour, will you? I'm going to need extra time for this venture."

"An hour it is," he agreed with a smile.

"Say, is she going to be coming out here, Sherrill?"

"On Monday. Why?"

"I wouldn't mind meeting her. Isn't that funny? I never connected her with the triple threat."

"A lot of people haven't, because of the name change."

"Monday, eh? That'll be interesting."

He left. She closed the door and went to the telephone to cancel her room service order. Then she stood facing the

speckled mirror over the desk, wondering how he could
have lied so outrageously with such a look of sincerity. The
image in the mirror was of an old crone, but suddenly she
didn't feel quite so bad about herself. He'd always been
charming, even gallant, and kind, too—a thoughtful, caring
man. And now he was living with Sherrill Raymond, of all
people. It gave her a strange feeling to think of Jamie living
with a famous author, one whose books she'd actually read.
She had a vague recollection of a small, large-eyed girl
sitting at a piano onstage. The girl had had an odd voice,
very deep and full; she bore little resemblance to the woman
whose photographs graced the backs of the books Anne had
read.

Hurriedly, she undressed and went into the bathroom to
fill the tub, mentally sorting through her clothes. For the
first time in years she was acutely aware of her body. She
looked and felt her flesh with sadness. She was a bony
stick with shrunken, drooping breasts and wrinkled, cadav-
erous thighs. Her body was white as paper and about as
appealing as an open grave.

She wished he'd telephoned so that she might have had
some chance to prepare herself. As she bent over the sink,
leaning in close to the mirror to apply a bit of makeup, she
sagged all at once and held on to the sides of the sink with
both hands. She was inundated with memories of herself
and Jamie—trips they'd taken, evenings they'd spent together, dinners they'd shared, early-morning conversations in
bed, making love. Her thoughts slid toward the nightmare
and she let them, gripping the sink hard, daring the nightmare to overwhelm her with the fear it always brought.
Nothing happened. She viewed the event much as she might
have watched a rerun movie on television: something she'd
seen before that didn't especially interest her. Taking a
deep breath, she straightened, wondering if she could possibly keep the horror at bay through an entire night. Maybe,
just maybe.

The food was standard, mediocre hotel fare. All three
ordered what they considered the safest choices: Jamie had
soup and a club sandwich, Dene had tomato juice and fish
and chips, and Anne had a chef's salad. Laughing, they

complained about the soggy bread, the horrible salad dressing, the bony fish. Initially, their complaints served as conversation, helping to ease the awkwardness of the reunion.

Dene was on edge and kept a careful watch on Anne while trying to appear as if she weren't. Her eyes moved back and forth between Anne and Jamie; she hoped she hadn't instigated a situation that might prove embarrassing to all of them. Anne seemed relaxed, though, even comfortable, and ate with more appetite than usual. She was more like her old self, but Dene wasn't sure she should trust appearances. Too often she'd seen Anne reappear, as if from the past, then slide back into herself even more deeply than before.

"Tell me," Anne asked, "about you and Sherrill."

Jamie looked over to see that Anne wore an innocent enough expression and was displaying, if surfaces were to be believed, nothing more than healthy curiosity. "You'll meet her on Monday and you can decide for yourself."

"Is she writing a new book?"

"She's just started a new novel."

"Oh." She worked on her salad for a few minutes, then looked over at Dene and smiled. "Stop staring at me," she said pleasantly. "I'm not going to do something unseemly. Dene," she told Jamie, "has taken on the role of my guardian in recent years—along with my elderly nephew, Charlie. I think it gives them both great purpose in life."

"Don't be unkind," he said quietly, sensing the onset of a scene.

"I'm not at all," Anne said openly. "It's the God's honest truth. I've turned strange and timid in my old age. Dene will certainly attest to that." She fixed her eyes on Dene, expecting her to reply. Dene said nothing.

"You're hardly in your old age," Jamie said, abandoning his sandwich.

"I'm almost sixty."

"Oh, horseshit!" Dene erupted. "You're fifty-seven, which is *not* 'almost sixty.' Stop trying to goad me. It seems to be your major occupation these days."

"All right. I'm fifty-seven. It's hardly adolescence."

"*Hardly*," Dene concurred, giving up on her half-eaten fish and chips, pushing the plate away from her with a look of distaste.

"And I look at least a thousand," Anne pushed on.

"If you say so." Dene felt completely worn out. This had been a bad idea; she'd have to apologize to Jamie in the morning. To her astonishment, Jamie suddenly started to laugh, holding his napkin to his mouth to muffle the sound.

"Share the joke," Anne urged happily. She'd forgotten how infectious a laugh he had, and how rarely he used it.

He took hold of Anne's hand and held it until he had his laughter under control. Then, wiping his eyes he said, "It's all such rubbish. You're just as lovely as ever. But the two of you have evolved into an old married couple. If you were gay, it'd be perfect."

"We're hardly that," Anne said. "Although I confess the idea's occurred to me more than once."

"Are you *kidding*?" Dene said disbelievingly.

"I'm not kidding," Anne said, enjoying Jamie's hand enclosing hers. "You're not exactly dogfood, you know. There have been moments when I've looked at you very seriously and wondered."

"But you *know* I'm not gay," Dene protested.

"I know that," Anne said impatiently. "Neither am I, for that matter. That doesn't mean the idea hasn't occurred to me. It wasn't totally repellent either, I might add."

"You defeat me." Dene turned to look helplessly at Jamie. "She defeats me. I swear to God she says whatever pops into her mind, hoping for results."

"That's possible," Anne said consideringly. "Life has become exceedingly dull in recent years. I mean, you must admit it's pretty pathetic when an old babe like me goes to the closet thinking she'll make a grand entrance and finds she doesn't have one goddamned thing to put on that she wasn't wearing when Cleopatra sailed down the Nile."

Dene gaped at her, then gave in to the laughter welling up into her throat.

"It's all so bloody silly," Jamie declared. On impulse, he lifted Anne's hand to his lips and kissed it. Anne smartly withdrew her hand and stared at him angrily for several seconds. Then she relented and allowed herself to relish the attention. "Let's relax and be friends," Jamie proposed. "We're all of us too old for this nonsense of trying to goad one another into overreacting."

"Hear hear!" Dene said. "I couldn't agree more. What about you, Grannie?"

"Don't go too far," Anne warned her. "I'm still sensitive about my age."

Again all three of them laughed. Everyone in the dining room, with the exception of the actors and crew who occupied several nearby tables, stared at them. Their laughter seemed unnaturally loud in view of the otherwise silence and it was into this scene that Sherrill walked.

She saw the three of them at once, at the table for four by the windows, and stood by the cashier's desk debating if she should interrupt. The hostess was working her way between the tables toward Sherrill, an armful of menus held to her breast. Sherrill smiled, indicated she'd found her friends, and started across the dining room. She felt everyone was watching her as she made her way toward the three people on the far side of the room. She arrived at the table and stood there uncertainly, able to say no more than "Hi."

Jamie looked up. She watched him fix on and recognize her—there were two distinctly separate processes—then he leaped up, sending his chair toppling backwards, to embrace her.

"I came early," she explained unnecessarily. "I didn't want to wait, so I thought I'd surprise you."

"It's great!" he exclaimed. "Great!" He beamed at her, completely forgetting Anne, who was watching with undisguised interest, and Dene, who kept her eyes shyly averted.

"Listen," he said, his arm around Sherrill's shoulders. "You've got to meet two dear friends: Anne Reynolds and Dene Whitmore."

Sherrill shook hands with Anne and said hello as she tried to absorb some sense of the woman. She wished she had the time to stop and study her; there was something about Anne that drew her. But she had to turn to shake hands with Dene. "I've seen some of your photographs in *Toronto Life* and a couple of other magazines. I love your work. Do you know of Sarah Moon? Some of your pictures remind me of her work, and others remind me of Diane Arbus. But they're always you, not anyone else. You do amazing photographs. The ones you did of Jamie are by far the best pictures I've ever seen of him."

Jamie could only stare at Sherrill, wondering how she'd known that Dene had done his glossies and how she'd learned as much as she evidently had about photography. He felt terribly proud of her, and a little shaky from her unannounced arrival. How like her, he thought, to act on impulse and surprise him. He'd forgotten how pretty she was, with her clear gray-blue eyes and wide-smiling mouth. She was drawing Dene out, bringing forth a Dene he'd never before seen: a confident, articulate woman of wisdom and warmth.

Anne, too, watched Sherrill, intrigued to think that this was the woman Jamie had chosen for himself. She wasn't beautiful, she certainly wasn't voluptuous, but she did have energy and a vigorous intelligence, as well as extraordinary eyes. The eyes were the woman, Anne decided, watching with fascination as Sherrill's knowledge and questions led Dene to expand and grow almost visibly larger. Within moments the two women were chatting away compatibly. Anne turned at last to Jamie to say, "How about a drink: I'm getting a little tired of looking at the remains of the meal."

"Good idea." He craned around, trying to spot their waitress. She was standing at the rear of the room by one of the service stations, engaged in conversation with another waitress. He signaled to no effect, then remembered to ask Sherrill, "Have you eaten, love?"

"No, but I'm not hungry. I've told you how much I hate flying. It always puts me off food for days. I'd love a drink though." She smiled at Anne, saying, "I'm sorry. I haven't even said a word to you. I've seen Dene's work, you see, and Jamie didn't mention she was going to be here."

That was interesting, Anne thought. Obviously everyone was keeping secrets on this trip. Dene hadn't bothered to tell her that Jamie was going to be there. And Jamie hadn't told Sherrill about either of them. Was he up to something, or simply trying to protect himself from his past? She had no idea who was trying to do what to whom, and attempting to unravel it all was giving her a headache.

"On second thought," Anne said, "I'm going to go back up to the room, read for a while, and have an early night. You three go on to the bar and I'll see you in the morning. I thought I might come out to the location tomorrow if the invitation still stands."

Dene said, "Sure it does. But you don't have to go up yet. Sherrill just got there."

"I'm right in the middle of a new Dick Francis. And frankly, these shoes are killing me. I'll see you tomorrow, won't I?" she asked Sherrill.

"Absolutely." Sherrill smiled, thinking what incredibly beautiful features Anne had. "You really are beautiful," she said disarmingly, then saw Anne travel through several stages of reaction just as Jamie had done a few minutes earlier. "Really," she added for emphasis.

"You," Anne declared, taken aback, "are very kind. I can easily see why Jamie's so smitten with you. Now," she stated, rising. "I'm going to truck off to my book and my bed."

She left the dining room. The other three silently watched her go. Dene wondered if Anne was upset. She hadn't appeared to be. But it was always hard to read Anne; her moods had been known to change without warning. She turned to look across at Sherrill, then at Jamie. They were, she thought, very right together.

Anne got into her nightgown and washed off the "light makeup," which took a bit of scrubbing and several rinses. She brushed out her hair and stood examining her reflection, deciding she didn't look all that awful for a woman nearly sixty.

At last she turned off the bathroom light and went into the bedroom to discover she'd left another cigarette, which had burned itself out, fortunately, in the ashtray. "Damn it!" she whispered, reaching for a fresh cigarette. It was a good thing Dene wasn't around. Dene made such a fuss whenever Anne forgot and left a cigarette going somewhere. It wasn't as if she was careless and left them perched haphazardly. She always left them resting in the center of the ashtray so that, if she did happen to forget, they'd simply burn themselves out harmlessly.

Chapter 33

Near midnight, Jamie looked at his watch. Sherrill noticed and said, "We'd better be going now. I've still got to unpack."

"Will you be coming out to the location tomorrow?" Dene asked.

"Is that allowed?" Sherrill asked Jamie.

"Of course, if you'd like to," Jamie responded.

"I'd love it. We'll see you in the morning, then." Sherrill said good night to Dene, who was staying on in the bar for one last drink with some of the crew.

"Where are your bags?" Jamie remembered to ask on their way to the elevator.

"The bellboy took them up to your room. I owe him a tip, by the way."

"We'll see him in the morning and settle up."

"Are you annoyed that I came early?"

He looked astonished. "Of course not." He placed his arm around her shoulders. "I couldn't be happier. I was starting to go a little crazy without you."

"That's nice." She smiled and patted the hand resting on her shoulder.

"I hope you're not going to mind the room. It's pretty terrible." He couldn't help remembering Anne's visit to New Brunswick years before, and her displeasure with the room, the hotel, the food—everything.

"I don't care about the room. I'm happy to be with you. I was starting to go a little crazy myself. No mess in the bathroom, no socks hidden in tricky places for me to find." When they emerged at the sixth floor, Jamie directed her across the hall and held open the heavy fire door that closed off the wing. "We're down at the end on the left. It really is a dreadful old hotel," he apologized. "But everyone's staying here. They spend a fortune putting a film together, then try to economize on the accommodations." As they went down the hallway, he told her who was staying in which room. "They're all downstairs in the bar now, except for Anne." He pointed to the door and dropped his voice as they went past. "She's in there."

Sherrill walked into the room and looked around. "It's not too bad. From the way you were talking, I really expected something awful." It was a small square room into which had been crammed two three-quarter beds whose heads sat against the left-hand wall. By the right wall was a plastic-covered armchair; farther along was a desk-drawer unit with a mirror on the wall above. Straight ahead, overlooking the street, was a window with an inside ledge running the width of the room. Jamie had set out all Sherrill's greeting cards on this ledge, as well as his books and some toilet articles. Between the chair and desk on the right-hand wall was another window. Both were covered with gaudy orange curtains, which Sherrill drew before hefting her suitcase onto the bed farthest from the door.

"I think I'll take a quick shower," he said.

"Okay. I want to get this stuff put away."

"There's a closet here." He indicated the door opposite the bathroom, which she'd failed to notice. "I left one side free for you."

In a matter of minutes, she hung away her clothes and placed her underwear and stockings in an empty drawer in the desk unit. As she stowed the suitcase in the closet she could hear the water running and Jamie singing as he always did in the shower. She smiled as she turned on the television set and then looked at the skimpy nightgown she'd brought along. Jamie's shirt lying across the foot of his bed looked more inviting. She undressed, pulled on his shirt, and put her robe on over it.

Jamie threw open the bathroom door, releasing a cloud of steam and hot air, and emerged clad in the new white pajamas she'd bought him before he'd left. The network news—an hour later on the East Coast—was just under way. She was half-listening to it as she watched Jamie. He looked very boyish with his hair wet-combed and beads of water still glistening on his neck. He moved toward her as someone rapped on the door. Their eyes met as they stood listening. Whoever had rapped at their door continued to run down the hallway rapping on every other door. A prankster, they tacitly decided. That sort of thing happened after midnight in hotels. People got some booze into them and reverted to childhood to play stupid, irritating games that without fail involved rousing other guests from a sound sleep. Jamie shrugged lightly and came to sit down on the side of his bed. She sat on the other bed, facing him. With their hands joined, their feet touching, they looked over at the TV set, to hear a news item about the rising bank interest rate. Jamie tugged at her hands and she turned to look at him with a smile.

"I missed you so much," she said. "I couldn't believe I was ever going to get here."

"I've never been so lonely in my life as I've been these past three weeks."

"The apartment was too clean, too quiet," she said, still smiling.

"Are you accusing me of being slovenly?"

"No." She laughed softly. "Having to clean up after you and Perry . . . it's proof that you live there, too."

He shook his head slightly, and she said, "What?"

"Nothing." He looked down at her hands, lifting them. "You've got good hands, strong, capable hands."

"Big, ugly hands."

"They're beautiful," he disagreed.

"You're prejudiced."

"That's true."

Someone pounded on the door.

"What the hell?" Sherrill exclaimed.

"I'd better go see who it is." He got up and went to the door. Sherrill stood slowly, her heart thudding heavily. Something was wrong. She could feel it. She'd been able to dismiss the first rapping at the door, but this pounding now seemed ominous. She stood near the foot of the bed and watched Jamie open the door. He turned and quietly said, "There's a fire. Get your bag."

Obediently, she bent to pick up her handbag as Jamie ducked into the bathroom, grabbed two handtowels, soaked them in cold water, and handed one to her before he stepped out into the corridor. Sherrill got to the door to see that the hallway was filled with thick black smoke. Anne was standing to one side of their door, plainly terror-stricken. Jamie disappeared into the black smoke. Sherrill called out, "Jamie, come back! We can't get out that way!" He reappeared and she realized he'd taken only two or three steps. As Sherrill stepped back into the room, Anne suddenly and violently shoved her out of the way and ran through the room to the window that overlooked the street. Sherrill dropped her bag and ran after the woman, afraid Anne was going to leap out the window. Sherrill had noticed as she'd drawn the curtains that there were no exterior window ledges, and she wondered if Anne, in her frantic haste to get the window open, knew that. Anne leaped up onto the wide inside ledge, dragged the window open, leaned perilously far out, and began to shout. Sherrill, still clutching the wet towel, turned to look for Jamie, only to discover she couldn't see anything. Not only was the room rapidly filling with thick black smoke but the power had failed. They were in total darkness.

"Jamie?" she called, then waited for him to answer, her heartbeat accelerating moment by moment as the realization came to her that they were utterly trapped in the room. They were six stories above the ground with nowhere to go.

"I'm over here," he called back, "trying to close the door. I can't get it shut."

How had it happened so quickly? Sherrill wondered, returning her attention to the open window and to Anne, who had a tenuous hold on the window frame and was leaning even farther out, waving and shouting in an attempt to catch the attention of the firemen in a truck that was just now pulling up in front of the hotel. She was alternately shouting for help and whispering in a thin, tremulous voice, "Oh, my God! My God! Please hurry up, *please!*"

Sherrill held the wet towel to her mouth with one hand and wrapped her free hand around the older woman's ankle, convinced that at any moment Anne would lose her balance and topple six stories to the pavement. After a few moments, Sherrill withdrew the towel from her mouth and turned, gazing into the choking blackness, to call, "Jamie? Are you all right? Where are you?"

It was several seconds before he answered this time. In the interval, she thought, *it's not fair.* They were going to die in this room and it wasn't fair. Why was this happening now when things were finally going to work out for both of them? *Please,* she thought, *don't let this happen to us.*

"I'm here," he answered finally, in a voice that sounded heavy and unfamiliar. "Keep the towel to your face!"

Her hand still firmly fastened to Anne's ankle, Sherrill dropped down to see that the smoke was only an inch or two above the floor. At this level, she could see the greeting cards and Jamie's comb lying on the carpet. She straightened and leaned past Anne's thigh to see that the fire truck had pulled to a stop and firemen were swarming about on the ground. Anne was still whispering, "My God, my God! *Hurry up!*" Sherrill tightened her hand on the woman's ankle, saying, "It'll be all right. You'll be all right." and wondered how and why she was remaining so outwardly calm. Her heartbeat had leveled off to a steady, rapid drumming in her chest and all she could think was that, whatever happened, she did not want to behave in a fashion that might reduce her in Jamie's eyes. It was vital to remain calm. If they were destined to die, then they'd die together. She couldn't believe it was time for either of them to die. They were going to get out of there, she told herself. But as it grew worse, she found it increasingly hard to believe they would escape. The speed with which the fire had overtaken them astounded her. The threat of fire, its menace, had never been real to her until that moment. Now it was too real, and there was nowhere to hide safely from it. She held the towel away from her mouth and again called out, "Jamie?"

The telephone rang. It struck her as weird. Listening, she heard Jamie pick up the receiver and say hello. She was further astounded to think that in the middle of a fire, when their lives were unquestionably imperiled, he'd stop to answer the telephone. They were both such polite, programmed people. Jamie was saying, "Yes, we know. No, we'd love to, but I'm afraid we're trapped in here." Then there was the sound of the receiver being replaced and Sherrill knew he had to be somewhere in the middle of the room because the telephone sat on a table between the two beds.

"Jamie, are you all right?" she called.

Seconds dragged by before he answered. "I'm okay. Stay by the window!"

Anne was waving her arms and shouting to the firemen, *"Up here! We're up here!"* and then, in a whisper, she prayed, "Oh God, hurry up! *Hurry up!*"

"You'll be all right," Sherrill told her again, her throat and lungs burning from the intake of smoke. It had the foulest taste and smell as it billowed out the window past her and Anne. Less and less air was available to breathe. The gushing smoke was pushing the fresh air away from the window so that only occasional fresh drafts pierced the hot black cloud. The firemen on the street below worked to extend a ladder from the back of the truck. Sherrill watched, leaning as far out the window as she dared, alarmed at not knowing Jamie's whereabouts. She risked turning again but saw only blackness, and breathed in more of the hot smoke. The heat in the room was building, the wall beneath the ledge on which Anne was perched was now hot to the touch. Sherrill bit down on the wet towel and shook her head as if the gesture might clear her thoughts.

Jamie struggled with the door but couldn't get it closed. At last he gave up, removed the wet towel from around his neck, and held it to his face as he groped his way toward the window, where he could discern a faint light. At his back he could feel tremendous heat and he wondered if the fire was actually moving down the hallway toward them. If he could have closed the door he might have been able to gain them a few more minutes. With the door jammed open, all the smoke and even possibly the fire itself was being drawn, tunnel-like, right into this room. He tripped over something on the floor, righted himself, and reached Sherrill at the window. She was very calm; they both were, as if Anne's hysteria were compelling them to behave quietly and with control. Sherrill turned at the touch of his hand on her shoulder.

"Don't turn around," he warned. "Try to keep breathing the fresh air." He was having terrible trouble breathing. His lungs seemed to have closed down and he could take in only small, wet breaths through the towel. His eyes were stinging; he was certain that the heat at his back was more pronounced.

"They're bringing up the ladder," Sherrill told him, then at once began to cough and replaced the towel over her mouth.

Anne was hanging out the window, with only one hand fastened to the frame for support. Sherrill's grip on the woman's ankle was so fierce that her entire arm hurt from the strain.

Anne couldn't think. She only knew the firemen had to
get that ladder up to the level of the window and that she
had to get on it. She was aware of Sherrill's hand on her
ankle and wished Sherrill would let go. The ladder was
slowly extending itself toward her and she held out her
arms, willing it to come close enough so that she might grasp
it. She didn't want to die. Her thoughts of death had always
been on her terms, in her choice of surroundings. She wasn't
prepared for this; it wasn't what she wanted. This wasn't
the peaceful solution to an unsatisfactory life; this was
accidental, unplanned, violent. She wanted to be down on
the ground, safely out of the billowing, choking smoke that
was rising upward over her and had all but cut off her supply
of fresh air.

Dene stood gazing up at the corner sixth-floor window.
Smoke gusted upward so that it was impossible to see who
might be up there. She knew it was Jamie's room, and she'd
had a glimpse of Anne hanging out the window. But then
the density of the smoke had increased, completely obscur-
ing her view.

It was taking forever for the ladder to extend itself upward.
She watched with her arms wrapped tightly around herself,
terrified. The top of the ladder disappeared into the smoke.
She held her breath, afraid to look away. Standing shivering
in the snow, she wondered if one of Anne's cigarettes might
have been the cause of this fire. No. Daring to look away for
a few seconds, she could see that the fire was in the room
next to the one she and Anne shared. There was an orange
light in the room that flickered and grew brighter second by
second. Anne wasn't responsible. Dene felt nearly sick with
guilt for suspecting Anne might have had anything at all to
do with the blaze. But hadn't they heard the alarm? When
it had sounded, everyone in the bar had jumped up and
gone running out to the street. According to what the people
all around her were saying, the only ones left in the hotel
were the occupants of that corner room. Where were Jamie
and Sherrill?

Returning her eyes to the corner window and the ladder
which had now arrived at its lower ledge, Dene saw a
black-suited fireman begin to descend backwards with painful slowness. Then, out of the smoke, a second figure

appeared, going forward down the ladder, facing the fireman, both hands fastened to the guardrails. A moment later she saw a third figure, then a fourth. Everyone on the street watched in hushed silence as the four figures on the ladder started their slow descent.

When the fireman and the ladder arrived at the window, Anne's presence of mind suddenly returned. She straightened, to stand slightly to one side of the window, saying, "Come on, Sherrill. Climb out! Hurry up!"

"You go ahead!" Sherrill urged. "Go on!"

"No, I'll be all right now."

Sherrill saw no point to wasting precious time arguing. She threw aside her towel. "Are you okay?" she asked Jamie, who was simply a presence she could feel at her side.

"Go on!" he told her. She braced herself to climb up onto the ledge and felt Jamie's hand boosting her. It was amazing, she thought, how that ladder and the fireman waiting to guide her down it represented a continuation of her life. She had no doubt whatsoever they would climb down the ladder and arrive safely on the ground. Gripping the near guardrail, she stepped barefoot on to the first rung.

"Are you okay?" the fireman asked, his voice muffled by the oxygen mask over his nose and mouth.

"I'm fine," she answered, then stopped, panicked. "Where's Jamie?"

"He's right behind you," the fireman assured her.

She had to stop, turn, and look back to satisfy herself that was true. Jamie smiled encouragingly and again said, "Go on!" She faced the fireman, took another step down, then thought to ask the man, "Where's Anne?"

"She's okay; she's right there, too."

The rungs of the ladder were very far apart; the guardrails were very low, so that she was forced to move in a half-crouch. One misstep and she'd slip between the rungs and plummet to the street below where, she could see peripherally, a huge crowd of people was gathered. Bent almost doubled, she took one long step after another, her feet numbed from the cold metal, her eyes fastened to those of the fireman, who every few seconds asked how she was. "I'm fine," she assured him. "I've never been happier to see anyone in my life."

"I'm pretty happy to see you, too," he said.

When they were perhaps ten or twelve rungs down the ladder there were several minor explosions. Glass showered over them as the window of the room where the fire was taking place burst from the intense heat.

Dene held her fist to her mouth, watching the four figures on the ladder creep slowly downward. The fireman, then Sherrill, then Jamie, then Anne. The noise on the street was clamorous—police walkie-talkies, calls coming over car radios, hoses being turned on, instructions being issued to the firemen as well as to the crowd. The fire itself made quite a lot of noise. The two explosions made Dene jump. The fire seemed to be reaching out in an attempt to wrap itself around the people inching their way down the ladder. Her stomach was knotted. She sank her teeth into her fist and continued to watch.

About a third of the way down the ladder it occurred to Sherrill that to the people on the street below she was as good as naked. Everyone could see her bare legs as they moved, taking her closer and closer to the ground. Behind her she could hear Jamie coughing violently. She wanted to stop and look back, assure herself he was all right, but she knew she couldn't stop. A few more minutes and they'd be on the ground.

Jamie watched Sherrill and felt a mounting pride. She'd remained calm and controlled; she'd behaved as effectively and sensibly as anyone could have in the situation. He was a little shocked by Anne's behavior but could understand it. She'd more than redeemed herself by insisting Sherrill go first down the ladder. Thinking about it, he realized that Anne had undoubtedly saved their lives. If she hadn't come pounding at the door, he and Sherrill would probably have gone to bed. Then, when the telephone call had come, they'd have gone to the door, opened it, and been asphyxiated almost instantly because of the buildup of smoke and fire in the closed-off corridor. Had Anne not burst into the room and thrown open the window, to shout and signal, the firemen would never have known the three of them were in the room. The black plumes of smoke billowing out the window and rising upward would have effectively prevented anyone on the ground from seeing them. Certainly cries for help wouldn't have been heard in the din of sirens and shouted instructions. There was an ironic element to all this that he was going to have to think about carefully. But first they had to get to the ground, and he was having great difficulty breathing. He was coughing nonstop, able to draw only minute quantities of fresh air into his lungs. Just make it to the bottom, he told himself. Christ! They'd come so close to dying. How was it possible that when he was on the verge of having everything he'd ever wanted he'd come so perilously close to losing it all? How could that *happen*? And why the hell hadn't he thought of smashing that second bloody window to redirect some of the smoke away from them? The perfect damned gentleman! Being respectful of someone else's property at the risk of one's own life.

He could feel his lungs closing, could feel a kind of lightness in his head. They had to make it to the ground, had to. He wanted his life, his future, his love. He cursed his flabby, out-of-condition body and forced his legs to work for him, his feet to reach down for the next rung and the next.

Chapter 34

Dene watched as the people on the ladder neared the bottom and then, one at a time, were lifted to the ground by the firemen. The full impact of the situation suddenly overcame her. An inner quaking started up, a sensation so violent she felt as if her body might detonate, sending pieces of her in all directions. People she knew and cared for had come very close to death up there on the sixth floor. Now that they were safely on the ground, the peril was greatly magnified.

Jamie, Sherrill, and Anne were completely coated in a black film so that their eyes and teeth looked impossibly white—they seemed like members of some minstrel show, done up in blackface. It wasn't funny, yet Dene had an

overwhelming desire to laugh. At the same time she could
feel sobs working their way up from her chest. It was a bad
dream she had no idea how to handle. The nightmarish
aspects of the fire were compounded by her realization that
if she hadn't stayed on in the bar for a last drink, she, too,
would have been up there, would have had to traverse the
terrifying length of that ladder. She knew categorically she
couldn't have done it. Therefore, she would have died in
that room. Trembling, she broke from the ranks of the crowd
and moved stiffly toward Anne, who stood in her begrimed
nightgown in the middle of the roadway looking around as if
waiting for someone to give her directions. Her white hair
was now black; she didn't look in the least like herself. As
Dene neared her, she felt sick with guilt for suspecting
Anne might have been responsible for causing the fire. She
found her momentum and hurried toward Anne, who, upon
seeing her, rushed forward to collapse into Dene's embrace,
saying, "I'm so ashamed, so ashamed."

"Why?" Dene asked. "God! You're half-frozen. Here, put
my coat on." She slipped out of her sheepskin jacket and
wrapped Anne in it.

"I went crazy," Anne admitted, her eyes wide and insistent.
"I didn't care about a *thing* except getting out of that room."

"That's all anyone would have cared about," Dene said
reasonably.

"But I didn't care about *them*," she tried to explain, twisting around to look at Jamie and Sherrill, who stood surrounded by half a dozen police and firemen. "I didn't think
about them once. Except at the end, when the ladder arrived.
I didn't want to die up there," she said fiercely, her hand
gripping Dene's wrist.

"It's all right," Dene said consolingly, directing her toward
the sidewalk. There was a restaurant opposite the hotel.
The owner came out onto the sidewalk, saying, "Bring her
in here where it's warm. A lucky thing I was still here. I
should've been home half an hour ago. Come in, come in.
I'm making coffee."

Grateful to be out of the cold, Dene led Anne into the
restaurant. Within minutes the place was filled with people
in their nightclothes—other residents who'd fled the hotel
upon hearing the fire alarms.

"Didn't you hear the alarm?" Dene asked, staring at the older woman.

"There wasn't any. Somebody went running up and down the hall banging on the doors, but he didn't *say* anything. I mean, if he'd shouted, 'Fire!' I'd have opened the door. I thought it was some kind of joke. When I finally decided to open the door and have a look, the whole place was filled with smoke. I couldn't see a thing and I couldn't remember where the fire escape was. I thought it was at the end of the corridor. That's where they usually are. But I couldn't *see*. So I ran along the hall knocking on all the doors. If Jamie hadn't opened the door ..." She trailed off and stared at the tabletop, her expression one of horror and fear. "I've been playing around with it for years," she said, slowly raising her eyes to Dene's. "Death. Thinking about it, how I'd do it. I don't really want to *die*, Dene. I got so goddamned angry thinking I wasn't being given a choice. I shoved that poor girl out of the way and went running for the window. I behaved like a lunatic. It was disgusting."

"No one knows how she'll behave at a time like that," Dene sympathized. "Forget it. Don't even think about it. What's important is that you're all alive. I think that coffee's ready now; I'll get you some." She slid out of the booth and stood up, only to lose her momentum. She stared at Anne, stricken once again by the reality of the fire that was still blazing across the road. Covering her mouth with her hands, she broke into convulsive sobs. Anne jumped up to comfort her, murmuring, "It's over. It's over now. Everything's going to be all right."

The world was suddenly entirely different to Anne. As she stood holding Dene, she could see the firemen at work and the crowd of people watching. She felt as if she were looking at the scene of her birth, as if something heavily ugly had been lifted off her chest, leaving her lighter, purer, and more aware than she'd ever been. She was filled with energy and wished she were in Toronto right then so that she could start putting into action some of the many ideas flooding her brain. She wanted to redo the house, to have her hair cut and restyled, to go out and shop for an entire new wardrobe. There were shows she wanted to see, and movies; records and books she thought she'd like to buy. All sorts of things.

This year," she said, "we'll have a Christmas tree. The whole works."

Dene lifted her head and could do no more than gape at her friend.

The fire chief waved over one of the ambulance attendants. "Take these two to the hospital," he instructed the young man, who then turned to Sherrill and Jamie and said, "If you'll come with me."

Sherrill was deeply frightened. Jamie seemed unable to breathe. He was drawing air into his lungs in shallow, rasping wheezes. She held tightly to his hand as they walked barefoot through the snow after the attendant. In the back of the ambulance they sat holding hands. Sherrill was unable to look away from Jamie's face, tortured by the agonized sound of his breathing. Ludicrously, all she craved was a cigarette; she wanted one more at that moment than she'd ever wanted anything.

"I love you," she said, wishing she could cry and get some of the anxiety out of her system. "I love you so much."

"I love *you*," he gasped, his arm secure around her.

In the emergency room at the hospital, they were given oxygen masks to place over their noses and mouths. Sherrill sat on the foot of the bed behind the drawn curtains, holding Jamie's hand as he lay on the bed, noticing how everything they touched was instantly marred by greasy black soot. She stared at her free hand, pushing away her reactions to what they'd just been through. All the time they'd been up in that room waiting to be rescued, she'd faced the possibility of death, confronting it head on and over and over, believing, yet unable to accept that death was stealing closer to them with each second's passing.

Painful arterial blood samples were taken from the backs of their hands, then there were chest X rays, and sputum samples. Eventually a brisk, breezy nurse squeaked on rubber soles into their curtained-off cubicle at the end of the emergency room to tell Sherrill, "Okay, hon, you can go. This fella's going off to the ICU."

"Why? For how long?" she asked.

"Don't know," the nurse answered, unruffled. "Somebody's waiting for you, hon."

"Can I come back to see him later?"

"You related?"

"She's my wife," Jamie answered, removing the mask from his face.

"No problem," the nurse said. "I think we'll get you into the shower, fella. Think you can handle that?"

He nodded as the nurse's hand efficiently replaced his oxygen mask.

"I'll be back in a few hours," Sherrill promised, standing down from the bed, still holding his hand. She didn't want to leave him; she had the irrational feeling she might never again see him alive. "Get some sleep," Jamie mumbled to her from behind his mask. "I'll be okay. You look after yourself."

She bent to kiss him on the forehead, reluctantly released his hand, and backed out past the curtains. She turned to look at the nurse behind the duty desk, feeling lost. The bright cleanliness of everything was shocking, dazzling. The nurse behind the desk looked up and smiled, "Your friend's around the corner in the waiting room."

What friend? Sherrill wondered, as her bare feet took her along the cold tiled floor away from Jamie.

Dene jumped up the instant she saw Sherrill and hurried over. "We've got a motel room for you, and some clothes. I thought I'd better come, make sure you were all right."

"I'm not all right," Sherrill said numbly, allowing Dene to lead her out of the hospital and across the parking lot to a rented car. "They're keeping Jamie in there. I feel like a refugee. I have nothing," she said. "Nothing. It's the most dreadful feeling. Have you got a cigarette?"

"Sure." Dene opened her handbag, lit a cigarette, and gave it to her. Sherrill couldn't help noticing the odd way in which Dene kept looking at her.

"What's the matter?"

"Nothing. I'm sorry." Dene shook her head, got the car started, then thought to say, "You must be cold. I brought a blanket. It's on the back seat."

"No, I'm fine." She took a hard drag on the cigarette and immediately began to cough. She took another drag. "I hated leaving him there."

"How is he?"

"I don't know. They never tell you anything in hospitals. Never. When I was having Perry they left us alone in the labor room for hours. Things were going wrong, but they wouldn't tell us anything. As if we were too stupid to understand the simplest things. They talk to you so carefully, like we're all backward children. How's Anne?"

"She had half an hour of oxygen, then was released. She was asleep when I left. She feels very badly about the way she behaved."

"Why?" Sherrill asked, mystified. "She saved our lives. If she hadn't got up on the window ledge and shouted and waved, no one would have known we were in there. Were any other people trapped in the building?"

"No. Just the three of you."

"We nearly died," Sherrill said in a soft, awed voice. "The attendant who brought us to the hospital told Jamie we had maybe another minute left in there. I think I'll get cleaned up and go back to the hotel."

"Okay," Dene agreed readily.

Sherrill glanced over to see if Dene was patronizing her, but she seemed not to be.

"You're a nice woman," Sherrill said. "Very kind."

"No." Dene shook her head.

"You are," Sherrill insisted. "You care. What time is it?"

"Around three-thirty, maybe four."

"Aren't you tired?"

"Exhausted. But I couldn't sleep if I wanted to. Standing there watching all of you come down that ladder . . ." She shook her head again. "You were brave as hell to come down that thing. I couldn't have done it."

"Yes you could have," Sherrill said firmly. "I promise you you could have. It looked like the safest thing in the world to me, that ladder; it looked half a mile wide and as easy as a staircase. I didn't think twice about getting on it."

Dene stopped the car in front of a modern new motel and led Sherrill along into the lobby and halfway down a corridor to a room. She produced a key and opened the door to a large, starkly clean double room. On the end of one bed sat a stack of clothes, some shampoo, a pack of cigarettes and some matches, a razor, a hairbrush, and a pair of sneakers. A similar assortment of goods sat on the foot of the other bed.

"It was the best I could do," Dene explained. "I cadged most of it from the guys on the crew and the motel staff here. Everyone's been fabulous. Nobody can get back into the Grand National before morning. Do you want to be alone, or would you like me to stay and keep you company?"

"Stay," Sherrill said, gazing down at herself. "I've got to get this stuff *off* me!" she cried, catching sight of herself in the mirror on the wall. She laughed, then started to cry, at once swallowed the tears and lit a cigarette from the pack Dene had left on the bed. Her hands shook uncontrollably, as did her legs.

Gently, Dene took the cigarette from her and said, "Why not take a shower? You really don't need this. I'll sit here and wait for you."

Sherrill walked into the white-tiled bathroom and stood blinking against the glare. Her reflection in the mirror struck her as so grotesque that again she laughed, then removed herself from the vicinity of the mirror and stood staring now at the spotless tub enclosure. Everything seemed distorted, unreal. She was fascinated by the slick gleam of the white tiles. At last she turned on the water and divested herself of the ruined robe and shirt. The blasting heat of the water was soothing and she remained motionless for quite some time, feeling the heat ease some of the tension. When she lathered up a washcloth and began trying to remove the black coating from her body, she could feel hysteria banking inside her. Here she was in some motel room God-knew-where, while Jamie was in the intensive-care unit at the hospital undergoing treatment for smoke inhalation. Everything either of them had brought to wear was in the hotel room and probably lost for good. The possessions didn't matter, but her feeling of nakedness, and Jamie, did. As she scrubbed away at herself, watching in horror as the streams of black froth flowed from her body, she imagined herself returning to the hospital only to find Jamie's bed empty and a nurse quietly saying, "I'm sorry." He couldn't die. It wasn't that critical. But there was such a real possibility that he could die that she found herself unable to stop thinking how empty and lacking in value her life would be without him. People went into hospitals every day to be treated for something small and relatively uncomplicated, never to emerge again. They went in and they died. Someone's error, or the patient responded badly to medication. It happened all the time. She tore the wrappings off two more small bars of soap and kept working. She couldn't get clean. The more she scrubbed, the more dirt there seemed to be. She washed her hair three times and still the rinse water was gray. She washed it again. The greasy blackness was everywhere—between her toes, under her arms, behind and inside her ears, in her nostrils, everywhere. The horror was complete. Her chest heaving, she continued to rub soap into her skin, feeling she might never rid herself of the black coating and therefore never be free of the horror. Enclosed in the stall, behind the opaque shower curtain, she felt as entrapped as she had while standing at the sixth-floor window of that smoke-filled room. She had to stop. After rinsing herself a final time, she turned off the water and reached for a towel. The towels, one after another, came away from contact with her skin bearing traces of soot.

"What time is it?" she asked Dene as she emerged from the bathroom.

"Almost five o'clock."

She'd been in the shower for over an hour. "I think I'm coming unglued," she said, reaching for the stack of clothes on the bed.

"I wouldn't be surprised," Dene said quietly. "I can't believe how calm you are."

"I can't either." Sherrill pulled on the too-large cotton shirt, wincing at its roughness against her rubbed-raw skin. She stepped into the jeans, which were a fairly good fit. "The clothes feel good," she lied, sitting down on the side of the bed beside Dene to put on the socks and the outsize sneakers. "I've got to go back to the hotel," she said. "It's not going to be real to me until I can see it."

"You should try to sleep."

"I couldn't," Sherrill stated flatly. "Why are you doing all this?"

"Why not?" Dene glanced at her watch. "The restaurant here'll be open in half an hour. I checked. We could probably both use some coffee."

"I could," Sherrill agreed, examining Dene's profile. "Tell me the truth," she said.

"The truth," Dene repeated. "Is this an appropriate time?"

"You bet," Sherrill said quickly, "the most appropriate

time there's ever going to be. I don't know what I'll do if anything happens to Jamie."

"Nothing's going to happen to him. They'll detoxify him, and after a few days, he'll be out."

"How do you know that?"

"I asked."

"Oh!" Sherrill nodded. "Tell me."

"Why? It's past history. None of it matters now."

"I want to put things into perspective. I watched the three of you in the dining room before I came over to the table. It seems like years ago, but it was just last night. I watched you," she repeated. "It was strange, like a family reunion or something."

Dene smiled. "He loves you, and he's happy. For the first time in the ten years I've known Jamie, he's happy. Nothing else is important."

Sherrill had to think about that, and to agree. "You're right," she said after a moment. "God!" she sighed. "I'm tired. I've never been so tired in my life. I want to call my mother." Abruptly, she reached for the telephone, got the long-distance operator who connected her with Fort Lauderdale information. It took only a few minutes, and then the telephone was ringing in her mother's hotel room. Her words a chaotic tumble, Sherrill said, "I wanted to call you, hear your voice. I'm sorry to wake you. Is Perry all right? There's been a fire. I wanted to let you know in case it gets into the papers or . . . Don't tell Perry, okay? I don't want him upset. They're keeping Jamie in the hospital, treating him for smoke inhalation."

They talked for several minutes; Sherrill agreed to phone again later that evening, then hung up, to sit staring at Dene. "It's so stupid," she said, making a failing effort to smile. "Now that it's over, I'm more scared than I was when it was happening."

Dene extended her arm around Sherrill's shoulders and Sherrill fell against her, quivering with fatigue and fear. Dene held her, stroking her still-damp hair, thinking how strange all of this was. She was glad she could give something, even if it was a contribution as minimal as clothes and cigarettes and a comb. "I'll drive you over to the hotel in a little while," she offered, somewhat intimidated by Sherrill's tiny structure, the fragile feel of small bones under a thin layer of skin. "We'll go get some coffee, then head for the hotel. The fire chief wants statements from everyone who was staying on the sixth floor. Evidently the alarm system failed."

"There *was* no goddamned *alarm!*" Sherrill cried, sitting away. "They tried to burn us to a bloody crisp!"

"They think it was an electrical fire. The room had been rented by some kids in a rock band, but they didn't get back to the hotel until long after the fire started. According to the chief, that fire had been smoldering for hours before it finally took hold."

Sherrill could feel rage racing along her nerve endings and had to make a conscious effort to control herself.

"How old's your little boy?" Dene asked.

"Nearly eight," Sherrill responded automatically.

"I always wanted a child, but I guess it wasn't meant to be. That sounds a little complacent, doesn't it? But I did really want one. You're very lucky."

"We were so incredibly calm," Sherrill said. "It was unbelievable. Jamie stopped to answer the phone in the middle of the whole thing, for God's sake! I can't believe he did that!" She laughed, a short raucous burst of noise.

"That sounds like Jamie," Dene smiled.

"I don't like him being there!" Sherrill said, feeling desperate. "I want him the hell *out* of there."

"Everything's going to be all right."

"You'd have made a good mother," Sherrill observed. "You know all the right noises."

"I've had plenty of practice in recent years. Anne's had a lot of highs and lows, more lows than anything else."

"Are you two gay?" Sherrill asked bluntly.

It was Dene's turn to laugh. "No. We're just old friends. I rent the ground floor of Anne's house. We met on an airplane, believe it or not."

"I didn't mean to be rude."

"It wasn't rude. I'm sure a lot of people wonder if we are. People seem to have a passion for categorizing. Have you ever noticed that? They want to know who and what you are so they can put you in the right slot. I have a lover," she said, and then heard a ten-year-old echo of Anne's voice as it spoke of the lover she'd had who'd moved on some months earlier. "It's funny," she said, "the way things happen. I'll have to phone Charlie at some point today."

Sherrill reached out to take hold of her hand. "I'm being a crazy person," she apologized. "I'm sorry. It's going to take me a while to deal with all this. I keep thinking of refugees and concentration camp victims, thinking I know exactly how they had to feel. Maybe it's a kind of survivor's mentality."

"There's nothing wrong with that. Come on." She tugged at Sherrill's hand. "I'm sure the coffee shop's open by now."

Sherrill sat a few seconds longer staring at the older, red-headed woman before again volunteering herself into Dene's arms, hanging on. Then she withdrew and stood up, jamming her hands deep into the jeans pockets. "What's this?" she asked, coming up with two twenty-dollar bills.

"Taxi and cigarette money. You can repay me later."

Sherrill smiled shakily. "Thank you."

"Come on. We could both use some coffee."

Jamie had been able to remain in the shower only for a few minutes; he'd found it too difficult to breathe in the steamy little bathroom. After managing to rid himself of the worst of the soot, he toweled dry, then allowed the nurse to install him on a gurney—the oxygen mask once again firmly in position over his mouth and nose—and he was wheeled to the ICU.

Now he lay awake in the all but empty unit, gazing at the ceiling and taking stock. One arm was hooked up to a glucose drip, the other to some different drip. An electrocardiogram machine monitored his heartbeat; the oxygen unit bubbled away as it fed fresh oxygen into his lungs. He hated the place and refused to succumb to what he thought of as a "hospital mentality," of believing he was ill and totally dependent upon the ministrations of the doctors and nurses who kept appearing to take yet another blood sample or to ask still more questions about his past medical history. He wanted to sleep but the hospital noises interfered. All he could think of was Sherrill. When the nurse had told her she could leave, Sherrill had kissed him on the forehead, whispering, "I love you," and he'd felt such a rush of caring he'd come close to weeping.

He wished she'd come back. He hated this bloody place. He wanted to be with Sherrill, to talk to her, hear her laugh, to hold her and make love to her. They'd been apart for three weeks. It seemed an impossibly long time. They were never going to be separated again, he decided. Somehow, in some way, they'd be together.

His eyes filled. He wished the damned nurse had thought to draw the curtains around his bed. A bit of privacy would have gone a long way. He continued to gaze at the ceiling, thinking carefully about Sherrill as the room gradually grew lighter.

Chapter 35

After making her statement to the fire chief, Sherrill was escorted to the now closed sixth floor by one of the firemen still on duty in the hotel. As the elevator doors opened she was assailed by the dampened smoke smell and felt nauseated and deeply afraid. In the grim light of morning, pieces of broken glass glittered the sodden carpet near the elevator. A crew of men was at work on the wing where the fire had taken place, although it wasn't immediately apparent to her what they were doing. There were half a dozen huge steel drums and the men were placing charred objects in them.

"Walk careful now," the fireman told her. "Mind your step."

She nodded to indicate she'd heard and stepped through the doorway, then stopped, staring at the wreckage. What had been the hallway was now a black cavern, and the room where the fire had occurred was simply a brick cell enclosed by exposed and twisted, blackened steel beams. Broken glass and bits of wire were everywhere; the floor was inches deep in plaster. The wet carpet gave sickeningly beneath the layer of debris as she stepped cautiously into the corridor and began to work her way down to what had been Jamie's room at the far corner. She smiled at the working men but found it very hard to breathe; her heart raced and her nausea was heightened by the aftermath stink of the fire.

At the doorway to the room she stopped again, a small involuntary sound of distress emerging from her throat as she looked in. The window sill gaped open but the curtains were gone. Everything in the room was of varying shades of black and gray. Upon first glance, it seemed that all of hers and Jamie's things had been destroyed. She felt as if she were viewing the battered remains of a stranger, and wanted to turn around and leave. Instead, she moved into the middle of the room and slowly looked around. All the cards she'd sent Jamie lay strewn about on the floor, some of them water-soaked, others charred. Her makeup was all over the floor, along with quite a lot of clothing, her leather boots, and Jamie's trench coat. She drew open one of the dresser drawers to see that the contents seemed undamaged. Encouraged, she went to open the closet door, exhaling gratefully at the sight of hers and Jamie's clothes looking as if they'd escaped damage.

The fire chief appeared in the doorway asking, "How're you doing?"

She had to swallow before she could respond. "It's rough," she said truthfully. "But I needed to come up here and see this."

"I know," he said. "Best thing you could do, though most folks can't handle it right away."

"It wasn't real to me. Now it is."

"How's your husband anyway? Forgot to ask before."

"He's being detoxified; he'll be all right. We're not married."

"Well, whatever." He smiled understandingly.

"Could I take some of our things with me?" she asked.

"We'd appreciate it if you could wait a few hours until the photographer's been in, and the inspector."

"My handbag. Could I take that?"

"Oh, sure. Just don't move anything, okay?"

"Okay."

She retrieved her bag from the floor between the beds, wondering how it had come to be there. She couldn't remember when she'd lost possession of it. She recalled Jamie telling her to get her bag, there was a fire. But once they'd returned inside the room from the corridor and Anne had gone charging past her to the window the sequence became a bit confused.

"You'll want to get some sleep," the chief said, watching as she examined her blackened hands with a grimace.

"I will eventually." She'd have to try and sponge off the bag, see if she could salvage it.

She took a last look around the room, then picked her way back down the hallway to the elevator. As the doors opened in the lobby she saw Dene standing near the telephone booth, waiting.

"I thought I'd hang around to take you back to the motel. Are you going to be able to save any of your things?"

"More than I'd thought. A lot of our stuff was in the closet."

"Great! Are you hungry?"

"No. Listen, I don't think I can go back to the motel right now. Would you mind driving me to the hospital? I really want to see Jamie."

"Sure."

It was a bitterly cold day. The snow of the previous night had frozen into patches of ice on the ground. As they left the hotel and crossed the road toward Dene's rented car, Sherrill turned to look at the sixth-floor windows. Upward rising trails of black stood out sharply on the gray brick of the building. "Christ!" she whispered, feeling the trembling start up again. They'd nearly died. It had come so close she could feel the presence of death like someone brushing against her in a crowd. She felt overheated; her legs had begun to ache. She turned to look at Dene. "You look so tired," she said, noticing the bluish shadows under Dene's eyes, the lines etched either side of her mouth. Her hair, silver and red, blew about in the wind and Sherrill watched, entranced by its silken length. Who was this woman? Why had she taken on the role of Sherrill's . . . What? Protector? Guide? Yet there was such a sense of rightness to Dene's being there that Sherrill couldn't imagine being with anyone else at that moment. Dene hadn't, at any point in the past eight hours, tried to inflict herself or her thoughts or opinions on Sherrill; she'd simply been there to provide whatever service she might.

"I think," Dene said, "I'll drop you at the hospital and go

back to the motel and see how Anne's doing. She took two sleeping pills, so she's probably still out like a light. I think I'll take a couple of Seconals myself."

Sherrill had another coughing fit in the car and spit into a handful of tissues. Black strands and clots. She bunched the tissues and jammed them into her shirt pocket.

"The word is people will be able to go up to the rooms later on this afternoon to check the damage and get their things out. I guess you'll be glad to get back into some of your own clothes."

Sherrill didn't answer; she was thinking about Jamie, trying to imagine how he might look in the intensive-care unit, telling herself he was going to be fine, just fine.

"Why am I so scared?" She wanted to start crying again.

"There's nothing to be scared about," Dene said confidently, placing her hand briefly on Sherrill's arm.

"Yes there is. Up until last night I knew I loved him. But I don't think I realized how much I love him, how much I really need him. He said I couldn't carry the whole load alone and in a way he was right. Not that I couldn't carry it, but that it's better to share. He gives me perspective, Dene. That's important. With people always after you, inviting you out not because they like you but because you're a celebrity, you need someone who accepts you for yourself, not for your talent. Jamie's the only man who's ever liked *me*, just me, not my singing voice, or my writing, or some *part* of me; he likes me.

"The entire time I was married to Drew, I kept waiting for whatever was going to happen next. Drew was something I had to get through until the next part of my life was ready to happen. I was convinced there had to be something more, something better than what I had, because what I had wasn't even what I wanted. He wasn't a husband; he was a competitor. I don't need that. What I need is Jamie, who has his own success and doesn't feel threatened by mine. I want him to be all right, to get the hell out of that goddamned hospital and *keep living*.

"You should be able to understand what I'm talking about." She turned to look at Dene's profile. "You're a successful woman. You know that when you're home alone you're just you, not the well-known photographer everybody's after.

Just you. You haven't bought the public persona any more than I've bought my own PR. Maybe when I was twenty I might have fallen into that trap, but I'm too old to buy it now. I'm home, alone with Perry, and I'm just 'mom' with supermarketing to do, cleaning to take in, laundry, and beds to make: all the ordinary garbage everybody has. Jamie sees that; he knows it. Because we're exactly alike. We both need someone to recognize the people in us and not be misled by the externals we've had to contrive in order to deal with our careers."

After a moment, Dene said, "You've just put into words something I've been thinking about for a long time. You're right. You're absolutely right."

After dropping Sherrill at the hospital, Dene went directly back to the motel. Anne was heavily asleep. Dene picked up the telephone and dialed Charlie's number. When he answered, she told him what had happened.

"Christ! How's Anne?" he asked. "Is she all right? Are you?

"I'm fine, Charlie. Listen," she said, then paused.

"What?"

"I've been thinking, thinking very carefully. Do you still want to?"

"What, get married? Sure I do."

"Okay. I want to, too."

"You mean it?" he asked.

"I love you, Charlie. I've got to hang up now. I'll talk to you later. Okay?" She hung up and swallowed hard.

At 7 A.M. a new shift of nurses came on. Someone came to read the electrocardiogram; someone else came to take another arterial blood sample and check the drips. They spoke to him as if he were a malfunctioning robot, or someone so simpleminded he could be trusted only with the least complicated of questions. He knew how easily one could be self-victimized by succumbing to hospitalization, and he had no intention of sinking into a state of belief in his own illness—as if he were the illness and not someone merely afflicted with a temporary disorder. Yet he did feel alarmingly weak, and he was readily able to oblige the nurses with thick black sputum samples. He longed to sleep, but the noise in the unit seemed to increase as the morning progressed. He wondered how they expected anyone to become well again in such a bloody noisy place.

The intravenous needles bothered him. His arms were itchy and sore; he felt anything but clean after his too brief shower in the middle of the night. He lay, trapped on his back by all the paraphernalia, and gazed steadily at the ceiling. Of all the damned irony, he thought, falling in love with Sherrill had to be the biggest surprise of his life. At first he'd been entranced by her, intrigued by her lack of pretension, her directness and intelligence. But very quickly he'd moved into a state of caring that went far beyond anything he'd previously experienced. He'd believed, years before, that he'd loved Lucienne. Side by side with his love for her had lived countless doubts and fears, none of which attended his feelings for Sherrill. There were no dark areas, no pools of resentment steadily filling day by day with an accumulation of thoughts and feelings gone unexpressed. Between them there existed an awesomely simple sort of truth and he found himself unable to imagine living alone without her.

I love her, he thought, and felt the full impact of his caring almost like a physical blow. She was the one, the one he'd always believed he'd recognize on sight. But time, experience, too many women, and too much time alone had dulled his perceptions. Did it have to take a disaster to make him acknowledge the truth? This possibility frightened him far more than the fire had. Until Sherrill had entered his life, he'd been evolving into a right old auntie who didn't want his records left without their dust covers, or his precious marmalade spilled on his carefully laid table. He'd been turning into the sort of person he wouldn't have liked had he encountered himself disguised as someone else. Sherrill had changed that; she'd changed everything. He could feel himself expand merely thinking about her. It occurred to him that he wanted to take the full responsibility for a commitment made with total awareness.

She'd said she'd be back in a few hours. By raising the upper half of his body and twisting partway off the bed he could see the clock on the far wall. Nine-thirty. She'd be coming soon and he needed to have his thoughts in order before she arrived. He collapsed back against the pillows,

wishing one of the nurses had thought to straighten the
bedclothes. Whatever had become of those infamous hospital
corners? This bed had been laid like a table, the sheets
tossed upon its surface by a hostess presented with the
arrival of unexpected guests. He could hear the sounds of a
trolley coming along the corridor and hoped they'd give him
some breakfast; he was ravenously hungry. He hadn't eaten
much of that dreadful dinner and that had been more than
twelve hours earlier. Bracing himself with his heels, he
managed to push his way back up into the bed so that he
was half-sitting. A nurse came by and he asked her to raise
the bed.

"Jeez, the bed's a mess," she observed, and deftly proceeded to straighten the bedclothes without disarranging
Jamie.

"Am I to have breakfast?" he asked.

"Hungry?"

"Starved."

"Let me check your chart." She went off to the nurses'
station, spoke with another nurse, looked at a clipboard,
made a brief telephone call, then made a note on the clipboard and returned to Jamie's side to say, "You get breakfast and you're off the glucose."

With one arm now free, he wolfed down soggy scrambled
eggs and two pieces of unbuttered toast, then drank the
unexpectedly good, strong tea. The meal seemed to act like
a sedative. By the time he'd finished the tea, he was yawn-
ing, ready for sleep. He pushed aside the tray table and
rested his head against the pillows, thinking it was probably
impossible to sleep but he'd try to nap for a few minutes.

Sherrill nervously approached the ICU. She had a migraine
and her legs ached so badly she could scarcely walk without
holding on to something for support. She stepped through
the door and at once saw Jamie in the bed nearest the door.
He looked terrible. The sight of him undid all her resolutions to be witty and cheerful. There was machinery all
around him; tubes and wires attached to parts of him. The
oxygen mask compounded the overall image. She sat down
in the chair beside the bed, relieved to hear that his breathing sounded easier. She wondered how long he'd been asleep,
then wondered how it was possible for him to sleep after

what they'd been through. She doubted she'd ever again be able to sleep without the aid of pills or several drinks. Every time she closed her eyes she was back in the hotel, trapped in the room, calling out Jamie's name while he took longer and longer to answer.

She wished she could smoke but there were signs everywhere in the hospital, large red circles surrounding cigarettes, with thick red slashes through the middle. An Esperanto of signs universally understood. Little areas throughout the place were designated for smoking; there was one directly next door to the unit. She'd noticed it on her way in and thought she'd go there now to have a cigarette while she waited for Jamie to wake up.

Taking care to be very quiet, she moved to get up from the chair—her thigh muscles protesting agonizingly—when Jamie opened his eyes, saw her, and smiled. She sank back into the chair, covering his immobilized hand with her own, completely unable to speak. His free hand lifted to lower the oxygen mask and he asked, "Did you sleep?"

She shook her head.

"I've been up all night," he said, "thinking. Mainly about you, about us."

"How do you feel?" she asked hoarsely, that disoriented feeling overtaking her again.

"I'm all right. I don't know what the bloody hell I'm doing in here. I hate hospitals."

"I'm sure they won't keep you long," she said, not in the least sure of that. His features were gray; even his lips looked bloodless. Without the mask his breathing was still labored and wheezy.

"I've been sitting here all night thinking," he repeated. "I think we should get married."

She bent her head and rested her cheek against the back of his hand, remembering how she'd married Drew, the speed with which it had happened. Now it was happening again. She knew she ought to be pleased, but she simply felt frightened. She could feel the tension in Jamie's hand and knew she had to say something but couldn't think of any way to express her feelings without hurting him. She lifted her head and, with a forced laugh, said, "You'll have to give me a minute. I wasn't ready for that."

His face shut down with disappointment and she squeezed his hand gently, groping for the appropriate words.

"It's not time yet," she said softly, searching his eyes.

"Oh, that's lovely," he said bitterly, turning his head away.

"Don't do that," she said sharply. "I need some time, Jamie." Oh, God! she thought. *What do I say? What do I do?* "I want to say yes," she said. "I know that's what you want me to say. In time I probably will. I do love you. But it's just too soon. I can't agree to something this important because you want me to, Jamie."

He couldn't conceal his letdown. He knew he was being unreasonable and tried to get himself past his dissatisfaction with her answer. "It's all right," he said, seeing how fearful she was of hurting his feelings. "Maybe I am going a little too fast."

"Why do we have to get married? What difference will it make?"

"It's the commitment," he said, "wanting to assume the responsibility for someone else. I want to make that commitment to you. That's what makes it different, Sherrill. It means you want to work at it and have it come out right. Otherwise, it's a year here and two years there and you waste your whole bloody life."

"I know that. I just need more time." She imagined being married and felt a different kind of terror. It wasn't quite the same fear she'd felt being trapped in a burning building, but something more general. She could readily hear the arguments with Drew, the snide comments about her work; she could hear them too clearly. While she doubted Jamie would ever stoop to that sort of sniping, it really was too soon to be completely certain. Her instincts told her he'd never be another Drew, but her common sense said, "Wait!" For a moment she could see the stage at the dinner theater, and Jamie standing center stage in the dark, waiting for her. He'd be there, still waiting, when the time was right. "I'm so tired," she sighed, resting her cheek once more against the back of his hand. "I went back to see the room. It was terrible, but I had to do it. I'm going back again later to get some of our clothes. The things in the drawers and closet weren't damaged."

"That's good," he said quietly, understanding the words she hadn't spoken. She was right; they did need more time. "Nothing's going to change," he said. "I love you."

"I know you do. I know that. I just need a little more time." She yawned, her hand coming to rest on his upper arm.

"It's all right." He stroked her hair briefly and felt himself slipping into sleep.

A nurse came by. She slid the oxygen mask back into place over Jamie's face, then went to the storage room for a blanket, came back and draped it around Sherrill. Neither of them stirred, but slept on.

Charlotte Vale Allen is an author of impressive and wide-ranging talents.

The publication of her recent personal memoir, *Daddy's Girl*, was met with unanimous critical acclaim. However, Charlotte Vale Allen had already established herself as a best-selling author of contemporary fiction, with sixteen novels published in the six years since she became a professional writer.

Born in 1941, the author was raised in Toronto. She left school in her late teens to become an actress and in the ensuing years lived in England and then the United States.

Charlotte Vale Allen is married to the actor and writer, Barrie Baldaro. She and her family divide their time between homes in Toronto and Connecticut.